RADIO BLUES

ASBURY PARK PUBLIC LIBRARY
ASBURY PARK, NEW JERSEY

RADIO BLUES

Gloria Nagy

ST. MARTIN'S PRESS   NEW YORK

RADIO BLUES. Copyright © 1988 by Gloria Nagy. All rights reserved. Printed in the United States of America. No part of this book may be used or reproduced in any manner whatsoever without written permission except in the case of brief quotations embodied in critical articles or reviews. For information, address St. Martin's Press, 175 Fifth Avenue, New York, N.Y. 10010.

Design by Judith Stagnitto

Library of Congress Cataloging-in-Publication Data

Nagy, Gloria.
    Radio blues/by Gloria Nagy.
       p. cm.
    ISBN 0-312-01810-X
    I. Title.
    PS3564.A36R3   1988
    813'.54—dc19   87–38259
                                                                                CIP

First Edition

10 9 8 7 6 5 4 3 2 1

For Vanessa Faye. My gift, my daughter, my very best friend.

I may not be normal but nobody is.

> Willy Nelson
> "I'd Have to Be Crazy"

Prologue
or
Beginning with the Grisly Ending

The Grim Reaper—clothes by Pauline Trigère, skull by Kenneth, black velvet cape by Norell—sliced through the freshly permed and frosted head of the famous radio and television therapist, Dr. Amora Sweet, testing for the first time the Sotheby's diamond-and-platinum scythe, and left immediately for California to contaminate several tons of Mexican cheese before attending a dinner in his honor in Bel-Air.

One immaculate slice from this James Beard graduate achieved what twenty years of psychoanalysis, four husbands, countless lovers, Herbalife, and prayer failed to touch: the greatest case of sibling rivalry since the Smothers Brothers.

1

You've Got The Right Key But The Wrong Keyhole

It was just like my sister to upstage me right on the eve of my goddamn fortieth birthday. Okay. It was, being that we were identical twins, also her fortieth birthday, but that kid always knew how to steal the thunder.

There is probably no better cure for the angst and self-pity that accompany the candles on the fortieth slice than opening your office door at 6 A.M. on a sunny late-September morn and finding your twin sister's decapitated, but still attractive, head in the middle of your *New York Times*. Snapped me right out of it.

Also, it was a terrible waste. That head was worth a

fortune. The orthodontia and hair alone! Add the expenses for two, count them, *two*, nose jobs (she wanted Jackie Onassis, she got Linda Evans), eyelid and chin reshaping, ear pinning, dermabrasion, the silicone cheek implants, not to mention facials, dermatology, and cosmetics. We're talking high six figures. What a waste.

Actually, though we began as identical twins, the head and I had little in common forty years later. I had not indulged in any of the above-mentioned enhancements and had also managed to stave off the Vampire God of exercise (on whose neck Amora panted daily) for most of my adult life, so there were those fifteen pounds. We barely resembled one another. Outside or inside. I liked to think that she had chosen to grow more attractive outside while the innards had slogged; I had let the outside down, but the interior region was, despite my imperfections and neuroses, a little English garden of health and beauty. At least until that gruesome morning. The damn thing had found its way down the hall to *my* office. This fact, said my new acquaintances at the NYPD, made it entirely possible that I was the next candidate for the ultimate mind-body experience.

I have always been a responsible person. I have been what might be called hyper-responsible. I have been so religiously responsible that until I was thirty-five years old I thought that people who laughed during working hours were frivolous. I am not the sort of person who disappears. Who vanishes leaving her only child, husband, job, friends, therapist, and dry cleaning in the lurch. I am the type who would stay at my elderly husband's side and give my seat on the lifeboat to the tubercular young mother. Loyal and steadfast, like my birth sign. Virgo. Sign of the nurse.

I read something once about a good life being a life in

which no part of the self is stifled, denied, or permitted to oppress another part of the self, but one in which the whole being has room to grow. I had not done this. I was as rooted and stuck as a potted palm. So, in some bittersweet irony for the Sweet sisters, Amora's head opened the way for me, loosened the soil; I started growing again—freed to become a person who guffawed before five.

Aroma and Amora Sweet. The Sweet sisters. Or, as my equally impaired childhood friend, Kitty Litter, used to say, The Taffy Twins. It is pretty hard to be taken seriously, to remain calm, cool, and good-humored when fourteen hundred times a day you must deal with name jokes. "I bet your sister's a honey." "Don't get bitter, sweet." "Bet your mother had a sweet tooth." Har-de-har. Even Hamlet couldn't resist. "Sweets for the sweet." The worst part began when sex entered our sugary little lives. How about "I never eat sweets."

Amora and I spent hours curled up on our pink-canopied beds thinking of new name possibilities. We also cheered ourselves up by thinking of how much worse it could have been. Sugar Spice. Ginger Snapp. Pepper Salt. When Amora got her Ph.D. she sent me a one-sentence note. "I could have been Dr. Pepper."

The main reason we never changed them, of course, was that it would have soured our relationship with Mom and Pop. The Sweethearts. That possibility was always more frightening than all those exchanges with bank tellers and blind dates.

My mother was Jewish (she is now dead and so previously or eternally Jewish). My pop is Italian. They did not live a conventional life. What foiled my therapy for years was how I could be so screwed up (responsible does not mean rational) when our parents had the perfect marriage. They adored one another. Until the day she died, they fell into one another's short olive-colored arms, hourly. They even looked alike, connected somewhere in past Arabian meldings, Mediterranean midnights, two ancient Semitic-tingled souls baying in the moonlight.

"Cara mia!"

"Bubeleh!"

They squeezed. They hugged. They anticipated one another's every wish. Everything was a loving compromise. Spaghetti with matzo balls. Gefilte fish oreganate.

"My Madonna!"

"My Moses!"

It was enough to make you lose your halvah marinara.

When Amora and I were ten my father sold his plumbing-supply business and moved us from Greenwich Village to a farm in the Adirondacks to fulfill his lifelong dream. My mother, who had never been north of Macy's, went with a brave smile. "This is a test of our love," she told me, stroking my wavy black hair.

"Jewish head, Italian heart. That's what we've given you." Sometimes she'd say, "Jewish head, Italian hands," or "Jewish head, Italian soul." The Italian parts changed. The head remained Jewish.

We went, kicking and screaming, into my father's dream. A Tuscany farm in upstate New York, with goats, chickens, and grapevines. Mr. Blandings and his dream house.

Hitler could have done bits on Pop's dream house and laid them in the aisles. Neither of my husbands nor Amora's ever got over Pop's creation.

Pop believed, as do all true Italians, that the dining room was the heart of the house. So, nestled on 150-odd acres of rolling, mystic meadows, he built a massive five-thousand-square-foot dining room and kitchen. The floor was stone, the ceiling was strung with Christmas lights that flickered and glowed from summer to winter. The walls were knotty pine, which was not in your authentic Italian farmhouse, but had been a very good deal from my Uncle Angelo. In the center of this enormous room was a plaster recreation of the fountain of Trevi, which could be converted into a Jacuzzi with the flick of a switch. Water jets shot bubbles from the plaster penises of cherubic bambinos to all the right pressure points.

To the north of the fountain–cum–hot tub was the largest dining-room table ever built on earth, including that in the *Last Supper*. A gargantuan oak slab that sat thirty without a leaf and had built into the center a lazy Susan large enough to rotate five pasta bowls, an entire hindquarter of lamb, several vegetable dishes, a twenty-pound turkey, and a whole provolone. The table was filled every single night that I can remember. This was not a childhood of quiet family meals. I still shout across the table even when it's just me and my daughter Vivika in the kitchenette.

At the opposite end of the room was what Amora and I snidely referred to as the "Dutch oven." A ten-foot-square fireplace with rack, most often filled with the crisping remains of one of Pop's flock. Searing animal flesh was the family fragrance.

Now, in Pop's passionate architectural frenzy to create the dining room of the century, he overlooked a lot of family necessities such as bedrooms, bathrooms, parlor. This reality hit him rather late in the building process, and so the bedrooms were thrown in to accommodate as many people as might be too sated after dinner and a dip in the fountain of Trevi to wend their way home. There were at least ten. And they all opened into one another. Finding the bathroom was the after-dinner game the guests played while Amora and I (who were never allowed the luxury of nudity in the privacy of our own boudoirs, and which created certain personal problems later in life) watched with sadistic glee. People lurching in and out of our rooms, kidneys swollen with Pop's homemade wine, desperation growing as the anticipated toilet grew more elusive. Our lips were sealed.

The exception to the chamber maze, with private entrance and plumbing, was the master bedroom, formerly the living room. At the last minute, money ran out, so the living room became their bedroom. This left no place for the grand swimming pool that, with the dining-room table, was an integral part of Pop's fantasy (he had been a swimmer in high school). So the swimming pool was put in their bedroom. Pop's ritual after dinner was to enter the living–pool–master suite, strip nude, dive in, swim some laps, and emerge by the terry-cloth robe my mother lovingly left for him. Then up the Astroturf stairs and into their bed. The outside wall of their room was glass so my Pop could see his goats and the mountains at dawn and the goats and sheep could see him and Momma going at it nightly, which they did with great gusto.

"My *Puttanesca!*"

"My Solomon!"

I have wandered from the point. The reason my sister and I were so insecure was not because we had come from a bad marriage, but precisely because we came from a great one. There was no room for us. We were always on the outside like the goats and the chickens, noses pressed to the hazy clouded glass, wanting to be in there with them where all the love and fun was. We never made it. Even after Momma died, when we thought we might have a crack at it. Her ghost replaced us. Like the prophet Elijah; a place was set at the table every night.

The most terrifying thing about Amora's murder was that it was so inappropriate. Nice Jewish-Italian girls from happy homes in New York State do not get beheaded on their fortieth birthdays. They die in their sleep at age seventy-eight of colon cancer in their Collins Avenue condos. (We had it all planned.) Little did we know that life was warming up, swaggering from the dugout to the mound, that famous left arm hot and loose, getting ready for the dreaded and always effective curveball.

For forty years I had fiercely believed that Amora was the winner and I the loser. Me victim. She star. She, the celebrated blonde Jane Fonda devotee, subject of *People* magazine articles, and a nationally renowned media shrink. Me, the "before" part of the photo.

We were both doctors of psychology. I'll give myself that. But my dusty little diploma hung on the spotted wall of my office at a halfway house and mental-health clinic for teenage runaways, while hers glittered in sterling silver on the gray suede wall of her Park Avenue offices. Not that she was without her little problems and private turmoil.

Amora felt that I had been Pop's favorite. She told me not long before the murder that she had always been competitive with me and that all of her perfection neuroses came from trying to be as different from me as possible to get Pop's approval. She had always competed. Even when we were still on training wheels. If my trike went two feet, hers had to go six. I was so terrorized by her maniacal glee at beating me that I just stopped trying to win at all. The alternative seemed to be a kind of accelerating fanatical competitiveness that was totally alien to my basically lazy and nonaggressive nature.

Amora's role model was Marilyn Monroe as seen by

Mary Poppins. It made her a real pain in the ass, especially by the time we reached high school. High school is where it all sticks to the pan. No one ever gets over high school. No one. What were the most formative years of your life? It's always high school. The only people who will disagree with the above statement after thinking it through are people who didn't go to high school.

In high school Amora was cheerleader; president of the student council; class princess; editor of the yearbook (she always laid out several dozen pictures of herself and none of me); drill-team captain; star of the modern-dance troupe (trees in the rain were her specialty); straight-A student; and voted Best-Dressed, Cutest Figure, and Most Likely to Succeed.

I was none of the above. But I had my niche. I wrote poetry and had a really eccentric but loyal and interesting group of friends. I was also voted Best Wit and Best Dancer (which drove Amora insane). Also, she had no friends. No girlfriends, that is, except one; but more about her later. Boys she had. Up until the bitter end.

I was okay as long as we were separated, but part of Amora's obsession with beating me made it essential that I be present as much as possible. She would change her schedule to get into my classes. Every class we shared I barely passed. I only really did well in subjects that were of no interest to her. I excelled in Spanish; she of course took French. "Spanish is a peon's language," she sniffed. It worked for me.

As we got older, I began to lose my steadfast commitment to failing for her sake. I started looking over my shoulder a little bit, too. And looking in the mirror. Frankly, it was a great relief to me when, in our senior year, Amora dyed her hair and had her first nose job. The less identical, the better. At last, I was an individual, rather than a rounder version of the same being, and so I began to look myself over more carefully. She couldn't stand what she saw, but I didn't think I was so bad. I liked to think of myself as of the Sophia Loren school. Earthy and natural. A little before my time, but I had my revenge in the seventies, when Amora was definitely out and I was definitely in. She never got over that.

After high school there were many years of little contact. I went west to college, she stayed east. I got married. She got married. I got divorced and moved back to New York. She got divorced and moved to New Mexico for post-doctoral work. She met a noted local shrink famous for his work with displaced Indians and his use of mescaline therapy, got remarried and moved to San Francisco and became a star. I got remarried and moved back to the Village.

Then, after fifteen years of Dodgem cars, she was offered a fantastic national news-radio job in New York and a featured weekly spot on the "Today" show and we were back in the same seething caldron.

And the sibling shit started all over again. Only this time it was working a little better for me.

Amora had, as the product of her first marriage, a thirteen-year-old son. Amora's son, Clive (after . . . of India) was sexually ambivalent. I had Vivika, who was sixteen. Vivika was not ambivalent. I was still married, fairly contentedly. Amora was recovering from flight from reality numero dos. Everything that she tried to even the score backfired. Our fateful exercise class, for example.

"Aro [my nickname because I was *straight as*], Amora insists that you come to Afro-Brazilian class with her at four." Amora talked about herself in the third person most of the time. She had done it for years but it intensified after she became famous. She had read somewhere that very famous people sometimes did that as a way of separating their real selves from their public selves. Which sounds good, except for two things. One is that trying to communicate with someone who does it is like trying to laugh underwater; and two, she mixed it up because she did it about her *private* self. Never on the radio, television, or, to my knowledge, with a patient. Some inner voice must have protected her.

"And what, pray tell, is Afro-Brazilian class? Do they teach you how to be one, empathize with one, or cook one?"

"Your sarcasm hides deep anxiety, dear one. It's dance, of course. You need it and I enjoy it. Besides, Amora wants to talk to you about something important."

"Sorry, I never talk and Afro-Brazil at the same time. It's bad for the digestion."

"First we'll dance, then we'll talk. I'll send a car for you."

I went, knowing that somehow a setup was in progress, but drawn by ancient, primordial forces. Womb bondings. Mingled amniotic fluids from our pre-birth connection. We had rolled together in eyeless, mindless silence. Floating in the placental algae of the life force. Closer together than anyone ever is. Two embryonic passengers in a black viscous elevator on our way to the basement of the universe. A split in the life force. An aberration, like a two-headed monkey. Crystalized, twinning, microscopic monsters. Freaks of nature, fighting for the same air supply, the same space in the shaft. Forming in tandem. Closer than intercourse, than plant to earth. We were God's doubleheader. Did we fight for who went first?

Maybe it was attenuated in us, germinating in Gemini, a severing sense of loss. Loneliness had stalked me all my life. And it stalked her too, though she did not admit it. I went down first and so it continued. We fought our twinning and lost the only chance at connection that either of us might have had. Cut. Alone forever. Twisting away from one another. Unwinding into the bright barren cold. Asundered.

I did surprisingly well in Afro-Brazil. This made Amora very quiet after class as we sipped our caffeine-free, NutraSweetened original Diet Coke with a lemon twist at the Odeon.

"What's the matter, Amo?" (Her nickname because she was loaded.)

She sighed and shook her head as if chasing away a thought too horrible to express.

"I'm not taut."

"What?"

"Not taut."

"What's not taut?"

"My face. I always thought it was taut, but it's not."

"Taut?"

"Not taut. I saw it. It jiggled when I jumped. I had my new sapphire-blue extended-wear contacts in and I saw it jiggle."

"*You* wore your contacts to an exercise class? A *mirrored* exercise class? That's really sick, Amora."

"Well, I thought I was taut. But I'm not taut."

"You're taut. You're plenty taut. You're one taut tootsie."

"I am not."

"You're taut enough. I mean, you're almost forty, for Chrissakes. Time to de-taut a bit."

"I am *not* almost forty. I am thirty-five, and at thirty-five one is taut."

"Oh. Yes, well. How silly of me to make such a

mistake. I remember now. I'm almost forty but my identical twin sister is thirty-five. Boy, that birth canal is a real bitch, ain't it?"

"Amora Sweet is a public person. And she has been quoted, in print, in several leading magazines, on her feelings about being thirty-five. Everyone *knows* that she is thirty-five. And you must not forget that fact, because Amora wants to include her *older* sister in some of her good fortune."

"She always was generous. What a woman. And so taut. We're talking taut."

"I am about to offer you an incredible opportunity."

"Does it involve being thirty-five and quite taut?"

"No. *Amora* is thirty-five. Aroma is older. The rest is a personal choice. If you would like to come with me to Dr. Piatneski, whom Amora plans to call immediately after we finish, we can see about tautening. Otherwise, what I pose is a chance for you not only to make some real money, but to join me in the public arena."

"No shit."

"Please lower your voice and listen very carefully."

"If I'm listening, I don't need to lower my voice."

"You're threatened, sweet sister. And you're acting out."

"Okay. Okay. I'll stop, but, please, no unsolicited therapy. You know what it does to me."

"Aro. How would you like to share my radio show with me?"

"Message is scrambled. More information needed."

Amora sighs. "All right. Let me be frank." She sighs again and a shiver runs through her entire body. "Aro, I'm burned out. I loathe the radio show. Talking to all those faceless, scummy people. You can't believe some of the calls and the letters! It's draining my positive energy.

I know it's why I'm losing my tautness. I can't keep it up! Five days a week plus my practice and the 'Today' show and the column and the speaking engagements and the social life and all. And, of course, there's Clive."

"Of course."

"I am at my wit's end, because after all, the show has made Amora famous and it is very lucrative, and believe me, there are hundreds of unqualified witches waiting to take it away from me, if I should slip or falter or, worse, God forbid, say something on the air, something terrible."

I lean forward. "Something terrible, like what?"

Amora leans in.

"Like, well, for example, the other day, this awful woman called in. She was a hysteric, that was obvious. 'I'm a lady poet,' she said. 'And before I tell you my problem I must know who your favorite poet is.' 'Yeats,' I replied. 'Yeats?' she said. 'Oh no. I don't think I could open up to someone whose favorite poet is Yeats. He's such a romantic. I don't think I'd feel safe with you,' she said. And I, well, I almost said to her, 'Who the fuck cares, you delusive old cunt.' I started to say it and my engineer cut me off. Can you imagine if it had come out? On the radio! My God! I need a break or I'll jeopardize everything I've worked for."

Tears form at the sides of her sapphire-contacted eyes.

"I'm really sorry, Amo. I always think of you being able to handle everything. I'm sorry I teased you."

She shakes her head—shaking the unfallen tears off into the air flow. "No. No. It's my fault. I put on too good a show. However, let me get to my point. Last night, during my facial, I had a brilliant idea. Radio, right? No one can *see* me. So, if my *older* sister, who is also a highly trained professional therapist with an untrained but otherwise identical voice, were to sit in for me now and again, I would get some time off and she would get the opportunity of a lifetime."

"Listen. This is very heavy. How about a couple of real Cokes with caffeine and sugar and everything?"

"How about a vodka martini?"

"You're on."

2

What Kind of People Listen to the Radio?

For the next several hours Amora and I discussed her proposition. She had an answer for each of my snide and skeptical questions. As chance would have it, one of Amora's lovers was James Mackay, the owner of WNRD, Amora's station. Jimmy Bob (as his intimates called him) was a seemingly nice middle-class Irishman from Connecticut who had suddenly appeared in New York business and media circles buying everything in sight. He was a flamboyant and mysterious mogul—the kind of guy rumors and blondes follow. And he had two rather printworthy idiosyncrasies: one, he employed a huge number of Chinese and was accompanied everywhere by three very kung-fuian bodyguards; and two, he was completely obsessed with country music, cowboy heroes, and rodeo shows. He was the proud owner of four hundred pairs of cowboy boots in every known reptile skin and enough suede and leather garments to have pulled the Comanches through the Ice Age. Jimmy Bob adored Amora not only because she wore black suede chaps, high-heeled snakeskin boots, and a smile during their "hayrides," but because, compared to his wife, Wanda, Amora was a real down-home gal.

Wanda Mackay had done one semi-selfless thing in her entire over-massaged life. She gave Jimmy Bob a child. Unfortunately, it was a girl (delivered by cesarean at the seventh month to avoid any unnecessary wear and tear on Wanda's lissome frame). The result, by age six, was a mini version of Wanda replete with scaled-down designer wardrobe, her own facialist and hairdresser, and a rather original banter.

Little Wanda to chauffeur: "I don't want to take the Mercedes to school today. *Everyone* comes in a Mercedes. I want to take the Rolls!"

Chauffeur, calmly: "I'm sorry, Miss Mackay, but your father has designated the Mercedes as the school car."

Little Wanda, precociously: "Listen, you faggot cocksucker, you do what I say or you're history."

Jimmy Bob did not much like it at home with this duo, and Amora's soothing, man-pleasing facade offered welcome solace. So, if Amora wanted her sister to sub— Amora, who would never do anything to embarrass Jimmy Bob: "Trust me, darling, my sister's a much better therapist than I am. She really cares about the masses and their problems. I'll handle everything. It'll be our little secret"— so be it, or so Amora said.

"Just climb up here and ride my bronco, little lady, and you can have any little old thing you require." Amora got her blue-ribbon ride and I got the tail of the donkey.

Martinis or no martinis, I did not make any commitment. I needed time to think. Even though it was after eight when I left her, I decided to walk and clear my head. I weaved up West Broadway, through Tribeca toward Canal Street. Rush hour was over. It was drizzling and the fresh mist felt soothing and cool on my untautened cheeks. The bag ladies were out in force. Scampering from dumpster to dumpster, rummaging, like Long Island matrons at Macy's Thanksgiving Day Sale, for Sprite cans and Heineken bottles.

I stopped for the light and watched one. Her name was Rachel. I knew her from the Grand Union at LaGuardia Place, where she lined up every morning to feed her soda-pop cans into the recycling machine. Sometimes she had a huge lawn-and-leaf bag and it took hours. She paid no heed to the shouted insults of the waiting junkies and less industrious peers. Rachel did her thing. Rachel carried a club in her bony filthy hand and had a half-dead pit bull for protection. No one messed with her.

I watched her now, her toughened eagle-beaked face intent on her work. The animal was tied to her bulging shopping cart with frayed surplus rope. I thought about Amora and the flip side. Wanda Mackay. Rachel. Me. Rachel. The victims and the valiant fighters. Or what? More and more I wondered about that.

Women were packing it in. For the first time in history. Bag ladies. Bag persons. Women were lying on Madison Avenue with crusted, lice-infested hair, jagged black toenails, and not an ounce of Oil of Olay in sight. Women. The backbone of society. The keepers of the family fire.

Through the centuries, the men went down, lost to war, drink, disease, insanity, or the pressure of daily life, but the women hung on. Apron ironed. Brave smile in place. Suckling the young on wizened, tired tits. Proud, mothering *and never giving up*. Well, hell. This was 1988 and they were giving it up all over the fucking place. Laying it down, spreading it out, and giving it up.

It had a certain allure. What if one decided, for example, that it was no longer worth it; that the rewards for leg shaving, chicken roasting, child rearing, husband pleasing, career building, exercising, nail buffing, moisturizing, fashion scouting, self-improving were no longer worth the toll? It was rather seductive to imagine sprawling, kicking back into a sea of lowered expectations and no responsibilities. No more shoulds. No more waiting for the dishwasher repairman, waiting for the plumber, waiting for the kettle to boil. I watched and I thought about Amora's proposition.

On the plus side, I certainly could use the money. She had offered me one-half of her day rate (I later found out it was only one-third). It averaged out to about five thousand dollars a month, or more than double what I was making at the halfway house, and it was a chance to do something really stimulating.

Needless to say, every time I listened to her show, I cringed in horror at her shabby skills and insulting advice, convinced with every fiber of my being that I could advise circles around her. I would be near the limelight for the first time, and who knew where it could lead?

One night, after months of excellent broadcasts, I would come unglued on the air, thereby ruining her career. I would then offer my undisguised services—the sweet Sweet sister rises to the top and saves the ratings!

Anyway, the whole thing had possibilities.

On the minus side, there was the rather obvious insult to my autonomy and self-respect, not to mention the emotional pitfalls of pretending to be the identical twin sister that had been the bane of my existence and the source of most of my self-destructive and infantile behavior. And something else, something harder to define: a desperation beneath Amora's control.

I wavered. And then Rachel turned her world-weary face and caught my eyes in her angry, despairing stare. And I understood something. The joke was on the bag ladies. There was no way out. She worked harder now to stay alive than she ever could have in Staten Island keeping house for Mr. Rachel and her hatchet-faced family. She worked like a vassal. Hardly sleeping. Never stopping. And in constant danger. Better to wait for a plumber a day, Aroma dear. There is no free lunch, not even in the garbage bins. Rachel and I crossed the street. By the time I got to Washington Square, I had made my decision.

We began with my sitting in the control room watching Amora do her thing.

Caller: "My name is Linda, and I'm thirty-six years old. Oh, Dr. Sweet, I can't believe I'm really talking to you! I've never missed one show! I—you've saved my life!"

Amora, mildly patronizing: "That's very nice, Linda. How can I help you?"

"Well, Doctor, I'm very depressed."

"Oh, that's too bad. How long have you felt this way?"

"Oh, off and on for about eight years."

"Really!"

"I'm legally blind, so I don't get out much. And I have terrible trouble with my weight. I weight about two hundred and fifty pounds right now and I'm only five feet two!"

"Oh dear."

"And I have four children under the age of ten, and my husband, he drinks and abuses me. He lost another job last week, and our unemployment's run out. I'm just depressed. I don't know why."

"Well, no wonder, Linda. You have a very negative attitude! No man wants to be around a woman who's depressed and negative all the time. First of all, you must start an exercise program. I know when I'm out of shape, I feel dreadful. Get out and get some exercise!"

"But I don't have the money and I need someone to go with me, and that means leaving the kids, and they're too little to be left alone."

"I'm sorry, Linda, it's time for one of our sponsors to intercede. We're out of time. Just think positive and cut out all refined sugar!"

"My name is Ida and I'll be seventy-six next month. God willing."

"How lovely, Ida, and how can I help you?"

"Well, Doctor, I'm a widow. My Harry passed away three years ago next month. God rest his soul. And, well, I met a fella. Lovely gentleman. Seventy-seven years old next spring, God willing, and we've been, well, we've been together for about a year . . ."

"Oh, Ida. You're a big girl. Do you mean that you and your gentleman *sleep* together?"

"No. No way! I have my place. He has his place. Rent-controlled. No. We do it and then he goes home to sleep."

"Oh, Ida, good for you!"

"Not so good. Here's the situation. He plays cards with three widow ladies in our building. Tuesday and Thursday nights. And I don't know. I get nervous."

"Ida dear, do you mean nervous or jealous?"

"Yeah. The other one."

"Oh, Ida. I don't think you have anything to worry about. Why, to be sexually active at your age. He's a lucky man."

"You don't know these women! Listen. He's taught me things—Harry, God rest his soul, would drop dead if he knew what he's taught me. He likes to fool around down there with my female parts. And at first, oy, I thought I would be sick with shame! Now, I don't mind. It's pleasant. It makes him happy. But he wants me to do it to him. To put his, you know, in the mouth. I would rather be struck by lightning! I would rather die! I told him. Never! Not even if he had cancer, never! But when he goes to play cards, I think, if one of those girls would do that, I'm a goner."

"Oh, Ida. I think he's a very lucky man. All I can suggest is go with him. Keep your eyes open and get into the group! I think you're just adorable. Let Ida be an example, girls! It's never too late!"

"Doctor, I know I'm a goner! That Esther, she's a real whore."

"Ida, I'm out of time! But hold on and we'll give you some sex-therapy referrals. Maybe overcoming your aversion to oral sex might alleviate your fear. Hold on, dear."

"I'd rather be dead!"

After a while the calls ran together. The woman who left her husband alone and dying of cancer because "he was bringing me down." The gay accountant who was passionately in love with his straight boss. The frigidos. The nymphos. Guilty adulterers. Sociopaths. Women in love with sociopaths. Mothers of sociopaths (Amora was very much into sociopaths). Transvestites. Alcoholics. Children of alcoholics. Child abusers. Potential child abusers. Former child abusers. Abusees of every form and shape. Homos. Homophobics. Widows coping with grief. Wives coping with rage. Everyone coping with anxiety and self-doubt.

The red lights gleamed, the phones flashed. People crowding the systems like quiz contestants, remaining on hold forever for a chance; a moment of contact with the life line. The answer. The hope. Dr. Amora Sweet. Saviorette. Am I all right? Is it all right? Tell me it's all right? She will not judge. The abuser and abused tap dancing with the A.M. Jesus. *All is forgiven, come home. Love, Mom.* A thirty-second secular chance at absolution.

My mind began to wander. I thought about things like how many different kinds of shit there were: bull, whale, rat, bunny, turkey. And the biggest shit of all. Shrink shit. This was definitely it. Shrink poo-poo. Then my mind flipped the dial to Amora's second husband, the prominent Jungian analyst John P. Harrington, host of a short-lived cable therapy show entitled "The Analyst and Analasand: A Dialogue." The dialogue went like this.

The arrogant, narcissistic doctor: "Elmer is our guest tonight. Elmer, tell me what's going on with you."

"I'm having migraines. I haven't had them for years. My mother died a couple of months ago and I've been having terrible headaches ever since."

"That's fairly in line with normal defense reactions. Let me tell you about myself, Elmer. Here I am, an educated, sophisticated professional. A respected doctor, a devoted husband and father. Sometimes, I curl up into a little ball and lie in the dark sobbing all night. 'I'm no one's child,' I wail over and over. I've done that periodically ever since my parents died. Let the grief get out. The headaches will stop. You know the way. I still wail and kick my feet and scream, 'I'm no one's baby! I want my momma!' Of course what we are searching for is the mythical mom.

Not the real one. The perfect one who would give us endless unconditional love and protection. The goddess mom. That is the tragedy of modern life. How far away the family myths have gone. When a parent dies we mourn the loss of our universal connection. When they go, there is no one between us and destiny. The brink, the finite nature of the universe is on us. We lose all fantasy of safety. Even if the real parent was a harridan, a demon. When they go, we are left alone with the reality that we will never get *it*. Never get the validation, the love, the fantasy bonding we have fought our way toward against all odds. The cord is clipped. And the pain is vast."

Not much of a dialogue. Amora left Dr. Dementia shortly after a whimsical family vacation in Florida, the point of which was a last attempt at establishing a working relationship with Clive.

Clive and his steppapa were not exactly the abalone and the rock. So, after three years of tension, they had departed on the trail of camaraderie. Somewhere around Palm Beach the scout disappeared and the trail ended in the Atlantic.

Clive and the doctor had taken out a paddleboard together. Clive, being sullen and ambivalent, did not want to go, and most certainly did not want to paddle. They went around and around in circles. This drove the doctor crazy. So, using all of his superb analytic training, the doctor shouted at seven-year-old Clive, "You're not a man!"

Amora, who is sunning on a nearby deck, comes to the side to see what the screaming is about. Clive eyes his mother and yells, "He said I wasn't a man—but he's the one. He's not a man! He whined about his feet being cold, but I never complained once!"

"I'll kill you, you little son of a bitch!" the doctor replies, throwing himself on top of poor Clive and trying to drown him while Amora screams for help from above.

During the day I sat in the control booth with Chen the screener and his helper, and O'Ralph, the producer, the people who sort out the loonies from the losers, who make sure no one insults Dr. Sweet or screams out her real age or hisses obscenities into the air waves. *What kind of people listen to the radio? Lonely people.*
At night at home I really started to get into the entire radio spectrum. Eighties radio. No more Fibber McGee and Jack Benny. Now we had semiliterate disk jockeys proffering the new music to alienated teenagers in New Brunswick. "Now, punkers and hunkers from Maine to Mars, we like got something so bad, so rad, so mad, so sad. Like, The Cramps."
The Cramps crooned "Vaaaalium . . . V-al-ium." I could hear Cole Porter sobbing somewhere. Then Prince, the Cabbage Patch doll of teeny decadence, wailed the love affair of Mickey. "I met her in the waiting room. She was masturbating a magazine. Oh, Mickey, Mickey . . ."
Tell the radio audience, Prince, how did the lyric line of "Mickey" develop? Is it based on a personal incident? And I know our young people are curious: Was it a gossip, news, or shelter publication? Was the magazine actually masturbating Mickey, or was she, in fact, performing the act on it? If so, how does one go about that? Is there any danger of contracting AIDS from such sexual activity? And lastly, but certainly of great interest, does chafing occur from continuous involvement?
DJs for every taste. The milky, marijuana'd fifties tones of the jazz station. "Hey, you are tuned to WKOL, Manhattan's primo jazz station. Like to take you back to the days of the giants. Let's trip down memory lane with

the man himself. Mr. Charlie Mingus and his golden implement."

"This is J. Arthur Fostwick, your host for 'Sonata at Sunset.' Now the lights dim, the curtain is rising, come with us to the land of musical enchantment. Tonight, in response to popular request, an hour of Gregorian chants performed by the Mormon Geriatric Men's Chorus, followed by the long-forgotten concerto of eighteenth-century Portuguese composer Ponce Sardinão."

The cooking shows. A demented chirpy female and a sonorous and jovial male announcer answer recipe questions from people that, God willing, will never invite you for dinner.

"Last Christmas, you gave out your chutney and cream cheese stuffing recipe. I lost it! Could you *paleeze* do it again?"

"Oh, I'm so glad you called! I forgot all about that! It is a goody, isn't it? Let's see now. First you take your blanched almonds. Then you add your softened cream cheese and a half pound of your marzipan."

"Mmmmmm. Patsy, our mouths here at the station are watering!"

There was something to this radio scene. Being a child of the late fifties, it had been of little interest. It was always there, but it seemed to be something to play while being felt up in your car or when the stereo was broken. TV without the visual. A nostalgic anachronism. But the more I listened, the more I understood. In its own way it was far more intimate, connecting, and seductive than the tube. A voice right next to you, like the ones inside your head, keeping you tuned in.

It was on the West Coast during my marriage to Amos Cohen, the Marlon Brando of Berkeley, who did a lot of speed and was up nights, that I first experienced the power of the radio waves. Amos opened the late-night talk shows to my callow sensibility. I listened to strange isolated people, people who lived alone, had insomnia, or both, and who could wax rhapsodic about Greek politics at three o'clock in the morning.

These people were so well informed! Not like the mainstream TV crowd. The "Dating Game" group. "Bachelor number one, if I let you kiss my car on the first date, what would you say?"

"Er, um, 'Wow,' I'd say. 'Wow, what a lobe!'"

These people, sitting by their AM-FM tuners, knew their foreign affairs. I hadn't thought about those California days or poor Amos for years. That's another thing I found out listening to Amora, the radio lets your mind wander rather pleasantly.

I kept visualizing a person who became my generic radio audience. It is a woman in her late sixties with short gray permed hair and a quilted powder-pink bathrobe, the kind with "flammable" warnings inside. She wears reading glasses and slightly soiled blue mules. She is sitting in her living room in one of those old-fashioned Queens apartments that she has lived in since the War of the Roses. She has a copy of the *New York Post* on her lap and a half-full cup of Chock Full o' Nuts all-method grind on the Early American side table that also holds her radio and reading lamp. On the floor is her cat.

The radio waves undulate outward from Astoria to Kew Gardens, sound transmissions busy disturbing the space between things. Widows and insomniacs, cats and canaries, the waves disturbing the surface of their lives.

Every single one of us has one. It is a necessary personal possession. Comb. Toothbrush. Alarm clock. Radio. Now, it can even go with us. Plug it into your ear and never be without those movements in the air, those voices in your head. Mind-gum. They curve in and out of all of our private places, the places where we are special, behind the doors where we are kings. No matter how empty, inconspicuous, and lonely our daily lives, we come back to our kingdoms. Out toaster oven, our favorite chair.

In the middle of the night, when the aging lady in the pink robe is most aware of her distance from everyone else. The endless distance of human aloneness, the silence of the swallowed scream. The twitch of hope moves her fingers.

"I would like to ask your esteemed guest, Mr. Ellsberg, do you really think that Bobby Kennedy was involved in the Monroe death? I can't believe that a man of your reputation could get into those gray areas. It sells books. I know that, I write myself, but Bobby, he was nearly a saint. Did you read *The Kennedys?* He comes off like the daisy in that weed garden. I don't think you can back any of this up . . ."

Radio waves sending the siren song from Akron to Indianapolis, "V-al-ium" soothing the loneliness like the purring cats and the hum of the Frigidaire. Being lonely myself, I really began to identify. When nuclear war hits, the tube will go blank forever. The radio will be our last connection to the rest of humanity.

As part of my training program I not only became rather obsessed with listening to it, but with hanging around WNRD every chance I got. Additionally, I practiced with Amora in her co-op at night.

"Now, Aro, I'm going to tape this, so you can hear how you sound. I'll be the caller and you respond as you think appropriate. I'm sure you understand the hand signals and the countdowns by now, so I won't go into all that. Let's take one. One, two, three . . . You're on."

"Hello. You're on with Amora Sweet. Who am I talking to?"

"I'm Emily and I'm fifty. Oh, Dr. Sweet, I am such a fan of yours! I can't tell you what listening to you has done for me! I saw you on the 'Today' show and you're gorgeous! I couldn't believe you could be so insightful and so beautiful. You are a real role model for American women!"

"Okay, doll. Cut the shit and ask the question."

Amora turns off the tape. "Just what are you doing? This is no time for jokes. I was hoping you'd be able to start next Monday."

"Sorry, sis, but do I have to listen to a press release before every question? Give me a break."

"I am trying to recreate a real situation. And many, many calls are from admirers like that. You must be gracious and patient with your compliments."

"*Your* compliments. I'm terrific with *my* compliments."

"Every job has its down side. Let's go on. You are a true role model for American women."

I, in my best Amora voice: "You're so kind. How may I help you?"

"Well, Doctor, it's about my husband. We've been married twenty-five years. Our children are grown, and . . . and [Amora sniffles, histrionically] he came home last week and told me he's fallen in love with his secretary and he wants a separation. I'm just sick. I can't sleep or eat. I don't know what to do. He says that he still loves me and he wants to keep living here but he'll move into the guest room (it was our son's room before he went away to school), and he wants to be free to see this woman whenever he pleases. He says he's very confused and that he needs room to explore his feelings. What should I do?"

"Tell Mr. Mid-life Crisis to take a fast train to inner space. Tell the turkey to sort it out at little Miss Muffet's place. Let her do the dishes while listening for the sound of a decision being made. Do not wash one more sock under any circumstances! Check for signs of venereal disease and make a casual phone call to a good women's-rights lawyer—"

Amora snaps the tape off, her alabaster face a tad on the crimson side. "Just what in hell are you doing now? Can't you be serious about anything? What kind of a therapist are you? Is that what you do with those poor little teenyboppers? Sneer at their sordid difficulties?"

"I'm sorry. You're right. You are absolutely right. I don't know what came over me. It was just such a set-up question. I have new respect for how hard it is to do what you do. Remember the dame that called yesterday and asked how you felt about anal intercourse? 'Why, I think it's a gas, dear. Excuse the pun. I just love it. Go for it. Tell the lucky devil you have my full support!'"

Amora sighs. Her color recedes, she rises and pours herself a sherry. I have not earned one. "Do you know what I wanted to say? I wanted to say, I think it's sick and disgusting, unnatural and unhygienic. Look at the fags . . . it's what they do and now they're dying like houseflies, dear."

We laugh together at the same thing at the same time. One of those fragile moments of human connection, when the wave is ridden together. Shore is reached simultaneously. A rare occurrence that goes a long way in marriage and in sisterhood.

"Oh my God, Amo. You really do need help. You poor thing! Why, just think of the possible scenarios of what you could say. Don't worry. I promise, I won't blow it for you. I'll be good. I'll be as ladylike and professional as your audience deserves. Let's try it again."

How blind I still was with her. It was just like our

childhood. Me so eager to please that one moment of potential humanity from her and I was Play-Doh in her creamy hands. I wanted so badly to believe that we were alike, that her magic could rub off, that we were the same inside, that I forgot all that I knew. The smile that never reached her phony blue eyes. The sudden coldness, the withdrawal the minute she had what she wanted. We had shared a moment of mirth and it erased almost forty years of reference material.

On my way back downtown that night, the reality of what I was getting myself into finally hit. I had been skirting it. I had not even told Vivika or Clifford, my husband. I didn't want any input that might have altered my decision. Now the moment of truth was approaching. The responsibility I was assuming was suddenly terrifying. It was harder work than it looked. Would I fail at what she did so well, thereby proving to her, myself, and our dear departed mother once and for all that she was better? The lights in our apartment were on. Tonight was the night of marital communion.

3

The Home-Life Part

My second husband Clifford Jergens was an art historian. He taught art history at NYU and wrote commentary for the *Voice* and some ritzy-titzy art journals. I married him because he was everything Amos Cohen was not. He wasn't Jewish, insane, outgoing, funny, or crude. He also wasn't like Pop: Italian, verbal, and earthy.

Clifford (never Cliff, not even as a teeny-weeny baby, this was not a Cliff), was a *serious person*. A true intellectual. A person who would never be found dead with a copy of *People* magazine by the john. *U.S. News* and *The New*

Yorker were too lowbrow for Clifford. Illuminated manuscripts were his idea of summer reading.

Clifford and I had been married for five years the night I told him about Amora's plan. He worked at home, and so it seemed as if we saw a lot of one another, the three of us crammed into Clifford's fortuitously rent-controlled apartment on Ninth and University Place, but we rarely intersected. It was one of those prewar jobs with little windows and dank hallways that always smelled of must and yesterday's bacon. I hated it. It is always a mistake to move into the lair of the lion. Relationships need neutral territory, space with no prior claims upon it; where neither person has looked at a certain vase on a certain table for twenty years.

"Where's my granny's Venetian vase?"

"Oh, I thought it might look nice on the windowsill."

"You moved Granny's vase? Without asking? Put it back at once!"

"Will not! I live here, too!"

"That vase hasn't been moved since Granny passed on. Put it back!"

Sound of vase flying through the air and crashing against table.

"Okay, it's back!"

But Vivika and I were beggars at the time and so not too demanding. I never ever felt that I lived there, or that anything about it had to do with me. I was a white-walls-and-light person. Clifford was an antique-and-forest-green type. The Reich's museum was his decorating style. Rembrandt and Van Eyck were definitely his look. Lately however, he had fallen under the spell of the SoHo scene, the new art. The trend that appeared to me to revere anything that looked as if the artist was either nine years old or serving a life sentence for mass murder, or both.

"It's fresh. A fresh voice!" Clifford would shout. Clifford never ever shouted, so I am overdramatizing to make a point. If you heard Clifford the *first* time, without asking him to speak up—*that* was considered a shout in our house. To Clifford, my normal speaking voice was maniacal raving.

"Clifford, it's a monstrosity." We wandered from a bronze caterpillar with a porkpie hat and tongue sticking out to a sort of Smurfette as seen by Arp. On the walls were floor-to-ceiling paintings of menacing cartoonlike hoodlums raping animals. "Michelangelo would have a stroke."

"No. No. He would embrace it!"

"No one would embrace a bronze caterpillar."

"It's new. It's art." Clifford shook his head and sighed at my blind ignorance.

"It's crapola, bunkie. I need detox. Get me to the Met, quick." We had our differences, as you may have gathered. Clifford looked like Donald Sutherland playing Ingmar Bergman. I think that is what first drew me to him; he was as unidentical, as alien to my small, round, dark-haired being as any earthling that ever lived.

Every day was a winter in Norway for Clifford. The world was seen through a fog of morose ambivalence and stern contemplation. He was what once would have been described as the strong, silent type. Dinner, when Vivika wasn't home, was often the sound of one fork clattering.

I did love Clifford. He was righteous, brilliant, and honorable. He was patient and thoughtful and terrific to Pop. It's just that Amora and I grew up with rather peculiar ideas about men and marriage. Somewhere between Scarlett O'Hara and Germaine Greer. It was part of our competition. Because the Sweethearts were so impossible to fathom and we were so pissed at our position, we didn't look on *marriage forever* as the way to go. We made a bet on our tenth birthday. Whoever had been married the most times by our sixtieth birthday was the winner. The winner of what was unclear. What was clear was that Amora was ahead. Two down. This made me a bit more philosophical about my relationship with Clifford. With Amos, I was so out of control that the contest hadn't taken on significance yet.

I got in the elevator with our next-door neighbor, Madeline, runner-up in the Sandra Dee at Fifty Look-Alike Contest. A petite spinster lawyer who lived with her ten cats and lost hope.

"Hi, Madeline. How's life?"

"I'm still in the same rut. I need a change. I need some adventure, but God, I've got rent control!"

"I know how that is. Could you sublet?"

"The babies."

"Sublet to a cat fancier."

"You hear such stories. I should come see you. I really need some professional help. My karmic bonding is off. I'm not happy, but I'm not unhappy. I have season tickets to everything. I have my little home all set up. I know where the best butcher, the best shoe repair is, but something's missing. I'm germinating. I may be a very young soul; I may have to wait till next time."

"Sounds like good planning."

"The only danger is that our souls are reaching the cutoff point. Soon they're not going to get through anymore. There's going to be a million souls trapped here, and no more reincarnations for a long time, not until the Age of Aquarius. And current belief is that it takes several incarnations to change just one bad habit; that's how hard it is to change."

"Do me a favor: Don't tell any of my patients."

"I know it sounds silly, but it's true. That's why I'm so scared of risking. I'm a secondary supplier. Not a creative person, not a primary supplier. I need a push. I need a man to call and invite me to move to Paris with him. Something to motivate me."

The goddamn elevator has stopped moving. I am now trapped with tiny Madeline and her chunky bosoms and her bag of cat food. "I think the elevator didn't make the cutoff. We may be here a while."

An omen. An obstacle between me and telling my family about Amora's offer.

"You wouldn't believe what happened last night. I had a blind date. A patent attorney from Syracuse, a friend of a friend. He came up and I said, 'How about going out for some coffee?' And he said, 'Listen, honey, I'll ball you or I'll buy you coffee, but make up your mind quick. I don't have time for both.'"

"I hope it was good coffee."

"I've had better."

The elevator passes through. We are reincarnated onto the fifth floor. "Night, Madeline."

"I really am going to call you."

"Call my sister on the radio. It's cheaper. You're doing fine. There's nothing wrong with a nice safe rut, kid. Enjoy."

"I do have my little world."

My little world had not seemed to miss me. Clifford was in his study, so I thought I'd start with Vivika, who was more overt and less dense, more volume-displaced by the biological phenomenon of teenage-a-mania.

Vivika was in her room eating a piece of carrot cake and listening to someone on the radio screaming what sounded like, "Fuck, Fucky, Fucka, Fucko."

"Hi, baby. Who's that singing? Is he singing 'Fuck'?"

"Of course. God, Mother, you are really out of it."

"They can sing that on the radio?"

"That's nothing." (Vivika is too bored to keep explaining current reality to her mother, who is neither current nor real). She changes the subject.

"Did you go out wearing *that*?"

"Yes. Terrifying, isn't it? It's not fluorescent, not made of latex, and not torn! People gasped on the streets. What are you doing?"

"Biology homework. What do you call it when you have a big lower jaw and your bottom teeth stick out over your top teeth?"

"An ugly face."

"Mother. You're so creepy."

"Ask Clifford, he's into that stuff."

"If I ask Clifford, he'll turn it into a great big deal. He'll pull out all those big books and it will take forever. God, he drives me so crazy. Everything is so *sixties* with him. He's so *herbal*."

I sink to my knees beside her carrot cake. "Oh, no! Not that! Don't ever tell him that! It would break his heart! You really hit below the belt. Oh my God! A sixties herbal!"

Vivika smiles at me. Her lovely wide-cheekboned face, the face that has always melted my heart, softens. For a moment my baby reappears inside the teenage posture. My baby's face. My buddy. My gift. Stuck together through thick and thin.

"You're cute, Mommy. Want some of this?"

"Just a small bite."

"You think small. Everything you do is small." A teenager is returning.

"Small and nonfattening."

"You don't take any risks. You never just let go, just get wild. You're so fearful. Small bites of everything."

"Go ahead, dear. You take the risk, eat the whole piece. Don't cry to me when your jeans explode."

"I wasn't referring to the cake."

"Well, for your information, I am about to take a huge bite. My first real honest-to-God mainstream risk."

"Is it fattening?"

"No. Maybe immoral. Possibly illegal. But absolutely dietetic."

Vivika thought it was a great idea, though she balked at not being able to tell her friends about it. I knew pretty well beforehand that she'd like it. Teenagers live in that brackish marsh of narcissism and tunnel vision, without a sense of consequence, so that almost anything dangerous is appealing. Words like jail, death, failure, cellulite hold no threat because they are totally unvisualized concepts in relation to their own Noxema-softened reality.

Clifford was something else entirely. I tiptoed in. He was sitting in his houndstooth wing chair with his feet up on his grandmother's needlepoint footstool, reading a tome on Gothic architecture.

"Have you gotten to the rape scene yet?" I lean over playfully and kiss his cool bony cheek.

Clifford does not respond. No chuckle, no nothing. "Shwash, hisp she, sh, sh shucumble clinic?"

"Could you repeat that? I didn't hear you honey."

"Where were you so late? Was there a crisis at the clinic?"

I saunter around in front of him and curl up on the Turkish prayer rug at his long slender feet. "Nope. I had a meeting with Amora."

This interests him. I can tell by a slight raising of his

left eyebrow. If Clifford won first prize in the New York State lottery, his jubilation could be charted by two raised eyebrows and a tight smile. "There is certainly a lot of sisterly communication going on of late."

"Yes. But it's not really about anything personal. It's about a job. I, uh, wanted to talk to you about it for a minute."

Clifford is intensely curious. I can tell by the way he recrosses his ankles and leans slightly forward. "A job? For whom?"

"For moi. I didn't want to tell you until I was sure about it. What she wants is for me to take over her radio show for a while until she catches up on things and gets some rest. She's totally exhausted, and since our voices are identical and I am a therapist, too . . . well, she made me a fantastic offer, Clifford. It comes out to about five thousand dollars a month and I don't have to give up my job. I'll just rearrange my hours. I'm nervous as hell, but I'm kind of excited, too."

Clifford is definitely paying attention. He has closed the volume on his lap. "I have a question. This does not in any way sound like your sister. Why would she want to make you a competitor? What if you do better than she with that ridiculous fraud she performs on poor defenseless souls? Why wouldn't she ask one of her less-threatening colleagues to take over for a while?"

Heh, heh, heh, I laugh nervously. "Oh, I think you've misunderstood. She . . . I . . . she isn't exactly going to introduce me or anything. It's more like . . . no one would know . . . like pretending that I'm her."

This is almost a two-eyebrow situation. Clifford stands up, lights his pipe, and begins to pace back and forth, looking like Abraham Lincoln the night before the Gettysburg Address. This goes on until I can't stand it anymore.

"Clifford. For Chrissakes, say something."

Clifford keeps pacing. "Since your decision has obviously been made without consulting me, I don't really see that my saying anything would be of any possible use."

The guy had a point. That was the trouble with having a serious conversation with a rational self-contained person. There I was flailing in the void and there he was being logical and firm-footed. "I'm sorry, honey. You're absolutely right. I should have discussed it with you sooner, but it all happened so fast and by the time I had sorted everything out, I was already rather committed."

"Not the most reasonable way of making life decisions."

"If I had been reasonable, I'd still be in the Adirondacks milking goats."

"Perhaps. Perhaps not."

"Clifford, you are making me so crazy right now. This is like 'Masterpiece Theater.' Real people don't have fights like this. Give me an opinion. Give me an emotion! Tell me I'm a stupid shit. Anything!"

"No."

"I'll throw your grandmother's footstool out of the window if you don't. I swear I will. Yell at me!"

Clifford stops pacing and sits down at his desk. "If you throw my grandmother's needlepoint stool out the window, I'll throw Vivika out the window."

Now we are getting somewhere.

"Okay. Okay. Fight dirty! You've got that sadistically cruel Viking streak. Ice water in your DNA. You win. Punish me with your withdrawal. Go ahead! I'll fill in the blanks. You think that I'm insane to get involved in something like this. I'm playing right into Amora's polished little hands. I'm a delusionary fool and I'm making a terrible mistake. One that could ruin my career and bring shame to my family!"

Clifford looks into my seething frightened yellow-brown eyes with his coolest, bluest stare and nods. Slowly. If you blinked, you'd have missed it. I didn't blink.

Have you forgotten everything you've ever learned, Aroma? Being a healthy post-therapy woman is knowing that you can't afford one teeny-weeny bite of poison candy. Can't even take a good long sniff. The way you keep ahead of your blind spots and old games is to recognize the danger signals and return the tempting gold-foil box, unopened. Amora was a great big plump chocolate-covered caramel with nuts and marshmallows. Only there was that one dab of cyanide in the center. I knew that! I had spent years working it through, grounding myself to live life as the back end of the circus horse. What was I doing? I was gobbling the yummy morsel. Ignoring the warnings of my inner guide and my Norwegian know-it-all. I did not know what I was doing or why. I only knew that I started next Monday.

4

The Arrival of Blood Relatives as Diversion

In the heat of the week's events and my Friday-night fight with Clifford, I totally forgot that Pop and my mother's sister, my Aunt Minnie, were arriving early Saturday to spend the weekend. I did not remember, in fact, until about one o'clock that morning, in the middle of our weekly lovemaking session. I had hoped that the anger of the evening had generated some sensual juice, but whatever juice had been generated had begun to evaporate by the time we climbed into bed.

Clifford tuned in the public-access station, which features a sporadic soft-porn series called "Midnight Madness." This amateur hour for the sexually frustrated begins with TV's "Only Nude Talk Show," which is followed by a toothy vile-mouthed former madam of a certain age named Vivienne who teaches vegetable masturbation and offers sexual tips with the help of an inflatable plastic man named Irving, whom she pokes, sucks and prods delightedly without any noticeable response from poor Irving.

From Vivienne, I have learned such helpful hints as "If you stuff a cold cucumber, a real rough one with lots of those tiny green bumps, up your cunt, you'll get a thrill no man can equal," and "A good firm toothbrush is a fantastic vibrator, and you never need new batteries." If properly handled, Vivienne could open the dental-hygiene and fresh-produce industries to an entirely new marketing strategy.

After my bath that night, I remembered that it was Friday and Clifford would be waiting for some marital frolicking.

Clifford always watches a few segments of "Midnight Madness" before frolicking; it's less premeditated than buying a real porno movie, but seems to help the glandular rejuvenation process.

Clifford is watching "The Only Nude Talk Show" on TV. After a few seconds of viewing it is not hard to figure out why it boasts that distinction. The host, a middle-aged New Rochelle version of Merv Griffin, whom one would hardly want to look at fully clothed, is sitting completely naked on a water bed (that's the set) next to a slack-mouthed blonde with black pubic hair and absolutely no tits, just two bluish-black nipples that seem to be glued to her chest. The host, Alvin, is fondling her black pubis with one hairy hand and holding a microphone in front of her purple-pink slackened lips with the other. His cucumber, which is neither green nor bumpy but surprisingly limp and puny, is seen between the rolling folds of his belly as he pops searching and incisive questions at Lydia, his guest.

"So tell me, honey, how do you like working at Club Paradise?"

Lydia, lolling: "It's like real nice. We get a real nice clientele there."

Alvin, sliding his hand up along her skinny thigh: "Really? That must be very stimulating."

Lydia, eyes rolling back into the place, where, if she had one, her brain would be: "For sure. At lunch we get your business types, your commuters. At night we get your workers and neighborhood types. I meet so many people from various occupations."

Clifford is glued to the screen as if he were watching Picasso glaze a plate. This is the only television program except for "Nova" and the "Live at the Met" series that Clifford ever watches. A hairline crack in his intellectual cortex.

Clifford's cucumber is also watching, its entire uncircumcised form as entranced as its master. I am not looking forward to this. It has been a long time since I looked forward to this.

"It's past Little Clifford's bedtime, and anyway, he's much too innocent to watch this filth," I jest. I have always referred to Clifford's cucumber as Little Clifford. In moments of extreme intimacy I have even gotten as carried away as to call it Cliffie.

Clifford does not respond to my attempt at mirth. Neither does Little Clifford, the traitor, whom I have always considered my friend and ally. He at least has a little spontaneity, a little personality, some spunk.

Lydia is now in a prone position, her spike heels digging into the water bed at a perilous angle.

Alvin holds the mike over her head and leers down at her.

"So tell me, Lyd, what did you do before you got into your present line of work?"

"I was President Reagan's personal physician," I respond, hitting the "off" button, much to the dismay of Cliffords large and small. I take Little Clifford in my hand, trying to make it up to him. I am forgiven. We begin the process of marital amour. I think about Clifford making love to Amora, which has always held an unhealthy eroticism for me. Tonight it just makes me feel like crying.

It was not always like this with us. If there was one thing we had in the beginning, it was juice. We didn't make love, we fucked. I have never much been one for making love. To me that was for Ali MacGraw and Ryan O'Neal, something you did in the movies with all your makeup on and someone standing behind you with a check for one million dollars. I have never really believed that love had anything to do with sex. I would prefer to think of love as a noble and highly refined emotion; majestic and coming from the finer parts of my consciousness. I never think of love in bed. Bed is for sex. Cuddling and hugging are for love. Fucking is for the other stuff.

For example, I wouldn't fuck my puppy, my pop, my Aunt Minnie, Amora, Vivika, or a host of other people I love. And even with everything I rationally know about love between a man and a woman being different, I still feel more like fucking when I am not so Ali MacGraw but a little more rapacious, a tad more Joan Collins.

The Madonna-prostitute syndrome, of which I am an avid student, is not just reserved for men. Oh no. I am a primary sufferer. It ruins my marital sex life. Husbands are supposed to be cuddly, safe, romantic, and friendly. Sex is supposed to be spontaneous, impersonal, and preferably with people who have no emotional place in your life. To whom you are not vulnerable. With an element of the forbidden about it.

Clifford certainly had all those elements in the beginning. He was even my first uncircumcised cucumber. But marriage ironed out all the hills and valleys. The forbidden became "Oh, that again."

The intimacy that should have rushed in to replace the passion never appeared. So there we were, neither friends nor enemies, neither passionate lovers nor cuddly bears. Two married people after a fight who knew how to masturbate with a white asparagus but not how to love each other or how to rekindle the torch; two married people slowly starving before the dying heat without a cinder or salamander in sight. Knowing when to baste the roast, how long to cook it, but without a goddamn match. We basted one another. We turned the meat over until it was ready. We knew how to do it to each other. We always ate. We got it hot and swallowed enough to satisfy ourselves, to keep from starving. We just never saw the flame dance anymore. When we were through and half-asleep, I remembered. *Oh shit, Pop.*

So much for my restful weekend to ready myself for Monday's debut. Having Pop and Aunt Minnie was about as restful as entertaining Yasir Arafat and Anatoly Shcharansky for a couple of days. I had no time to ponder my conversation with Clifford or look even casually down from the wobbling ledge on which I sat.

At seven I woke Vivika. "Baby, Grandpa's coming. Up! Up! You clog the toilets and I'll loosen the washers in the sinks."

"Jesus, Mother, this is getting ridiculous. Can't you just take him shopping or something?"

"And break his heart? Your grandfather gets all his ego gratification from fixing things. If he comes and there's nothing to fix, he feels worthless. Do you want your only living grandparent to feel worthless?"

"Oh, brother. You really do the job. No one understands how horrible it is to have a shrink for a mother. Someday I'll write a book!"

"I'll write one first. No one understands how terrible it is to have a teenager for a daughter. Now please, hurry! Aunt Minnie's coming too, which means they'll be here before eight to catch us with the beds unmade."

"Oh, God, Mother, my whole weekend is totally wasted!"

"Just think of how many more you have to waste than your poor ma."

My Aunt Minnie was sort of a short Jewish version of Clifford. Aunt Minnie's philosophy of life went something like "Why smile when a frown is so much more logical?" A positive comment, to Aunt Minnie, was "Thank God, his heart got him before the cancer." She meant well. Which is what we all say about relatives who drive us totally out of our guilty little minds. Actually, I'm never so sure they do.

From a professional point of view, if the world were populated by Aunt Minnies, shrinks would be part of ancient folklore. People like Aunt Minnie think an interior life is having shelf lining in your linen closet. Things are simple. Negative and simple. "One day you get up, you go to the bathroom, you turn on the light, you look into the mirror, and you're old" is one of Aunt Minnie's favorite observations. She's great at dinner parties.

Aunt Minnie on the Carson show:

Johnny: "So, Aunt Minnie, how's the world been treating you?"

Minnie: "Not so good as it's been treating you, Mr. Money Belt. Mr. Big-Time Goy. Mr. Polygamist."

Johnny—laughing raucously: "Oh, Minnie, you're something else."

Minnie: "I should be so lucky. If there was a God, I'd be a cockroach, living cozy in my little corner. That's all I need, Mr. Wimbledon Box Seat. A scrap of hair, a dry-skin shaving, some spilled chicken fat. Just a quiet place without aggravation from this rotten, stinking world."

Johnny: "Ed, take Aunt Minnie backstage and give her a nice hard shutup. That's what these Hebrew broads need to loosen them up."

Ed picks Minnie up and carries her off to thunderous cheers. Minnie is heard screaming offstage: "I'm clean. Not like these whores today! I'm clean as the day I was born! Go ahead, you Irish Jew-hater. Stick me. Everyone else has!"

Aunt Minnie and her battered husband, Seymour, used to run a dry-cleaning business in Radner, Pennsylvania. Aunt Minnie did the bookkeeping, which kept her away from the customers. At first, she had covered the customers out front and business was terrible.

Aunt Minnie did not know how to talk to people.

"What's that on your skirt? Blood? For shame. A grown woman like you still doesn't know how to menstruate? I never had one drop of God's curse on fabric since I was thirteen. Such a mess."

"This is your third broken zipper in a month, Mr. Zappetti. If you must behave like an animal, at least have the good sense to buy better quality."

To eighty-five-year-old Mrs. Polachek: "Why spend six dollars to clean a sweater when you may be gone before it's ready?"

Finally Seymour figured it out and they traded places. Business boomed. One day a nurse with dirty white uniforms smelling of French perfume and nicely rounded like their owner came in. By the time the uniforms were returned, Seymour and the nurse had done some pressing of their own. Aunt Minnie was left with her dark little house and the largest basket of bitterness and obsessive-compulsive revenge fantasies in the Northeast. When my mother died, her only comment was, "It figures. The good die young. That bastard shiksa-whore lover will live forever." Somehow even my mother had gotten rolled up into her Seymour obsession.

The only person who had ever made Minnie smile, including Johnny Carson, was Pop. He would bound across his castle–cum–dining room, his whole stocky being generating warmth, his barrel chest obscuring whatever neck he may have once had, and clasp poor old dried-out, mothball-smelling Aunt Minnie to him, his round balding head gleaming in the reflected light of his twinkling Christmas bulbs. "Mamma mia! How's my gorgeous dame! Give an old man a big thrill. Give us a big smackaroonie! I've made your favorito, mia cara. *Pasta e fagioli* and pickled herring. Let's dance, angel eyes."

To Pop, Minnie was all that was left of his wife on earth, in a direct way. We were more obtuse, especially Amora, who no longer looked like a Sweet. (Pop's father was given the name Sweet at Ellis Island. His name in Italian was Dolce. The translation was haltingly offered by my grandmother and that was that.)

Amora did not look, act, or talk like us. She sat among us at family meals like Princess Di at an African tribal dinner. Pop loved her, but he couldn't for the life of him figure her out. And me, well, I was too close. It was one step from incest, I was so much like my mother in looks and attitude. Aunt Minnie was his best bet.

I was right, too. They did get there before 8 A.M. and caught me with beds unmade, dishes in the sink, but, thank God, the toilet was stopped and the washers were all leaking.

"Get me a wrench," was the first thing my pop always said. He set to work at once, saving us from our city helplessness and the inept craftsmen of pre-war apartments.

Vivika and I got Aunt Minnie all to ourselves.

"Aunt Minnie, would you like a cup of coffee?"

"Too much acid."

"How about a nice cup of tea?"

"Gas."

"Some Danish?"

"I'm off sugar. Got a touch of diabetes."

"A piece of fruit?"

"Makes me belch."

"How about a bagel?"

"My dentures."

"Rye toast?"

"Too bland."

I could hang in there as long as she could. I was fueled by the power play as much as she was. We would go on till we both died of starvation or until Vivika lost control and began screaming in hysterics, blowing my cover.

"Some lox and onions?"

"Fattening."

At this point Pop enters, face flushed with success, a slightly moldy Tampax dangling in his fingers (Vivika didn't have to be so damn efficient). "I got it. Toilet's purring like a kitten. How's about some breakfast? Hey, Minnie, what if I whip us up one of my mushroom frittatas?"

The sides of Minnie's mouth twitch in what might be considered a smile. "Sounds fine, darling."

Saturday night Vivika had a date, or as close to a date as eighties teenagers seemed to come, which meant that several girls with no last names and a few boys with no names at all went somewhere and did something until it was late enough to worry their parents. Then they went home. Clifford took Aunt Minnie to see *Shoah*, a nine-hour documentary about the Holocaust, their idea of a rooting-tooting Saturday night. I had Pop all to myself.

After dinner, Pop and I cleared the table and sat back down with a large plate of homemade Amaretto cookies and a bottle of his Adirondack dago red. It never occurred to either of us to move into the comfort of the living room. Having basically grown up at a table in a house with no living room, we were never really at ease unless we could rest our elbows in front of us and see some sort of edible within reach.

Pop was feeling nostalgic. So was I. "The Village makes me miss your momma so much, I can hardly stand it, baby. I was takin' a walk this afternoon and I thought I'd go sit in Washington Square Park, like the old days. Your momma and I used to wheel you two dolls over there in your double stroller and sit in the sun, so pleasant.

"Now! Ay, Madonna! Junkies. Lunatics. And to be perfectly frank, the so-called normal people up there look just as *pazzo*. Those old professor types running in circles in between the drug dealers, huffin' and puffin'. One guy was readin' a book while he was joggin'! Cops all around. Some old broad with one shoe on yellin' about Armageddon and all those *pazzi* with little radio sets in their ears just runnin' around in circles like they was on a country road in Maine, for Chrissakes, dodgin' the bums covered with dirt. Poor lost souls. And then all the so-called normal people, walkin' that New York walk, fast and stiff, like they all had breadsticks up their prosciuttos. 'I'm a busy man, don't bother me. I'm very busy and very important. Don't be poor or sick or crazy in front of me. Shoo, shoo!'

"That's the whole thing about New York. No one gives a shit what you do, as long as you're busy. Even if you've got a day off—nothin' planned—walk fast! Look busy! Like you're rushin' to some summit meet. 'Outta my way, blind man, I'm very busy!' They don't even see those folks lyin' in the street, wanderin' around in a haze, freezin' their asses off. It's important, baby, not to stop seein' them. It's important for Vivika to see them. You stop, and somethin' dies in your heart. No matter how busy you are, it won't fix a dead heart."

"Oh, Pop, you're so wise. We should put *you* on the radio."

"Don't think I haven't had the idea. If that guy from St. Paul can make the cover of *Time* magazine talkin' about all those dried-up Norwegians, whatta ya think I could do with crazy Italians." Pop gets up and paces for a moment, which is always the signal a sensitive subject is about to be raised. He sits back down closer to me and pours us each a fresh glass of vino.

"Speakin' of the radio, how's your sis? Never hear from her. Listen to her show, though. Wouldn't miss it. Can't understand most of it. Bunch of whistleheads, lookin' for a dame, can't hardly run her own life, to solve their problems. Guys in love with guys. Ladies with ladies. Thirteen-year-old children, knocked up already. I'd rather talk to my goats. They got more serenity and a lot more sense. But I worry about her. Did I tell ya that Clive came up and spent a week with me?"

"No, Amo didn't even mention it. And I've seen a lot of her lately. How strange."

"You have? I didn't think you dolls were so close. But, baby, if you're seein' her a lot, maybe you could say somethin' about, about . . ." Pop pauses and takes a big gulp of wine. I decide to pitch in and let him off the hook.

"About Clive?"

Pop nods, unable even to say the word. "Does she know about him?"

"Know what? That he's probably gay or that he's very unhappy?"

"Madonna! The one is enough, ain't it?"

"More than enough. But it's only part of his problem."

"I didn't know it could show up so young. Promise the Virgin you'll never repeat this, but he, well, he tried to kiss my housekeep's son on the lips. May God forgive him! Your sister should get him some help. Specially now with all this AIDS stuff. The world is turning into a great big *putrido formaggio!* My only grandson. No more Sweets! All gone; all the male line gone when your old man goes. It would break your mamma's heart. She always saw herself with lotsa grandkids. Ayyy. Talk to her, baby, The kid's unhappy. Maybe they can fix him. Change him around. He's still a bambino, for Chrissakes!"

My heart is filled with red wine and love. I take my poor pop's strong calloused hand. "I can't, Pop. She wouldn't accept it from me. She doesn't respect me enough. She has absolute denial, in public anyway. If I can help, somehow, by talking to Clive directly, I'll try, but you know Amora."

Pop sighs. "*Sì, sì.* I know Amora." He kisses me, then sits back watching my eyes.

"So, how come the sister act all of a sudden?"

—52—

Now it is my turn for a gulp of wine. I stall, munching my sixth cookie. What to do? What to do? I have never lied to my pop, not once in my entire life, not even when anyone with an ounce of sense would have.

"Okay. I'll tell you the truth like always. But you must swear on the Virgin that you won't tell a living soul, and especially not Aunt Minnie!"

"My word of honor. As a man!"

"She offered me a job. Sitting in for her on her radio show."

"So, big secret. Millions of people will know."

"*No one* will know. Remember when we were kids and we'd fool you and Momma by trading places, pretending to be one another? Well, it's like that. I'm going to pretend to be her for a while."

"This city has made you nuts! All I ever heard from you was how you wanted to be different, be yourself. So why?"

"I could say for money, because she's offering me a lot of money. But I know that's a cop-out. I'm not sure why, Pop. But I'm committed. I start Monday. Pray for me."

My pop puts his head into his big strong hands and shakes it back and forth. "My grandson's a *strano*, and my dolls have gone New York City. The dirty air has poisoned their minds! If I had any sense, I'd grab you and Vivika and take you home with me. This place is *malato*."

Pop sits up, tears fall from his beautiful brown eyes. "Tell the truth, baby. This Norwegian. Does he make you happy? In the bed? Like a man and woman. *Uomo e donna.* Like that?"

"Sometimes."

"Sometimes! What kinda answer is that? What does he say about this plan? This deception?"

"He says that since I have already made the decision, there isn't much to say."

"Ay! That's what you married? A guy that looks like a Giacometti, a great big stick with no balls connected to the paddle? Shame on you, Aro. Never marry someone you can control! Never! Better to fight to the death than to manipulate and win! You wanna turn into one of those Busy People, rushin' around Manhattan pushin' old women with no teeth outta the way? I'll listen in, kid. I'll listen. But if it gets too much, you come back to the mountains and let your old man clear your head. We tried. We took you dolls outta this gladiator pit, and you couldn't wait to climb right back in!"

"I know, Pop. Please don't think you failed. I carry the farm around with me. It helps. I guess, well, she never wanted to be me. She just wanted to defeat me. But I wanted to be like her. I want to see if I can do it. If I'm as good. And it's the first time she's ever needed anything from me. She's always been trotting on ahead."

Pop fixes his burning browns on my teary ones. "You be careful, kid. I hate to say it about my own flesh, but I don't trust your sister. There's something missing there. Something wrong. Anything happens, you come home."

"Thanks, Pop. I promise. I will."

That Sunday it helped a lot to know that if catastrophe occurred, I could hole up in a mountain hideout. It helped. But it was rather like throwing an ice cube into a steam engine. My anxiety increased as the day progressed. By the time Pop and Aunt Minnie departed, I was about as calm as a carrot in a Cuisinart.

Then Amora called.

"Aro, I must see you. Right away. Meet me at my place in twenty minutes and wear dark glasses and a scarf."

"Do I bring my Beretta too, or just the sword in the umbrella?" (I'm always sarcastic when I'm nervous.)

"Amora has no time for jokes. Please just do as I say."

Off I went looking like the Jackie-O impersonator at a Halloween party. Even Clifford and Vivika noted this.

Vivika: "Oh my God! You're not going out like that? You look ridiculous! Totally retarded."

Clifford: "You're going to your sister's like the spider to the fly, like a character from *Diabolique*."

I buttoned my trench coat, ignoring both of them. They exchanged blank but knowing stares.

Vivika: "Please, Mother, if you see anyone I know, *don't* say hello. *Paleese!*"

Clifford: "Oh, she won't. She's on secret assignment. She's on her way to a chhhsssssgsd."

Vivika: "What? I didn't hear what you said."

I fled. The subway was on time and uncrowded. I sat down, feeling invisible behind my Sophia Loren Optiques, taking in my fellow travelers. A Spanish girl with a short black skirt sat across from me, snoring. Her legs had fallen open, giving the slavering pimple-faced degenerate next to me a perfect view. Next to her was a Betty Boop blonde with huge staring, unblinking bug eyes. She looked like a living skeleton, eyes that overtook their sockets. The mother in me wanted to close the Spanish girl's legs and give Miss Pop Eyes my glasses. But I maintained my aura of camouflage. Three teenage hoodlums with hostile faces and ghetto blasters jumped on. Everyone's eyes shot the other way. I'm invisible; can't get me.

At Fifty-first Street a crazy one-legged derelict in a wheelchair slid into the car, screaming at everyone and waving a dirty paper cup. "If youse assholes are gonna refuse me, I'm gonna make trouble! Gimme somethin', youse citizens!"

Now we were trapped on both ends. The hoods and the wheelchair. Gimme, gimme. A middle-aged man in a suit and tie turns red in the face with his own helplessness. The train bumps along. Everyone starts easing forward, about as inconspicuous as our intruders. Fifty-ninth was going to be one helluva mass exodus. Maybe Pop was right. Maybe the city was rotting my mind. I get off at Fifty-ninth Street and so does everyone else, including our tormentors. I walk the five blocks to Amora's feeling unsettled.

I need a few minutes to myself, to think, so I duck into a coffee shop and sit down at the counter. "Regular coffee and rice pudding." (I always order rice pudding when I'm trying to think.) A man and wife sit next to me staring ahead.

"I'm givin' up on the fucking TV; it's all crapola. Just the ball games and the news from now on. The rest is garbage. Don't compare to the radio."

"There's something good on Monday. A rerun movie about AIDS. With Sylvia Sidney and Ben Gazzara."

"Sylvia Sidney has AIDS?"

"No. No."

"Ben Gazzara with AIDS? That's your idea of a good movie? I'm gonna unplug the fucking thing."

I couldn't think next to them. I moved down. A young couple came in.

"Maybe you've never been in love like that. When you can't even say 'I love you' because the feeling's so deep. Talk is cheap. It's easy to say 'I love you'; it's actions that count."

"I read that somewhere."

"No. That's my original thought. I learned that from life."

"Boy, it sounds awfully familiar."

I take my cup and my pudding and move to a table. Cabs and room service. I'm on my way to cabs and room service. No more mingling with the masses. Fame and fortune await me. I couldn't concentrate on Amora. I take several deep breaths to offset the caffeine and sugar load that were further unsettling my shaky little being. *Okay, Aro, easy come, easy go. If she's canceling out on you, it will be a blessing in disguise. If it's something else, you'll just stay calm and listen hard. Like the radio. We have the choice each moment to act rather than react. Remember your own psychobabble.*

I pay and put on my raincoat.

"Ben Gazzara don't have AIDS. It's his son. He's a lawyer."

"Figures. They not only lie and steal, now the gonifs give you the fucking plague, too. At no extra charge."

Amora was in her pink satin bathrobe. She looked as if she had just gotten out of bed.

"Jimmy Bob was here." (She had just gotten out of bed.) "Did anyone see you come in?" She is overwrought. One of her eyelashes has slipped sideways, making her look as if a spider were crawling up her cheek.

"Just the huddled masses. No one specific. Oh, the doorman."

"Good. Good." Amora heads for the liquor cabinet. I follow. My outfit makes me feel cool and superior. I decide not to take anything off. Amora pours herself a double Remy Martin and turns away, heading for her white silk couch. Offering me nothing, as usual. Better anyway. A clear head is needed.

"Where's Clive?" I decide to stand, keeping my edge and trying to keep the conversation light.

"Clive?" A moment's pause, as if she were either trying

to remember who Clive was or where she had misplaced him. "Oh, he went to a movie with my secretary. It's so bloody awful trying to have an affair with a child around. The poor dear's seen every play and movie in New York three times."

"Better than MTV."

"What?" Amora is preoccupied. She also has no idea what MTV is, which is a sure giveaway of an uninvolved parent.

"Why don't you and ol' Jimmy Bob go to a hotel?"

"Oh, God. That's so cheap. So tacky. And besides, we could be recognized! It's bad enough as it is. That witch Wanda knows something. She's, he thinks, she's hired a private detective. He's afraid someone may have been following us. Oh, God! I can't stand this! I can see it now all over the front page of *The Enquirer.* 'Beautiful Radio Shrink Is Home Wrecker.'"

I begin to get the drift. "Don't worry, Amora. They save the front page for movie stars; they'd probably put you back with the 'Giant Marries Dwarf' and 'Lady from New Jersey Gives Birth to Three-Headed Werewolf.'"

She didn't like that. She took a long, deliberate sip and fixed her icy cat eyes on me. This usually intimidated me, but she had never done it with a false eyelash crawling toward her nose before.

"You enjoy my anguish, don't you? Your jealousy has always poisoned our relationship. You could have been like me. You could have improved yourself. You're lazy! You were the favorite. They gave you all the love. All that was available in that *asylum* we grew up in. I was never like the rest of you. Never! I'm special. I made myself special. I've scratched and clawed to get where I am. I've earned this! Do you hear me? It's so easy for losers like you and Father to scorn me, because I did the impossible! I became a star. On my own! No one gave me anything! And no one is going to destroy what I've worked for! No one. Do you understand? If someone gets in my way, I'll remove them. Whatever it takes, I'll do it. No one's going to touch me! No one!" Amora throws her glass against the wall and falls forward, sobbing hysterically.

I remove my glasses, trench coat, and scarf. The game is no longer in any of my repertoires. I was never any good at games and I was playing a master.

Also, my feelings were hurt. It's quite one thing to call yourself a loser or to suggest the possibility tearfully to your best friend or husband, who, you know, will immediately contradict you and reassure you and list all of your various attributes and accomplishments. It's quite another thing to have your direct competitor and, in some ways, mentor, fling the dreaded moniker in your disguised little face. It really hurt. There I was, a ridiculous figure, jumping like a puppet on a string to the command of a sibling on whose charity I had been poised for departure on an all-expense-paid cruise. Humbled. Humiliated and sniped. That's what she really did think of me. And I had trotted docilely up to the mound and stood waiting for the ball to smack me in the nose.

Even so, I was able to steady myself enough to realize that I was not really the object of her palsy. Somehow her Connecticut cowboy and his frau were the catalyst.

I sat down beside her. "I'm sorry, Amora. I've had a very bad day. I guess we both have. But that's all academic now, anyway. I guess the deal's off."

"Off!" Amora shoots up so fast, I fall backward into her satin pillows, losing my balance and sliding onto the floor, just missing the edge of her cut-glass coffee table and saving my nearsighted but deeply appreciated left eye.

"Are you mad! It's more important now than ever! I

must get away until she gives up and calls off her hounds. I've asked for time off at 'Today.' I'm leaving for Paris tomorrow."

I couldn't help thinking, as I climbed back onto the sofa, that for someone who needed me desperately, she had certainly shot her mouth off. Then it hit me. She was not going to be around for my debut. I was not only jumping off the platform, I was flying without a net.

"You mean you won't be here? But you promised! You said that you'd be right there if I needed help. What if I freeze! If I'm such a *loser*, God only knows what could happen."

Amora calmed down. Fast. As if someone offstage had just yelled "Cut!" "I didn't mean that. I was upset and angry. Do you think I'd entrust my entire career to a loser? I have absolute faith in you."

She did. I wasn't.

"Listen, Aro," she said, quietly taking my icy hands in her warm identical ones, "Jimmy Bob and I have it all planned. Wanda will hear me every day and think that I'm in New York. And if you'll wear the disguise—I even have a blonde wig just like my hair—then if she does have someone watching, we're covered all the way. She'll think Jimmy Bob is out of town on business. So she'll give up. Only he'll really be in Paris with me. We must have time away, time to think. Too much is at stake for both of us. The station's community property.

"Jimmy Bob is a very powerful man. He heads an empire. You know how I am about powerful men. I can climax just watching a powerful man walk into a room. If he's wearing an Italian suit, I can come twice. It's just the way I am. I need a man like him. I've been looking a long time. And time's running out. My biological clock is ticking. I can't let him get away. I want him desperately. And I'll do anything to get him!"

I know I should keep my mouth shut. I try. I can't. "But you're still young. Only *thirty-five*. There will be other men. Remember our bet. There should be several. It hardly seems worth risking your reputation for."

Little did I know that I had the answer to the whole potato right there oozing out of my own mouth. Just add the word "Why" and mash. I hate hindsight.

She smiles ironically. "Touché, sister dear. We know the truth. Dr. Piatneski said he couldn't do any more work on me for three years. I don't have a moment to lose. I want Jimmy Bob and all he stands for. And that bitch is not going to stop me." I wait for Alexis Carrington to storm in and point a pearl-handled revolver at us.

This was not like my normal Sunday night, and that could only be for the good. Better than a Kurosawa festival at the Bleecker Street Cinema followed by dinner at Clifford's favorite Japanese macrobiotic restaurant. "I'll have the tempeh grots and vegetable soba and the tahini-miso spread."

I was scared, bruised, and ready to burst into tears. But I was not bored. I hadn't felt so alive since Amos Cohen and Berkeley.

"Okay, Amora. I'll go for it. Two things. I want your number in Paris, just in case, and I want you to look me in the eyes and tell me that you're not keeping anything back. That there are no more little surprises likely to leap out and zap me."

She played it well. Perfect eye contact. "You have my word. Now you know everything. I'll leave my number and also the keys to my apartment, so that you can stay here. Clive would adore it, and frankly, it would be much better for our plan."

"Gee, I don't know. I'll have to work on Clifford first. He's not exactly jubilant about this."

"Use your wiles. It's very important—for Clive."

"I'll try. One other thing. When will you be back?"

"I don't know yet. I'll contact you."

"I would certainly hope so."

"A check will be sent to you from my office each week."

"Great. Well, I'd better go. Good luck. I hope you know what you're doing, Amo. This is the big time."

"I am well aware of that fact, sister dear. Just play your part. Make me look good. Leave the rest to us."

That's probably the last thing Judas said to Jesus.

5

You Can't Be Too Rich or Too Thin, But You Can Be Too Everything Else

The most amazing, ceaselessly amazing, thing about getting older is that you keep reclaiming parts of yourself that you had cast off like last year's trend, only to find, twenty years later, that the darling polka-dot mini is right back in style.

I had totally forgotten what a ham I was. I had neatly packed away all my exhibitionist, senior drama club impulses. Boom, there they were. All those years of playing to myself in the bathroom mirror, all the birthday parties when I had to be the center of everyone's attention.

Boom. Heeeeerrre's Aroma. What a sweet smell. What a great gal.

I *loved* being on the radio. It was so much better than television. I didn't have to look good, I could scratch my nose; I was invisible, but powerful. A deadly combination. And I wasn't even risking anything because I was her; she'd take the praise, sure, but she'd also catch the flak. There I was, just like a real media star, with my engineer, my screener, my producer, my Styrofoam coffee cups, my doughnut holes . . . *my audience*.

The only problem was that I was rather like an overstimulated three-year-old who has been encouraged by adoring relatives to do her goldfish imitation. After the shyness goes and the first clap is heard, look out. *Gotta sing. Gotta dance.* I didn't just want to do homilistic therapy, I wanted to rule the air waves. The one-liners that ran through my head. The heart-wrenching anecdotes. And there was this Anne Sexton poem that I used to practice in the car with a little catch in my voice. I was dangerous before a mike. I took a lot of deep breaths and tried to get ahold of myself. For the first time I understood the phenomenon of the instant celebrity, the struggling actor who finds himself in a hit sitcom and turns into the greatest jerk on earth. He'll do anything. Shows up at the opening of a Diet Pepsi. More. More! I've been anonymous all my life and now I'm a star! *Gotta sing. Gotta dance.*

Well, I wasn't a star. But I was on the radio and I took to it like a wonton to duck sauce. I went into character as Amora with chilling ease. But the advice was mine and it was different. I could tell by the mail. People noted it. *My fans* sensed it. And it was mostly positive. Highly positive. I could also tell by the reaction in *my booth*. Chen, the screener, and O'Ralph, one of the only nonOriental producers but a cousin of J.B., were obviously thrilled. After all, they were going along with the deception because it was that or the pavement, but they sure as hell didn't like it. They were there to keep me looking good and they were smiling. How about my Katharine Hepburn impression right after the staton break? I resisted. I tried to be mature and do a good job.

"Hello, you're on with Dr. Amora Sweet. How may I help you?"

"Dr. Sweet? This is Bob. I'm thirty and I'm really nervous."

"That's okay. Just take your time."

"Well, I, my dog died and I can't seem to handle it. I can't stop crying. I feel so foolish, but it just hurts so bad."

"How long ago did he die?"

"A month. He was hit by a car. I found him. He had dragged himself over to the curb, you could see the blood where he crawled. He was the most wonderful dog. He was like a friend."

"What else is going on in your life? Any other upheavals?"

"No."

"What about in the past?"

"Well, my brother, he died two years ago. He had AIDS. My family threw him out. I never even saw him sick. He just disappeared."

"Did you mourn him?"

"Like cry and stuff? No. It didn't feel real. I never even knew he was gay."

"I think that may be what you're doing. It's pretty scary to see your family reject your sick brother. There's a lot of grief in both his loss and the loss of the fantasy that your family would be there for you no matter what. You turned to the dog, and when he died, there was no barrier between you and the loss. Does that feel right to you?"

"Yes. Yes, it does, it really does."

"*Your reactions are appropriate. You may want someone to talk to during this process. Hold on and we'll give you some referrals.*"

Gotta sing. Gotta dance. This is what I understood about psych life at this point. Growth comes in one giant howl of reality. This is followed almost immediately by rage, mindless spastic rage at the truth. Then comes the grief. Wrenching, fetid sadness. Then there are moments of acceptance, when one feels strong, grown up, and headed for glory and happiness ever after.

The responsibility for this grown-up and joyous new persona becomes too enormous and is followed by a spasm of denial, resistance, and regression. And so it goes. And this is the good news: The other suckers never even get to the awareness stage. Mental health is damn hard work. Being a grown-up is no place for sissies. The people who were trying, who were struggling with the frothing bulls of reality, no matter how peculiar their own little herd might be, for them I had enormous compassion and seemingly endless energy. The gamers were a different kettle of calamari.

"*Dr. Sweet, this is Sherry. I'm twenty-four and I'm very attractive. I mean, men say I am.*"

"*What's going on with you, Sherry?*"

"*Well, I have this relationship with this man; he's lots older and very successful, he's sort of a father figure, I guess. He says he loves me and wants to be with me, but he's still with his wife.*"

"*Yes.*"

"*Well, I know I should stop seeing him. I mean him being married, but he's so good to me. So I've started seeing this other guy. Younger and really cute, so now I don't know what to do.*"

"*Sure you do.*"

"*Pardon?*"

"You know exactly what to do. You've found a way to get all your needs met without having to be really involved."

"Well, I guess, but I want to be committed. I don't want to be lying to one man and another like this forever."

"When it gets too difficult, you'll do something else."

"Well, but that's what I thought you could do, tell me what I should do. I'm so confused."

"It's very convenient to be confused when you don't want to make a decision. I can't tell you what to do. You're doing what you want to do. Enjoy it while it lasts."

Oh, no, no, no, sugar plum. I'm not going to roll around on that neurotic water bed with you. I know a mind fuck when I see one.

Gotta sing. Gotta dance.

"Dr. Sweet, I'm Brian. I'm thirty-five and I'm gay. And I've got a problem with fantasies. I, well, I seem to be obsessed with AIDS fears. I have these weird thoughts all the time."

"Can you give me an example?"

"Well, I know this is going to sound really weird. My lover, Perry, thinks it's absolutely bizarre, but I was at a cocktail party and there was this bowl of pretzels and all these people were sticking their hands into it and I thought, what if someone with AIDS went into the bathroom and jerked off and didn't wash the semen off his hand and then he came back into the party and took pretzels out of the bowl and then some other person picked up a pretzel with some of the guy's stuff on it—could they get AIDS? I have hundreds of thoughts a day like that. I make lists in my mind of all the people I've slept with who could have given it to me and I make puzzles of how to pass it. Like a hetero guy has a one-nighter with a chick who got AIDS from a bi guy and then years later this hetero guy marries a hetero girl and he gives her AIDS and she gives it to their baby. Thoughts like that all day long."

"Well, Brian, I'll tell you one thing: It's going to be a long time before I dive into the pretzel sticks again."

So, I'm not perfect. So I had a little lapse.

The most fun was the monologue. This was not the kind of monologue I would have preferred, more David Letterman or Richard Pryor, but it was good enough. At the beginning or end or both of each program, I got to pontificate on the topic of the day, which was the topic of my choice, and since no one ever remembered the topic or addressed their question to it, what it basically meant was that for several minutes a day, out into the satellites, out across the highways and byways of my native land, I got to give my philosophy of life out loud without a sullen husband or a patronizing teenager in sight.

Gotta sing. Gotta dance. I floated home each night, my mail under my arm. More. More. I was energized. I was obsessed. I loved it. I was doing shtik on the airwaves. Radio waves were moving me along. Wave good-bye Aroma. Wave a fond farewell to old Aroma. I had caught the big wave, a great fat swollen tidal, and I was soaring along, heeding no rock, no coral reef, no bottom. No severed blond heads.

A week passed in this euphoric fashion. There was no word from Amora or Jimmy Bob. I began to feel as if it were really my show. I had become a hybrid. A combo Aro and Amo. I began wearing more makeup and paying attention to things like whether my stockings were color-coordinated with my shoes.

Vivika was not entirely impressed with this new aspect of her so familiar mother's life.

"You were great today, Mommy. You look pretty, too. I like that lipstick."

"Why, thank you, darling."

Vivika gives me one of her sideways stares. One of those mother-daughter competition stares. One of those maybe-my-mother-isn't-quite-as-nebbishy-and-safe-as-I-had-figured stares. "You're talking funny."

"Funny? Whatever do you mean, darling?"

"That's what I mean."

"What?"

"That. That 'whatever do you mean, darling' stuff. That's not how you talk. That's how Aunt Amora talks."

"Oh. I must be doing it unconsciously. Maybe it's an improvement."

"No. It totally weirds me out. You're not going to like dye your hair or anything gross, are you?"

"Certainly not, sweetheart."

"See. You did it, again! 'Certainly not, sweetheart.' It gives me the creeps. You're getting just like her."

"From your mouth to God's ear. Mind your tongue. That's a real shitty thing to say to your mother."

"That's better." Her face relaxes. "What about geek breath? Does he like miss her?"

"Don't call your cousin that. He's really a very sweet kid. Oh my God! I just realized I haven't even called him. How irresponsible of me. I've been so engrossed, I just completely forgot! I think I'll go up there tonight and stay with him. Want to come?"

"Are you nuts? All he wants to do is try on my clothes and have me tell him about like Matt Dillon's love life. I'd rather be grounded."

"Suit yourself. Tell Clifford I'll call later on this evening, will you, dear?"

'You did it again!"

"Oh, fuck off, kid. I'm entitled to clean up my act every now and then."

"That's better."

The closer I got to Amora's, the more my euphoria seemed to slip. I was wearing my disguise. We had agreed that when I used her apartment I should wear it, just in case the detective was watching. With my hair covered and all, I could be mistaken for her, thus proving that she was in town. As I breezed past the doorman, it also dawned on me that that was why she had encouraged me to use the apartment. In fact, she had really entreated me, so I was way behind schedule.

The maid had the night off. Clive answered the door. A pale, skinny thirteen-year-old with hyperthyroidic green eyes, wispy, close-shaven, mouse-colored hair, large soft ears, and a fey wistfulness that made me want to clasp him to the warmth and protection of my bosom.

"Why, hello, Auntie. What a nice surprise. Amora said you'd be coming. I've been waiting patiently. Would you like some fettucine with caviar? I just made some. I hate to eat alone."

"Don't run a guilt number on your old aunt, Clive. I feel bad enough about not coming sooner. Give me a teeny break, okay?"

"So sorry. I guess I'm just my mother's son."

"That is not a genetic transference. Running guilt numbers is not in the DNA. You can knock it off any old time."

Clive gracefully leads me into the salmon-pink kitchen, where he has set the marble table for one, down to sterling flatwear and a pink candle. He deftly adds a second place setting, brings the fettucine, and places it on the table next to the salad of arugula and warm goat cheese. He motions for me to sit.

"You're right, Auntie. I can really get into the self-pity thing. Amora says it's my way of getting attention."

"Does it work?"

Clive comes around behind me and serves like a waiter at Lutèce. "Not really."

"Maybe we can think of something that will."

Clive goes even whiter than normal. "Would you care for a glass of wine? We have a really tasty Chardonnay from California."

"No, thanks. Are you changing the subject?"

Clive is suddenly a child again. He has momentarily dropped his chic New York fag routine. His eyes fill with tears. "You wouldn't tell her that I'm—you don't mean that, do you?"

"No, sweetheart. I just meant that if you're not reaching her and you need to, and of course you do, maybe there's a better way than by being a gay pip-squeak yenta. You're trying to reach her by hurting her and that's not the way to play your mother."

Clive nods and lowers his head. His thin shoulders heave.

"I saw my shrink today. She asked me how I felt having my mother away and I said that she was always away, even when she was right next to me." Clive looks up, his frightened frog eyes breaking my heart. "I have this feeling inside, Auntie. I can't describe it, but it's like a hole. And it's always there. Even when I'm doing something fun, like cooking or playing the piano or sewing something. Even then it never goes away. It even gets cold in there in the winter, like a cave. I keep trying to fill it up or something. But nothing makes it go away. It just feels empty in there."

I put down my fork and reach my arms out to him. "Come here and sit on your old aunt's lap. Right now. Come on." He comes, meekly, curling up and sinking in without resistance, his long slender arms wrapping around my neck, hanging on for dear life.

"Clive baby. Sometimes that feeling, that empty feeling, sometimes it feels like that because there's a part of ourselves we don't let ourselves experience. When we don't know what we feel, it's like a part of ourselves is missing. That's what makes us feel lonely and empty. You are one smart kiddo and very sensitive. If you can let yourself have those feelings that scare you, that emptiness will go away. It may mean telling Amora the truth, too. But you don't have to be afraid of that. I'll help you. You don't have to do that alone and not until you feel ready. Your grandfather and I love you very much, and even if I have been a real shit, not coming sooner, I am always there for you. Do you believe that?"

Clive holds me tighter, nodding his head into my neck, his tears hot and sticky against my skin. I am very glad I came. I decide to move in with him until Amora comes back. At this moment he needs me more than Vivika and Clifford do.

We sit together rocking gently, feeling some of our mutual loneliness melting. I am getting as much comfort as I am giving, though he would probably not understand that. Children never do realize how much strength we get from hugging them, from wiping their tears and blowing their noses. All that "There, there, everything is going to be all right" is as much for our own well-being. That is part of the supreme selfishness of parenting. Even when we seem most selfless in our comforting, we are getting our most primal needs met. The doctor inside the patient. The mother inside the child. I can give Clive something that he needs and that I need to give and that Vivika no longer seems to require and that Clifford has, to my knowledge, never required. It feels wonderful.

The phone rings. Clive stiffens and sits up. The phone keeps ringing.

"Honey. We should answer the phone. It might be your mother."

Clive shakes his head violently. "No. It's not. Don't answer it!"

"Why not?"

"It's that horrible woman. She keeps calling and demanding to talk to Amora. I keep telling her that she's in the shower."

"What horrible woman?"

"Jimmy Bob's wife."

"Wanda Mackay?"

Clive nods, covering his ears with his slender hands.

"Oh my God. She doesn't know your mother's out of town, right?"

"Of course not. Amora beat that into me with her mascara wand. But I can't keep stalling her. No one takes *that* many showers."

"I'd better do it. I'll have to pretend I'm Amora. I'm not really ready for this."

I extricate myself from Clive and both of us dash for the phone by the microwave. I grab it on the sixth ring, a sure sign the other person means business.

"Hello. How may I help you?" I've gone instantly into Amora's radio greeting. That will never do. Get it together, Aro. Remember, this is the big time.

"Who is this? With whom am I speaking?" demands a shrill, slightly slurred female voice with Southern intonations.

"This is Amora Sweet. And who is this?"

A moment of silence. "You must be squeaky-fucking clean, dearie. Your skinny little cunt must be shiny bright, just the way that s.o.b. likes it."

This was not your usual kitchen phone call. "How dare you talk to me like that. Don't you ever call my home again or I'll, I'll" [a small feminine catch comes into my performance, my voice cracks delicately], "or I'll call the police."

"Oh, I wouldn't do a stupid thing like that. Think of the bad publicity. I know you're fucking my husband. And I know he's there!"

"You must be insane! I have no idea what you're talking about! I'm having a quiet dinner with my son. I haven't seen your husband for weeks. You must know that he's away on business. Ask anyone at the station. If you are having marital problems, that is hardly my concern. Goodbye!" I slam down the receiver.

"All right!" Clive is applauding wildly. "You were great. You do my mother better than she does. That was terrific!"

I take a small bow. "Thank you. Thank you. It was nothing. The mere culmination of a life's work."

While we are basking in our glory, the phone rings again. Clive and I stare at one another.

"What now, Auntie?"

"I'd better answer it."

My hand is shaking. "Heloo." This time I let a little Bette Davis slide into my voice.

"You can't fool me, you bleached-out pussywhip."

I slam down the receiver, waiting for the line to clear. I unplug it before she can dial again. I was rather enjoying her descriptions of the fabled Amora. I hate to admit that. But I was. After a week of "I adore you, Dr. Sweet. You are so beautiful, sexy, glamorous, intelligent, sensitive." Not once did any caller ever say, "Hey, you really look like a peroxided pussy, Doc." Better that Amora was not here to take that call. People shouldn't have to hear that about themselves. I could use the information a lot more constructively. My self-esteem soared.

"Come on, Cliveala, now I'm starved. Let's microwave the noodles and pig out. Then we'll really take a shower and hit the sheets."

"Grand idea." Clive is smiling. Tearing my heart. "Auntie, I'm really happy you came. This is just neat. I hope Vivika appreciates you."

"Thanks, pal. The grass is always greener, though. If you talked to her, she'd probably give a view of her home life that would harden your noodles."

"Oh, no. We've talked. She thinks you're weird, but basically a good mother."

"She said that?"

"In a manner of speaking."

"Well, well. Wonders never cease."

"But will Wanda ever cease?"

An ironic thirteen-year-old is always a find.

"I don't know, pal. But at the moment, I would say the odds are against it. She's got a full tank and she's dying to race."

"Well, maybe we can put a little sugar in her engine."

"Well, at least a little NutraSweet."

6

Penis: The Noun, The Adjective

Clive and I prepared for ambush on Park Avenue while Amora and Jimmy Bob were having a little powwow of their own in a suite at the Meurice. For ten days they had lost themselves in a cowboys-and-Indians version of *The Story of O*. Ten days of drugs, champagne, and nonstop sex. No little side trips to the Boulevard St. Honoré. No hairstyling or manicuring. No quiet little dinners at La Perusse. They never left the room. My Amora, for whom sex was always a trade-off, was trading it off. By the time Jimmy Bob dismounted he would be so mind- and member-blown that La Wanda wouldn't stand a chance.

My sister as a teenager used to describe the male organ as if it were a character in a Stephen King film.

"Can you imagine if you enlarged a male genital, the way they do with spiders and flies and things in the movies? Can you imagine how horrifying and grotesque it would be? People would run screaming from the theaters! And *that's* what we're given and expected to fondle, and stick inside of us, and, even more disgusting, put in our mouths! God could not exist, or he would never have allowed such a revolting thing to be thrust on women as their only way to procreate. Sometimes, just thinking about it being there, between men's legs, under their clothes, is enough to make shivers of nausea run through my entire body."

Amora had done a lot of shivering and a lot of throwing up. She had overcome her distaste for Godzilla in gabardine because it was very, very important to her image and her goals to be desired and adored by men. By the time Jimmy Bob entered the picture she had sucked and inserted enough of the revolting little danglers to provide the entire cast of *Gremlins III*.

She was an expert. She often gave me lessons.

"Aro, you don't know a damn thing about flirting. You must learn how to be seductive in a ladylike way; let your eyes linger just a beat too long: pretend to brush against a man accidentally; listen as if he were the most fascinating being on earth. It's very important to learn these things. Flirting is an art. Women who learn the art walk off with all the best men. Just look at me."

"I'm not the type. I hate flirting."

"Every woman's the type. It's easy. Just remember that

they are different from us. Their little things are outside and our little things are inside. That makes them more vulnerable and more susceptible to all kinds of stimulations. I've found that if I just let my eyes wander toward a man's organ, he'll blush and I can see it perk up. Use your God-given power over them! You've got a child to raise. Be smart!"

Well, I did all right. But I was not about to start casting lingering glances at strange penises to secure my future. I lived vicariously through Amora.

This was in the seventies, after all; before AIDS, herpes, chlamydia, and God only knows what else. This was the decade when women were told to go get 'em. Fill the silver screens with the forbidden alien things. Stick the little monsters any old where. Up, down, in, out.

Men wandered through singles bars with Polaroids of their erected sets in their pockets. "How'd you like to take that home with you, baby?"

What did they know? We were the ones gobbling the damn things up like ten-cent ice-cream cones. They had a product that was suddenly extremely marketable. It was like finding a bunch of old coins that you'd had in a jar since you were born and discovering that they were Spanish doubloons. These guys had fallen into the honey pot. *Women, women everywhere, running fingers through your pubic hair. Never asking you to share, never asking if you care. . . . No dinner for two, a hot dog would do, a beer and a screw. Women everywhere, already bare before you'd even combed your hair. Every bozo had a spare.*

I hated the seventies. Men and women treated one another like shit. And even worse, women also treated themselves like shit. The seventies wasn't the Me decade, it was the Prick decade. Sort of like the pyramid form of ancient Egypt. It was our icon. Women were told that they were free and equal, and somehow, in the translation, that became a sexual challenge.

I'm free and equal and I'm gonna get me some meat to beat. We got that. Did we ever. We ruined men for a good ten years. Every single member of the species thought he was one little hot bologna. The word "creep" ceased to exist in their ethos.

I knew women who slept with people they wouldn't have shared a cab with five years earlier. Sexual revolution, my Aunt Minnie's underpants. I'm convinced that it was all the deodorant, douching, hair spray, and heavy breathing that messed up the ozone layer. We threw the entire ecobalance off. Every mother's son had a golden pole from which desperate but equal women could vault into oblivion.

Everyone wanted the goddamn things. Women and other men. The price went up. Men got over the cheap thrill of having any woman they wanted; now they became choosy. *I have a golden wand and I do not have to let just any old pussy wave it.* Beautiful women and handsome homos competed for the same thing. *Here! Oh, please! Stick it up here! Mine's juicier. Mine's tighter! Please. Oh, just once!*

Well, the score got evened. Boy, oh boy, did it ever. Now it's not just an engorged horror-show actor from which to duck screaming behind your butterlike-flavored popcorn. Now it has runny sores and plague squirting out of it. Ahhhhh! Run for your life! Now they can't even give it away.

Sex? Oh, that was nice. I remember that. Like panty girdles and chlorophyll gum. Icons from the past. "What's sex, Mommy?" a child of the next century may ask.

"Oh, that was something we used to do for pleasure and to have babies before the Age of the Diseases. It doesn't happen much anymore."

* * *

Except in Paris. In Amora's hotel room. That was definitely a seventies scene. (Well, Amora was really more sixties, if you want to nitpick, more Pillow Talk than Hard Core, but if Rodeo Porno was what Jimmy Bob wanted, she was more than willing to oblige.)

"Ride me, filly, ride me home. Ye-ahhhhhhh!"

Amora bounces demurely up and down on top of Jimmy Bob, who is lying back on the stack of French-lace-covered pillows wearing his cowboy hat, his boots, and a silly grin. Amora is clad in similar garb.

"Oh, Jimmy Bob, what a man you are! I'd do anything for you, anything!" Her newly lifted white breasts jiggle before his half-closed eyes.

"Uuuuweee. I love those titties. Gotta get me a handful of those milky melons." Jimmy Bob grabs Amora's breasts in his hairy gold-ringed hands and caresses them as if they were about to produce a dairy product.

Amora's cheeks are red as she increases her canter. "Oh, darling, you know that drives me just crazy. Oh, oh, I'm going to come. Yes, yes, yes! Ahhhhhhhhhh!"

"Yahhhhhhaaaaaaaaaa!"

The maids had taken to gathering in the hallway to listen to this literal translation of the act of amour. They fought over who delivered the room-service trays and changed the sheets. The sex-crazed Americans with the Chinese bodyguards were the talk of the hotel. Jimmy Bob and Amora were oblivious.

On the eleventh day, Amora woke up from her trance.

"Oh my goodness! What day is this? What time is it?"

"Hell knows, my little coyote. Come on back here and give your old dude a great big wet tongue kiss. Lasso my mouth, cactus flower. Then I'm gonna ride you around and around the ring. Mmmmmmmm."

Jimmy Bob or no Jimmy Bob, when it was time to snap to, there was no one like Amora for switching gears, even in midmount.

Amora stood up. "Not now, dear. I must call New York. Why, anything could have happened. My child could have been kidnapped. Aroma could have had a stroke. God only knows what."

Jimmy Bob pulls himself up to his full six feet and several inches and swaggers naked, with his rope unfurled, across the Aubusson rug to his little lady. "Now, now, honey cake, don't you fret. I left explicit instructions with everyone that if any old thing happened out of the ordinary, to call immediately. Matter of fact, I did check in yesterday, while you were bathin' your magnificent little assemblage, and Chen said that your sis is doin' just great. And, even better, she's been staying uptown with your young'un."

Amora has obviously mixed feelings about this information.

"Oh. Well. How reassuring. Clive must be thrilled. He's always liked her. It's his way of punishing me, I suppose. I'm so pleased she's adequate. I was a teeny bit afraid she might not be able to handle the pressure. Her career has been rather provincial, after all. Well, I feel better. But I should call. What kind of mother must you think I am?"

"Compared to that dry hole I live with, you're the fucking Madonna." (Jimmy Bob tended to drop his cowboy drawl when the subject of his wife and daughter came up.)

"You know what that kid of mine asked me before I left? She wanted to know if seven was too young for a platinum American Express card! That Dress Hanger has ruined her. But I'll show 'em. I'm not gonna let her get away with one copper penny. I'll rot in the clink first. Not one Visa card! Nada. I don't know how yet, but I'll fix her! That idea of yours—to have your sister set us up with an alibi, so we could get away and think things through—that was brilliant! That must have confused the crap out of old Wanda! Now come on over here and give your cowpoke some great big sloppy kisses. We'll call your son right after lunch. It's too early there, anyway. Bring that ass to Daddy. Rrrrrr."

Amora put on her best dance-hall grin. But her heart was no longer in it. During the entire ride, as she bounced along over hill and dale, her lover man growling beneath her, images of Clive, Wanda, Chen, and Aroma sped behind her lifted lids. She felt a cold chill in the middle of the heat of Eros. Something wasn't right. She could feel it.

Amora had damn good antennae. We were, after all, not identical twins for nothing. That's the one thing all the studies show. This crazy intuition about one another. Now that I was at Amora's, *I* was horny as hell and *she* was uneasy. She had good reason to be. Poor Amora, in her haste to flee with her Thoroughbred, had not devised a plan with her usual cold-eyed cunning. It never occurred to her that a woman as desperate as Wanda Mackay might not give up so easily.

When Amora finally phoned, Clive was at school. I didn't tell her about the calls from Wanda because it seemed useless. Why ruin her tryst? She didn't seem to want to hear any reality, anyway. She also seemed relieved that Clive wasn't there, probably correctly anticipating one of his martyr numbers (though we were working on that).

She would be gone another two weeks, she said— some business of Jimmy Bob's to attend to. I said fine, feeling like someone had punched me in the stomach. I liked living her life. I was not prepared for returning to my own.

The next day was Saturday. I had made it through my second week with flying colors. Clive and I were having breakfast and watching *Key Largo* with Humphrey Bogart and Lauren Bacall, gobbling Clive's Eggs Expresso and working on our third croissant. Clive was leafing through a copy of the *Ladies' Home Journal.*

"What's high blood pressure, Auntie?"

"Clive, you don't have high blood pressure, you have hypochondria."

"What's that?"

"It's when you think you have high blood pressure and you're a perfectly healthy thirteen-year-old."

"I've read about thirteen-year-olds with all kinds of horrible diseases. Kids get everything grown-ups do. Can a thirteen-year-old have a heart attack? I've been having a lot of funny pains in my chest."

"That's from all the breast-beating you do."

We are interrupted by a loud knock on the door. We both jump. Lauren has just called Humphrey a coward and run out of the room crying. And I thought they had a perfect relationship.

"Auntie, the door!"

"I heard it. One of your friends?"

"No! No! I don't have any friends! Besides, no one can get up here without being announced. It's almost impossible!"

"I bet it's Vivika. The doorman knows her. She said she might come by and go to the movies with us."

"Really? Did she really say that?"

"Well, actually, she said, 'I'll come if you make Clive promise not to talk about Matt Dillon.'"

We have tiptoed into the living room and are approaching the peephole. I have this really keen gut feeling that it is not Vivika. I peep.

In the hall, outfitted in twin Ralph Lauren pantsuits, stand Wandas large and small.

Inside, outfitted in stained flannel nightie (me) and a huge pink Madonna sweatshirt (Clive) stand us.

The knocking is becoming borderline banging.

"Oh my God, it's Wanda! Clive, run and lock yourself in your room. I'll have to let her in. What does your mother usually do Saturday mornings?"

"The same thing she does Saturday afternoon. Sleep."

"I can't say that! She might insist on seeing. Oh, shit! I'll think of something. Run!"

"No. You need me. I want to stay."

"Go! If you hear any shooting or screaming, dial 911 and put on some serious boy's clothes, please. We may have to run for it."

Clive is off, a pale pink flash of disappointment. I take a deep breath and open the door, hoping that my best professional expression is masking my panic.

The Wandas take in my entire unwashed, egg-stained being in a long, sweeping smirk.

"Who on earth are you?" Wanda Woman demands haughtily.

"She's nobody, Mommy. Just some slob."

I ignore the lizardous munchkin, wishing I were the Firestarter and could reduce the brat to a smoldering briquette.

"I might ask you the same question."

"I am Mrs. James Mackay, and this is my daughter, baby Wanda."

"How nice for you both. You must have the wrong

apartment. Now if you'll excuse me, I'm lunching at Le Cirque and must see to my ablutions."

"Is this not the apartment of Dr. Amora Sweet?"

"Yes, it is, but Dr. Sweet is away visiting her widowed father for the weekend."

"You really expect me to believe that?"

"I have few expectations."

Baby brat puts in her two cents. "Next you'll be telling us she went to the North Pole to visit Santa Claus."

"No, actually, that's next weekend. She's going to stop on her way to a birthday party for the Tooth Fairy."

"She's being rude to me, Mommy. Fire her!"

"How dare you speak to my child like that! Who are you anyway? What are you doing in that cunt's apartment?"

"Tsk, tsk. Such language for a budding young feminist to hear. Very bad for the self-image. I don't really think it is any of your business who I am. Now please leave, or I'll call the security officer. He never should have let you up here, anyway."

"Just try it. I have several intimate friends in this building. I've known Gus and the doorman for years. You'll make an even bigger fool of yourself than you have so far."

"I'd love to stand here and listen to value judgments, but I'm really very busy. 'Bye."

I start to close the door just as baby brat hurls her miniature Hermes shoulder satchel into my face and flings herself against the frame. This leaves me with two choices. I can let them in or I can splatter the evil midget all over Aroma's peach-colored wall. I choose the second option. Fortunately, I reconsider. This kid is not worth life in prison.

Clive sneaks out of the bedroom dressed in his most macho garb—Miami Dolphins sweatshirt, Levi's, high-top sneakers. The kid even has a volleyball in his hand.

I slam the door behind the Wandas and move protectively toward Clive. "It's okay, pal. This is Mrs. Mackay and her . . . her . . . *offspring*. Your mother works for her husband."

"Right on," replies Clive in a sort of Eddie Murphy street-kid rasp.

"Uuwwwww. Mommy. That's her son. Gross."

"Listen, Thumbelina. I don't care whose kid you are; you speak like that to me or Clive again and you're out of here."

"Mommy, that hag is threatening me!"

"Now, now, darling. Calm down. This is very hard on Mommy. Sit down and be a good girl and let Mommy talk to these . . . these . . . people."

"Oh, how nice. Validation. At last."

The minimonster settles herself on Amora's silk sofa, takes a bottle of Chanel nail enamel from her satchel, and begins painting the baby nails on her pudgy little fingers. Wanda throws her purse and Gucci scarf on the peachy-pink settee and pauses, breathing rather loudly for obviously dramatic effect. "This is not easy for me; I'm sure you can understand that."

Clive and I nod. I resist, this time successfully, making any sarcastic remarks.

"I haven't slept in weeks. I seem to be having some sort of breakdown. My motto has always been that I pinch life, it does not pinch me. I am not the sort of woman who fights over a man. But I have a child to consider." (The child is carefully applying her third coat of shocking-pink polish and nodding with approval.) "I went to my facialist yesterday, trying to relax and clear my mind of all this sordid business. She looked at me quietly under the magnifying light for some time before speaking. Finally, she turned off the light and took my hand. 'It's starting,' she said, and there were tears in her eyes. Aging is much harder for a woman like me than you could ever imagine." (Large firm nod from Shirley Temple.) "I am used to a certain life-style. And so is my child. I will not let a tacky little whore like Amora Sweet take my husband away from his family. I'll fight to the death."

This upsets Clive. "Auntie. What does she mean?"

Both Wandas reply in unison. "Auntie?"

Advantage Mackays.

"Wait just a minute. *You* are the cunt's sister?"

"Don't be ridiculous. Clive always calls me Auntie. I'm his godmother. A very close friend of the family." The fact that my sister had chosen to keep me, like a very dark secret, in the closet of her life was certainly working to our advantage.

Baby brat jumps up, knocking over her polish and sending streams of pink enamel flowing over the side of Amora's marble-and-glass table onto her eighteenth-century Persian rug.

"She's lying, Mommy!"

This confuses Mommy, who seems to be operating under the influence of the barbiturate bottle. "Sister? Jimmy Bob never mentioned a sister, dear. But then Jimmy Bob never talks to us, anyway. Jimmy Bob is just no fun."

"I could have had my own career, you know? When he was madly chasing me all over Dallas, I had been approached by television. I write, you know. I could have had my own interview show. I wanted to interview the city's artists, poets, architects, and the great divorce lawyers . . . the people who are shaping Dallas.

"But now it's too late. It's started. Day by day I'll begin to see the fine lines. The little puffs. The splitting ends. The slight dropping around the neck. A hardly noticeable spreading about the waist. And the obvious things. The knees. The backs of the arms. No more bikinis. No more sleeveless dresses. Do you know what happens to women like me when our husbands leave us? Do you?"

Clive and I clasp hands, wide-eyed. We shake our heads.

"We end up selling Indian jewelry in Sante Fe and sleeping with one another! I will not let that happen! Do you understand me? You tell that over-made-up ugly duckling! You tell her to leave him alone, or I, I know things—I could destroy him—I, I know the truth about his, about his . . ." Wanda swoons and falls backward onto the aforementioned pink settee. Baby Wanda moves, a little slowly for my taste, to her side. I dash to the kitchen for a glass of water and to clear my head. Clive stands frozen in his tracks.

"She's fainted! She's fainted dead away!" Baby brat chants as if we had done it on purpose.

I have no idea what to do next. I run back and lift her expensive frosted head (she and Amora must have the same stylist) and put the water glass to her lips. She takes it from me and gulps it down. Acting does dehydrate one. The scene has played itself out. I stand up, excruciatingly aware of my slovenly appearance. "I am terribly sorry for your unhappiness. But I must repeat, I am only a family friend. I am staying with Dr. Sweet's son for the weekend. She will be back on the air on Monday. To my knowledge, and I know just about everything that goes on in her personal life, she has only the most businesslike relationship with your husband. Now, I really must insist that you leave. These children have been upset enough."

Wanda revives. She takes a hankie from her purse and dabs at her eyes. Then she takes out her Evian spray, Clarins moisturizer, and L'Oréal lipstick. "Yes. Yes. I've said what I came for. I must pull myself together. Thank God I have good help to take care of baby Wanda during this. I can barely get out of bed these days. I don't know what ordinary people do during a crisis. All of those women who raise children without staff. I fear for my darling baby girl. You tell the cunt that. She is, after all, a mother. Though God knows what kind."

Clive stiffens. "She's a great mother. You shut up about my mother!"

I reach for him just as baby bitch makes her move. "Don't you yell at my mother, bug-eyes!" She lowers her curly little mug and heads for him. Clive takes aim, and before I can intercept he sends the volleyball smashing into her head.

It might as well have been an ax. Hysteria prevails. We all run in circles chasing one another.

Baby Wanda is shrieking bloody murder. She and Clive are pounding on one another. Wanda and I are pounding on one another.

The doorbell rings. We all stop, like characters in a silent movie when the crank freezes.

"Yes, who is it?" I croak in what is an attempt at casual elegance.

"Security, Dr. Sweet." (Thank God he didn't say which Sweet.) "Is everything all right? I've gotten a couple of calls about a fight!"

"Oh, my. So sorry. Clive and I were rehearsing a scene from his school play. We must have gotten carried away. Please forgive us."

"No problem. Have a nice day."

"You, too."

The four of us pull ourselves together, behaving like lovers leaving the motel room. "Yes. Well. So nice to see you again." Wandas large and small smooth their hair, pick up their matching Hermes bags and Gucci scarves, and depart without further ado. I suppose they felt the point had been made.

Clive and I fall down in a heap on the floor and lie motionless. Little did we know this was just a cold reading. Rehearsal hadn't even begun yet.

7

Start Spreading The News: I'm Leavin' Today

I have never been to a formal New York bash. I mean formal as in a-thousand-dollar-per-ticket dinner dance in the Sculpture Garden at the Met honoring Prince Charles with Norman Mailer and Pat Buckley doing a mean cha-cha-cha and Mr. and Mrs. Donald Trump providing solid-gold towers as gifts for the ladies. A BASH. Where the jewels are Winston, the gowns are Balenciaga, and the ambience is somewhere between "The Sun King Meets Kitty Carlisle" and "Leona Helmsley as Seen by Andy Warhol."

The people who attend these bashes, sweeping down

the corridors of the Waldorf, Lincoln Center, or the Plaza, look as though they had just arrived that very minute on Earth. A little bemused. A bit flushed. A sly smile of curiosity and modesty at their good fortune curving their glossy lips. They appear to have it all knocked. Life for these fair fauns seems to be just one floating fox-trot after another.

The truth is, nobody has it knocked. Not even Mrs. Wanda Mackay, who the very evening of the morning of our melodrama in Amora's living room is herself sweeping across the lobby of the Pierre, coiffed and seemingly carefree as the waiters and busboys and fans watch enviously, believing the grand *bugia* of the bashers everywhere. Nobody has it knocked.

As fate would have it, the glamorous Mrs. Mackay's escort for the evening, a benefit in honor of the founder of the Save the Brownstones Society of America, is Richard O'Ralph, the producer of—you guessed it—WNRD's famous call-in therapy show.

This was, of course, no mere coincidence, but a carefully planned selection. It had been Wanda's intent long before our encounter to pick whatever porous little brain was handy in order to gather information about Cowboy Jim and the Cunt.

It was a grand night for a bash. One of those late summer evenings when the air is crispy-clear and the sky between the glimmering phosphorescence of the bastions of world commerce shines like royal-blue satin. The magical power that lies at the core of Manhattan pulses like an overwound pacemaker. The city on such nights lights the world. It glows with radiant beams of strength. It is hot. It is the center of the universe and just being in it makes you special; more alive and more worthwhile. Manhattan mania. A twinkling glass-and-steel playground for the elite. Whish. Swoosh.

Creamy beauties and dapper gents who belong at the center of such a world come out on such nights. Feeding the myth and the magic; blinking at the klieg lights and the flashbulbs with that slightly Cary Grant wonder. "What's all the fuss? Just landed, you know, old sport. Don't know much about the problems here on earth. Read a bit in the car on the way over. Bloody shame about poverty, crime, and all. Don't have any of that where we came from. Rotten luck, that."

Wanda fit right in. Whisking by in red taffeta on the arm of *our* producer. All went well until his unfortunate decision to have a fourth drink. Then came mention of what a smashing job *Amora's sister was doing with her show.*

Nobody has it knocked.

I took Clive home to spend the rest of the weekend at our apartment. By Monday, Mrs. Mackay's visit seemed to be something we'd dreamed. I packed some clean clothes, kissed Vivika and Clifford (who was barely, even for Clifford, speaking to me), and took Clive to school on the subway (a treat for him). Then I went right to the station. Waving a jaunty hello to the security guards, I breezed down the hall through the door marked "Private, Staff Only," and into my own little office, which had been set up down the hall from Amora's. First I read my fan mail.

Dear Dr. Sweet: I must admit, I was never really into you, but lately I have really enjoyed your show. Your insights are much more intelligent and compassionate. Thank you for being there. A recent convert.

Dear Doc: Like your style! You seem different somehow. Funnier and a lot more hip. Keep the faith, Jerome.

Dear Sweet stuff—I bet you are, too. I've got a great big hard . . . Gotta sing. Gotta dance.

I put my mail in my own file and called Chen, my screener, who really ran the show. Chen was rather like a Chinese Mickey Rooney. He'd grown up in Hong Kong, then gone to Rome and worked as a waiter in a Chinese restaurant near the Piazza Navonna for ten years before coming to New York and somehow landing in radio. He was bright and endlessly enthusiastic, but between his Chinese, Italian, and English malapropisms, his communications skills made him a rather bizarre choice for the job. His briefing notes were conceptual art pieces. "Victor is having problems with his mother-in-law" might come out: *Rictoria no lika his illegal mamma mia.* In addition, his spelling skills were reminiscent of a Ma Bell operator on an acid trip. "Yes. This is Station WNRD. That's *W* like in right, *N* like in knife, *R* like in lasagne, and *D* like in okeydoke." You had to be there. Actually, once you learned his code, it wasn't so bad, and when he padded in and flashed that Andy Hardy smile, he could have sent the briefs in Turkish, for all I cared. Amora loathed him, but Jimmy Bob had exotic and secret ties to Chen. Chen was an employee for life, and she didn't mess with him. Chen and I, however, were becoming blood buddies.

Chen appeared, not looking up to his usual elated state.

"Morning. Morning, Doc. Hope you happy as a woodpecker."

"I think I'm more like the tree this morning. You don't look so pecky yourself."

Chen shakes his head and wrings his small, smooth hands. "Oh, bad vibes, Doc. Serious goof-up. Mr. Jimmy Bob is gonna be very bummed out."

I feel the Saturday encounter moving back into my horizon.

"What is it? Is it about me?"

"Molto bad scene. Mr. O'Ralph took Mrs. Jimmy Bob to big fiesta Saturday night and he got a lot of buzz on. He slipped it out about what a hot job you doing taking your sis's place. It's gonna hit the fan belt. We gonna get it."

"Oh no! Has she called here?"

"No way. Not a ring a linga. But I got female instinctive. Bad Karma around here now. You be careful."

"She might call in, Chen. Do you know her voice?"

"Sì. Sì. Anywhere. Don't you have fear about that. Anyway, she knows where her jam's buttered. She hurt the show, she hurt Jimmy Bob. She do that, no lira. She be cool about that stuff."

"She came to Amora's on Saturday. Clive hit her kid in the head with a volleyball."

"Good boy. Should have used a bowling ball."

"You know baby Wanda?"

"Extremely. When I first come here, I work for Jimmy Bob as cook. I live there. One day small Wanda say to me, 'Make me pork chop suey . . . Now!' I say, 'I only got chicken. I make chicken chop suey, if you ask with politeness.' She say, 'Listen, you slit-eyed pecker-breath, I don't have to be polite to servants.' I pick her up and put her around my lap and spank her buns. And I'm out of there. But Mr. Jimmy Bob, he loved me. He felt so sad. He put me in here. Now I'm big shot. Those two dames is bad news. I protect you. Don't worry your hand about it."

"Thanks, Chen. I'd better start working on my monologue. Let me know if you hear anything else. Where's O'Ralph?"

"Lying down on his office. Got one big hangout. I bring him aspirin and blood fairy. He scared to face you."

"Tell him it's okay. It was bound to happen sooner or later."

"Oh, boy. That will cheer him out. You some nice cup-cookie. I wish you'd be here for good."

"Me, too, Chen. Thanks."

I went to work on my opening remarks. I wanted them to be really good. Somehow I had a feeling my coach was getting closer and closer to pumpkin time.

I was on before I had time to consider the possible consequences of Chen's news.

"Good morning. This is Dr. Amora Sweet, and for the next three hours I'll be with you, hopefully sharing thoughts and problems that we all face in dealing with life's stresses. The topic for today, though you are free to call with any question, is Loneliness in Modern Life. There is a term in Eastern philosphy called **mu**. It means nothingness, total emptiness. I have talked to many people who have described moments of that kind of aloneness. Loneliness, while it is often different from aloneness, is equally hard to express as a feeling. It is often masked by depression, anger, restlessness, alcohol and drug abuse, anorexia, obesity, and a variety of other contemporary maladies. It is not a state of being that most Americans feel comfortable with. It doesn't fit our self-concept as a society. To be successful in our society means to be loved, busy, have a rich social life, et cetera. To many of us, this translates as not being lonely. So when we are, it can be very frightening. Everyone is alone. Most of us are lonely at times. We can be lonely for our childhood. For a person or time when we felt bonded and completely received and understood. We can feel psychic loneliness. Physical and emotional isolation. Some of the most profound loneliness exists in large cities where one is surrounded by people all the time. There are people who live as recluses who are seldom lonely, and married people with large families who feel an almost paralyzing sense of isolation. Why?*

"Well, the theories are almost as numerous as the sufferers. First, it is part of the human condition, but it can become crippling and destructive if it moves into the forefront of the person's view of the world. This is usually the result of information received as children, from a parent with an alienated or paranoid world view. Very often, the child's needs are not met by such parents and the struggle to create what has been called The Fantasy Bond becomes the psychological MO for such a person. They grow into adults who see the world as the parents saw it and yet are driven to keep trying to get such a person to validate them. Obviously, this becomes a vicious and destructive cycle that can be broken only by what they call, in Al-Anon, the three A's: awareness, acceptance, action. We can all learn to use our loneliness in positive and creative ways. Artists and writers have long extolled the virtues of solitude as a creative impetus. It is also a door to our unconscious, a way into feelings that we might otherwise push aside and not explore. The more we honor our feelings and accept them as good, no matter how painful or uncomfortable they may be, the more we will grow and the stronger and more satisfying our lives will be. Please call and let's discuss this."

Cut to station ID and commercial. Chen gives me the okeydoke sign. O'Ralph pokes his sheepish head in and nods approval.

"Now available for a limited time, New York's first official duck-stamp print. A beautiful limited-edition print depicting a graceful flight of Canadian geese over Staten Island . . ."

I sip my cold coffee, basking in the glow of my own babble.

I am filled with power. I love this darkened booth, this aloneness; I am connected only to myself. Everything depends on me. Behind the glass, people signal and scurry, getting ready. My listeners wait. I am risen.

Radio is the perfect place for lonely people, for talker

and listener, all of us perched in our own isolation, connected by invisible currents, connections that are broken by a flick of the finger, a flash of thunder, an overworked battery. Connected. Broken. I wait in my dark aloneness for another human voice to reach out to me. Carried through space on an invisible wave. Zapping the loneliness for a moment. I am a responsible person. I am a lonely person. Everything here depends on me.

The radio makes me want to cry. I turn it on and tears fill my eyes. Radio is about loneliness. Voices without faces, traveling through space. Shooting stars burning out. My listener, the woman in the flammable robe, pours another cup of java and turns to the baseball game. This is the way God must feel. Sitting before the galactic control board watching the buttons light up. "Help me! Answer my prayer!"

I am a godlet, doing my part. "It's okay," I want to whisper to everyone else on earth huddled by their radios, overwhelmed by life. "It's okay. I feel like that, too. We're all going to make it. Don't be afraid. God will be right back after the station break; I'll just sit in for a while. Voices flying through the light, soaring into the night sky, sealing our emptiness with sports news, weather reports, financial advice, and rock 'n' roll.

"Dr. Sweet? This is Hilda. I'm forty-three years young and I've just become sexually awakened."

"Congratulations, Hilda."

"Well, thank you. Only, the problem is that it isn't my husband who's awakening me. I'm having an affair with a much younger man. I never knew I could feel like this. I just want more and more. I never thought of myself as a sexual person before."

"Do you have a satisfying relationship with your husband?"

"No. Not really. We're great friends, we really love one

another, but there's never been any sexual energy. But I'm very confused because I do care about my marriage and yet I don't want to stop. And even worse, I find that now I'm attracted to all kinds of other men. It's like someone turned on a switch or something and I'm afraid that I may just lose total control of myself and—"

This very intriguing conversation is interrupted by the appearance in the control booth of Wanda Mackay. I could not hear her but I could see her gesticulating wildly in my direction and having a silent-movie fit. Lights were flashing. Chen was jumping up and down. O'Ralph had his hand over his ears and poor Hilda was left hanging, her libido waving in the breeze for all of America to judge.

"*Due to technical difficulties, the Dr. Amora Sweet program will not be heard. We offer a repeat of yesterday's 'Real Estate Investment for Widows.'*"

I did the only mature and professional thing. I ran and locked myself in Amora's office.

The bloody cat was out of the Gucci bag. Wanda Mackay's shrill Texas soprano echoed down the halls, causing secretaries to grit their teeth and cover their word processors. For five minutes the earth shuddered, time stopped, and then silence. She was gone. We all let out our breath and peeked our heads out into the corridors. I had been spared. Chen and O'Ralph appeared, looking like recently freed skyjack hostages. I beckoned them in.

"What happened?"

O'Ralph slumped in Amora's Queen Anne chair (which is not so easy to do). "The eagle has landed."

Chen sat down on my desk. "Oh, wow, Mamma! That one bad scene. Mrs. Mackay was popping her fork. She say she going to Paris and kill the adulterators. Big bluffing. She not going nowhere but her law man's office."

"You're such a fucking optimist, Chen." O'Ralph

slumps deeper. "She is threatening to expose our little scheme here. The station could be ruined."

I try to appear calm. I try to swallow. The inside of my throat feels like a Gore-Tex rainwear lining. "Would she really do that?"

"No way, José. She won't cut off her toes to spit in her face. It's a smoke scream. Don't be nervous, Doc."

That is always a throwaway line. "I think we'd better call Amora and Jimmy Bob and tell them to come home, fast."

"I'm not so sure, Aroma. There are two ways to go here. One is to light the flares and call in the cavalry. The other is to do absolutely nothing and proceed as if nothing had happened."

"I like column two, O'Ralph."

"Wait a minute, you guys. How can we possibly just paddle on along when she could nail us to our consoles at any moment?"

"Chen has a point about not endangering her security. She might threaten, but she'd be really stupid to go public."

"Right on. She not going to rock the moat. She and her punk love the loot too much. We just walk smooth and carry a big Dick. She calming down real speedy."

"I hope you're right, but I think we've got to call Jimmy Bob. We can underplay, but they have a right to know what's going on here. Too much is at stake."

Chen and O'Ralph exchange loaded glances. Oh, that hindsight again.

"Okay," I say, in my most convincing three-year-old-masquerading-as-grown-up manner, "which one of you wants to place the call?"

O'Ralph's eyes widen like a close-up shot in a teen horror flick. Chen's eyes do the sidewise equivalent.

O'Ralph swallows so hard his lips curl. "You want—you want—*us* to call?"

"Well, you run the show. You've worked for him for years; don't you think it's more professional?"

The buck is being passed so fast, it's sizzling.

"You don't know him. You don't really understand the, uh, other side of him. He doesn't like to be, he's . . . he's . . ."

Chen to the rescue. "He not like bad news deliveries. He like to be big boss. Not bothered with dirty details. When he take off his cowboy hat—gotta devil loose. Better you make the ring-a-ling. He better about chicks."

They are both shaking in their running shoes. I am certainly not interested in a pissing contest with my only two allies.

"Okay, guys. I'll do it." Two noticeable sighs of relief. I wasn't the least bit afraid of Jimmy Bob. Was I missing something?

Chen and O'Ralph nod meekly. We all gather around the phone. The Three Stooges preparing to meet Snow White and Prince Charming.

The line was busy in the little love nest on the Rue de Rivoli for some time. That was because Mrs. Mackay was burning it up. Actually, she probably could have made herself heard without the phone, such was the depth of her rage and rancor. By the time we got through, we were more or less like the duplicate telegram no one bothers to open. He was a pussycat.

"I want my buckaroos to hold the fort. We will not be blackmailed by some Park Avenue hussy. Jimmy Bob will not let his troops down."

Amora could be heard weeping in the background, with just the right amount of damsel in distress to ensure still another ride around the Alamo immediately following our pep talk. They would be home at the end of the week.

Wanda (our leader assured us) would not do anything rash. We should carry on as usual until further notice. I prepared for the bitter end of my newfound success.

The station was on Forty-sixth and Seventh, in a serious skyscraper owned by Jimmy Bob and bearing his name. I decided to walk back to Amora's. I need a little air and some time to think before I faced Clive and called Clifford.

So much had happened in my life in the last month, not just to the content but to the form. I had found something out about myself that I could not put back in the closet.

I was becoming aware of how many of my life and career decisions had been based on a knee-jerk reaction to my goddess-twin rather than coming from the true part of myself. If she was glamorous, I would be plain. If she was thin, I would be portly. She famous and wealthy, I scraping by on my higher principles and smug self-righteousness.

I was no better. That was the first light bulb. I was no different. That was a floodlight. I was sort of a failed version of myself. *That* was the marquee at Radio City.

Okay, while I was at it, if this was a truth tantrum, then I might as well go the distance. I liked her world better. I loved the radio. I liked an apartment with silk couches, Grand Marnier in the crystal decanter, and a doorman. I would rather be making it with Jimmy Bob at the Meurice than attending a lecture on the "Historiated Capitals of Early Romanesque Cathedrals" with Clifford.

I had done all the right things for all the wrong reasons, only to wake up weeks before my fortieth birthday to find out they weren't even necessarily the right things.

In little more than a year my only child, my raison d'être, my center of gravity, would sashay off to college, and there I would be, the clown without the circus, living a life created by default. If Amora is a diamond, I am the rhinestone. Talk about a life script. I had written myself the part of handmaiden in my own fucking play!

I was a fraud. I was every bit as jealous, competitive, and greedy as Amora, and in addition, I was a self-deceptive loser. (This was not, as you may have gathered, an "I'm okay, you're okay" kind of walk.)

I headed up Madison, tears of remorse and self-pity clouding my newly opened eyes, buffeted by the crowds of Busy People.

New York is not great when you're feeling like this. I was so down that even the bag ladies seemed to be more spritely, attractive, and on top of it than I was.

People whizzed by, all looking taller, smarter, better, and more worthy. All with a place to rush to and a damn good reason for being there. By the time I reached Amora's, I was dragging what was left of myself like the loser of a cat fight.

I couldn't go up and face Clive like that! I limped around the corner into a mock-Irish pub and ordered a glass of wine. *So this is how it begins. Self-respect shattered, career in shambles, Helen Morgan née Aroma Sweet takes to hanging out at neighborhood taverns numbing her pain with John Barleycorn, until one night as she staggers home to her one-room walkup, she slips on an unscooped dog poop and slides into the path of a crosstown bus.*

A soft-faced young man with eyes like a live-action Bambi bounces onto the seat next to me. I can feel him watching as I sip my drink. Well, what the hell. Why not pick up a handsome youth on my way down the big tube to oblivion? What possible difference will it make as I slide in front of that bus, if I've added to my list of mistakes a quickie with Bambi?

"Excuse me, but aren't you Dr. Sweet from the Village House?"

Oh, that Dr. Sweet. I turn, disappointed that his attention had nothing to do with a fatal attraction to the doomed lady.

"Yes, I am."

"You probably wouldn't remember me. I'm Gabriel; I was in one of your teen drug-abuse groups several years ago."

I make eye contact. I don't remember. Another character defect or the beginning of Alzheimer's, another possible ending to my ironic and wasted life. No, the bus is better. Cheaper and less humiliating. I'll stay with the bus.

"Gee, I'm really sorry. I can't place you."

"Well, I'm not surprised. I was a mess. Really totaled. Long hair, a beard, and I was stoned most of the time."

"You look pretty together now."

"Oh, I am. I'm in the Navy, actually. They're putting me through school in computers. I love computers."

"That's great."

"I've had fantasies of running into you like this."

"Sounds like a pretty dull fantasy life."

"Not really. I mean, I never got to thank you for what you did for me. I never would have gotten straight if it hadn't been for you. You were really tough, but you didn't bullshit and I heard you. Not right then. I dropped out of the group and sank a little deeper, but one night I was in really bad shape and I remembered something you said in group, something about it never being too late to change, and that once you surrender the game, you find hands all around helping you up. You said, 'You have everything you need.' Something like that. And I did it. I let it go. I never got high after that night. I always wanted to thank you. You really saved my life."

Now outside of *Miracle on 34th Street*, this is about as close as one comes to an intercepted pass from the Great Beyond.

"Gabriel, if you sprouted wings and flew out of here, it would not surprise me at all. I really appreciate those kind words tonight."

The bus can wait. I have not been totally useless. I helped save this archangel's life and he has just reciprocated. I open my purse and prepare to face Clive, feeling the cooling hand of self-acceptance gently covering my fevered brow.

"Oh no, please, Doctor. Let me buy you a drink. It's the least I can do."

"Thank you. I accept." I look at him more closely. "I know you, now. You sat in the back wearing a T-shirt that said something about nuking the universe and you never said a single word. You just smirked. I thought you hated me."

"I thought you were one foxy dame."

I didn't realize that archangels could be so perceptive. "Well, you've made my day, Gabriel. Good luck."

"Thanks, Doctor. I've got it, the best. Never give up. Just like you said."

I said that? Heh heh. A definite hold on the Alzheimer's and the bus. I was ready to face Clive, and whatever happened next was in the hands of the archangel and his boss.

I knew something about myself that I had not known before. It did not fit my self-image or my previous line of defense. It was like that really great black dress that year after year you can always count on, always looks good, a real standby. And then one night, when you really need it, the damn thing betrays you. Nothing has changed and yet it doesn't make it anymore. It doesn't even fit the same. It's all wrong. Dead. Finished. Outgrown. That's where I was. I had slipped it on, expecting the old magic, and there I was in a potato sack.

At the moment it was the sack or bare ass in the snow. But I was getting ready for a new wardrobe. This was not something that could be fixed by taking up a hem or letting out a seam. This was a major purchase.

When I got upstairs I found Clive sitting in the dark listening to the all-news radio. I reached for the light.

"No, Auntie! Don't. A crazy man killed two little kids by pounding nails into their heads."

"In here? All the more reason to turn on the lights. Don't you know that listening to that is bad for you? Turn on some music."

"It's too late, I'm into it. He raped the little girl first and sodomized the boy."

"Clive!" I hit the lights. Clive jumps up and throws himself at the switch.

"No, Auntie. Someone's watching us."

"Someone's what? What are you talking about?"

"Look out the window. Do you see a small guy with a mustache, hat, and a black leather trench coat, very Calvin Klein, leaning in the doorway directly across Sixty-fifth? The building with the black wrought-iron entrance?"

I creep to the window and peer out. There is the watcher as billed. "Yes."

"He followed me home from school. He's been there for hours."

"Oh my God! You poor baby! Why didn't you call me at the station?"

"I tried, but the switchboard was all jammed, and then I turned on your show and it was some real estate for dead people or something. I thought maybe the guy in the raincoat had machine-gunned the place. I thought it best to lie low until someone contacted me."

I kick off my shoes and Clive and I tiptoe into the kitchen, shut the blinds, and light some candles.

"Honey, it's not that I don't believe that that man is following you, but I do think a little less "Miami Vice" might calm your imagination some."

"I don't think he's after me. I think it's you or my mother he's shadowing."

The Gore-Tex has relined my throat. "Well, we're safe now. Why don't I make us some dinner and I'll tell you all about what happened today."

"I've already done it." Clive glides to the oven and flings it open. "Voilà! Poulet à la Clive avec moutarde et fines herbes."

My throat had a lump as big as Clive's volleyball. This could be our last supper. "Considering you expected my machine-gunned body to be momentarily discovered, you went to an awful lot of trouble."

Clive grins and shrugs his bony shoulders. "Grandpa always says no matter what happens, face it on a full stomach."

I sit down and hold out my arms. "Grandpa's right. Come give me a great big hug, then we'll eat. Then we'll talk."

After dinner, we got ready for bed. Clive climbed in and I held him in my arms and told him the whole story. When it became clear to him that what I was really telling him was that his mother would be home soon and I would be going, his whole skinny being shook with sobs. I held him until he fell asleep and then it was my turn. When I'd pulled myself together, I tiptoed into the living room and peeked out the window. The guy in the doorway was gone.

Clive and I left together the next morning, our mutually puffy eyes covered by dark glasses, looking nervously over our shoulders for our chic shadow. I walked him to his school door, then caught a cab and went back to WNRD.

I checked in with Chen and O'Ralph, who were subdued and about as relaxed as hockey pucks. Then I went to my office and leafed through my mail. On top of the pile was a pale-purple handwritten note smelling of expensive perfume. There was a New Mexico postmark and no address. I tore it open, feeling a large fist tighten over my chest. The note said: *Time is running out. The money or the media. Your choice.*

A new form of poetry? A code? Maybe Amora was a spook for the CIA? I became so engrossed in this message and its possible meaning that when Chen gave me the signal, I had not even thought about my opening remarks. I raced into the studio and plunged in.

"*Good morning. This is Dr. Amora Sweet; it's so good to be back with you after yesterday's technical problems. Since we lost so much time yesterday, I'm going to skip the opening thoughts. Let's just begin.*" Not bad, I thought smugly as the board lit up and the cosmorama began.

"*My wife has trouble having an orgasm. She can only come when she helps herself with her finger. She thinks I'm failing her as a husband. If I do it with my finger it doesn't work the same. Maybe my finger needs to be in a different position . . .*"

"*I have a problem with the shape of my head. My soft spot didn't close and my head is pointed at the top and it protrudes in the back. When I was little my mother tried to make me feel better by telling me that it was like curly hair—first nobody wants it, then everybody wants it . . . well, I'm still waiting for pointed heads to be in.*"

"*My husband came home late one night and woke me up and said, 'Our son was killed one hour ago.' No warning. Just like that! It's been three years and I can't get over it. I have nothing to live for . . .*"

"*I called some months ago about my problem with erections. Well, I still have the problem, but I've found out something very interesting about my penis. It goes up inside its covering and if I rub it, like a woman's vagina, I can have an orgasm just fine . . ."*

Three hours whizzed by. Me and the flashing lights and My People alone with Our Radio, pulsing along to our private drummer. No one interfered today. The show went perfectly. We all let out a great big loud sigh. I went back to my office. Chen and O'Ralph trailed behind.

"Good show, Aroma." O'Ralph gave me a peck on the cheek.

"What a turnup! Lots of weird situations today. Maybe it's a full spoon or something."

"Maybe. If we can get through this week, we should be okay. Jimmy Bob and Amora will be back Friday. So I guess that's my last program."

We all look glum at this pronouncement. Then Chen remembers something.

"Hold your courses! Dr. Amora sent telex. Said, 'Tell my sister to stand still until further instructions.' Maybe there's something up her blouse?"

"When did that come, Chen?"

"Yesterday evening after the tit hit the pan."

I feel a little better. Then I remember the note. I pick it up and pass it to my team. "I got this in the mail this morning. It was addressed only to Dr. Sweet. Does it make any sense to either of you?"

O'Ralph studies it. Chen studies it. O'Ralph shakes his head. Chen nods his head (which means the same thing, in Chinese or Italian or both, as O'Ralph shaking his head).

"Must be some 'in' dialogue of Amora's."

Chen and O'Ralph depart and I take advantage of the quiet to plan my monologues for the next few days. Most likely my final remarks. A feeling of terrible sadness creeps through me, filling every corpuscle. The black dress has got to go.

On a whim, I call Clifford with the madcap thought

that he might have heard the show and want to meet me uptown for dinner.

Vivika answers.

"Hi, sweetheart. Did you catch the program?"

"For a minute between classes. Really, Mom, it's like totally disgusting, some of those people. I don't know how you stand it. It just grossed me out."

"Compassion comes with age. Why don't you come uptown with Clifford tonight and take Clive and me to dinner?"

"Dwayne has passes to the Palladium. It's a party for Scum and the Sponges. I did all my homework so I could go. You promised that next time someone had passes, you'd let me. I have my Betsy Johnson all ironed and my hair's rolled."

"Why would you possibly want to do that when you could have dinner with your parents?"

"Mommy, you are so creepy. Thank you lots. When are you coming home? I miss you."

"You do? That's the best thing I've heard all day. I miss you, too. It looks like my gig is over Friday, but I'm not sure."

"That's cool. How's the geek?"

"Don't call him that! He's fine. Frankly, I would love to bring him home with me. He really needs more than he's getting here."

"Oh, no! Oh, no way. If you think I'm going to share a room with that freak-out, you're crazy! Forget it. Just forget it!"

"This is not the time to discuss it . . . I'm sorry I mentioned it. I'm really concerned about him. He's a sweet boy and he adores you."

"Well, he's about the only male who does. I look so gross. My skin's all broken out and my hair is pathetic. And on top of everything, I'm getting my period and I'm fat as a hog. Totally retarded."

"Well, at least you don't have a pointed head."

"What? What are you talking about?"

"Nothing, baby. I'm sure you will transform that disgusting mass into a gorgeous young woman by Palladium time. Is Clifford there?"

"In a manner of speaking. He's locked in his study again. He could have croaked for all I know. Not a sound is coming from behind the door."

"Will you knock and tell him I'm on the phone?"

"All right. But don't get your hopes up. He's working on one of those magazine pieces. I love you, Mommy. 'Bye."

"Me, too, sweetheart." I wait. I hear a knock, then a bang, then another knock. Another bang. Then Vivika loses it and begins pounding and shouting. "If you're alive, pick up the phone. If not, I'm calling the police in five minutes!"

"Hsssshl."

"Clifford? Is that you? I can't hear you."

"I'm working on a piece for the *Voice*. I can't concentrate with all these interruptions."

"I haven't called in two days."

"Shusssslkjssdfk hlll time."

"Could you repeat that, dear?"

"When I'm working on a piece, I lose all track of time."

"I don't suppose you heard the show today?"

"Don't be ridiculous. The orgasms of housewives in Queens is not exactly my idea of topical information."

My feelings are hurt. But I still feel I deserve it. I choose to ignore the slimy remark. "I don't suppose you'd be interested in taking a break and meeting me for dinner?"

"No. I'll be working all night."

"What if I come home for an hour and fuck your brains out?"

"You're beginning to sound like your callers, Aroma."

"Okay, okay. I get the picture. Why don't you send me a note when your withdrawal is over. Or maybe something more dramatic, stigmata bursting forth on my instep or something."

"Husssskkhgkdlls khdk ftheekwkhl to your senses."

This time, I did not ask him to repeat it. I pick up my briefcase, put on my now standard street garb, trench coat, hat, dark glasses, and go home to Clive.

The man in the very Calvin Klein followed me all the way. I decide not to burden Clive with this information. I also decide we should stay in for dinner. While I reheat the remainders of Chicken Clive, I make several passes at the window. The skinny guy in the black leather job has been replaced by a tall blonde in head-to-toe Norma Kamali. I have kept all the curtains closed (or drapes, or draperies, whatever upscale curtains are called). I am fairly strung out. Clive, with his highly charged antennae, doesn't miss a beat. When I leave the room to get Amora's mail, he dashes to the window. When I return I am even more strung out because there is another one of those lavender envelopes. I open it. It says: *Ménage in the moonlight—such a pretty sight.*

"Clive?"

Clive leaps like Cynthia Gregory in Swan Lake.

"I'm sorry, honey. I didn't mean to frighten you."

"Now I know why you've been acting so funny. There's a transvestite in last year's Kamali watching, the same as the guy last night."

"How do you know she's a transvestite?"

"Give me a break, Auntie. *I know.*"

"Well, whatever it is, I don't want you to be frightened. I can't really call the police without starting a whole mess, but if either of them approaches you or calls or anything, you let me know immediately. I don't have any idea what's going on. But it would seem that they're private detectives and they're really just staking us out trying to get evidence for Wanda. I don't think they're going to bother us."

"Did you hear about the teenager in Brooklyn Heights who was raped and strangled in her own bed with her school scarf?"

"No! Will you stop with that stuff! We're perfectly safe here. I'm sure when your mother gets home, she and Jimmy Bob will sort all of this out and Wanda will back off." I nonchalantly pass the missive across the chicken. "Clive, does this note mean anything to you?"

"Yes, it means that someone has very bad taste in perfume." Clive is silent, his huge green eyes flashing across the strange message. "Amora got one almost like it before she left. She seemed a little bummed out about it. Why?"

"Oh, nothing. I just thought maybe it was some kind of love code or something. I was just curious."

To be on the safe side, Clive and I slept in Amora's room with the light on and the door bolted and a chair in front of it. All done casually so as not to alarm him, of course.

The rest of the week went well. That is, no more Wanda. Our two shadows, which we had taken to calling Sherlock Holmes and Miss Watson, were omniscient, but seemingly harmless. And every day, one of the purple stinkbombs arrived. I saved them all for Amora's imminent return.

On Friday I did what I expected to be my last show,

had a tearful farewell drink with O'Ralph and Chen, raced to Clive's school to pick him up, and jumped on the downtown train to Vivika's school for the Girl's Independent School League Volleyball Tournament.

There was my pride and joy: a powerful, beautiful, strong young woman, with all of Amos Cohen's moxy, leading her team to victory.

The underdog team of all time. The school hadn't won a game of any kind in twenty years and they were up against the current champs, St. Zelda's. The preppy rats! By the second game I had made silent injury wishes against every single smart-assed uptown member of St. Zelda's, including their rather androgynous female coach, who for some peculiar reason was wearing white tails and high heels. She wanted victory so bad, the cords in her neck shook when she gave her pep spiels.

Vivika's team didn't look as if they could hit a dead fly with a sticky swatter, but they had guts. They hung on and refused to be intimidated by the prissy misses from the Upper East Side. YAAAAAAHYYYYYY! Clive and I, two misfits, underdog and closet victim, really got into it. It was as if our own fates hung on the outcome of the game. With one point between them in the top of the tie-breaker, Vivika sent a crashing open-palmed slam over the net, right into the shoulder of a particularly obnoxious little number from Zelda's, and the game was over. Clive and I jumped up and down screaming with joy. Vivika had done it. Hurrah for the underdogs! We were winners after all! Hallelujah! Then out of the corner of my eye, across the sock-smelling moisture of the crowded, hysterical gym, I see our shadows. Both of them, at opposite ends. So does Clive.

"Auntie. They're here! How could they have followed us here?"

"I don't know, honey. Unless . . . ?"
"What?"
"Unless they're following Vivika, too."

We try to wend our way through the crowd of elated teachers and parents to Vivika, who is in the midst of passionate embracing with her fellow players. By the time we reach her, she has been carried out, waving over her shoulder to me. We run after her, but she goes in the van with her team to some celebration or other. Our shadows seem to be gone, also. I run to her teacher, who yells something about pizza and that is all I could get.

I grab Clive and hit the nearest pay phone. Clifford is out or not answering. The machine goes on.

"Clifford. I'm worried about Vivika. I think someone may be following her. Or me. Us. I can't explain now. When she comes home, keep her there and check the street. Look for a small thin man in a Calvin Klein trench coat or a tall, blond transvestite wearing Norma Kamali. I mean we think she's a . . . she might be a very large girl. I know you don't know fashion. Just look for *big shoulders*. Gotta take care of Clive. 'Bye."

Oh, to be a flea in a tree when Clifford picked up that message.

I decide to hang around downtown until Vivika gets home, so Clive and I jump in a cab and head for my favorite restaruant in Chinatown, Sung Fat. This place is so Chinese that the menu is not translated and you order (for those of us not fluent in the tongue) by pointing to whatever the famished Chinese who pack it in are devouring.

Clive and I share a table with a stony-faced married couple who were slurping up a hideously gelatinous bowl of noodles and intestines. We do not point to this.

While we gaily down our sissy dishes, Clive listens to

the all-news station on his Walkman and I try to sort out my highly disconnected thoughts.

In two days my sister will return. There is some question about what she will want from me after that time. We are being followed by two strange trendy people. Odd-scented notes are coming in the mail. I want to take Clive to live with me. I don't want to go home and face Clifford. I am worried about Vivika. I am going to be forty before you can say "Mongolian Beef." I am anxious.

"Listen to this, Auntie. A man beat his mother to death with a metal pipe because she wouldn't cook spaghetti and meatballs for his dinner."

"Clive, take that thing out of your head. Someday it's going to freeze in your ears and you'll spend the rest of your life listening to garbage on news radio."

"He wasn't even Italian!" Clive takes off his earphones and gives me the most wistful smile since Charlie Brown met Snoopy. "I sure have fun with you. Every day is like an adventure. I never have fun with Amora. Everything is so serious and phony. It's never like real life. The only way I even know she's human sometimes is that I hear her having her spells at night."

This perks my interest. "Spells?"

"*Mais oui*. She puts on this 'my life is perfect' act. But when she's losing it, she locks herself in her boudoir with a bottle of brandy and splits her seams. Screams, yells, pounds on pillows. She murders pillows. Wow, she can really get into it with a pillow. She strangles them and beats them with her fists. Then she just cries and howls. Like one of those hounds in the old Dracula movies. Wooooooooooooooooooooo!"

The inscrutable colon gobblers stop slurping and stare at us.

"Chill out, dude. We're being watched."

"Get down, Momma! You're into Vivika's lingo. Right on!"

"It has its uses. Tell me, without any more demonstrations, please: Does this happen often?"

"More and more often. She may just snap her strap one of these days." He is trying to be flip but his eyes fill with tears. "Know anyone who wants to adopt a thirteen-year-old fruit with a hyperactive thyroid?"

"You'll be beating them off with sticks, pal."

I must be very careful what I say here. I set down my chopsticks and give him twin cheek kisses. "Clive, baby, the absolute best part of these last few weeks has been our times together. You are really like my own kid and it will break my heart to go home without you, but the fact is that you not only have a mother who, whatever her problems, does love you, but you also have a father. That hardly qualifies for entry in the orphan's guild."

Clive sneers. "My father. That worm brain. He's so scared of Amora that he won't even call us up. He sends me telegrams on my birthday and Christmas. Telegrams! I don't even know what his handwriting's like. Probably can't write or read, either. She must have been pretty desperate to let that snail crawl on top of her."

"Clive, knock it off now! I only met him once, but he was very nice. He just wasn't very strong. He was from a terribly rich family and he adored your mother. He's been awfully generous. She never really gave him a chance to be a father to you. She left him when you were still a baby."

"Oh yeah? Well, nobody would stop me from being a father to my son. Not that it's likely that I'll ever have a son or a wife or a home with a yard and a fireplace and nice neighbors or anything, anyway. Not likely. But if I did, I'd never just let him go. I'd fight for him. I'd do anything to be near him!"

Clive drops his head and sobs quietly. His large soft ears are bright red and his whole body shakes with pain. The innard eaters stare blankly at the grieving boy. I entertain the thought of pouring their viscous broth over their shiny black heads.

Instead, I hand Clive a Kleenex and gently touch his back with my palm. I pat.

When I was a child and in pain, my mother would do that. She'd softly, so gently, put her warm hand on my back or my chest and just pat, pat, pat. She never said a word. She never had to. Her hand said it. It talked a blue streak. There, there, there, baby, it said. Everything's going to be all right. Feel my hand, how warm and strong it is. Don't be afraid. Don't be sad. I'll pat away the pain and fear. I'll always be here.

Clive calmed down. Our tablemates departed. I pour cups of steaming tea and we open our cookies. "Beware of dark strangers," his said. "You are going on a long journey," mine says. I call home.

"Mom! We won! We really won! Oh my God, I don't believe it!"

"It was wonderful. My heart still hasn't returned to normal beating. When did you get in, honey?"

"About twenty minutes ago. I told Clifford."

"Did you get an eyebrow?"

"No. I almost got a half of a lip curl. Not too bad."

"Honey, I know this is going to sound really weird, but did you notice a small man with a big mustache in a black trench coat or a tall blonde woman wearing Norma Kamali when you left the game? Or anytime this week?"

"Mother, you are so paranoid! I don't believe you! I picked up the message on the machine. You sounded like something from "Cagney and Lacey." No one is following me. Don't be crazy!"

"Just the same, if you see anyone like that, you get home fast and call me immediately. Promise?"

"Promise, unless they rape and mutilate me first, in which case I'll call you after."

"Bite your tongue. I know I'm overreacting. But then I'm always overreacting. So at least I'm behaving normally. Clive and I are very proud of you. I'll call later. Did, uh, Clifford hear the message?"

"No. Lucky for you. I erased it. I don't really think that would be too cool right now."

"What a classy kid. I owe you one."

"Dwayne has new passes to Tunnel this weekend. Okay?"

"Okay. But having the tradeoff ready so fast doesn't look good in the big book."

I round up Clive and we head uptown. Our shadows are nowhere in sight. By the time we zoom across Fifty-seventh and Madison, I feel terrible. I assume I am carsick from the maniacal Israeli driver who seems determined to give us our money's worth. "Can you please slow down? There's a child in the car."

"Child, smild. In my country, he'd already be in the army, killing Arabs."

I just make it to the bathroom. I stay there heaving up things that have been resting long before Sung Fat took spoon to wok. Nerves, I think. Better that than salmonella.

The thing about projectile vomiting is that it really gets your priorities straight. No time for self-pity or idle fantasies. No time for paranoia or wardrobe indecision. There is you. There is the bowl. There is the desire to stay alive. Period. It went on well past midnight. Finally, whatever was left inside me had surrendered. The last Milk Dud and grilled-cheese sandwich. The piece of tomato and last month's egg cream. There was nothing left. I was purged. I staggered into the shower, brushed my teeth until my gums squeaked, wrapped my newly slender and shivering body in some male's terry-cloth robe, and crept out to merciful sleep.

Clive was lying in the dark huddled at the foot of his mother's bed, his face drained of color. "That was great, Auntie. Can you do it again?"

The kid had wit, which was fortunate. He was going to need every wry ounce of it.

I fell into a heavy sleep. When I woke up, Clive had left without me, and I barely had time to limp into my clothes and get to the station. As I fell into a taxi, I saw Sherlock across the street. It was not Sung Fat's rancid peanut oil. Nerves. Definitely nerves.

I remember everything about that Friday. I had breakfast in a coffee shop (grilled corn muffin and regular coffee). Two women in unseasonably early fur coats sat at the corner next to me.

"I never cook anymore, except for my dog."

"That can be very trying."

"Oh, it is. He's very particular. He won't touch anything greasy, and if I make the same thing twice, he refuses to even taste it. He loathes leftovers."

"I had a Siamese like that once. She would only eat veal sautéed in butter and garlic."

"I had eyeholes cut in my Hermes carry-all so that I can take him with me to Le Cirque for lunch. I never leave him alone."

"Good idea."

On the subway I sat next to two women formerly of Scarsdale.

"I've been in a depression for six months, ever since we moved into the city."

"I've been here two years. I'm still depressed."

"Scarsdale was my world. I had my beautiful home, my garden, my friends. Now I've got filth and crime. My husband loves it."

"My husband loves the Fifty-ninth Street Bridge. Our apartment faces it. Our bedroom faces it. Not the river, like normal people; the goddamn bridge! He sits in the window and stares at it for hours. Someday I'm going to blow it up."

"There's a black with a silver pistol running around our neighborhood raping women and stealing their purses."

"I was never depressed in Scarsdale."

Chen was wearing a red sweater. O'Ralph had a new blue suit. The first commercial was, "When precision counts, don't take any chances with your tool."

The lead news item was a new report from the EPA listing 403 major chemical leak sites in the Northeast. Five Eastern Airlines passengers had been caught free-basing in the john.

I had a call from a frustrated husband who described making love to his wife as "Romancing the Stone."

A battered wife called to ask how she could stop her husband from chasing her around the yard with a carving knife when she displeased him.

"You can't," I said.

"Well, he's not like that all the time," she said.

"Well, how many times do you have to be dead?" I said.

"Beg pardon?" she said.

"Once," I said.

"Well, I'm committed to the relationship. I'm not perfect either," she said.

"Do you chase him around with a knife?" I said.

"No," she said.

"Then you are more perfect than he is; get out of there and get some help," I said.

"Well, but he can be very sweet," she said.

"Othello was nice to Desdemona, too," I said.

I talked to a fourteen-year-old girl in California who

had just had her second abortion, and a seventeen-year-old track star who had gotten drunk, crashed his father's car, and lost his left leg. A man with terminal cancer wanted to know how to tell his eight-year-old daughter. An Oregon woman called whose husband wanted her to join a bisexual cult. It was not a lighthearted day. Bad vibes, man.

"Well, that's all for this week. It's been great hearing from you; have a nice weekend. Here's a little mental-health hint. At every moment that there is pain, there is also growth. Our lives are about becoming. It is the journey that we must embrace, not the destination. And everything on the journey is valuable. Have a happy weekend and a magnificent journey.

"This is Dr. Amora Sweet, thanking you for listening. I'll be back with you same time on Monday."

Gotta sing. Gotta dance.

I said good-bye to Chen and O'Ralph, who were as anxious as I was. None of us had heard a word from the Americans in Paris since Amora's last telex. I stacked her mail in a neat pile, separating out the lavender notes and putting them in a mailing envelope in her desk drawer. I dawdled tidying up, putting off the moment of departure. I had cut my time at the clinic to two afternoons and Saturdays since Amora left and they were expecting me back on a regular basis next week. My stomach knotted. I didn't want to go back. I wanted to stay here. I felt fragmented and abandoned like one of the street people they pick up, plop in the hospital, and then dump back on the sidewalk. "Here's a fiver and some hot coffee. Good luck." I didn't seem to fit back into anything. Guess what, Amora, old sis, old pal, old bean. A funny thing happened while you were humping with the Huguenots. I fell for it! I did. All my worst fears, right out there in the open. You were right, you vixen, you. I was jealous. I did want to be you. Even worse. Now that my own life has lost its meaning, you're coming back to claim double victory. What a woman!

I put my head down on her polished maple desk and bawled. The phone rang.

"Dr. Sweet."

"Auntie?"

"Clive? Are you all right?"

"Relatively. Amora called from the airport. She's on her way. Can you come home now?"

The itsy-bitsy spider climbed up the water spout. Down came the rain and washed the spider out. Up came the sun and dried up all the rain and the itsy-bitsy spider climbed up the spout again.

I kept singing that in my head all the way home. It was sort of the nursery-school version of the myth of Sisyphus. I was going home in anticipation of the great deluge. I was really worried about Clive.

Sherlock and Miss W. were both in their places. I turned my head, pulling my hat lower (I had lost so much weight that, with the wig and scarf and all, it was possible that they still didn't know which sister I was), and raced up to Clive.

He had showered and outfitted himself in the style to which Amora was accustomed. On the marble table (still bearing the thus far unremovable traces of baby Wanda) he had set up her favorite champagne, a fresh pâté-and-cracker assortment, and a heart-shaped handmade card that said "*Santé*, Amora." His eyes were red from either the shower or crying, or both.

"Tell me all, baby." I led him to the couch and held him in my arms. One for the road.

"I don't have much to tell. She called, she sounded fairly weird, a little nervous. She said she was on her way here with Jimmy Bob and she hoped we would be here to greet her. That we all had a lot to discuss. That's it."

"Okay. We had better give them the entire scenario. Both of our fashion plates are downstairs. Seems like a terrible waste of money, hiring two of them to watch us."

"Maybe they'll stop now. They don't seem to know about each other. They're always in different spots."

"Maybe."

There was a tapping at the door. We both leapt and ran for it. Clive peeked out and then flung it open and jumped back as if to avoid impact with someone.

Amora swept in looking wan and tired despite her exquisite new Chanel suit and hat. "Thank God!" She threw her purse and cosmetics bag on the floor, tossed her hat after it, kicked off her sling pumps, and collapsed on the couch. "Champagne. Fast!"

Clive sprang into action. Amora reached for the glass, pushing aside his handmade heart without noticing it.

"Where's Jimmy Bob?" I managed to croak out in the heat of my hurt at her rudeness. Clive's lips trembled, but he held on.

"Bringing in the bags. The last two days, we shopped."

There is a crashing and panting. Jimmy Bob staggers in, sinking under the weight of four oversize Vuitton suitcases. He drops them, staggers out, and reappears with four more.

"Next time, we'll hire a mule train; my lumbar region is done for." Jimmy Bob tips his ten-gallon gray suede hat with the Indian beaded band, loosens his silver-and-turquoise string tie, and lowers his endless beefy frame next to Amora.

"How's my little cowpoke?"

Clive winces. "Fit as a fiddle, Mr. Mackay."

"Good!" He turns to me. "I don't know if we can rightly thank y'all for doin' such a splendid job. I'll never doubt my little lady's judgment ever again. You did us proud."

The Gore-Tex is back. Is this the moment when the proud but vanquished heroine turns in her gun and walks slowly off into the mist? "Thank you, Jimmy Bob. I really enjoyed it."

In fact, Jimmy Bob baby, I enjoyed it so much that I thought maybe we could cut a little deal. My own show, por ejemplo. *Nothing fancy. Just five or six hours a week under my own name with possibly a syndicated column in one of your magazines or newspapers. Now that I've gotten the hang of it. We'd be the new eighties version of Ann and Abigail. Just think of it! A few pounds off. A little frosting. The nose. The chin. The tits. Voilà! We're identical again. Whaddya say? I promise I'll go the distance for ya . . . do my best . . . pretty please, with buffalo chips on top?*

Amora pours herself another glass of bubbly, then pours one for J.B. They toast one another, eyes locked, as if Clive and I were statuary.

"Amora, I hate to be a mood breaker, but there have been some pretty weird things going on while you were gone, most of which we don't understand, and I really think it's time to talk."

Jimmy Bob's face tightens—ever so slightly, the grin never wavers—but everything goes cold for just a second. I see what Chen and O'Ralph were talking about. A peek at the underbelly.

Amora sighs. But then Jimmy Bob pats her small white hand with his big hairy one and winks and I lose this insight; envy wipes it right out. Oh, to have a man to protect me. How does it happen that women get that? I mean get it without giving everything up. It's a knack. Amora is about as fragile as the Sixth Fleet. She just knows how to play helpless. Men have always fallen all over their silly selves to rescue her, dropping their double-ply cashmeres at her pedicured little feet. I always sneered at the phoniness of it. *I* was a feminist. *I* did not need a man who would open doors and take burdens from my emancipated shoulders. Muggers, bullies, rapists, thieves—let me at 'em! Child support? A pathetic cop-out. Alimony? Beneath contempt. I would do it on my own. I would change my own tire and repair my own car and pick up my own dinner check, thank you very much. And in addition, I would be my own best friend, financial analyst, therapist, laundress, and gourmet chef, and assume total responsibility for my child, my career, my sexuality, and my health. I am Woman, hear me roar. I can do everything!!!!

Sure. Two feminists sitting on the curb. "Fine mess you made of this one, Ollie." Helen Reddy has run for her life, Jane Fonda is one step away from a full-page spread in Ripleys. Won't somebody stop her before she achieves again? And even Gloria Steinem has dyed her graying mane blonde and is being seen on the town with rich and powerful marriage prospects.

I wanted a man to put his big hairy hand on mine and pat it. "Now, now, little lady, the Duke will take care of everything. Don't you fret." There. I admit it. I may be burned in effigy at NOW meetings all over the nation. But I wanted it, that Friday afternoon.

I had married two men who had fulfilled my feminist insanity. I trained them right. I asked for nothing, and that's what I received. Certainly can't blame them. At least Clifford was civilized about it. Amos Cohen was an entirely different matter.

Amos Cohen was the wild man of Berkeley. Only James Dean had ever done for a cigarette between the lips what Amos did. He stalked the campus with a brooding insouciance, a sullen eroticism that was the cause of many moistened undies among the aspiring bohemian ladies of Oakland. I thought he was a creative genius with whom I would have a wildly romantic and exciting life.

In reality it was more like the Audrey Meadows role in "The Honeymooners." Amos married me, I am now convinced, because I was the first girl who had ever refused to sleep with him. We would drive each other berserk with stolen moments of rumpled frustration. The backseat of his roommate's Chevrolet. The wet marshy grass behind the dorm. Party closets. I refused to go to a motel with him or to surrender my cherished chastity. Actually, it was the best sex, our almost-sex, that I ever had in my entire life, and to this day, I am much more turned on by the idea of a grapple on a sofa, a tryst in a Audi 5000, or a little hands-on beneath an overcoat at the movies than by a big comfy bedroom scene.

We married a week after graduation. We did it. The foreplay was a lot better. An ego like Amos's didn't require sexual performance. He always thought letting me touch him was my reward.

I remember the exact moment I realized that I did not really love him. We had been married a year and I was working full-time and going to graduate school (I am Woman, hear me self-destruct). Amos was not working and not going to graduate school. Amos was taking a lot of drugs (paid for indirectly by *mio*) and writing a book of poetry. It was a laborious process because Amos thought the conventional ways of writing—using a typewriter or lined paper—were bourgeois and noninspiring. So Amos wrote only on rolls of white toilet paper. Every water drop became the makings of artistic tragedy. The nadir of the project came when a drunken buddy of Amos's, who was sleeping on our foldaway, got up in the middle of the night, couldn't find any TP, and used the first half of the manuscript to wipe his ass. Things were not great.

Amos, on this morning, came into the kitchen wearing a jacket and tie, slacks and regular shoes. I forget why. But it must have been something really important. I had never seen Amos in anything but jeans, boots, and his usually torn or sweaty T-shirt with sleeves rolled up and a pack of Marlboros tucked in the left one, his muscles flexing as if they were on some sort of hydraulic pump. That is what I fell in love with. That is what I married. That is what he was married in.

The suit did not work. In the suit he just looked like a stocky, ill-kempt rube. Since there was little to admire in his personality (demanding, selfish, and narcissistic), and from the look of the toilet paper, Robert Graves was not going to lose any sleep . . .

My life is barnacle on the Ocean of Garbage. Shit and seaweed cover me. Neptune sucks himself off. Beneath me sharks belch the sea-god's seed into the grotto of infinity . . .

What had I left? I had my romantic fantasy, which had now been struck a fatal blow by a polyester drip-dry and a polka-dot tie. I did not let on that this had occurred, however. (Especially not to myself.) I did something much more sensible. I stopped breathing. Now, it is known as hyperventilating. Then, it was just suffocating.

Finally, I went to see the school shrink, which was not as easy as it may sound. This was the sixties, remember. Between the suicide attempts, LSD freak-outs, school-induced schizophrenia, identity crises, and drop-in, drop-out conflicts, there were lines around the block waiting to dump the latest load onto the new gods of healing. Nothing was from your body. The mind was the message.

"There is nothing wrong with me," I said defensively before the poor therapist had even asked my name. "I just can't breathe."

"I have a perfect relationship with my husband. I just keep losing my air supply."

It took about two months. One morning I walked into my session and out of nowhere, totally without any previous awareness on my part, out jumped the truth. "I don't love my husband. I don't respect him. I don't want him to touch me. I've made a terrible mistake!"

Then two things happened. First, I started breathing like a son of a bitch. The second thing was that my mother died. So I stayed. I was too shattered to leap off the Pacific shelf into the big unknown. I supported Amos (who had by now forsaken poetry and taken up jazz saxophone). I finished graduate school. And then, just about the time I was steady enough in the world without the rock of mother love to lean against, I got pregnant. Wouldn't you just know it.

I Am Woman, hear me scream hysterically . . .

Vivika was born in 1972. Two years later I finally left Amos, who at that time was heavily into out-of-body experience. Whatever that means. He did not try to stop us. He never kissed Vivika good-bye, or, from that day to this, wrote her a note or sent her a present. Vivika's idea of fatherly love comes only from Pop and whatever spilloff Clifford lets her wade around in. Probably for the best. Pop is a much better bet. The last I heard about Amos, he was working as a claims adjuster for an insurance company in Napa Valley. Marlon Brando can relax. I am invincible. I can do anything. Bullshit.

Jimmy Bob is now rubbing Amora's neck.

"All-righty, amigos; let's powwow."

Clive and I sit forward obediently waiting for the peace pipe to pass in our direction. Jimmy Bob slams down his crystal tulip glass and stands up, towering over us.

"Now, Aroma honey, why don't we start with you. Give us an account of recent happenings."

"I'll try to be as concise as possible," I begin, already seeing the glaze of boredom in Jimmy Bob's twinkly blues.

"Everything went fine until Wanda, Mrs. Mackay,

started phoning. Clive and I put her off as long as we could, but then she showed up here with your, uh, daughter, and then she came to the station. That blew your cover story. After that, however, we didn't hear anything more from her, but we've been watched day and night by two detectives. I assume they're detectives. A man and a woman, but they aren't together. They were down there when I came in. And—" (before I can get to the part about the weird notes, J.B. interrupts me).

"Watched?" Amora and Jimmy the B, J.B., Jimmy Bob, or Mr. Mackay or Sir, exchange a quick but meaningful glance. I am beginning to think that this conversation is not what it seems. Another setup in progress?

"Yes. Clive and I assumed it was Wanda's work."

"Oh, yes. Of course. Two, you say?"

"Yes. Two fashion types. A small dark man and a big blond."

"Transvestite." Clive chimes in, pleased with himself.

Amora and Jimmy Bob exchange another meaningful glance and turn on poor Clive.

"How would *you* be knowing something like that, young'un?"

Clive's floppy ears are turning purple right before our eyes.

"I saw a movie once. She, uh, I looked through my telescope. She had big hands and stuff, she didn't look like a real woman. It's just an observation, sir."

Amora glares at him. "Children have no business seeing movies about things like that. I forbid you ever to use that word in this house again."

"Transvestite?"

"Jimmy Bob, he did it again!"

"But, Mo, Amora, it's not a bad word. It's in the dictionary. 'The practice of wearing the clothes of the opposite sex, often as a manifestation of homosexuality.'"

"Jimmy Bob, he's memorized it!"

"Now, now, honey pot. Boys will be boys. Clive, son, don't be saying that again and upsetting your momma."

"Yes, sir." Clive sinks back into the silky cushions, his ears like two large grapes against the white pillows.

I am losing my patience. "I think, with all due respect, we are getting sidetracked here. Frankly, our news doesn't seem to be much of a surprise to you, so maybe we should reverse the order and you tell *us* what's going on."

Third meaningful glance exchange.

Amora sighs one of those "oh, woe is me, why should a person of my specialness be forced to deal with such as this" sighs.

"Very well, but I think it best that Clive leave the room."

Tears fill Clive's eyes.

"With all due respect, Clive has been a rock through all of this; he's not a baby, and I don't think that's really fair at this point. The time for shielding him has long since passed."

"If you say 'with all due respect' one more time, I'm going to scream."

"Now, now, ladies. Let's all calm down. I am the tie-breaker here. I agree with Amora. Clive, son, you wait in the other room. We'll fill you in at the appropriate time."

Nothing like a fair vote. I cannot bear this. I take two deep breaths and say my mantra and try to recall everything I've learned about positive fighting, which in my experience only works when you're not really mad. I feel humiliated and small.

Clive gets up slowly, his eyes heavy-lidded like a cartoon frog. His thin shoulders hunch forward. He shuffles out.

Just as he gets to the door, he stops. His body straightens and he turns. A sly smile curls his trembling lips. "*Too* bad, I was just going to tell you about my conversation with Mrs. Mackay's lawyer and . . . the death threat. Well, some other time, perhaps."

I love that kid.

Fourth meaningful glance, henceforth known as M.G. Both in unison:

"What conversation? What death threat?" Both rise and run to the bedroom door, behind which Clive has slipped.

"Clive dear! We were rash; come on out, now. You *are* a big boy. I think we should reconsider our decision!"

"Come on now, buckaroo. Let's have a little man-to-man. Open the door, son. I've got a gigantic steak dinner with your name on it waiting for ya, later."

Clive turns on his radio full blast and does not acknowledge the highly amateurish manipulators at the door. I feel great.

Finally they give up and return to me.

"I bet he was just making that up. Do you know what he's babbling about?"

"Clive does not babble and he never tells lies. As you well know, Amo. I'm sure it's nothing serious, though." I smile pleasantly. "Now, as we were saying . . ."

"Aro. Things have happened that we are not at liberty to discuss. I'm afraid the situation with Wanda has gotten pretty ugly and poor Jimmy Bob's entire empire is threatened by certain information that has fallen into her hands. Things are quite complicated. Also, there is my career to think of. You can imagine what a scandal could do now. Jimmy Bob is doing everything in his power to control that dreadful woman, but we just don't know what she's liable to do next. And so we have a proposition to make to you, dear."

This is the part where the coach would ask for time

out, the film editor would freeze the frame, the lawyer would approach the bench, Johnny would putt into a station break. I nod.

Fifth M.G.

"Well, Aro. First, you have done quite an adequate job sitting in for me, but sadly, now that Wanda Mackay knows, it's much too risky to keep up the pretense. However, she, uh, has made it very clear in her demands to Jimmy Bob that one of the starting points in her divorce agreement would be that I no longer conduct my radio program. You can see her point."

I see it. I see it.

"However, I am not about to take a thriving career and just throw it out the window, so what we had hoped was that you might continue as yourself. We would do a brief press release and you would just continue. Hardly anyone would even notice. Listeners don't really pay attention to those silly details. It would be Dr. *Aroma* Sweet in lieu of Dr. *Amora* Sweet. The program stays the same, but we wouldn't be doing anything illegal and Wanda would have no grounds for complaint. It would certainly be a big career boost for you. I would keep the 'Today' show, of course, and the column, and clinics would go on as before. And then, when all of this messy stuff is over, I would just return. I think it's really a brilliant plan, don't you? Of course, the money arrangement could stay the same, too."

Someone should yell "Cut" now. "Excuse me, just a minute, I must have a glass of water." I jump up and head briskly for the kitchen. My trainer rushes to my corner with septic stick and wet towel. I pour a glass of Perrier and press the bottle to my throbbing head. I must think clearly.

I am being offered a dream come true. Myself and I

on the radio. Big-time stuff. Why? Really why? It seems impossible to believe that my sister could want that Connecticut Okie badly enough, no matter the money or the loosening flesh, to turn her most prized possession, her public, over to her most fearsome rival. She never even shared the key when we went skating.

Once again, I know somehow I'm being had, but the reprieve is so heady, the opportunity so enticing, the chance to stave off a little longer my coming to terms with the quality of my own life and relationships so powerful that I decide to act as if I do not really know that I am the mouse heading for the glue trap. I gulp down the fizzy cold water and refill my glass. It's not champagne, but it's not dishwater, either; sort of like my self-image. I reenter casually.

"Well?" Amora and J.B. are practically panting with eagerness.

"I have several questions first."

"Of course, dear." Her smile looks a little bit tight to me.

"When would all of this take place?"

"Let me handle the technical aspects, honey bun. We will make two announcements on Saturday and Sunday that Dr. Amora Sweet will be taking a leave of absence and her show will be conducted by her sister and closest colleague, Dr. Aroma Sweet. Which means, little lady, that you can show up as usual on Monday."

"I see. And for how long?"

M.G. number six.

"Why, that's kinda hard to say. I would imagine it could run as long as six months, maybe longer. You know how divorces are, heh, heh."

"When you're poor, they're simple. Someone takes the bed, someone takes the TV, you split the tapes and sell the car."

"Oh, for the simple life, eh, Amora?"

"There's no such thing, darling. Is there, Aro?"

"No such. Oh, also, Amo . . . dear, what you said about the money. Somehow that doesn't seem fair, considering I'll be doing all the work. I think eighty-twenty makes a lot more sense, sort of like a finder's fee or agent's commission. Only long-term." I smile demurely.

It is hard to smile with clenched teeth. But if anyone could manage it, she could. "Fine, dear."

"Oh, one last question, for now. You must understand, this is all very sudden. I haven't had any time to sort things out" (which is obviously just fine with Dale and Roy). "What about Clive?"

In unison: "Clive?"

"Yes. Well, this is all going to be rather hard on him, and the two of you are probably going to want some private time together, so I thought possibly you might want him to stay with me for a while."

Seventh meaningful glance. Eight and they win a trip for two on the "Love Boat."

"Why, what a lovely thought. What a good idea. How kind of you, Aro. You know, it would be even better if he could stay here, where his home is. Jimmy Bob has taken a suite at the Carlyle and I can stay there. I know that's a lot to ask of you, being away from your family for months at a time, but it would be much better for Clive. You really don't have room for him at your place, and he's a bit old to be sharing a room with a teenage girl."

"Well, I don't know. I guess we could work out some arrangement during the week and then be in the Village, or everyone could come up here on the weekends. I'd have to discuss it with Vivika and Clifford." Can't wait!

"Good idea! Can you call them and we can settle it right now?"

"Oh, no. I'd better go home and do it. I'll get back to

—135—

you later. But I'd be glad to take Clive home with me, if you'd like. He can sleep on the couch; it's quite comfy."

They win the "Love Boat" cruise.

"Why, that would be so nice for him. Thank you, dear."

"I'll go get him."

I saunter to the door. "Clive, it's Auntie. May I come in, please?" The door swings open so fast, I stumble and fly into the room. The door slams behind me.

"Were you sitting on the knob?"

"I heard. I'm packed, let's go."

The subway was jammed. I passed the time trying to reconstruct the encounter, reading the graffiti in front of me. *Suck cat pussy get tongue AIDS.* Clive listened to his all-news station and relayed what he considered interesting events. "Divine died of asphyxiation. An eighth grader brought a shotgun to school and wasted the principal."

Two blue collars with grease-stained hands pushed in next to us.

"Hey, Joe, you hear 'bout your friend Tony?"

"Say what?"

"He passed. Last night. Heart."

"I just had lunch wit' him."

"Well, he passed, anyhows."

"Jeez, ain't that somethin'. Such a hearty guy."

"They laid him down in Brooklyn Memorial."

"Oh, yeah? My grandparents are buried there. Nice."

"Yeah. Real nice. We tried to put my old man there but they was too crowded. Hadda take him out to Long Island."

"That's good. Long Island has more class. Everyone wants to be put out there."

"Yeah. I got a plot there—had it since I was a kid. All paid for."

"Nice."

A young man gets on, looking from a distance like a golden god. A mass of yellow curls, large blue eyes, and tan copper-tinted skin. He is dressed in the rumpled corduroy look made popular by the Kennedys. He looks like a Kennedy. As he pushes closer, the glamor fades. The blue eyes have the dazed glow of a drug-busted brain. Vacant spaces behind the turquoise.

He sits down next to a pretty, intelligent-looking young woman who is holding a flute case on her lap. Her fine-boned face is lowered over her book. There is delicacy about her chiseled cheeks and her long, slender fingers.

My eyes wander down to her legs. The legs do not have any business on her body. They are gross. Thick and broken-veined. Without shape or grace. Swollen and heavy. I become fascinated with this body. The top and bottom so unalike, so out of balance. Ironic. Her body is ironic. Her body and his body. Golden-perfect boy with fried gray matter. Delicate artist with crude stumplike extremities. God's justice.

I look at Clive, smiling benignly, his lop-eared sweetness lost in bad news. Blocking out his hurt with the woes of the world. Mixed bags. Tricks or treats. Most of our lives are Halloween sacks. Combinations of yummies and bad jokes. Spiders and caramels. I see us all lined up in boxes on our way to Long Island, the *in* burial ground. Layer on layer, wave on wave, subway car after subway car. It all ends the same.

I turn my head. A man with a face eaten away by cancer is reading the *New York Times*. At Fourteenth Street, a tall black dude wearing a button that says "At War" jumps on, flinging a wheelchair into the aisle. In it sits a pretty black girl with neatly braided pigtails, fuzzy green sweater, and no discernible lower body. A human paperweight. She holds out a plastic cup and chats gaily with the silent averted eyes of the, however barely, more fortunate. Everyone on the car except the Kennedy God gives her money.

Nausea wells up in my throat. I am suddenly exhausted. I need a vacation. The old New York City burnout. The moment when the invisible shield that stops the force of human energy, human despair, human rage from overwhelming you each day melts. You see everything. You feel everything. Time for a week in Bermuda, dear. Right.

When we get home, I am so tired I can hardly walk. Madeline gets in the elevator with us.

"How's life, Madeline? Have you met my nephew, Clive?"

"Never had the pleasure. Hello, young man. Are you a cat person? You look like a cat person."

"No. I'm a canary person."

"Oh. Well, maybe next time." Madeline pats his head. Clive gives me a look. I avoid eye contact.

"Anyone invite you to Paris yet?" I ask.

"Oh, you remembered. How telepathic you are. I was just thinking about that. Not yet. I went out with an accountant who told me I had just the right amount of cellulite. That's the first compliment I've had from a man in years. Maybe it's for next time." The elevator stops, we depart.

"What does she mean about next time?" Clive whispers.

"Reincarnation, kid. She's into it."

"She's out of it, is what she is."

"We're all out of it today, baby."

I brace myself for reentry. We tiptoe in. The apartment is dark and musty. Of course it is dark and musty, even with the lights on and the windows open. No one is home. I turn on the kitchen light. There is a note from Vivika informing me that she is spending the night at her friend Chandra's house. These new names, these hashish-induced made-up names. Whatever happened to Jane, Judith, Carol, Susan? Now it's all trend names. A name to set my child apart. A name like no other. The more obscure, embarrassing, and unpronounceable, the better. A star name that no one who meets her will ever forget. Raphene. Ariadne. Chindrika. Phoenicia. Makes a more interesting tombstone, someday, I guess.

There is also a note from Clifford reminding me and Vivika that he will be in Boston for a few days on a student jury at BU. I had completely forgotten. My relief is mingled with a deep longing. Lonely longing. I am too tired to eat. Luckily, so is Clive. We reheat some leftover pizza and I tuck him into Vivika's bed and collapse into the imcomparable comfort of my own.

8
Nobody Likes a Dead Head

By Sunday, I had worked out a temporary plan. Clive would stay with me downtown until Clifford returned; then he and I would go back to Amora's and stay during the week. On the weekends Vivika would come up or we would go down. Clifford, too—providing that when I told Clifford he still wanted anything to do with us. Clifford and I were due for *a serious talk*.

Vivika took Clive's presence surprisingly well. His obvious adoration melted even her diamond-hard teenage heart. Vivika would sleep in my room, which she liked, and Clive would sleep in hers (which she didn't like but agreed to after various perks and incentives had been offered by her anxious and over-eager mother).

Sunday afternoon I called Amora at the Carlyle, taking but a moment to ponder why she had already abandoned her luxurious lair when she had it all to herself. Oh well, no accounting for taste.

Jimmy Bob answered. He sounded distant. The cowboy drawl had gone home to Connecticut.

"Oh, hi, Jimmy Bob; is my sister there?"

"No. She's not. She's away."

"Away? She just got home."

"Not really away. Out. She's out."

"Oh. Okay. When will she be back?"

"I'm not sure. Late."

"Late? Too late to call me back?"

"Yeah. Too late."

"Is, ah, anything wrong? You sound kind of funny."

"No. Everything's good. Just got me at a bad time."

"Oh, sorry. Well, will you tell her that I called and I'm keeping Clive with me in the Village for the week, until I work things out with Vivika and Clifford?"

"I thought we agreed you'd stay uptown." (Sound of cowboy charm turning back on.) "I sure don't want to upset your sis now. She's so concerned about that young'un."

"I know. But after all, you are making rather sudden and profound demands on my life. I do have one, and I can't just flip it around like a trained seal, you know."

"Now, now, little lady. Don't go gettin' your choler up. I'll do my best with your sis, but it sure would be kind of you, if you could try—seeing how hard it is and all—to come back uptown sooner. For the boy's sake."

"I'll try. But frankly, since Wanda already knows that

Amora has a sister and that you two were together in Paris—why keep up the pretense?"

"Some things are just too knotted up for a rookie twirler. Your sis and I need your trust on this one. Please, dear lady, out of the kindness of your heart, we need a little more of your time with the disguise. Keep my wife and her hired gun off track a bit longer. It behooves you, darlin'."

"Guns."

"Pardon?"

"*Two* hired guns."

"Right. Right. You . . . you're sure about that now? Can't rightly figure why she'd have two workin' the same times."

"Beats me. Maybe it's an introductory special. Two for one. Limited offer."

"Heh, heh. Oh, you are one funny lady. Well, maybe so."

"Well, uh, please tell Amora to call me, even late. And I will try. I'll keep wearing the disguise, too. But just for another week. I'm starting to get paranoid."

"Well, we wouldn't want that, now."

No. We sure wouldn't want that.

Jimmy Bob did not seem happy, but really, what could they do? There are definite benefits to having the edge, doing the favor, being the martyr. I tried not to use those dirty tricks so well performed by our dear departed momma, but war is war. I felt better. I was beginning to get really excited about Monday morning. My emergence from Amora's closet. My mind raced. Maybe my own PR man. A new hairdo. Wash the gray out. Some new clothes. A little more pizzazz couldn't hurt. Even without the show.

Sunday night Clifford called from Boston. We had our serious talk.

"Clifford, I know we've really drifted apart, not just because of all this, this is just an excuse. I'm finding out things about myself that are extremely unsettling, but I need to let the truth in. Please try to understand, even if you don't approve."

"Whmsssss the sssdh mssss matter of sssye."

"Honey, I can't hear you."

"It is not a matter of *my* approval. At this moment our growth is unparallel. We are moving in different directions. We have what might be described as a metaphorical impasse. You seem to be seeking twists and wiggles, while I am committed to a linear path. A life in a straight and orderly line. At this moment we are protecting ourselves from one another in order to pursue the path appropriate for our individual needs.

"We are both adults" (*speak for yourself, Buster*, I thought) "and this sort of problem is often a marital hurdle. We will weather it. But at this moment we are alienated and in need of things other than one another's approval."

Whew. When the guy talks, the guy talks.

"What does *that* mean? Are you interested in someone *else's* approval? Is that why you're so cool about it all?"

"How eastern European of you, Aroma. Why would you immediately jump to infidelity as the meaning of my remarks? Search your own conscience first, wife of my heart. As a matter of fact, I have buried my sexual enthusiasm under a pyre of melancholy. I am in my Nordic neuter phase, such as it is. That is part of my desire for calm and space between us. It is my signal that I need silence and aloneness."

"But you always need silence and aloneness."

"That is a feminine interpretation of reality. What do you tell your patients about the adverb just used? Unfair, Aroma. Not always. Just often."

Whimpers, sniffles, and sobs.

"I'm sorry I made you cry. I have great difficulty with this kind of communication. It doesn't mean that I don't care. It only means that I cannot easily express feelings."

"*Vous*? Never. I know that deep inside there's a semihysterical tap dancer dying to break out."

"That is a projection and that is not the point."

"All right. I'm sorry. At least we've communicated our positions. When will you be home?"

"Thursday."

"Can we have dinner together?"

"I think that would be a very good idea."

"I'm really sorry, honey. 'Bye."

What a cop-out broad. For what was I apologizing? There was a good example of why Clifford could get away with talking to me as if he were reading it off the Balfour Declaration. When I give derelicts money, *I* say thank you.

After I pulled myself together, I went in to kiss the kids good night. *The kids*. I liked the way that sounded. Vivika was lying on the floor reading *Gulliver's Travels* and listening to a Monkee's tape of "Daydream Believer."

How dare she browse in the private domain of my youth! The Monkees were my time—she has hers, her Bruce Springsteen, her Madonna. Get your mitts off the sixties!

Something about that song was unbearably painful to me that night. My heart filled with yearnings, Daydream Believer and aspiring Homecoming Queen yearnings, for the first huge bite into life. For the time of the Monkees and the Beatles, animal images fitting our raw and unquenchably innocent energies. Monkees, Beatles, Rolling Stones; gathering nothing, spinning along the underground of electric possibilities. Plugged into the big socket night and day. So much of the time now my body feels unplugged. I plug it in for sex, then pull it out, the old sexuality and the socket syndrome.

I felt so old, standing there. So numb.

Just before all of this madness with Amora started, I had lunch with my unmarried friend Amber. Amber is not her real name. Her real name is Edith. Amber fits her better. Amber is a bit, well, flaky. She is into things like psychic surgery and electromagnetic therapy. Very heavy on the tarot cards and the palm reading. Amber was having an affair with "one of my fire-walking friends." She went on to describe in rather unnecessarily vivid detail the "boundless passion and weeping with joy" that engulfed them. I listened like Amber's senile maiden aunt. I had almost forgotten that kind of rapture. I think I had wanted to forget it. (It had, after all, gotten me into a lot of trouble.) But I felt empty. And sad. I still had a few sambas in me after all.

I stood in the doorway feeling as if I were on the top of a Ferris wheel standing up in the swaying basket. If I leaned forward, the wheel would turn and down I would go, falling, out of control, away from the form of my life. Totally up for grabs. One cancer cell busting loose into inner space, without the crossing guard to stop it. If I leaned forward, I was a goner. I wanted to hold still. Stop life here. No more time passing, no more quick glances in the mirror hoping not to catch sight of a new little line or crinkle that hadn't been there the day before. No more facing the realities offered at forty. All the things I would never be, will never change, rearrange, or rewind.

I know less and less, I thought. I used to know everything and now I know nothing. I will never be a tall blonde beauty who whisks into a drawing room in Paris, smiles sensually, and asks, "What language are we speaking tonight, darlings?" *I have no more time to waste* was the thought that came to mind. No more time for self-pity and past guilts. Future fears and laziness. Growth is anti-laziness. I had written that down and put it on my desk. You can't just stay there swaying back and forth in the basket forever. It's not a fucking cradle, you know.

Even if it were, the wind would get you, anyhow. It's okay to balance up there for a while, get your bearings and all, but the fact is, kiddo, that you are going to go down, just like everybody else. You don't know *when*, but you do have something to say about *how*. Better swaying gently and joyously in the breeze, watching the stars and the sunrise, breathing in the sweet summer air, rocking a little faster now and then, baying at the moon a tad, but gliding rather than pitching forth, than giving up and hitting the ground before it's necessary. Not one second before it's absolutely necessary. The first half of the ride is over, pal. You wasted a lot of time getting up here. Dozing off, screwing up, not paying attention. The second half is up to you alone. Use it, don't lose it. If it's Eleanor Rigby you want, it's Eleanor Rigby you'll get, Aroma Sweet. So cut the shit. Sit down and buckle up; the best part of the ride is beginning.

I took a deep breath and kissed my growing-up baby girl, who was just spreading her skirt out on the seat, just closing the safety bar, just beginning. I held her tight. "Wish me luck tomorrow, sweet pea."

"I do, Mommy. I love you."

"I love you, too, baby."

Clive was sitting up in bed with his all-news station plugged into his head. His eyes were almost closed, but he fought it, not wanting to surrender one event connecting him to the world, giving him the greatest illusion of control. "A guy from Morocco went berserk at a shopping mall in California and stabbed his wife to death at Taco

Paco with fifty people eating lunch. He dragged her out of the booth and tried to cut her head off right there by the Pepsi machine."

I lift the earplugs from his orbs, copping a motherly feel of the soft furry flesh. So cute, so friendly were those protuberances.

"You'll have nightmares."

"I only have nightmares when I'm awake."

"Those are called daymares."

"Really?"

"Possibly."

"You know what the guy said when they arrested him? He said, 'No future. I have no future.'"

"Neither does his wife."

"He was smiling."

"Clive. Enough."

"Are you nervous?"

"Who me? Vibrating."

"Don't be. Now you can be yourself. You'll shrink circles around her."

"Now, now. It's not a contest between your mother and me."

Clive looks deep into my tired red eyes. "Yes, it is."

"Just what I needed in my mid-life crisis, a kid with all the answers."

"I love you, Aro. Thank you for bringing me with you."

Tears are falling all over both of us. "I love you too, pal. Don't ever thank me again for things like that. It's bad for your self-esteem, which we will continue to work on."

"I'll work on yours while you work on mine."

Vivika was still up, so I couldn't fall into the luxury of mindless slumber. I poured a cup of tea and went into Clifford's study, all by myself. I had never done this before.

I had always waited for an invitation. My heart beat faster, a crime of trespass was in progress. I sat down in *his chair* and flipped on the TV. It was tuned to "Midnight Madness." An enormous fat woman with double rows of false eyelashes and lots of rhinestones hanging between her large lugubrious breasts was holding a microphone over the unmade water bed, on which sat tonight's guest of honor on . . . "The Only Nude Talk Show on TV." The guest was giggling and twirling strands of her jet-black Barbie-doll do in her fingers. She had not bothered with jewelry but did have on a pair of ankle-strapped silver pumps.

Fat Lady: "So, Athena, what are you like in person, when you're not performing at the Pussy Lovers' Lounge?"

Athena—giggle, giggle, twirl, twirl, tongue moving over glossy purple lips: "Well, I'm real shy until I know someone."

Fat Lady: "Shy? Boy, I don't know. I saw your routine with the flashlight. That don't look shy to me."

Athena—blush, giggle, giggle, twirl, twirl: "Well, but that's impersonal. In private with a guy, I'm real shy. But I should be better after my tit job."

Fat Lady—reaching out and grabbing one of Athena's melonlike morsels: "Gee, I don't know, they feel pretty good to me."

Athena, sighing: "Uh-uh. They're losing their firmness."

Fat Lady: "So what's a job cost?"

Athena: "A good job—five thousand. You can get a bad one for twenty-five hundred—but it feels like a rock in a sock."

For some bizarre and unconscious reason, this act turned me on. There I was plugged in without a socket in sight. I toyed with the idea of the always pleasant and supportive right hand, but somehow to do that there in Clifford's office was not really appealing. And Vivika was in my bed. "Pass, passion," I whispered. "Glad to have you back, but I can't go out tonight, sorry." I got up and walked over to Clifford's desk, braver now by the combination of "Midnight Madness" and the knowledge that there was no chance of Clifford flinging open the door in a Learian rage and smiting me. I sat down. I began to poke around. A voice in the back of my head said, "Stop, kiddo. Get up and get out of here while the getting's good." Another voice said, "Stay. The truth will set you free." A third voice said, "You always were a snoop. How dare you invade the privacy of someone you trust! You hypocrite."

The truth won. I began peeking in drawers and opened mail. So far so good. Dry and expectable. I was just about to leave for the privacy of the bathroom, where I would give my right hand some much-needed exercise, when a note paper slipped out of an invitation to some SoHo gallery opening.

The handwriting sent all the alarm bells screaming into my mental defense zone. *Danger! Young single woman's handwriting. Proceed with caution!*

> *Oh, Cliff. I still shudder with pleasure when I think of that last night. I lay on my bed feeling windswept, tingling with life. I must get used to this man, this not-like-any-other man—this special being dropped to earth to pleasure me. This highest, tallest, strongest, wisest Cliff. My Viking god. Come soon again and sail me into the sunset of ecstasy. My body quivers at the thought of you. Oh, I am out of breath in this fond chase.*
>
> *Daffy*

Two simultaneous impulses. Both involving hysteria. One of the rolling-with-laughter variety. The other, the other . . . I mean now, really. Poor Shakespeare. And, Daffy? As in Duck? Poor her. Get this girl some help, fast. And Clifford? So much for the Nordic neuter phase. And Cliff? I fought a mad desire to call all of my women friends and read it to them. I could see her in my mind, this Daffy Duck, this recent recipient of Little Cliffie's favors. A Bard College type. Broad-beamed and heavy-breasted. Long, tangled braid. Dirty toenails. Passionate about the Renaissance. The two of them entwined making gentile love to one another. "How eastern European of you, Aroma," he had said. Daffy Duck is not Jewish.

The rat. I, like Jimmy Carter, had self-righteously contained my adulterous lust in my mind. He, the Scandinavian swine, had unleashed it all over NYU. (This was so obviously a student that I wouldn't even bother with an FBI check. Academic wives have a nose for 'em.)

Then came the pain. Splattering grief. Spastic sobbing coming from so deep, so far away, that the power of it amazed me. *It's always there,* I thought, every single hurt, every single betrayal of trust, every sniped feeling, every rejection, every loss. It's all there; entered, dated, and checked into some gigantic computer calendar of the spirit, lying dormant beneath our flip and with-it facades, our ability to cope with life in an adult and rational manner. It's all still there. The name of the girl in the third grade who invited you over for dinner and wasn't there when you arrived all dressed up and excited—Suzie Bock! All of it. My mother's hand the last time I held it, all the warm, comforting, patting flesh gone. A bone held beneath mine. A cold, bloodless bone. All of it came back. I sobbed the universal sobs. I cried for everyone else on earth. Like Jesus cried, I thought. The release of all human hurt, grief folded into rage into eternity. When it was over, I took a bath and climbed into bed beside my sleeping daughter, feeling envy for her innocence on this bumpy, rutted human road, set my clock, and fell into a heavy feverish sleep. I didn't know of anything else to do.

Monday morning I put on my Jane Pauly act, cool, dry, and able to cope. I got the kids off to school and made it to WNRD without giving in to the overpowering desire to hop on a plane to Boston and tear my husband to bloody, disemboweled shreds.

The A-Team was there to greet me. Chen, O'Ralph, and J.B. himself. We discussed the topic of the day: guilt (always good in a pinch). I went into my *own* office, now with my name prominently displayed on the door, to prepare. Amora's office had been locked and her name removed. This was all rather hard to absorb.

I worked on my opening remarks. "Guilt is probably responsible for more ruined lives than all the evils of modern life combined. We are all victims of it in varying degrees." Pretty heavy, Aro, for the first shot out of the bag. But I had a lot of first nights to make up for.

"Guilt is . . ."

A knock, followed immediately by Jimmy the B's smiling face. Didn't anything ever rattle this guy? "Just wanted to wish you good luck, honey; from your sister, too."

"Thanks, Jimmy Bob." We were now at the familiar stage. I make a mental note to get Chen drunk and pick his mazelike psyche about J.B. Just where did all his money come from anyway? Even Amora didn't seem to know anything about him. And why were there all those Chinese around him all the time? Hardly the companions of a Wild West fanatic.

"Did you hear the announcements?" J.B. inquired.

"I sure did."

"Well, Wanda seems to be appeased. She showed up here yesterday to supervise the removal of your sister's name from her office. We're havin' to sneak the poor darlin' down here to pick up her mail and such."

"One thing, Jimmy Bob. Your wife and I did not have the happiest of meetings. Why would she agree to let me do the show?"

"Beats the bull turds outta me. But first off, she doesn't have a clue that it's temporary, and she's greedy enough to know that a total change in format means a big loss in ad money—your sis's show is our biggest daytime money machine. And, for some reason, she doesn't seem to see you as a threat."

Well, I asked for it. "I see. Another thing. Amora didn't call me back, and we have a lot of arrangements to discuss. Will you please have her call tonight?"

"Sure thing, honey. Knock 'em dead."

Before I started, O'Ralph made another announcement and even read a short bio of *my* career. Unlucky at love but . . . I forgot how that went. And then I was *on the radio as myself.* No imitation Amora. *My* voice, *my* style, *my* advice. Let 'em try to stop me now. The three hours went by before I even took a sip of my cold coffee. I had come home. I loved it.

The crew opened champagne. Chen and O'Ralph were jubilant. "To our new star," said O'Ralph.

"I blink to that," offered Chen. I, for once, said nothing. My combination of emotions, joy and anguish, rolled around together like the Pillsbury dough boy and the butter pat. So this is what it was like at the top. Lonely.

When all the fanfare was over, I took the remains of the bottle of champagne and went back to my office. For some reason (guilt, guilt), I really wanted to talk to my sister. All the bitterness and anger seemed to have been washed clean by my moment of equality. Parity with the primal threat. I wanted to tell her the truth, tell her all the feelings that I had gotten in touch with since this whole cacophony began. I wanted to tell her about Clifford and how much I loved Clive, and how much I loved her. I wanted to say I was sorry for my part in our turbulent and tortured history. I wanted her to know. I called three times and left messages at her apartment and the Carlyle. She was out of reach. I remembered that I still had a key to her office, so I decided to put it into a letter instead. Much better idea, anyway. J.B. had said he was bringing her down for her mail, so the timing was perfect. I wrote my sore and throbbing heart out. I sealed it in my stationery and put it right on top of her pile of mail where she couldn't miss it. I relocked her office door and returned to my own. I decided, since the letter writing was going so well, to bang one out for Clifford. As I began, just before the riven edges of my psyche splattered into tirade, I remembered that I had forgotten to tell Amora about the lavender notes in her desk drawer. Oh well, I'd tell her when I spoke to her. I had now, as Chen would say, bigger zits to fry.

When I finished, the champagne was flat and so was I. I turned off the lights, picked up my missive of matrimony, and went home. Queen for a Day.

On the way downtown I realized two things. One was that I didn't want to go home to Clifford's apartment. I did not want to be there right now, period. What did I mean, *right now?* I had never wanted to be there. I would gather Clive and Vivika and take them uptown. It was what Amora wanted, anyway.

The second thing I realized almost made me leap into the lap of the bald-headed cretin with the six-inch steel pipe in his earlobe who sat to my right, lost in whatever thoughts a person with a six-inch steel pipe in his ear loses himself in. (I could have chosen the lap of the gentleman on my left, who had a rather nice ponytail and a large silver spider in his ear, but he had a suitcase on it.) The thought was, *Friday is our fortieth birthday.*

Pop had planned it for months. We—meaning Clifford, me, Vivika, Clive, Amora, and various friends and relations—were to arrive Friday night for the big feast on Saturday. Oh my God. Tears squirted out of my eyes. The guy with the pipe winked and handed me a surprisingly clean Kleenex. I guess he knew about discomfort. *I don't want to be forty this week.* This was not how I planned it. Maybe I could wait, like Amora, until I was famous. Then a simple little soiree à la the *Ms.* shindig for Gloria Steinem's fiftieth. Five thousand of my closest friends and legions of admirers who would crowd the reception line drooling in awe at my firm upper arms and legendary accomplishments. Definitely. I'll wait to turn forty at a better time. Anytime. Just not this week. I had a hunch Amora felt exactly the same way.

Forty. Shit. At twenty I thought by forty I would be toothless and farting at the dinner table. At thirty I thought by forty I'd be Virginia Slim. At thirty-five I thought by forty I would be serene and sure of my path. So much for projections. Now I could start on fifty.

"Thanks for the Kleenex," I said, rising as my stop approached. He gave me a salute and grinned. He was cross-eyed and had three teeth missing. I wondered how it would be to make love to someone with missing teeth and a pipe in his ear, and what the future would hold for such a fellow. Wondering about this got me home.

Clive and Vivika were both there. "We heard you! It

was great, Mom! You're a star! My friends are all like raded out!"

"Thank you, thank you. I was almost mobbed by fans on the way home. It's all been too, too much." I could feel my frozen smile cracking and sliding inward into my real face.

"Listen, kids. Something's come up and we're not going to stay here this week after all. Amora really wants us uptown, and it's a lot easier for me and for Clive to get out in the morning. Viv, I know it's a little more hassle for you, but so many of your friends are uptown and you'll have that fantastic white silk bedroom all to yourself. And we'll go out for dinner to celebrate. We all deserve a break. Okay?"

The questions and protests lasted long enough for both children to exert whatever amount of power they felt they could get away with. When they were totally sated with pulling my chain and making it hard for me, they gave in, almost immediately reversing positions, embracing the enemy plan and running off to pack. I packed rather lethargically. I knew it was psychologically dangerous for me right then to stay within strolling distance of Clifford's study. I had lost ten pounds since the whole Amora chapter began, and her closets were flowing over with clothes. I could always borrow a few looser garments if need be. I called her at the Carlyle again and left an urgent message. Then I called her apartment to make sure she hadn't changed her mind. Her housekeeper was there. No, Doctor had not been home but had left a note that I might be staying. She would get everything ready for us. She would? How nice. We cabbed it uptown, dropped our suitcases, and dashed gaily off to Gino's for dinner. Gaily, gaily we toasted one another; my little gypsy band.

We decided to walk home, it being one of those Indian summer nights, when summer is shaking hands with autumn and all is well with man and nature. I gave myself over to the pleasure of my debut. Live in the moment, I told myself, Friday is another century. All the way back I felt uneasy, as if someone was following us, but we saw no one. The doorway across the street was vacant. At the moment I no longer gave a damn. I didn't even bother with my disguise. Screw 'em if they can't take a joke. Up we went, to the luxury of Porthault and Chanel-scented drawers. A woman's home, created out of her own needs. Everything here was hers. I sighed in awe at the magic of it. A bed of my own to roll in. To spread out and loll in. To cover with my books, my glasses, my Snickers bars. To share with no one. Heaven.

Now that I knew I would be staying a while, I unpacked my things, making space in her Upper East Side drawers for my downtown belongings. One drawer, filled with silk panties and stuff, wouldn't slide back in. Something seemed to be stuck at the back of it. I pulled it out. In a plain manila envelope caught between the back of the drawer and a French lace push-up bra was a complete set of Amora's dental records. Funny. Even Amora couldn't be vain enough to hide her dental records. Must be changing dentists and hasn't sent them out to the new gargoyle yet. I put the folder right back where I found it—hidden under the undies. God forbid she should think I was snooping.

I took a long shower and fell asleep sprawled all the way across the movie-queen bed; on top of the covers, the way no married person ever can.

At five in the morning I sat straight up in bed. The doorbell was ringing. I jumped up and ran into the living room. I peeked through the peephole, but no one was there. Must have been some drunk coming in from a big night, I thought, trying to catch my breath. My bare foot hit something on the rug. I knelt down and picked up one of those lavender notes. This one had not been mailed. There was no postmark or stamp. No drunk. Hand-delivered. I tiptoed back into bed, turned on the reading lamp, and opened it.

Double your pleasure—Double your fun. Which Twin has the Toni? We know what you're doing. Now it's double indemnity—tonight.

I read and reread this, looking for meaning. I was frantic to reach Amora and tell her about the notes. It was still too early to call. Sleep was definitely out, so I took a shower, got dressed, and made the bed. It was now 5:45 A.M. I left a note for the kids saying I couldn't sleep and had gone to the station early, grabbed the note, and hit the street.

It was still dark, the sun just starting its east-side journey between the buildings. The city was all mine. I bought a paper and went to my favorite all-night coffee shop for breakfast. Two good-looking young men who looked as if they had been up all night sat at the next table chain-smoking and drinking black coffee.

"I kept feeling like I wanted to go home and then I realized I was home. Man, what a bummer."

"That's your trouble, Louie. That's always been your fucking trouble. You're a baby. You want someone to lead you by the hand. It's *your* fucking career. It's *your* fucking business. And *I'm* not your fucking agent!"

"We're talking fifteen years of tap and voice."

"Go back to the land of the has-beens and may-be's, man! Nobody gives a shit how you get there. You arrive alive or you don't."

"I don't wanna go back to the Coast. I go brain-dead on the Coast."

Two transvestites sway in and sit at the counter.

"I love your hair that way. I've never seen it so spontaneous."

I order a second coffee to go and walk to the station, feeling as if I am not the only screwed-up person lurching around the streets. There is a comfort and safety in numbers.

I smile at the security officer and saunter through the cool quiet corridors, using my special keys and the entrance marked "Private, Staff Only." Make way for WNRD's newest star! I pass Amora's office, so dark, so cold. I shiver. The urge to talk to her is overwhelming. I reach my office. I fumble with my coffee container and my purse. I take out my key and put it in the door. The door is open. I must have forgotten to lock it in all the confusion yesterday. I turn the knob and switch on the light.

The next thing I remember, I am on the Italian leather couch, well worn with afternoon delight, in O'Ralph's office. The station nurse and several police officers are standing over me.

I have finally achieved my darkest wish. I am an only child.

Clive heard about his mother on his all-news radio station. Vivika was told at school—before, however, anyone was sure which twin's *tête* was on the plate. Clifford heard in Boston. Splashing in the tub with his rubber ducky, no doubt. Pop heard from Aunt Minnie. Not what one would have hoped for any of them.

The next twenty-four hours was like a B-movie montage of every police mystery made before color. The ones starring Sterling Hayden, Mark Stevens, and/or Victor Mature. The moment I was fully conscious, adequately tranquilized, and the bump on my head bandaged, the police moved in.

"I want to talk to the kids. I want to talk to my father," was all I said for hours. Finally they sent a police escort to pick up Vivika and Clive and deliver them to me in the police ward of New York Hospital. They clung to one another, eyes wide with bewildered innocence; that first slap in the mug of real life. This was not pumping into the Walkman from the mystical amorphia of a radio receiver. This was a live broadcast from the Leader of the Pack.

Clive's whole frail body was shaking. Vivika was so giddy with relief that my head was where she had last seen it that she was able to rally forth into the role of older sister.

The detective in charge of the investigation was one Pincus Mallony, an Irish Jew from Staten Island with a cherubic full-moon face, rosy cheeks and matching lips, a thicket of black curly locks, and the sexiest, greenest eyes that I had ever seen not attached to a Burmese cat. He was as wide as he was tall, and built, as Pop used to put it, "like an elephant's ass."

"I know youse have had a terrible episode here and youse wanna go home to the family, but we need to keep youse here under observation for youse own protection, till we get some answers here. This is a fucking nightmare we're dealin' wit' here. We got a fucking psycho on our hands here."

Lieutenant Mallony (soon to be Pincus) did leave me alone with the kids for a while. I was pleasantly doped up and still in what might be described as a "state of shock," meaning that I thought I was handling myself with perfect calm when, in fact, I was one small step away from the screaming meemies.

Mostly I just held them. Vivika kept saying over and over, "Oh my God, I don't believe it."

Clive was silent. He spoke only once to ask a question. "Where's the rest of her?"

Where, indeed?

Clifford was being rushed back from Boston to pick them up. A police guard for the family had been arranged. Clive's real father had been notified. Reporters were everywhere, from my shelter in the Village to O'Ralph's racquet-ball club. It was all over TV and all over the radio. This was not the sort of fame I had in mind, guys.

The list of suspects was already long. I didn't know it yet, but I was about to join them.

The questioning went on for hours. Out it all came. Taciturn I was not. I told Mallony and his boys every last crumb of the little I knew from the day Amora made me the offer to Wanda Mackay and the crazy notes.

Notes? They had found no notes.

No little perfumed lavender notes in the left-hand top drawer of her desk? Not a one.

I asked for my coat and pulled out the last one that I had received that fateful night. Mallony's baby-greens glowed.

"Yo, get this to the lab—do a Speedy Gonzales on it."

The only thing I left out was my letter to Amora. I had completely blocked that. I was not ready for any memory involving grief yet (shock has its upside). That letter was too close to the loss. If, after ten years, it was still not really acceptable to me that at any moment my mother might not reappear and suggest a fast tunny sandwich at Blimpie's, then how on earth could the barely day-old decapitation of my alter ego be real? I forgot about the letter.

But the cops had found the letter. A troubled relationship? A pathological sibling rivalry? Jealousy? A motive as good as any other.

At that moment the list of suspects included the following: Amora's first and second husbands, O'Ralph, Chen, Wanda Mackay, Jimmy Bob Mackay, the writer of the lavender notes, the entire radio audience, and me.

The list continued to swell: her yoga teacher (wouldn't you just know), her masseuse (ditto), her decrepit housekeeper, Mrs. Sanchez. The Calvin Klein trench coat, the Norma Kamali blonde, and someone named Armand de Bouganville.

My personal favorite was baby Wanda, but no one seemed to go for it.

It was quite fascinating to think about who the suspects in your death would be. What people would say about you. Better not to know. Better to leave believing that your view of yourself and your world was accurate; imagine finding out that people who you assumed saw you as centered, productive, and normal, really thought, "I always had the feeling she'd end up like that." It makes one pause.

Clifford appeared looking even grimmer than usual. He was questioned. The kids were questioned. He took them home. I stayed in a private room, remembering all those crime shows where the material witness gets it—air bubbles in the IV, poison in the box of bonbons, a silenced bullet from the bedpan orderly, or the always popular deadly hypo in the middle of the night. I did not feel the least bit safe in spite of Lieutenant Mallony's assurances. "Hey, yo! Don't worry 'bout it."

If *I* had not done it, the word on the street was it was entirely possible that the slicer would fillet again. They were, after all, not very sure that *she* and not *I* was the target. The head had been found in *my* office, after all.

This scenario was saved for day two. It took a little while for it to sink in. When it did, let us say, I did not take it like a trained mental-health professional.

"Let me get this straight" was the last coherent sentence I uttered for several minutes. "Who," I shrieked, "would want to kill *me*?"

Who indeed?

So there I was. In less than forty-eight hours I had made my radio debut and discovered my husband's infidelity and my sister's murder. And they say blondes have more fun.

On the eve of my fortieth birthday I found myself in a locked police ward under the paranoid protection of a crude but cunning tom-eyed tank whom I found it increasingly hard to keep my hands off; the Patty Hearst syndrome, I suspect; both a potential murder victim and murderer. I remember at one point thinking, well at least we don't have to go to Pop's birthday party.

There was no body, there were no witnesses, no fingerprints (except mine), and nowhere to hide. Every time I shut my eyes, I saw a shadowy figure clutching a huge ax in a black-gloved hand standing over parts of my sister. Not much of a dream choice. I quickly developed insomnia. A highly practical solution.

9

The Fright Or Flight Part

The best thing and the worst thing about insominia is that you have a lot of time to think. That second night, I thought. I realized that they were extending my recovery for reasons other than my head bump. Observation for possible concussion, they called it. They had isolated me completely from everyone else. Also, the questions had taken on an increasingly aggressive tone. Anyone who watches Angela Lansbury knows that it is entirely possible to sneak up on your sister, chop off her head, drag her bleeding body somewhere completely invisible, clean up all trails of blood and associated yuck, run back to the scene, knock your own head on the desk, and wait to be found—all within the ten minutes from when I waved hello to the security guard to when he found me.

Aha! Mallony's smarter than that. I could have sneaked out hours earlier, done the dirty deed, and then just pretended to discover the head. Death had been placed at somewhere between midnight and 6 A.M. (no body makes it harder to pinpoint). Well, so much for alibis. It was time to call a lawyer. I didn't have a lawyer. I didn't trust lawyers any more than I trusted doctors or policemen. Or dentists or shrinks. I decided to admit to myself that I was not a trusting person. I was not a damsel-in-distress type. I was completely miscast in this role.

Another thought. Clive. His father was probably wending his way to snatch him up and carry him off at that very moment. That was almost unbearably painful. I could not let him go. Not now. He needed me now. Of course, since his father was a possible suspect, maybe the police were keeping him home and under surveillance. I didn't know anything.

I did know that I wanted out and that legally they couldn't keep me. In the morning I would ask to be released. I would go home and get the kids and get in the car and drive to Pop's as fast as a person in my condition could go. While I was devising this plan, feeding my need to have control over something that was happening to me, the night nurse came in with a pill. I refused the pill. The night nurse didn't like that. I asked for some tea and Jell-O, if it wasn't too much trouble. It was. I watched *The Letter*, with Bette Davis and Herbert Marshall. Now that's a murderess. If Mallony saw this movie, he'd know that I could not possibly have done what he was probably right now, at this very moment, convincing himself that I had done. What was guilt all about, anyway? I had certainly fantasized about Amora's death from childhood on. Many a time I had fought the impulse to leap on her and beat her to a bloody pulp. What did that count for? "No, your honor, I didn't do it, but, boy, I thought about it a lot."

"Twenty years!" sayeth the judge.

About the time that Bette was meeting her dead lover's mysterious vengeful Oriental wife for the payoff, Night Nurse Ratched returned with a tray of tea and melting Jell-O. "Thank you," I said. Nothing, she said. I picked up the paper napkin to avoid drooling melting Jell-O on my nightie and a little torn paper with pieces of glued newspaper letters fell out. "You're next. A double header," it said.

So much for police protection. For the first time in my entire life, I was not solving a problem in my head. I put the ship on automatic pilot and turned off everything except that much-touted but little trusted inner adviser. I was up and into my clothes and out of there before the tea was cold. I left the psycho note with one of my own for Mallony.

I crept down the back stairs and out the emergency-room entrance. If you ever have the misfortune to be in a New York City Hospital emergency room, you'll have no doubt about my easily waltzing past the staff. I was wearing my nightgown, my trench coat, dark glasses, and my ratty Banana Republic safari slippers, and I was by far the most together person in the room. The police had my purse, but my keys and a twenty-dollar bill were in my coat and they hadn't found them. I flagged down a taxi and whizzed across town to WNRD. I didn't know exactly what I hoped to find, but somehow it seemed that Amora's office might hold some answers. Bits of information had been floating across my battered brain. Who was the second tail? Who took the lavender notes? A psycho wouldn't know about them. Or the dental records. Without a body the police had made a positive ID from the dental records. But I'd seen her records in the apartment. Could they have been copies? Must have been. But why? It was her head, all right. I saw it again in the morgue. The perfect frosting. Even the icy fake blue contacts. While I pondered, I waited for Ed, the night guard, to sneak off for his reefer break. I had seen him do it before. He left right on schedule. I crawled down the hall, below the range of the TV camera, and slipped my key to Amora's office in the door. There was a police tape across it, and I neatly undid it and replaced it behind me. I was in.

I had no flashlight, no matches, but there was enough light coming through the window for me to see. The police had obviously gone through everything, but let's just say I was highly motivated.

I started going through her bookshelves. I looked under, in back of, through volume after volume. Nothing. And then, as I was about to give up, my eye caught sight of a book that didn't seem to belong among the erudite psychoanalytical tomes of which Aroma had been so fond.

It was our high school yearbook. Lincoln High School—Patriot—1966. I grabbed it. As quickly as I could, I replaced the other books and crawled to the door. Footsteps. Ed was making up for lost time. I curled up in the corner in back of the door, waiting for him to finish his night check. To pass the time, I opened the dreaded memory bank.

A face from the past fell out. Several pictures of the face. Sarah Jane Milano. Amora's bosom buddy. Her alter ego. Sarah Jane had been Amora's idol. Sarah Jane started out looking the way Amora ended up looking. That was the face Amora wanted. It took a while, but by the time of Amora's first marriage, which was the last time I had seen

Sarah Jane, Amora and Sarah Jane looked like the twins and I looked like the obscure distant cousin. Sarah Jane was not a nice girl, to put it in late-fifties vernacular. To bring it up to date, Sarah Jane was a drugged-out bimbo shiksa whore. She wore a T-shirt that said "Fuck first, ask questions later." I didn't like Sarah Jane.

Amora worshiped her. She didn't like her, either, but she was obsessed with her. They were inseparable all senior year. Sarah Jane was Amora's only female friend, then and after—as far as I knew, anyway. I was pushed out. I was jealous of Amora and Sarah Jane. God! What a time to dredge all that up! Next, I'd be really into it—leafing through the old Patriot looking up the old gang, seeing how young I looked, how fat I looked, as if I had not just escaped from a police ward and was hiding from armed security guards in the cold dark corner of my murdered sister's office.

The pictures of Sarah Jane were recent. I could tell by the earrings (Elsa Perretti hearts), the watch (Rolex), the hairdo, and the outfit (Donna Karan). Bet Mallony wouldn't get it that fast. But what I didn't get at all was what our yearbook was doing in her office. These were memories Amora found so repulsive that she had re-created her biography—putting herself in a fancy boarding school and eliminating all mention of her twin and her childhood in the sleepy old Adirondacks. And what was Sarah Jane Milano doing stuffed into it in the here and now?

Ed finished his rounds and I forced myself to close the book, hide it in my coat, and stealthily, like an Agatha Christie heroine, make my way to the fire exit and out. Out is easy. I decided, on my way down to find a cab and get to the Village, that we were going about crime prevention backward. Everyone breaks in; we should work on the out.

A cab appeared out of nowhere and I was in the Village ten minutes later. "Wait here," I said to the kindly Lebanese driver, who had nothing to do at 3 A.M. anyway.

I tiptoed in, trying not to wake Clifford. Vivika and Clive were curled up together in her bed, in itself a sign of deep trauma. I woke them, putting my finger to my lips and pantomiming our departure. They seemed to understand instantly. They jumped out of bed, threw some clothes in their backpacks, and were out the door in record time for two kids who think a shower is a forty-five-minute experience. I stopped long enough to write a note to Clifford. I put the note on the kitchen table, his first morning stop. Then I paused. Should I leave my letter? Inner adviser said, "Go for it." I pulled the crumpled communiqué out of my coat and set it next to the departure note. I packed bags of Oreos and Fritos for the road. Oreos could pull one through almost anything. The kids were in the cab and our driver was grinning madly, caught up in the odd happenings breaking into the routine of his nightly cruise. A rumpled woman with her head bandaged fleeing in the night with two sleepy children. He dropped us at the all-night garage where I kept my old Chevrolet, a gift from Pop long, long ago. When I leaned forward to pay him, I caught sight of the *Post* lying on the seat next to him. NO LEADS YET IN BIZZARE RADIO SHRINK BEHEADING. Underneath were two large photos, one of Amora (flattering), one of me (un-)—that sort of thing could never happen if one had a PR man. I lowered my head and told him to keep the change, put on my dark glasses, and hit the garage. I decided to play the odds that the Puerto Rican garage guys, who were not exactly Anglo newspaper devourers, had heard nothing about me and my sister. No one blinked when I told them my name. The black bomber screeched into view. The three us fell in and we were off.

Vivika sleeps in the back and Clive sits up front with me. He is very quiet and I notice that he does not turn on the radio or pull out his Walkman. I don't want to push him into talking about it. I don't really know if *I* could talk about it.

"Auntie?"

"Yes, baby."

"What's going to happen now?"

"I'm not sure, pal. I just feel it would be much safer and less stressful for you kids to be out of the middle of all this for a while. And for me, too. But I probably won't be staying with you. I may have to disappear for a bit."

"Why?"

"Well, let's just say that it's in my own best interests."

"That's no answer."

"You're right. I can't give you an answer. I just don't want you to be worried about me."

"I know why. Because whoever killed her is still out there and could try to kill you, too."

"I should have known you'd be too smart for me. You sure don't give yourself a break, baby."

Clive puts his hands over his eyes. "I don't want you to go. I'm frightened. I don't want him to come and take me away."

"Your father?"

"Yes. Please let me stay with you. Take me with you."

"I can't, baby. You know I can't. But if you stay with your grandfather, I think we can get a court order so that your father can't take you now. I'm not a very safe bet as far as the courts would see it at the moment. Understand?"

His fuzzy brown head nods up and down between sobs.

"She'll never be able to tell me now. She'll never say it."

"Say what, honey?"

"That she loves me. That she's sorry for hurting my feelings. I always thought that someday, like in the movies, we would have this big scene and she would tell me that, and then we would forgive one another and have this wonderful relationship."

"What if you think about her being somewhere now that is all-seeing and all-forgiving and she is seeing you and saying just that to you. Would that help?"

"I don't know. Maybe."

"Clive, what's happened is a terrible, frightening thing. Frankly, I haven't dealt with my feelings about it at all yet. I'm still sort of numb. But anything that you feel is okay. There isn't any guidebook for something like this. I can't make it go away, God knows I wish I could. I think it's much harder to lose a parent that you have a lot of anger and confusion about. It's going to take time for you to sort it out."

Clive starts laughing and crying at the same time.

"I said something funny?"

"What you said—it reminded me of my camp counselor. Last summer, we were talking and he told me that his mother had died. He said that the police called him and told him that his mother ran into a tree and was killed instantly and his first thought was, poor tree."

I start to laugh, too. Vivika wakes up and we tell her. We all laugh with a certain nervous hysteria.

"A bunch of sickos we've got here. Pass the driver an Oreo, please."

I stop for gas and coffee and call Pop. "I've been expecting you," he says. Oh, to go home again. How different it seems now. The glow of light coming through the windows, a pot of soup on the stove, loud laughter, dogs barking; a place of perpetual welcome. I have never really felt that anywhere but my parents' house was home.

What a scary thought. What a dirty trick to long for what you couldn't wait to discard. The illusion of safety and time standing still. Now the clock is ticking like crazy, the meter never sleeps for grown-ups; home is a bad joke, a mythical temptation, the Medusa disguised as the angel.

Pop never could understand why we wanted to leave. In the Old Country familes stayed together, birth to death. The young cared for the old, the feeble were propped, the misfits protected. No one left. Husbands and wives moved in. Each family was a bastion, a mini-kingdom, a wall against the world of loneliness and indifference. Maybe it was a better way. Freud was really the beginning of the end of that. The minute those heavy-duty relationships were psychoanalyzed, forget family life. We all bought into that. Maybe it was solid modern thinking. Maybe it was one gigantic mistake. Maybe we were meant to cleave unto our own, fighting and struggling and taking care of each other. It had even less reality for Vivika and Clive than it had for me. I wanted them to go home with me. To a place that felt like home, anyway. To breathe in chimney smoke and feel cared for. No TV dinners and "Mom's working late." Some time with a parent figure who had nothing more important on his mind than them. A place where they could mourn the loss of one of their own together, howling like tormented beasts in the night, with no neighbors to pound on the pipes.

How lucky I was to have such a place to go, I thought. Tears blurred my vision, making the road wave before me. Wouldn't it be wonderful to be able to go back in time to different moments in your life and do them over? How many moments of my childhood I wanted to go back and revisit now. How many moments in Vivika's childhood. Moments when I had failed her and failed myself. Moments with my mother. There I was at the top of the

Ferris wheel again, no way back, no detours to the past. Clive had fallen asleep beside me. No, he would never hear his mother tell him that she loved him and that she was sorry. Except maybe in his own head. That would have to do for both of us. I was glad that I had written the letter to Amora. I would keep in mind the thought that she had read it before she died. That she knew I loved her. That I was part of her and that I was sorry.

Our welcoming committee consisted of Pop, Aunt Minnie, Pop's best friend, a Brazilian musician named Pepe Pampas, and his hunchbacked old housekeeper, Shauna, who looked like Quasimodo's ugly sister but scored high on the loyalty and cleanliness scale. I can only compare the reunion to the airport welcome-home of the Iranian Embassy hostages and their loved ones. Everyone fell into passionate tearful embraces. Except, of course, Aunt Minnie, who stood off to the side, her mouth set in a Lucy tight line, her arms folded, shaking her head and muttering something like "The sins of the flesh reap the wrath of Abraham, Isaac, and Jacob." All she needed was flowing robes and a beard and she could play the part on television.

We were bathed, fed, and put to bed. I was out in an instant, the first real sleep in days. The first safe pillow on which to rest my fevered brain. We slept all day. Pop woke us for dinner.

We were all starved and ready for a little cheer. Pop had risen to the occasion. The fountain was cascading. Verdi was floating through the cavernous room, the fire pit was roaring, and the table was filled with food and candlelight. The kids loved it at Pop's for many reasons, and being allowed to drink wine to their heart's content was one of them. Pop ran around, filling our glasses, planting kisses, making nice. The man had buried his wife and would soon bury his hideously murdered daughter (the details of how you bury a bodyless person had not been solved and the head was still in the police morgue), but the life force was so powerful in him, the joy and gratitude for each day on earth so passionate, that he was not only able to handle his own grief, but ours as well. Dinner passed in a pleasant glow of wine and delectable tastes. I sat sandwiched between Aunt Minnie and Pepe. I tried to keep turned toward Pepe because I knew Aunt Minnie was just waiting for an opening.

Pepe lived in a beautiful estate on Antigua. He came from a wealthy Brazilian family, and before retiring he'd had his own band and played all over the world. I was crazy about Pepe.

"So, Aroma, when you coming to my island and starting to live your life? You are a beautiful peasant and you live like an old nun. You need to run in bare feet. To swim naked in the moonlight. To be a natural woman, not one of those New York phony baloneys. I play for those women. I listen to those women for thirty years. No good! They all so dry, they snap when you bend them. No juice in any of them. All they know is clothes and money. I play for one woman who talked her husband into buying her a Thoroughbred horse because she say, 'Well, it's better than wearing a dead animal around my back.' Some logic. *Corações de papel*. Paper hearts, they have. Dried-out paper hearts. You have fire. You come to the islands."

"How about tonight?"

"You serious?"

"No. But maybe soon."

"Good. You say the word. Give me time to work with my new gardener. I want my garden to bloom for you."

"What happened to Mr. Yokitani?"

"Ay, yay, yay. You don't know what that Jap do to my

soul! He don't love the flowers. He love the rocks, gravel, sand. I beg him. I plead on my knees. I want petunias! Bougainvillea! Like Brazil. He do what I say. But he don't love them and they know it. Six hundred bucks a month and all my roses die! I tried the Mexicans—they love the flowers, but the Mexicans, they not like Brazilians, nothing like us. They crazy. They love the flowers, but they hate the work. The Jap, he works but the heart is only for the shrub, the dirt." Tears fall from Pepe's brown puppy eyes into his plate.

I lean over and give him a kiss on the cheek. Aunt Minnie can bear no more.

"So, big tragedy. So no petunias! We've got the *head* of a family member in the New York morgue and you're going to cry about some rose petals? You should be ashamed!"

Pop stands up to intercept. Clive is deadly pale. "Hey, Minna mia, whatever a man loves, is the same. It's no better to love one thing than another. Pepe cries for our pain, too. You say *scusa* to Pepe. Come on now." Pepe's wavy dyed-black head hangs in shame. I keep patting his hand.

Minnie doesn't give up easily.

"I know all about the way men love. Flowers or shiksa whores. Maniacs with axes. I'm not impressed, thank you very much. I meant no harm. I know Pampas a long time. I just call them as I see them."

"Put your glasses on." I open my mouth, losing my cool and giving Minnie the moment she has been waiting for.

"Oh, I see. Now I'm to be insulted by you. Now that your society whore of a sister is dead, you get cocky. Well, someone has to speak for decency! This family has the curse of the unclean on it. Your uncle started it and it continues. We are cursed with the sins of others. Your sister has paid for her wantonness. Your mother has paid for marrying a gentile, and you . . . you, too. You think you're better than me because you sleep with that goy? Because you ran off and had a baby by a man who never stopped to send his only child a picture postcard? Big fancy education! A lot of good it's done us! The whole thing is *meshugge*. You and your sister were too good for us, well, look at what's happened. Some fancy successes! For shame!"

Pop has somehow moved across the table and lifted Aunt Minnie up from under her shoulders, gently but firmly.

"I think Aunt Minnie is a little overwrought. Too much vino, Minna mia. Never could handle my vino. Time to call it a night." She lets him lead her out, her back as straight as the Duchess of Windsor's. Clive and Vivika are crying. Pepe is crying. I am crying. Shauna can be heard bawling in the kitchen. A perfect "first night at home" dinner. Never fails. Someone always pops his cork. I silently add Aunt Minnie to the list of suspects.

When everyone is asleep, I tiptoe across the great dining hall to Pop's bedroom. I can hear him swimming laps in the dark. I almost see my mother's ghost holding a fluorescent towel, her hair cascading down her back, smiling patiently, waiting for her man to come to her. I knock as loudly as I dare, but he can't hear me. Finally, I open the door and peek in. He is swimming back and forth in the moonlight, slow, steady strokes, swimming out his grief. I creep in and sit down at the edge of the pool near the door. I wait for him to finish. He swims a long time in that slow, steady way. I know he is naked though it is too dark to see him, and I don't want to embarrass him. I don't know how to let him know I am there without either embarrassing him or scaring him to death. Finally he stops for air at my end and sees me.

"Wanna swim, *bambina mia*? It's good for the soul."

"I'd love to."

"*Bene*. I get out. You get in. I leave a robe for you at the other end."

"Thanks, Pop." I wait for him to swim back and get out; then I slip my flannel nightgown over my head "like an old nun," as Pepe said, and lower myself into the creamy, shimmering, night-lit water. It is a magic swim. I seem to have boundless energy. I dive. I float. I skim the water like a dolphin, like Esther Williams with a flower in her hair and smile perfectly fixed. My mind is clear. Life is totally embraceable. I glide across the water filled with joy and strength. The path before me is limited to two concrete walls faced with Italian tile. First I reach one side and then the other. Those are my goals. Back and forth, come up for air. Kick and roll and dive and stroke. I am alone in a watery universe, in a womb of my own. Without a mirror image. Floating in the windowless safety of the night sea. Rolling around and around, blind but all-seeing; safe in the dark warmth of primal protoplasm. Reborn. To stay here in this buoyant blackness forever; that is my only goal.

When I surface, it is as if I have awakened from a trance. I haven't felt so clean, so calm, and so filled with self-love for a very long time. I climb into my mother's huge white robe and curl up on the Astroturf at the side of Pop's bed. For the first time I really understand something about my parents. The incomparable pleasure of doing it exactly as you want, not caring for one single moment whether the entire civilized world is making fun of your choices. At that moment I would have put "Swimming pool in my bedroom" at the top of my eternal Christmas list.

We sat in the dark not speaking.

"Pop, I've got to talk to you."

"I'm all ears, *cara*."

"I don't want to upset you, but I don't want to lie to you, either. I ran away and the police will probably trace us here fairly soon. I got a note while I was in the hospital, under police protection. Pop, it said, 'You're next.' I'm going to leave the kids with you and just disappear for a while. I don't want to be anywhere near any of you until this maniac is caught. I have this weird feeling that I can figure it out, if I just have some time. Also, Pop, I think that I'm one of the suspects and that makes it even more complicated. What I think would be best is for you and the kids to go with Pepe back to Antigua. The police will have a hard time tracing you there. You would all be much safer. Whoever killed Amora knows a lot about us, and they can certainly track us down here. Will you do it?"

"Will I do it? How can I not do it? For the children, I would do anything! But I don't like this. I don't want you alone like that. Where is your husband? Why in hell are you doing this alone? This is crazy. *Pazzo!* You tell me the truth, *cara*. I don't understand this!"

"Pop. The truth is that just before the murder I found out that Clifford was having an affair and I'm so hurt and angry that it never even occurred to me to ask his help. Things were pretty crummy before, and after all of this, I don't even know what marriage I have left. That's another reason I need some time alone to think. I just had to get out of there.

"I may even be wanted! You know me. Always the good girl. Never turned in a homework assignment late; here I am a fugitive from the NYPD! Aunt Minnie wasn't all wrong, you know. In our own ways, Amora and I haven't done such a great job of it. That's all I can say. I don't know what comes next."

My poor pop shakes his shiny wet head.

"Pop, when Amora brought Clive up here, did she, uh, do anything unusual?"

"Ha! Everything she ever did, to me, was unusual. But for her, no. Spent a lot of time in her old room. Lookin' through scrapbooks, stuff like that. For Clive, she said."

"Old yearbooks?"

"*Sì*. Took some with her."

"I see. Pop, do you remember Sarah Jame Milano?"

"Sure, sure. Amora's *puttanesca*. Father was a bookie. Funny you should mention her. Your sis talked to her on the telephone, coupla times, when she was here."

"Who called who?"

"Lemme think. Uh, I think, both ways. Back and forth."

"Pop, do you have the phone bill for that month?"

"Sure. Keep everything. Your momma thought I was crazy, but see, you never know! Wait a minute."

Pop scoots around me and disappears into his dressing room. I sit curled up by his bed. Somehow I feel as if I'm being pulled forward by some invisible, but friendly, force. I feel strong. I feel sad. Sadder than I have ever felt in my life. I wonder if one feeling has to do with the other.

"Got it! It was July—after school was out!"

Pop is grinning so wide, all his gold teeth peek out. He is helping. I take the bills and open the July statement. There are three calls placed to one number. I stop there. The number is in New Mexico. Santa Fe, New Mexico. Like the postmark on the notes.

"Thanks, Pop. This is really helpful. Can I keep it?"

"Sure. Whaddaya think? Give your old man a clue?"

"I don't know yet. I promise as soon as anything makes sense, I'll call you. I've got to do this by myself."

Pop stands up. He paces back and forth, his wiry little legs bouncing him forward.

"I'm gonna give you money and I'm gonna give you my new car. And I'm gonna give you a gun. You want to take off like a *fugitivo*—you go strong. But I tell you. I don't have another *morto* in me. You be smart, *cara mia*; if you get into trouble you call the cops. You call me. I refuse to bury you, too! I'm old and my heart is swollen. One more pain and it burst like a big red balloon. *Capisci?*"

"Sì, Papa. *Io capisco.*"

"We go to Pepe's. I send word to the kids' schools that they are under the care of their grandfather. I teach them. You come there when you can."

"I will, Pop. I'll send letters. Don't worry."

"'Don't worry,' she says! You tell a father not to worry while his only living child is running around the highways with a murderer chasing her!"

"No one knows where I am, Pop. I'm safer in your car than in the police ward. Scary but true."

"*Sì, sì.* This is some world we got here. I tried to keep you out of it. I did what I could. Such strong women! No way to protect you girls. No way to tell you nothing! You make your pop feel like a *castrato*. Like an old fool. I tried to tell you that there's nothing out there. Only inside is there anything. To live in fear, in competition with the whole world, without ground you can stand firm on. For what? So when you die, they write one small paragraph in the big-deal *New York Times?* I never really knew your sister, but I know you. You are so like me. Big talker, but inside you are a *gelatina*. Not tough. Soft and sweet. You don't have cunning. You don't know how to play the game out there. You're smart, but you ain't tough, *cara*. That world out there can just chew you up. Don't fool yourself. If you win out there, you win by using your courage and your heart. You never beat them on their terms. That's why you suffered so much with your sister. You were always trying to beat her at her game. Always running into the same wall. Choose a different building. Don't try to win in that neighborhood."

I climb up and put my head on his strong broad shoulder. "Oh, Papa, I love you so much. I don't know what I would do without you. God bless you, Papa. I'm so sorry I've hurt you."

"Don't be sorry. You have to live your life. I have to let you. That is the hardest thing between parents and children. I sit on my tongue but I still try to live your life for you. Someday I will be gone and you will have to be able to do it by yourself. Without anyone to come home to. That is why I don't try to stop you now. This is necessary for you. My forty-year-old baby. Happy birthday!"

"Oh, Papa, I'm so scared. I've always been scared. I'm always trying to play it safe because I'm scared of life. Scared of life and scared of death. I've just stuck myself in a corner. Always trying to second-guess my own life, and now look at me!"

"Trust God, *cara*. Nothing is an accident. Maybe you need to test your own spirit. Maybe you need to walk into your fear. Where are you going?"

I stop crying and sit up. I realize that I know. "Santa Fe, New Mexico."

"Perchè?"

"Somebody told me they have nice jewelry there."

I left Pop's before dawn. I had one suitcase, a shiny new racing-green Toyota, a stack of Pop's favorite Willie Nelson and Frank Sinatra tapes, a thermos of coffee, a six-pack of diet Coke, an envelope with $20,000, the red wig my mother had worn when her hair fell out from the chemotherapy treatments, and a gun.

The car and the money were my birthday presents. Half of the money had been intended for Amora. The car was a departure addition. I left Pop standing in the dark, his hands on his hips. I felt somewhat like I had felt the day I left home for college.

There is an enormous adrenaline rush the moment daily life is ruptured. Even when the rupture is caused by a catastrophe. The moment the daily routine is thrown asunder, life is not just dwindling by in a daily stream of used cotton balls and dried-out Lipton tea bags; it's energizing. A crisis in the middle of daily life, whether a hurricane or a beheading, frees one up. It's rather an attenuated version of the vacation phenomenon: "In forty-eight hours I'm outta here" repeats and repeats in the ear. Deadly dull chores are done briskly, loose ends are left swaying in the breeze. There is the enticement of adventure, the anticipation of pleasure. Coming home is the pisser. There are all the swaying ends, plus dozens of new ones. A notice from the IRS, that totally forgotten American Express bill, notes from the dentist about the plaque-removal appointment, the gynecologist about the yearly Pap test, and nothing to look forward to. No more anticipation to energize you through the piles of inertia-producing details of daily life. Daily life should, in a proper world, be looked on only as the time between vacations or life crises.

So while I was basically terrified not only of the police and the slicer but also of being on the interstate highways zooming off into the unknown all alone for the first time in my entire life, I was not, on the other hand, bored. This was not like a trip to the dry cleaners or a thank-you note to Aunt Minnie. This was certainly a break in my daily life.

There was also this incredible feeling of freedom. Of omniscience. Of peace. I was all alone and totally under my own power. My life had become, suddenly, very simple. I was going to New Mexico. I was trying to figure out who had murdered my sister. I was trying not to become the next victim. Enough to keep me off the streets and out of the pool halls, but no more. No room for the scourges of the middle-class, middle-aged American woman. No secondary-gratification dilemmas. I was skipping a generation. I was back to the basic immigrant guide to survival. Rule number one: Survive.

I slipped Willie Nelson into the slot and whizzed across the New York State border into Pennsylvania.

I popped open a diet Coke and turned up the volume, my mind entertained by visions of myself as one of Willie's Gals, a trucker, perhaps, hauling the big loads with the guys. *"Ten-four, Yellow Dog, this is Mountain Dew burnin' it up on big 80. Last turkey to Tulsa buys the cold ones." I'd toss off my city clothes, braid my hair, slip into my skin-tight Levi's (that would no longer cut into my vagina like a double-edged blade and give me instant bladder infections, not to mention the fiery red ridges etched into my abdomen for hours and resembling the world atlas, not for the new Aroma). I'd just slip into my boots, toss my Stetson on, and take off for Montana to ride, rope, punch some cattle, spend time with the fellas delivering lambs and calves up-country where it's thirty below most winters. Herd some sheep, meet Clint Eastwood, and roll around for a while in our fleece-lined jackets, until the road called me and I had to be movin' on. Clint, you're one helluva dude, but I'm not the settlin'-down kind. I'm still driftin', honey man. Maybe we'll meet again in the spring, when the snow melts and the purple sunset falls across the Rockies. I leave him on his knees, sobbing in lonely acceptance of the love he could not tame.*

I was so buzzed by the caffeine and the fantasies that I didn't even pause at the Pennsylvania border. When I whizzed into Maryland, I realized that I was starving and in desperate need of a ladies' room.

What America has created in its highway system is a

kind of super-enormous board game. A repeating pattern that eliminates any cultural or regional differences but creates a false sense of security and feeling of familiarity. This applies to towns off the highway with signs that say FOOD, GAS, LODGING.

There are always three semi-seedy motels boasting color TV and twenty-two cable stations, air conditioning, and ice machines; at least one nationally advertised burger place, a pizza joint, and a taco or fried-chicken establishment. Two gas stations, a 7-Eleven, a family general store, a café with jukebox, and that is about that. The one thing that they cannot stamp out and standardize are the people. They are regional. The crowd at the McDonald's in Altoona, Pennsylvania, is nothing at all like the group at the Pizza Hut in Pratt, Maryland. And I was not like any of them. I slipped on the red wig and dark glasses. I was not going to be caught in a Burger King in Flintstone, Maryland, by some news fiend with a copy of the local tabloid with my picture staring out at him. I'd been to the movies. I'd seen all those ridiculous fugitives who never changed their appearance and were nailed in the first reel. They'd have to get up pretty early in the morning to put that one past me.

I entered the McDonald's off Highway 40 just across the Pennsylvania border trying to look as inconspicuous and cooled out as possible. Inside I felt as if I were flapping around in a Big Bird suit. I have never, not on my worst day, been this paranoid or self-conscious. I was more paranoid than Vivika, who always feels that every single person on the street is there only to check her out and pass judgment. But then, she's a teenager and that's normal for her. I decided it was also probably normal for me, given the circumstances. I ordered a Quarter Pounder with cheese, my first, I thought, with a certain holier-than-thou smugness, managing to walk to a table without dropping it, losing my wig, or beginning to squawk and hop around like the creature I felt myself to be. Every pair of small-town beady eyes seemed riveted on me. I chose a booth by the door, near my car. On the table someone had left a day-old copy of the *Philadelphia Inquirer*. Inside the second page was my photo with the story of my flight. SHRINK TWIN FLEES POLICE GUARD AFTER RECEIVING DEATH THREAT. NYPD LAUNCHES SEARCH. MOTIVE FOR BIZARRE KILLING STILL UNKNOWN. There was a biographical sketch on me, Amora, Pop, Jimmy Bob, et al. It was unclear whether the search being launched was for my protection or because I had become, by my departure, the prime suspect. I decided not to dwell on this. I chose instead to worry about the fat and sodium content of the foodlike substance I was devouring and to eavesdrop on my fellow patrons.

What kind of people hang out at McDonald's at ten o'clock in the morning? Lonely people. Here was the radio audience on a coffee break.

I allowed myself a quick fantasy to keep me company while I sipped my non-dairy-creamered coffee.

A darkly handsome television repairman who has stopped for a quick cup of java spies me in my booth. Something about the way I cock my head to keep the brown soggy lettuce strip from winding around my mouth touches him. I look up, in that startled, doelike way of the ingenuous damselette. My dark glasses meet his earnest, kind brown eyes. He approaches. I find myself pouring my heart out to him. He is a strongly built man, many years my junior, used to a life of simplicity and hard physical work.

I find myself surrendering totally to his quiet, gentle strength. Later, back in his trailer, he takes off my glasses and wig, and tears of joy at my sensual, earthy beauty fill his eyes, which are already brimming with passion, thus causing a sort of sizzle in the ducts. I am quivering with emotion. Slowly he undresses me, kissing each new part of my womanly body. It takes him a long time to pry me loose from my Calvins and rub blood back into the red atlas of my abdomen. By then we are both ablaze with desire. He mounts me, his large, hard, workingman's penis sliding into me in blind, pulsing ecstasy. I am lost in a whirlpool of lust and joy. I am out of my mind, living only for this moment, this feeling. He thrusts above me steadily, lingering, then jabbing again, each stroke sending paroxysms of orgasmic release through my entire being, until we are both limp with sweat and release. He is better than Clint. He is My Man.

I move into the trailer. I take to running errands with large pink curlers in my hair and no bra beneath my nylon drip-dry housedress. I spend "quality time" having coffee with the other women in the trailer park, sharing tales of hardship and despair, comparing our men, and worrying about the new cocktail waitress at Ed's Coffee Shop Café.

My days pass aimlessly. I browse the cosmetics counter at J.C. Penney. Have my daily Quarter Pounder, read the local papers, clean the trailer, plan Spam casseroles and meat-loaf dinners for My Man, and fuck my pink-rollered brains out. I am Woman. Living the way women were meant to live. The way Jerry Falwell and the Pope noddingly approved. I read Jackie Collins novels at the laundromat and long to be pregnant with my simple, hardworking man's baby.

"Hey, pecker-nose—you're hogging the French fries."

"Fuck off, dick breath, I paid for 'em."

There is nothing like a table full of teenagers to bring one back to reality. I scan the room. Not a TV repairman in sight. Two lethargic youths in McDonald's attire with gray teeth and acne scars are cleaning up. Not at all like the television commercials. No great-looking, burstingwith-vitality young people singing and dancing their redblooded, well-nourished hearts out while filling your every need. *You deserve a break today* . . . They shuffle by, leaving my half-eaten pile of burgeresque edible untouched. A lady and a man have taken the booth in front of me. The lady is holding a milkshake-like synthetic compound in one hand. In what would be her other hand, but is in fact a tiny stump of an arm, she is holding a cigarette. The cigarette is smoldering in a weblike prehensile little knot that I suppose would be called two fingers. She slurps the chocolate froth, then swings the stump toward her face and inhales deeply on the cigarette. I try not to stare. I cannot, of course, keep my eyes off this unbelievably fascinating sight. I envy her nonchalance. My dark glasses and red wig no longer seem worthy of a second glance.

I tap-dance my way between the sullen clean-up crew, carrying my own trash to the disposal bin, singing from my heart. So get up and get away . . . to McDonald's . . . I blow Big Bird a kiss. I take one last look around for My Man and I am out of there.

10

My Mother the Car

What kind of people listen to the radio? Roadies. Traveling salesmen, commuters. Runaways, recycled hippies, wanderers. Retired folk in their Winnebagos seeing the great U.S. of A. Car thieves. Hell's Angels, child molesters, serial killers. Peter Fonda and me. Like I said before, lonely people.

My goal for the second day was West Virginia by nightfall.

West Virginia. It sounded as exotic as Nigeria. Do they lynch Northeastern Jewish-Italians in West Virginia? Do they speak English or local dialect? Can you drink the water? Are vaccinations required? I was whizzing through the mountainous beauty of Maryland's national parks region into the deep, dark unknown.

By this time, the green Toyota had replaced Pop's farm, my apartment, New York, all safe harbors. It was now my haven, my home. Strong, dependable, fully heated or air conditioned. I knew how to control it. I had developed a feel for it. It was mine. When the tapes were on, I zoomed along, totally protected and oblivious to the world around me. No radio reports of murder or mayhem to cloud my fantasies or create anxiety. No disturbances in the field. After a while, this serene isolation would get to me and I would flip off the tape and hit the nearest all-news station. There I would puff myself up with enough fear and depression to last for one hundred miles or so, then slam Willie back and spend the next hundred miles calming myself down and regaining my sense of total safety and peace.

I have certainly heard the statistics of highway accidents, but I never feel safer or more in control of my immediate destiny than behind the wheel and on the road. There were moments that I had the same feeling as swimming laps in Pop's pool; joyous and invincible. It was almost the way it had been when I was little and my mother would hold me in her lap and sing to me. Totally secure. The beige leather bucket seat was my new mother's lap. I liked it in here. I could turn the bad news off anytime I wanted to. It felt so safe I even spent that first night off the road curled up in the backseat.

I crossed into West Virginia without being stopped at the border by foreign-sounding men in plaid short-sleeved shirts with tobacco juice dribbling from the corners of their mouths. This *was* an adventure.

I patted my wig into place and swung my new green Japanese mama-san into the parking lot of a knotty-pine-sided hovel called Rose's Place. It was the only place within sight or point on the map where lunch looked possible. I was ravenous.

There were five or six empty Formica-topped tables and a hand-printed menu on the wall. The menu listed pizza and assorted sandwiches and homemade soup, chili burgers, fried chicken, and cold drinks. The Four Seasons could relax. Rose was nowhere in sight. In her place there was an ancient Indian man with a large goiter hanging like a rooster's cockle from his neck and a filthy white apron tied up under his shoulders. It took him about fifteen minutes to make his way around the counter and over to my table. I debated getting up and meeting him, then decided I might hurt his pride or break some ancient sacred code or God only knows what. By the time he reached me, I was almost faint from hunger.

"Good afternoon. What's the daily soup?"

He shook his weather-battered head back and forth, making the goiter bob around. "No soup."

"Oh, gee, that's too bad. I sort of felt like soup. Okay, I'll have the chili and a tuna on whole-wheat toast and a diet Coke."

Now the head and goiter were into serious movement.

"No chili. No Coke, no tuna."

This guy and the mythical Rose should go into business with Aunt Minnie. "Well, what *do* you have? Maybe that's a better way to do this."

"Pizza. Pepperoni. Root beer. Chips."

This was obviously not going to be one of my Immune Power Diet journeys. "I'll have one of each."

Before he could begin his return trip, the door opened and an entire family of Mexican Indians entered.

They were noteworthy because, from the newborn baby, through the gaggle of children of various ages and sexes, to the mother, father, and granny, each one of them weighed in at about 250 pounds, and none of them had a visible neck.

The sight of this family of probable food buffs did not visibly disturb Rose's surrogate, but it caused considerable agitation in me. If he started taking their order before plopping my frozen pepperoni in the micro, forget it. They might as well eat my hypoglycemiated remains. I regretted the false euphoria of my caffeine and sugar load. I would not make the same mistake on the rest of the trip, I promised God, if he would just let me have my lunch before my fellow diners. I would not even look at a cup of coffee for a thousand miles.

The family did not acknowledge my food server. He did not acknowledge them. They pushed two tables together and sat across the hovel from me. No one spoke. That may be because it is more difficult to speak without a neck; where does one put the necessary equipment, vocal cords, voice box, et cetera? It may also have been that when you are that fat and very hungry, conversation is not a priority. It was also possible that they had just had a huge fight in the pickup and were not speaking to one another. Thinking about this got me through the agonizing death march that my food server was making between the counter and the kitchen.

Before I had time to scavenge my purse for a remaining Oreo or Frito crumb, the door opened again and, lo and behold, another family arrived to sample the local specialties de maison! This family might have been the subject of a Taylor Caldwell novelette. "Poor white trash" is what Aunt Minnie would call them. A mountain man wearing mud-stained jeans that fell a wee bit too far below his navel and underwear for the Jordache look, no shirt to protect his skinny, pale, hairless chest from the elements, a ratty nestlike beard, bare feet covered with who only knows what brownish substance, and a narrow, mean, slitty-eyed face. Behind him trotted his baby-doll wife, her black-rooted blonde hair in the always-fashionable-on-the-highways pink rollers, two rows of purple eyelashes, cutoff jean shorts that rode high on the milkmaid thighs (very white and covered with suspicious-looking bruises), spike-heel slip-ons, and fluorescent-green toe- and fingernail polish. Following immediately behind the happy couple were the two blondest, cutest, dirtiest little boys I have ever seen. They chose the table directly beside mine. Starvation was starting to look like the lesser of evils.

This family sat glaring into space, also silent. They had necks and were not obese, but the possibility of a fairly smarmy exchange of words did seem viable. Then one of the mucous-nosed, greasy-fingered little boys squirmed in his seat.

"Put yur ass back in them chairs 'fur I beat yur skulls in," said the mountain man. This father had obviously not been following the issue-oriented Movies of the Week on ABC.

His wife sat motionless, chewing a now discernible mouthful of bubble gum, which popped against her teeny-baby face and was casually picked off by one of her inch-long green nails.

Such an aura of violence radiated from this guy that I found it hard to breathe. I did not know where to look. I was trying fiercely to become invisible. I sat absolutely still in my chair.

Something crashes in the kitchen. Then silence.

The mountain man is not as patient as the no-necks.

He rises to his full puny swagger and yells at the kitchen door. "Hey, man, git us some beers out here, pronto."

I am feigning serious interest in a copy of *Newsweek* with Donald Trump on the cover that by some miracle had been stuffed into the side pocket of my purse and forgotten for months. What I am really thinking about is what it would be like to be married to the mountain man.

I waddle along behind him on my spike heels, my bruised knees, quivering from hours spent tied to the motel bedposts, hardly holding my weight. Obviously a premature ejaculator, my mountain man gets off by tying me up and beating me with various auto parts and/or kitchen utensils. This is a guy who pees on you, puts out a Lucky Strike in your belly button, and gives a nice hard crack across the face with his ring hand because the toast was burned. I marry him at fifteen, produce six babies, and die seven years later of old age.

The beers appear on a tray. (My food server may be old and slow, but he ain't stupid.) I discreetly try to rise and leave. My food server raises one flinty shaking arm to stop me.

"Coming up," he croaks.

The no-necks are still sitting in passive stony silence, the patience of the gods at work.

The dirty adorable little boys squirm again. Mountain Man grabs the closest by his hair and half-lifts him out of his chair.

"You're askin' fur it. Yur gonna git somethin' to remember when we's in the van."

I am having a great deal of trouble dealing with this and am very close to ripping off my wig and making a statement; grabbing up those poor helpless babies and fleeing in my racing-green samurai.

(Me, rising.) "Why, you son of a bitch. Why, you filthy,

disgusting swine! How dare you treat your child like that! In the name of decent people everywhere, I am making a citizen's arrest! Don't move or I'll shoot!" (The fact that Pop's gun is in the car is irrelevant in the fantasy world.)

I sweep up a startled innocent under each arm and back out of the restaurant, leaving the bubble-gummer and the cretin speechless before the face of justice.

Tears of sorrow for the babies who will not be rescued today well up behind my glasses, but before I can open my mouth and lose my bonded front teeth, my pizzalike compound and iceless root beer appear. This is what one could call an eating-for-survival lunch. I swallow whole chunks, using the cud technique; pizza to be digested later in the privacy of my vehicle. The no-necks watch me out of the corners of their silent but ravenous eyes. My food server makes it from me to the mountain man, knowing what side his maize is buttered on. The no-necks are probably cannibalizing their own fat supply by now.

While Daniel Boone is ordering ("Brang us two of them pepperonis and keep the cold ones comin, old man, ur yur butt is buckshot"), I throw more than enough money for lunch and a Vitamin B-12 injection on the table and creep out.

I slide behind the wheel of my mother, my friend, and ease out of Rose's Place, as grateful as I have ever been for what on other days has seemed a fairly short straw. I keep feeling that someone is following me.

The Mirage Motel in Jane Lew, West Virginia. The manager and his pink-rollered mother (on the road, pink rollers are the Burberry scarf of instant acceptance), graduates of the Norman Bates School of Motel Management, assign me to room 3C—the deluxe double right by the heated pool and ice machine. I register, exhaustion and cold sweaty anxiety creeping down my back. *Mrs.*

Emma Standish, Bangor, Maine. I can always say the car is borrowed. "Mom's" four hundred cats are scratching their way up and down the kitty pole. The fetid semisweet smell of Purina and cat shit wafts across my already queasy senses.

Son of Mom gives me the once-over. "What's a gal like you doin' out here on the road all by your lonesome?"

"I'm a documentary filmmaker, scouting locations for a series on the dying Indian culture."

The most absolutely marvelous thing about being on the lam, moving outside of the social confinement of one's real life, is that anything goes. I can bullshit my way across America. I can bloody well be whatever I want to be at the moment and lie my little synthetic red head off and it doesn't count.

A sly quixotic smile fills Son of Catwoman's bony face. "Is that right? I'm a writer myself; been working on the definitive study of General George Custer and Chief Crazy Horse. It's been a real rough experience, though. I had seven years of notes stolen from me right out of my locker at the Greyhound bus station. Twice."

"Twice? You mean two sets of seven years of notes?"

"Yep."

"Two sets of seven years' worth of notes, totaling fourteen years of work, stolen at two different times out of the same locker?"

"That's a fact."

"That's unbelievable."

"I took it bad. Hit the bottle real hard. When I read all of the crapola that those academic hotshots keep publishing, it makes me so mad, I just have another drink."

Mom nods her sympathy. "My son's a genius. He could have a Literary Guild Alternate Selection and a *Reader's*

Digest series easy, when he pulls himself out of his little down spell."

I take my key, knowing I should just smile politely and back out of there. Maybe it was all the cats. I was curious.

"May I ask *why*, after the first time, did you take another seven years' worth of notes back to the same locker?"

"Law of probability, I guess."

"Bad luck." Mom pats his hairy hand.

"Once would be bad luck, but twice . . . maybe you'd better think about why you don't want to write the book." Spastic-twitching shrink limb, radio psychobabble had left its mark.

I wait for mother, son, and cats to leap over the plywood counter and attack me. Mom does in fact, stiffen. Son seems to shrink. "Maybe you've got somethin' there. 'Scuse me. Gotta use the porcelain convenience."

Mom glares at me, double-checks my signature, hands me two threadbare towels and a discount coupon book to the best eating establishments in Jane Lew, and assures me for the third time (I am still not a trusting person) that the pool is *really* heated.

I open the door to 3C, expecting Robin Leach to leap out of the two-hanger cardboard closet and do an on-the-spot interview for "Lifestyles of the Rich and Famous." There is a lumpy bed with an out-of-order vibrator machine, a TV that is receiving *one* of the twenty-two advertised cable channels, a shower that on first test emits a trickle of rust-colored cold slush, and a bureau. It feels like heaven. My back and legs are one second away from the lower-body version of lockjaw and I am blind with exhaustion, but too nervous to sleep. A swim will be just the thing. I change into my exercise leotard, the closest thing to a bathing suit I have available, grab the towelesque cloth, taking my purse, which now contains my money and my gun, all I need on earth, and limp barefoot in the dark across the gravel drive to the pool. I pause on my crippled toes, then dive in.

Penguins would freeze to death in the Mirage pool. I come up so fast I almost propel myself back onto the cement. I am so cold I just keep swimming, afraid that if I stop, so will my heart and the movement of blood through my veins. I swim blindly in the dark until I am panting. I realize as I pull myself up onto the steps that I am also sobbing. The smack of the cold had broken through my protection, my numbness. I am shredded with grief. Faces whiz behind my chlorine-clouded eyes. My sister. My mother. My husband. I cower on the steps, shaking with loss and cold, my lips purple and shivering the way they used to when I was small, when leaving the pleasure of the water was so great a loss that only when I was caught, betrayed by my purple shivering self, would I go. The air was still and cold and the sky was dead-black, rural black, and the quiet so intense, so unbearably powerful and empty, except for the sound of my moaning woe.

Someone is there in the dark with me. My head shoots up, catching the sky full of blinding lights, stars pulsing in the jet air.

Norman Bates stands in the shadows, his hands in his pockets. Slowly I move my frozen fingers toward my purse. I was living on the outside now, cowboy rules. Anything could be real and anything could happen.

"What do you want?"

"Sorry, ma'm. I didn't mean to scare you. I came to warn you about the pool. Mom always tells people that it's heated, and it's been broke for a good ten years."

"A little late, but thank you, anyway." I climb out, wrapping what I can of myself in the towel and clutching my purse against my shaking stomach.

"I'll walk you back to your room. I have a flashlight."

"Thanks. I'm fine. I can manage." I trip almost immediately and stub my toe so hard that a whole new wave of sobs engulfs me. "Please, if you don't mind, I'd like to be alone."

"Sure. I understand. Got the blues. Get them myself. I just wanted to say that what you said in there . . . well, you made me think about things. I went into the john, that's where I do my best thinking, and I figured out something. I figured out that it was my mom what stole my notes, so's I'd stay here. I think I knew it all along and it was my excuse."

I stop crying and look this creepy stranger right in the face. Not worried about him seeing me sobbing and shaking, without my disguise or my defenses. I look him in the eye in a way that I do not ever remember looking anyone in the eye; without a shadow of self-consciousness or fear.

"What a brave and lovely thing to find out about yourself. You've taken a very big step. Congratulations."

"How did you know that?"

"Oh, just something I picked up on the radio."

"Most people don't bother; people been coming in that door day after day since I was a kid. Nobody ever bothered to talk with me before."

"I'm glad I was able to help."

"I'd like to do something to help you back."

"Oh, thanks, but that's not necessary."

He reaches into his pocket and in lieu of a butcher knife he offers forth a pint of Harveys Bristol Cream sherry. "I bought this for Mom, but I'd like you to have it; seems like you could use it, tonight. What with the pool and the crying and all."

Old programming starts to open my mouth with a polite refusal, but I am still looking into this man's eyes. The sherry has become like the pepperoni at lunchtime. A highly desirable commodity.

"That's very kind of you."

"I'm going to leave here and head for a city with a great big library and I'm going to start my book again. Lots of those notes are in my head still, anyway."

"Don't change your mind. Don't back down when your mother starts on you."

"No way. I'm behind that now."

"Well, good luck."

"Good luck to you too, ma'm."

I run the shower until the rust slush turns to decent hot, yellow water. No shower has ever felt so good. I find Flickin' Chicken in the coupon book and a box of fried junk is brought across the parking lot to my very door. I flip on a "Fugitive" rerun, which is perfectly appropriate, and settle into my formerly vibrating bed with a plastic glass full of sherry and a greasy feastie. I realize with some pleasure that it is the first time I have been alone in a motel room in my entire life.

11

Dream When You're Feelin' Blue

That night on the road at the Mirage, sleep crawled out from under my musty, mushy bed and sucked me down into its feverish pulsing womb. Deep, deep sleep. Surrender to the black magic of unconsciousness. I float down into it, arms outstretched, reaching back into the inky stillness for my other half. Amora. Seed sister. I float head over heels, reaching toward her, but she is gone now. The dream changes. I am running toward her across Penn Station. I am an embryo but I'm all dressed up and running toward her, so glad that she is alive. She walks slowly, her face blank, her blonde hair blowing behind her.

I keep running, my unformed eyes sealed shut, calling to her. But I can't find her. *Amora. Amora.* My mother appears and they embrace. They turn away and walk off together and I am left alone. I am sobbing in the blackness. I do not understand why I am so alone. My mother turns and whispers coldly, "You have what you always wanted. Go away." I stagger off.

A train is passing. A train for Santa Fe. I jump on. I am Amora now. I am beautiful and sexy. I enter a compartment and fling off my coat, exposing my lush nakedness underneath. The door opens. Gene Autry comes in. He grabs me and pulls me down onto his erection. I throw my head back in ecstasy and abandon. "Don't stop," I pant. "Don't ever stop! I'm free! It's my turn!" Soon the compartment is filled with Western stars. Roy Rogers and Dale Evans. Willie Nelson stands behind Gene, caressing my round milky breasts. Kenny Rogers sticks his tongue in my ear. The Lone Ranger arrives. Tonto thrusts his wiry brown cock into my sensual mouth. I float above them, an island of rapture and joy. *Amora. Amora.* I am alone. Clint shoots open the window, hanging from the outside of the train. "Why Santa Fe?" he inquires. Wanda Mackay bursts in yelling at him and smashing at his fingers with her Maud Frizon pump. "Because that's where women like her end up!"

I oversleep. I cannot seem to pull myself back to reality. I have always used sleep as a refuge, as a personal game preserve when things get too heavy, when new truth is too close. I sleep, dreaming of sleep, waking in layers to find that I am only dreaming another dream without waking up. Curled on my side in the pre-birth heat of effortless existence; no expectations and no responsibilities. No success and no failure. No conflict. Now I am back there alone; not sharing the space in the womb like a college dorm room, never unique from the very first second. I curl around my primal sleep all alone now. Free now. In the distance I hear my travel alarm as if from inside a coffin or a closet. Far away, back on the surface, where the fear is. Where the pain is. Where the rest of my life is waiting for me to call the morning meeting to order. I struggle toward it, away from the toasty suspension and back into the present. The diving bell bobs, sways violently, and then shoots me up into the sunlight.

I surface. It is 9 A.M., much too late for an outlaw to start the day. My heart is flopping wildly in my chest.

I must reach Indiana by nightfall to keep my schedule. I buy coffee in the vending machine by the pool, thus breaking my solemn oath. I decide not to make any more solemn oaths, at least not until I reach Santa Fe. I also buy a Twinkie. Of course this tastes better than anything I have ever eaten. Can my very own pink rollers be far behind?

I throw my stuff into Mama-San and I am back on the road. Soaring down the byways along the Ohio River heading for Kentucky, farther and father from home.

I bounce around with Willie for a while, wondering if he still respects me after what he saw in the train compartment. Then I make my first mistake of the day. I hit the radio dial.

Three stories precede the one about me. The first concerns a sixty-seven-year-old woman with agoraphobia who, after not leaving her apartment for thirty years, has just graduated from college. The second features a nurse arrested after the discovery that during the past fourteen years she has murdered all *nine* of her children (her husband never noticed anything out of the ordinary). The third is about Siamese twin boys who must change sex in order to be separated. The options are making one a boy and one a girl or making them both girls. That must have been a helluva parent-doctor meeting. I was not really prepared to be next. Obviously I had been slipped in by the news director under the bizarre-human-interest category. There was an all-points bulletin out on me. Also on Pop and the kids, who had "vanished from the family compound in the pastoral Adirondacks." All suspects had been cleared; police were still searching for the writer of the strange notes and moi. The body had not been found. The murder weapon, which was believed to have been a Chinese meat cleaver, the kind they use on Peking ducks, had not been found. The police believed that the crime was either the result of a violent argument between the twin sisters over the dead sister's lover Jimmy Bob Mackay (give me a break) or the work of a psychopath who would most likely still be stalking the surviving twin. Police spokesman Lieutenant Mallony then issued a plea for Dr. Aroma Sweet to turn herself in to the authorities for her own safety and thus clear her good name. The police were also following up on leads resulting from fan mail received by both doctors, patient lists, and crank letters and calls.

The Gore-Tex lining was back in my throat. My wig was slipping around on my overheated little head. I must see to my disguise as soon as possible.

I stop for lunch, choosing a town near the Kentucky border large enough to house a "Salon de Beauté." Flinging off my wig and adopting what I hope is an air of irritable haughtiness, I stride into the salon, checking first to make sure there is no television on which my picture could possibly be flashed. None. The radio is tuned in to one of those rolling-surf stations where all the music sounds as if it is emanating from a drunk tank filled with Hungarian violinists. There are several green plastic chairs, two shampoo sinks, two dryers, a dusty stack of

Redbook and *Ladies' Home Journal* magazines with people like Lady Bird Johnson and Grace Kelly on the covers. Old Clairol posters on the walls and two framed needlepoint samplers that read "Amway Is Forever" and "Christ Has Risen" (or was it "Amway Has Risen" and "Christ Is Forever"?).

A bleached blonde of middle years and many miles is sitting contentedly under one of the dryers reading a copy of *Daytime TV Stars* and nibbling from a bag of Cheetos resting on her well-padded knees. She smiles and gives me a little two-fingered wave with what appear to be newly polished digits. No one else is in sight. The dryer lady points to the door with a sign that says "Enter at your own risk" and shouts, "She'll be right back, honey!"

I nod, picking up a March 1979 copy of *Redbook* with Amy Carter and her mom on the cover, and try to keep myself from hyperventilating. This is the moment when the sweaty, beery local sheriff, responding to a tip from a motorist, bursts in with his gun drawn and splatters me all over the green linoleum.

The ominous door opens and out comes the last type of person on earth one would expect.

A walking *Vogue* cover. A tall, gorgeous, ebony-haired woman with cheekbones you could hide quarters in and a perfect, aristocratic, angelic face. Though she is wearing your basic white beautician's smock, it could be the new Courrèges summer look. I am speechless.

The creature winks and flashes a blinding, perfect, Ultra Brite smile. "Hiya. What a fuckin' treat. A new faze! I'm Mona, doll. Where'ya from?"

"Oh, I'm Gretel Johnson." (Gretel Johnson?) "I'm originally from Hawaii" (Hawaii?) ". . . but I live in Las Vegas now." (Las Vegas?) "I've been back east visiting relatives. I'm on my way home."

"Vegas? Boy, do we have some yackin' to do. I spent years out there. Went right from Brooklyn, practically. What kinda look you want?"

I have never been to either Hawaii or Las Vegas. "New. Really new. I was thinking of short and red, actually."

"Heavy. I love a challenge. How 'bout a makeover? Do the eyebrows, the makeup, the works. I got a bag full of tricks from my model days. I can make you look so new, your own ma won't recognize ya."

"Great. That's just what I'm looking for. A new me."

Mona sets to work. I am still so dumbstruck by her beauty—and the contradiction of her being in a place like this rather than the back of some bulletproof stretch limo on her way to meet her lover, the recently deposed head of some poverty-stricken Third World empire, and the further incongruity of her voice—that I don't even stop to consider what this "new me" might turn out to be. If it's anything like Mona, it will do very nicely.

While Mona cuts, she smokes, she talks, and she slugs down cans of diet root beer. She seems to accept the rather unusual facts of my arrival and requests at face, or "faze," value. Frankly, I don't think it would have much mattered if I had arrived in a werewolf suit requesting a waxing. She likes an audience.

Mona pauses in her monologue about hair color and her intensely negative feelings toward Linda Evans and Joan Collins, takes a long drag on her cigarette, and stares at herself in the finger-marked mirror.

"Look at that. Look at that faze! I don't got a drop of makeup on today, neither. You wouldn't believe what I look like with my makeup on. Fuckin' unreal. Drop dead! The turkeys in New York used to cream in their jeans when I walked in. Never had no women friends. They were all green. Green!"

I myself feel a tad lime-ish. I am also incredulous. Not even Amora ever talked about herself like this. In fact, I have never heard a woman, no matter how attractive, describe herself in any terms other than ironically negative. Each flaw magnified as if she was watching herself through a microscope. Every freckle or crease inflated galactically.

"I supported my whole lousy family from the time I was thirteen. You shoulda seen me at thirteen. I made Brooke Shields look like Howdy Doody. I had hair down to my ass and I was about twenty pounds heavier. More tits and hips. And tan. Real olive-complected. I was modelin' on Seventh Avenue before I had my period. All those old cockers thought I was eighteen. Not that they really gave a shit. I had more hands up my skirt than the fitters had pins. Hey, let's get wild. I'm goin' real short on the sides. It'll bring out your cheekbones and make your nose look shorter."

I am still thinking about all the guys with crème fraiche running down their Calvins. I don't know whether I am so intimidated by this being that I can't speak or I have my first case of puppy worship. I have never really thought about the power of sheer physical beauty before. Goddess beauty. Not Amora's recreated, never quite believed good looks or the regular normal attractiveness of almost everyone we meet in the course of our urban lives, but beauty that shapes a destiny. Beauty like money or fame or nobility. Beauty that alters the course of your life, trapping you inside like a ghost locked in the china cabinet of other people's fantasies.

Mona wacks off a wad of my hair. "So how'd you get to Vegas?"

I wince. "Well, there was this guy." I knew that was a safe line. You ask a man how he ended up someplace, he always says, "Well, there was this job." You ask a woman, she always says, "Well, there was this guy." My theory holds. Mona jumps right in.

"Oh, babycakes, do I know that one! There I was, this incredible-lookin' piece of ass, talent scouts and model agents followin' me down the streets, into the subway, the whole bit and my family lickin' their lips 'cause I was gonna make us all rich. I was like a racehorse. Every loser in the whole facockta family was linin' up tryin' to get in on the Mona action; I was only fifteen at the time, remember, and I met this guy."

The blonde from the dryer is cooked. She waddles over to Mona, brushing the Cheetos crumbs off her pink smock and pantomimes, "I'm dry," as if she were still under the dryer and unable to hear. Mona puts down her scissors and takes a long slug of soda.

"Hold everything, babe, back in a sec." She whips out the pink rollers with quick confident motions and begins the comb-out, to the delight of her patrona, who eyes me in the mirror as if I were doing a survey for *Cosmeticians Gazette*. "This Mona here, she's something! Magic hands, we call her. I don't know what this town would do without her. My old man moves himself into that bedroom a whole lot faster since Miss Mona's been workin on me. I always wanted to go blonde, but I never had the guts. Now my old man says it's like having a new woman. She even dyes my privates to match! Only my hairdresser knows for sure!"

"Lissen, with that son of a bitch you live with, I'd dye your ass to match if it'd help."

"Oh, Mona! You're something. If he could hear you talk, he'd never let me come in here again."

Now we are having a three-way conversation with the

mirror; somehow it is more intimate and less embarrassing.

"I'd love to see that peckerhead try. I used to eat better meat than his flabby ass for breakfast. You wanna hear somethin'? Her old man, he has this thing about not hitting a woman. Big macho deal. So what he does when he gets tanked is, he makes her stand out in the yard and he throws plates at her."

The blonde giggles cheerfully. "We went through five sets of china the first year we were married."

"Can you believe it? And that's nuthin'. Junie here has this trouble with her jaw; it's called TMJ. Her jaw goes off its hinge or somethin' and it hurts so bad she can't even open her mouth to eat. Has to suck straws, live on egg yolks and protein drinks and that kind of shit. And this ass-wipe she's married to, he wants her to suck his dick all the time. Are you ready for this? So I said to her, 'Look, every broad in America would like a certifiable reason not to have to do *that* again, and you've got one! Bring him a note from your fucking doctor. An official medical excuse.' Junie was too shy. So I went with her. You should have seen that quacker's face when I told him! 'Listen, Doc, my friend's old man keeps making her suck him off and it's killin' her, it hurts so bad. Write her old man a real heavy doctor-type note explaining why she can't do it no more.'

"He did it, too. Real serious and usin' a lot of big words. Wrote it out on a prescription pad, like *'Take two aspirin.'* Her hub went crazy. But he backed off. Only trouble is now she's got a pinched nerve from all the hand jobs. Can't ever win with the fuckers."

Junie nods agreement. She is now all rosy-cheeked and curled. Mona knows her stuff. I smile at her in the mirror, acknowledging her plight and thanking God that Prince Charming never appeared in that McDonald's leading me to a life like hers. *And yours is so much better?* a smart aleck voice in the back of my head whispers. I have a strong desire to clasp Mona and Junie, my fellow sisters, to my breast. But my breast is covered with dark wet hair, so I stay in my seat.

Junie dusts herself off and slips out of her pink smock, revealing a nicely rounded figure stuffed a little too closely into a baby-blue jumpsuit. "I don't want you to be thinking that my Clarence is a monster or anything. He's really not a bad man. He's churchgoing and he's a good provider. Don't let Mona fill your head about him. Mona's had so many beaux, she don't know how hard it is for us gals to find a decent one. She's spoiled."

"Spoiled, shit! No man ever spoiled me. I'm no eyelash batter. Men are business. As long as you keep that straight, you're cool. Except for the first one, the one big thrill—first love—after that, if you get your shit together, you see it like it is. Men are for sex. For making babies. A place to rest when you're on your ass. They bail us out. They cushion the ride. We do our job. They do theirs. No free lunch. All the best relationships work like that. Services provided for services rendered."

Junie stuffs some money into Mona's smock. "Oh, Mona, I love you so. You're so wild. The things you say! Isn't she wild?"

I laugh. "Four million feminists have just fainted."

Mona picks up her clippers and grabs a hunk of my rapidly disappearing locks. "Fuck feminism! It didn't change shit. Just made it worse. More confusing. That's why I'm *here*. That's what feminism did for me! Blew away my common sense and my whole fucking life."

Junie gives Mona a sympathetic hug and waves goodbye to me in the mirror. "Don't give up hope, Mona, dear. Your prince will come."

Mona watches her leave, shaking her gorgeous head. "Do you believe that? The poor broad's married to the worst dip-shit that ever slid out of the hairy hole and she's just packed her senses up and gone permanently out to lunch to keep the fantasy going."

"Very hard stuff for some women to face."

"What ever happened to 'The truth will set you free'? That's my style. Now where was I?"

"You met this guy and went to Las Vegas."

"Oh, yeah. I met this guy. He's eyeballing me at Maxwell's Plum and he's to die for. I mean very together. Old. Must have been forty and I'm like fifteen. He just stands at the bar drinking brandy from this huge snifter-type thing and smoking little cigars and checking me out for real. I mean the vibes were fucking electric. This goes on for hours. And I am really getting into it.

"And I'm givin' him like my really heavy icy stare and he's just smiling, like he really knows my shit. So this goes on till very late and my date, who is totally wasted by then, he goes to take a piss and Mr. Cool puts down his cigar and comes over and he says to me, 'You're mine. Get your coat.' Just like that. And he motions outside to this unreal Rolls Royce limo, that I find out later is one of only fifteen in the world. People like the fucking Queen of England have them. And there's this chauffeur in the front and I mean, I'm this kid from Flatbush Avenue! No one in my whole fucking family ever made it through tenth grade and this like mysterious stranger, this movie-star-type dude is rapping me out of my mind. And I'm a very hip kid. Very street-smart and cool, but this guy just zapped me. He took my arm, very laid back, and out we went."

I am so engrossed I have not even noticed that most of my hair is gone and is now being covered witht thick dark-red glop.

⌐209⌐

"Just like that? Did he take you home?"

"Home? Get serious! I never went home again. I got into the back of that car and lost my cherry on the way to the airport and got on the plane for Vegas and didn't see New York again for eight years."

"What about your parents? They must have gone crazy!"

Mona snickers. "Yeah, real crazy, until I sent the first check. After that, they were thrilled out of their teeny greedy little minds. I put my kid sis and brother through school, bought my folks a real house, paid for my granny's cancer surgery, helped my Uncle Moe open a butcher shop. I was the fucking golden goose. They calmed down real fast, record time, I'd say. Tilt your head back and close your eyes. I'm gonna do your brows."

I do as I'm told, not wanting to dam the flow from Mona's amazing mouth. "So there I was set up in this penthouse on the top of the primo hotel on the strip with my mystery man. It didn't take long to figure out he was mob. You know, I never knew his real name. His Sicilian birth name. Never to this very day. For the first year I think all we did was fuck. I never had anything like that. In fact, outside of Nico, I never had an orgasm ever again with no one. Do you have them?"

(Who, me? Little old me?) "Well, yes. I mean, it depends. But usually." I don't want to make Mona mad. I think of changing my answer.

"With a cock. I mean not orally or like a finger diddle?"

I decide that she is working from an enormous head start and I am entitled to my little piece of the rock. "Uh-huh. Yep."

"You're really lucky. Never happens for me. I'm dead from the waist down. Except for Nico. He blew my mind.

We'd fuck all day and then I'd get my shit together. And we're talkin' *together*. Emeralds, sapphires. Sables. And we'd go out. People would stop in their socks and just stare at us. He really got off on that shit. So for a year I was just like a kid in a candy store. Then, and Nico saw it comin', he says to me one morning, 'Goddess'—that's what he called me—'Goddess, you need something to do.' And next thing I knew he had built a revue around me—I was headlining in Vegas. I was sixteen, couldn't even legally be in a casino, and there I was. Goddess, The Showgirl of the Century!

"I loved it. But I was so stupid. I never even saw a cent. He took care of everything. I never asked one fucking question. See, he had a wife already. Planted back in New Jersey somewhere. And his family, they never did talk to me, not for years. So I was like this lonely princess. Five years we lived like that. Then I got pregnant and Nico said that was it—he was going to see the head of the family and appeal to his sense of honor. He would get a divorce and marry me and we would lead a normal life. He went away, back east, and I kept doing the show while he was gone. I was so lonesome, I coulda died, never had no friends then. I mean, who could I relate to? I waited and waited. One week, one month. I was startin' to show. And no Nico. And no way to reach him. I pleaded with his bodyguards, his people who protected us, to let me talk to him, but they couldn't do it. I never saw him again."

I start to sit forward and almost blind myself with the dye brush. "What!"

"Easy, honey. It's not happenin' to you, for Chrissakes. They had him killed. Seems his wife was the daughter of one of the all-time bosses and Nico had betrayed the family by staying with me. Not by having me, that woulda been okay. But by not goin' home, livin' the big fat

American lie wit the ugly wife and the chubby bambinos. So one night after the show—I was in my sixth month then and taping myself every night to go on—I come upstairs, so tired and so scared and so lonely for my Nico and there's these two meatheads in front of my door and all my stuff is in suitcases on the floor and they say, "You're outta here. Nico's not comin back. The party's over, bitch!' Just like that! I'm pregnant and I've got no place to go. They hand me an envelope with five thousand bucks in it and that is that. I was totally freaked out of my skull. Nico's cook, Sarah, she took care of me like a daughter, she took me to her house, let me stay, and I called my family. The minute they heard that the candyman had melted, they turned the whole scene into outrage at their tramp of a daughter who disappears without a trace and then calls home when she's committed a sin and has no place to go. It was clear I couldn't go back there, so when I got myself in some kind of shape I rented a motel room, moved my sables and shit in, and waited for the baby to come. That got me through. Knowing I'd have Nico's kid. But God wasn't through punishing me. The baby was born dead. A little boy. So there I was. Twenty-one years old and totally fucked. I went back to the motel, got into bed, and didn't get out for six months. If it hadn't been for Sarah, I'd have starved myself to death. When the money was gone, I started selling the furs. I hocked the jewelry. And then one morning I woke up and shit, I was still gorgeous and I was still young, so I went back to work as a showgirl. I did good. I couldn't dance worth a damn, but I looked like I could. I could fake anything. And the men started to call. I went out with everyone you ever heard of, from Sinatra on down. I could tell you stories that'd straighten your hair. I just didn't give a shit. My heart was broken. The more I didn't give a shit, the more the guys wet their pants for me.

I built up a little fortune all on my own. Plenty of johns wanted to marry me, too! Nice johns. Rich. Good guys. But I was stupid. I had put my life in the hands of a guy and gotten dropped on my head. He broke my heart and he left me with nothing.

"I never even knew he was dead till years later! So fuck men. I didn't need any of them. I'd make it all on my own. So I turned down all offers. I wined and dined. I fucked and sucked, but I was frozen. I wasn't even really there. Then I got busted. This guy really fooled me. He was on a sting operation, after the big-time prostitution rings, the mob stuff, and I was just a fly in the paper, but I was in jail and that was the end of my showgirl career and it cost me a pile to get off. So when I got out I left Vegas, did the LA bit for a while, messed myself up with drugs, went through most of the stash, and here I am, Nowhere's Ville. Don't even have a real license to do this shit. Bought a hot one off a crack-head in Nashville. That's why I stay out of the cities. I had to do somethin' while I figured out the rest of my life. The women here just love me. They've thrown a net around me and they won't let any hick prick bother me. Crazy scene, huh?"

Mona and I were made for each other. I mean, who else could top a story like that? My inner guide was on automatic pilot. I knew I could trust this woman and I knew I needed to trust someone. When she was through, I told her *my* story.

By the time I was transformed, we were friends and my nightfall arrival in Indiana was a forgotten goal. When Mona paused in our sequential monologues to close up the shop and get some beers and food for us, I looked at my new self in the mirror for the first time. I was much thinner than I had been in years (okay, than I had ever been). I did not resemble Amora or the old me. Here was this high-fashion punk redhead, with the new short look, sort of a girl's version of Sal Mineo, and all sort of rusty red. She had changed my makeup colors to bronze tones and plucked my usually substantial eyebrows into high feathery arches. I did not remotely resemble the *Daily News* head shot. This was the new look of a reborn only child. There were no twin twitching limbs belonging to this lady. I loved it. I loved Mona. I even loved myself.

Mona lived at the back of the salon. She invited me to stay over and I readily agreed. Mona had some ideas for me. Mona knew about the outlaw life.

By midnight we had worked our way through two double cheeseburgers, a six-pack of Rolling Rock, three orders of fries, a giant-size bag of Hershey kisses, and were slow-dancing to Mona's old 45s. "Took a walk and passed her house . . . LATE LAST NIGHT! All the shades were drawn and pulled . . . WAY DOWN TIGHT! Two silhouettes on the shade . . . SILHOUETTES, SILHOUETTES, SILHOUETTES, SILHOUETTES . . . TWO SILHOUETTES ON THE SHADES!!!!"

There is nothing like music from your adolescence to bring out the inner yearnings of the adult soul.

Around us in Mona's cluttered cozy room, filled with photos of her wondrous face and every known cosmetic and hair preparation, were fancy clothes and furs that she had managed to hold on to and that she insisted I try on. She showed me how to walk to look more confident and taller; she explained the importance of eye contact in turning men on.

I was feeling a little romantic and teary-eyed from the music. "Does that song get to you?"

Mona lay back on black silk sheets and smiled. "Yeah. Romance. Innocent fucking romance. I remember this kid from junior high. A Spic. My family woulda never let me bring a kid like that home, but he was the sweetest, cutest guy. My first kiss. Magic. We're talkin' weak in the knees. Nico was a whole different scene. You know?"

"Mona. I don't want to play doctor with you, but if it's any help, no one goes from years in sexual frenzy to total frigidity without a reason. You were hurt and you shut down, but you can start up again anytime you want. You just have to get more scared of being invulnerable than being vulnerable. There really is some nice person out there for you. All men aren't like the johns you knew. You have a distorted idea about men."

Mona looks into my moist mascaraed eyes for a long time, as if she is debating whether to let go or not. The *or not* wins. "Oh, yeah? Some *nice* guy like your Clifford, for example?"

"Please don't cloud the issue with facts. Just because I may not have it either doesn't mean it doesn't exist. Besides, marriage is much more complex than that. I'm not Clifford's victim. I am equally guilty and I used him, too."

"Sorry. My mouth. I always shoot from the fucking hip."

"That's fine as long as you get your own leg out of the way."

Mona lights a cigarette and pours herself another beer. "Shoulda got champagne. Only they don't have any decent champagne in this burg. Just cherry fizz water with rubbing alcohol or some shit." She sits up and pulls her smock over her head, revealing a French-lace bra and undies and a body that looks airbrushed, even in person. As if she is reading my thoughts, she shrugs.

"Everything's good but the tits. Too small. You've got great tits. Men are really into that shit." She reaches into a drawer and pulls out a silk kimono, ties it around her waist, and falls back onto the bed, keeping her eyes on me like a precocious child checking out the grown-up scene. "Okay, so how about you? Where was your big love?"

Took a walk and passed his house late last night . . . Like I said, 45s are always dangerous. From somewhere so far away from consciousness that it pops out as if I had just plucked a worm or spider from my mouth comes a name. "Reuben. Oh my God! Reuben Mars."

A wave of longing sweeps over me. A physical, palpable longing for romance. Sheer romance. Pure, movie, mad, falling-in-love-weak-kneed-for-the-first-time romance.

"Reuben Mars. He was English. He taught Art History at Berkeley. We circled one another for ages. I was mad about him. We went out for months. I was such a kid. I didn't know what to do with him! He seemed so old. He was probably twenty-six and I was still a professional virgin. The semester ended. He went back to England. I met Amos Cohen. God! How many dreams I've had about him. After Amos, I had a lot of fantasies about finding Reuben. When I went to London, I looked his number up in the phone book and called. It was an answering machine with his voice. He owned a gallery there, a crafts gallery, and the voice said that he was in America at his new gallery and to leave a message. I panicked. I just hung up."

Mona is inhaling deeply and looking at me slyly. "Where in America?"

"Oh, Jesus, Mona, that was years and years ago."

"Where?"

I sit forward, almost dropping my beer into my lap. "Oh, shit. Santa Fe. Yes. Heh, heh. Waddaya know."

"Hey, Doc. Wanna hear my theories on unconscious motivation?"

"Oh my God! That is *not* why I'm going there! Don't be ridiculous!"

"So, why Santa Fe?"

Before we can ponder this question any further, there is a loud knock at Mona's front door. We both leap up. Mona tiptoes to the window and peeks out. I follow right behind her like a newly rescued orphan pup.

"Who is it?" My heart is pounding.

"It's Junie! She's crying and she's all bloody. The shmuck musta been into the china again."

"What kind of man behaves like that?"

Mona waves to Junie. "What kind indeed. He's the fucking *sheriff!*" Mona stands up, realizing the impact of this information at the same moment I do.

The sheriff! "What do we do, Mona? What if she's told him about me?"

"Calm down, baby. Let's just stay cool. I'm gonna check her out. You just settle down. Have another beer. Have a smoke. Just stay cool. I'll be right back."

Stay cool. That was like telling King Kong to wait for the elevator.

I put my ear to the door and listen to the agitated Junie and soothing Mona out front in the salon. Mona is cleaning Junie up. Junie is relating between hysterics the events of the last several hours in rather graphic detail. My worst fears are being confirmed.

"It was real bad this time. Real bad! Oh, Mona honey. What he made me do! We were having dinner. I made my ham-and-bean casserole, special, just the way he likes it, but he was in a mean mood when he got home and he started drinking bourbon, which is always a bad sign. I was trying to make conversation, snap him out of his glums, and I mentioned that a tourist lady, traveling all alone, had come in to have herself made over, and suddenly he was real interested, wanted to know all about Gretel. It was real weird. I mean, he's never interested in girl talk! I tried not to tell much, I don't *know* much, but I was worried for you. Then he gets up and he goes out to his car and brings in a newspaper photo of that psychologist from New York, the one that's sister got her head cut off, the one we always listened to on the radio? And he says, 'Is that her?' Oh my goodness! Mona, it was! It was Gretel! And I says, 'No! I never saw that woman before!' And he goes nuts. He made me strip bare and lie down on the cold brick steps out by the barbecue and he stood over me, smashing my momma's French teacups all around me. If I hadn't put my hands over my eyes, he'd a blinded me! And then, when I still wouldn't tell, he pulled down his pants and did it in my behind. Like the homos. It hurt so much I thought he'd split me in two, and so, finally, I told him the truth! I told him it was Gretel! But he was too drunk to go looking for her. He made himself some coffee and I just ran out and came here. You've got to warn her. He's gonna come! If he wasn't such a egomechanic, he'd've called his men to do it, but he wants to make the arrest himself. Get the glory. If she's still here, you've got to get her out, fast! He didn't ask about her car and I don't know what she was driving, thank God, cause I'd a told him. But he knows she looks different. I didn't say how. I swear I didn't! Oh, Mona! I hope I didn't do something bad for her! He was really torturing me and I cracked! I'm such a coward."

I am sobbing against the door. This woman, who has never seen me before, and whom I had barely acknowledged, has risked her life trying to protect me and she thinks she is a coward. I open the door and walk over to her. Mona has wiped the blood from her forehead and hands. I kneel in front of her and take her soft white hands in mine. "Don't you ever call yourself a coward. What you did is the bravest, kindest thing anyone has ever done for me. I will never ever forget it. Thank you." Mona pulls us apart. "Hey, let's chill out now. We've got a mess on our hands. Junie, you split. Fast! Get back there before butt-breath knows you're gone. I can handle him. If he comes near you again, you go to his own fucking jail and have them protect you. Don't let him know you were here. Go now."

Junie smiles at me and gives me the funny two-fingered wave. The fingers are now bruised and bandaged. "Take care, honey. Thanks for what you said. He'll have to kill me to get anything else outta me." She struts to the door, her head high. She has crossed a threshold of her own. My instinct is that he won't hurt her again. Bullies always know when the game has changed.

Before I can tell her not to endanger herself for my sake, Mona has pushed me out of the salon, shut the light, and is frantically rummaging in her cluttered dressing-table drawers. "I gotta connection in Santa Fe. You call this dude. He owes me. You just tell him Mona from Vegas. He's cool. You'll be safe with him. Here!" She pulls out a gold-embossed personal card, scribbles her telephone number, and jams it into my pocket. I am so totally terrified that I hardly know if I'm standing or lying in a screaming heap on the floor. My fantasy of the beery sheriff with the Smith & Wesson is coming closer to reality. Mona half-leads, half-pushes me outside to my car. Thank God, I'd had the sense to park it around the back. All those *Dirty Harry* movies finally paid off.

We are running in a half-crouch. "Mona, do me a huge favor. Will you call my father and tell him I'm okay? Don't tell him where you are or where I am. He's staying on the Island of Antigua at the home of a Pepe Pampas. It's listed. Call from a pay phone, collect. Okay?"

"You got it, babycakes. Now listen carefully. Don't go through town. Take the road right back there to your left. It goes all the way to the highway, but no one uses it. I'll take care of the sheriff. I know his action. When he gets outta here, he'll think he's the fucking King of Siam."

I slide in behind the wheel. "Mona, I . . ."

"Yeah, yeah. Me, too. We'll say it all next time. You smooth out now. Get your stuff together. You've got some mean shit ahead for a while. Now go . . . Go."

Mama-San starts right up and I ease out of the gravel drive with the lights off, leaving my new friend in darkness.

12

The Way Things Really Are . . . Or Are They?

***S**he drove all night, not daring to stop, her head pounding with exhaustion, trying to reach the border while her brave and beautiful friend submitted to vile unnatural acts forced on her pure virginal flesh by the sadistic drunken sheriff.*

I took back roads and I didn't stop except for gas and a double black coffee until I'd crossed the Wabash and slid into Mt. Vernon, Illinois, where I dragged my bleary body into the Oasis Motel run by an Indian (turbaned, not feathered) who quoted the rate—twenty-five dollars if you use one vibrating queen-size, thirty dollars if you used both. I collapsed in an overstressed puddle on the nearest bed, being careful not to touch the other one.

Dreamless sleep. I was actually ahead of schedule because I had driven straight for ten hours—I, who had never been able to manage a two-hour drive without an acute case of muscle spasm and claustrophobia. When I finally woke up, it was dark again. Good. The cover of darkness, so touted by maniacs and vampires, suited the new, no longer night-blind, Aroma just fine. I took a bath, soaking my aching but slenderized bones in a midget-sized fiberglass tub with a little soap machine that controlled the dose. I used *both* towels. He didn't mention an extra charge—so I just threw caution to the whatever. When I got out, and the steam had cleared from the mirror, I got my first long look at myself. Even I didn't recognize me.

I checked my maps and decided on Dodge City, where no doubt Kenny, Roy, Clint, and Tonto would have rented a suite and arranged for a rootin'-tootin' night among the cornstalks or whatever it is they have in Kansas.

Then, following the only lights burning, I found the nearest restaurant, which was, surprisingly, an American-Chinese establishment filled with an office party from the Mt. Vernon Auto Insurance Agency. Fine by me. While I waited for my Midwestern version of chicken chow mein and sweet and sour pork, I tried to pull my thoughts together.

I started a diagram on the paper place mat.

First question: Who would want Amora dead? Second question: Who would want me dead? Third question: Who would want both of us dead? Answer: *I haven't a Chinese clue.* What is the missing link? A fortune cookie with the correct answer? No. *A motive!* Aha. Okay. Let's start over. Who would have a motive for killing Aroma? Okay.

Besides me and Clive. Who would have a motive for killing me? Besides Daffy Duck or one of my former patients. Aha? Former patients. Which former patient? What kind of people listen to the radio? Duck cleavers? Radio patients. *Aha!* So, we would then have your paranoid schizophrenics, your psychopaths, your frothing, frolicking fringe. Well, at least it was a small, definable mass.

I went on this way through my entire cornstarched version of Sino cuisine and several wake-up gallons of green tea. On the tube this stuff looks a lot easier. What I needed was a motive and a clue. A clue. Well, that I had. Notes with a postmark. Phone calls to same postmark. Old home-town friend suddenly reappeared. Dental X ray hidden in a drawer. Jimmy Bob and his Chinese henchmen. Chinese cleaver? But the motive. Why would J.B. do it? Why would Sarah Jane?

My fortune cookie, which was accompanied by a stick of the twin's gum, Doublemint, of all ironic touches, said: *Wear life like a loose garment.* A shroud maybe? So much for outside help. I paid the check and peed out about half the intake of green tea and prepared to move on. When I reached into my coat pocket for my glasses, out fell Mona's gold-embossed, hastily passed card. *Sarno Stucci. Rancho Estrella. Santa Fe. 453-9999.*

I had a destination. Now all I need was a motive and a strong bladder.

I whizzed through Wichita, my head spinning with possible suspects. Frank Sinatra was crooning in my newly exposed ears. *I took a trip on a plane and thought about you . . .* I had stopped listening to the radio. Better not to know. In my head I saw the sheriff, still drooling with lust after his savage attack on Maid Mona, leading a posse of neo-fascist brain-damaged deputies in a wild madcap pursuit of the green Toyota. (Mona tried not to tell him, but that hot soup-tureen ladle in her privates was too much even for her.) I must stop thinking these thoughts.

I took a walk in the rain and thought about you . . . I thought about that. Had anyone ever taken a walk in the rain and thought about me? I doubted it. Leave it to ol' blue eyes to bring out the melancholy middle-aged mourning of the dying ember of *fatale* status. Tears rolled down my cheeks. Just once I wanted to be a woman whom Frank Sinatra thought about on the Continental shuttle to Newark.

That made me think about Reuben Mars. *That* made me think about Clifford. *That* brought me around to Jimmy Bob and Amora. Was he devastated? Was he falling into his sour mash in some honky-tonk dive and tinning the barkeep's ear? *Quarter to three, no one in the place, 'cept you and me* . . . Was he deranged with grief and doing a Charles Bronson, combing the city for her murderer? Was he secretly relieved to be out of the maelstrom and richer by half of the community property? Or was he . . .

This thinking brought me back to Mona. I saw myself at fifteen standing at Maxwell's Plum watching the handsome stranger approach. *You're mine,* he says. *Come with me.* Unbelievable. All of my life I had been afraid to do anything that wasn't acceptable behavior. I would no more have thought of running off and having my overripe cherry popped in the backseat of a strange man's car than of going to midnight mass in my underwear. But what if I had? What if all of us good, play-by-the-rules, try-to-be-a-nice-person, good-friend, and responsible-human-being girls, what if we all walked out of Maxwell's and went to Las Vegas? Stop hiding in the crowd, Aroma . . . what if *you* had? Easy. No one ever asked me. Thus no conflict. No regrets. But the possibility of just letting life lead; of acting on chance and impulse, not always trying to control the script . . . I envied that. Of course, one might well argue, cheekbones or no cheekbones, Mona's impulsive actions had not really led her to the daisy patch, now had they. True. But she was so *alive*. Her life was still all opened up. Not shut down with the confining pathways of child-rearing, house-running, career-building, pot-roasting. Anything could happen to her at any moment! And she would not be afraid to follow the piper. Hop the Orient Express, jog the Road to Zanzibar.

Somehow this was all tied up with romance. Not real romance, because that was never the same, but young girls' yearnings for romance, for that time before any of it was real. The time before cherries and pimples popped and hopes were torn by reality. Before courses were chosen and commitments made, when life was just an endless horizon, spreading before us as far as the soul could see. Anything. Anything might happen. Nothing had been tried. A magnificent luscious candy box with not a bite taken. No half-eaten mistake sneaked back into the corner, no nougat posing as caramel. Romance.

I was really getting into this thought game, miles whizzing past effortlessly, when my tire blew. Luckily, reverie had slowed me down, and by some miracle I was able to get over to the side of the road without splattering like a little green splotch against the side of one of those warriors of commerce that terrorize the highways in the wee hours.

I skidded to a halt. Whew. That was the *good* news.

Then the bad news hit. I was alone on the road to Dodge City in the middle of nowhere in the middle of the night and being stalked by the police. I also had absolutely no idea how to change a tire or even if there was a tire to change. Please, God, if you get me out of this, I will never whiz past a stalled motorist without stopping to help ever again.

I take a deep breath and open my door. I get out, leaving my turn indicator flashing and the lights on. I inspect the damage. The front right tire is shot. Shit! It is really dark. It is really quiet. I am really scared.

I hear something from down below, down in the dark off the road. Footsteps. A coyote or a madman? I start to run back around to the car when an arm shoots out and grabs me. A relatively young man with a shiny bald head and full camouflage attire stands grinning at me in the moonlight. My throat closes. I feel as if someone is pouring sand down it.

Terrifying stranger: "Hey, lady. Don't be scared. I'm here to help. Got a flat? Wow, it's a bitch, too. Trunk open?"

I nod.

Terrifying Stranger: "Man, you should see your face. You look like you seen a ghost. I ain't going to hurt you. I'm a vet. Name's Art."

Me: "Hello, Art." My lips are still trembling. I am thinking about the gun in the purse on the floor of the backseat. Art's eyes have a glazed watery look. I think of my internship and of all the seemingly sweet and helpful Arts who smiled when relating the disembowelment of favorite aunts and family cats.

Art has flung open the trunk and pulled out a spare tire and hidden portable jack and is whistling as he raises Mama-San for her surgery. I place myself in a good getaway position and decide to humor him, since, even if he plans to grind me into fettucini after he's through, the guy is *really* fixing my goddamn tire. Somehow I find my voice.

Me: "Where did you come from?"

Still-Terrifying Art: "I come with the night. I'm the Highway Helper. You ever heard of me?"

Me: "Well, I'm from out of town. Are you related to the Hamburger Helper?"

Terrifying Art finds this mirthful and laughs loudly: "That's funny! You're a funny lady! Hamburger Helper. Ha! I'm gonna use that. No, ma'm. No relation. I'm sort of like Zorro, I guess. I just travel the roads helping people in distress. It's my karma. It's an after-Nam thing."

Ah. A Vietnam vet. One of the guys who, for some self-indulgent and infantile reason, was not able to go from napalmed babies to a career in computer software. I manage to take a breath. In my new life-style, he seems okay. Certainly not okay for old Aroma, but probably an ideal traveling companion for outlaw Aroma.

Me: "Have you been living this way for a long time?"

Less-Terrifying Art: "Few years. I was a Green Beret. Special forces. Air ranger. Career soldier. Know what air rangers do? Well, they drop into the mountains and they try to find the enemy's position and pinpoint it for the pilots, so they can blow the suckers away. But the Cong, those little bastards, were smart; they fanned out in cloverleaf patterns. They were everywhere. So it was real easy in the jungle to make a mistake. If we did, you know what happened? Our pilots dropped the goodies on *us*. We got blown up by our own artillery.

"A whole lot of us did, too, but they don't call it that in the reports back home. No way, José. No way. You make a mistake up there, you're history. Nothing can scare me after Nam, nothing and no one. I came home, did all the jerky shit all the guys did. Lost all the losses. Job, wife. Self-respect. But I didn't want to end up like all those other guys living in the wilds, hating the world, pretending they're Rambo. I love people. I love every little smelly one of 'em! I wanted to make up for all the death, all the suffering; do my little part. The thing is, nobody helps nobody no more.

"So one night, 'bout four years ago, I was in my jeep heading home and this Indian woman runs out into the road, flagging cars, and of course no one stops, so I stop. And her mother is in the back of her pickup and she's having a heart attack. I resuscitated her. Got them to a hospital and man, I felt so good afterward! I felt like, reborn. So I started driving around looking for people to help. *Kansas City Star* did a big story on me, even the *LA Times*. Some people from Hollywood are coming around, want to do a movie for TV on my life. Ha! Pretty wild, huh? So far, no one's done a negative trip on me. People get freaked at first, when they see me, like you did; wow, you should have seen yourself! I don't think anyone was ever that freaked before. Part of the problem is my head, some virus I picked up over there, all my goddamn hair fell out. The medics say they don't know why and they don't know if it'll ever come back. So I look pretty weird, I guess. Once folks get over that, they love me. I'm a pussycat!"

My pussycat has deftly thrown off the old tire and is wrenching the screws or plugs, or whatever they are called, into place. He stops suddenly, grabbing at his back.

Me calm now and concerned: "Are you okay?"

Art the pussycat: "Yeah. It's my back. I have a lot of trouble with it."

Me, understanding: "Oh boy, I know how that is. My husband had sciatica and he could hardly move for a week!"

Art, sweetly cracking Clifford's Nordic nuts: "I took one in the spine at Cam Lok."

So much for Ben Gay therapy.

We chat on. I have now let down at least half of my defenses, which is more than I usually let down with anyone, anyway. This man touches me, he makes me want to cry. He makes me want to give him a big flour-dusting hug and let *him* cry. I am growing fond of this guy. I stand there as he tells tales of people he has met as the Highway Helper, thinking about what he would look like with hair and a gray mohair suit (always a dangerous sign).

Over my shoulder I see a highway patrol car slowing down, and turning on the big lights. The stop-or-I'll-shoot lights. I must have gotten that look back on my face because Art jumps up remarkably fast for a man with a bullet wound in his spine.

"Are you okay?"

"I, no. The police are there. The police! I can't talk to them, I . . . oh my . . . Oh God, I! I—"

Art puts his arm around me. "It's okay. Don't be afraid. I know all these guys. You just wait here. Don't say anything. If they come over, I'll do the talking. You just look pretty and smile."

I nod. The patrol moves toward us, slowly. Art walks toward them, waving his arms overhead like the chopper guys on the ground always do in war movies. He doesn't even know my name, I think. If they ask for my registration, I'm a goner, I think. He thinks I'm pretty, I think. Then I stop, because I am too scared to think.

Art stands talking to the police for several minutes. I close my eyes. I hear laughter. Good sign. I hear a door open. Bad sign. I hear footsteps. I hear a motor. I open my eyes. Art is beside me, grinning like a marine version of Humpty Dumpty. "It's over. No sweat. Wanna grab some chow?"

Art retrieves his jeep from the access road below and I follow him to a trucker's café, where we settle in with cold beer and hot plates covered with enormous greasy animal bones smothered in barbecue sauce. I make a promise to myself that I will play the Greta Garbo role if it kills me. I will maintain an air of mystery and not reveal anything personal. This oath lasts, as usual, as long as the first plate of ribs and second pitcher of beer. I have never been able to keep my mouth shut at any kind of table on which food is served. Besides, I trust this guy. The same way I trust Mona. Maybe he'd like Mona. Maybe I should call Mona and have her meet us? Maybe I should just shut up and get back on the road.

Art listens intently, his high-domed bald head shining in the reflected light from the bar/pool hall at the rear of the restaurant.

People on the outside of the American Dream, those who have not signed up for muppie, yuppie, or even guppie status, they are not alarmed by my sordid tale. They have seen life from the obtuse angle of the disenfranchised. These are the people who leak. The faucet may get turned off, but the dripping goes on forever. They have seen one bad thing too many. Lost one too many battles; fought one too many fights, spent too many nights face to face with the rabid demons. These people wear their pain, their vulnerability, on the outside. No matter how well dressed or camouflaged they become, they leak. People on the inside can sniff it, wiping the drops off their Ralph Lauren polos in fear and discomfort. Once you leak, the hurt and loss inside drips from your rusty plumbing; you never belong to the American Lie again.

I am dubiously lucky, I think. I have not started dripping yet. I am still part of the "in" crowd of regular folks; I can pass, like the Pod People; my pain, my wounds still waterproof, smug in my conviction that nobody can tell what's inside; what the prices have been.

It is very late. I am suddenly exhausted and I have had too much emotion, animal fat, and suds. I feel dizzy and nauseous.

"What's up? You look a little pale. Are you okay?" My leaking stranger touches my hand. Tears pop out of my tired eyes and smack against my chin. Thoughtfulness always wrecks me.

"I just need some fresh air. I'll be all right."

Art is up in a second, has thrown money on the table, and half-carries me out into the starry cool middle-American night.

I take several deep breaths. I do feel better. We walk to my car, carefully parked out of sight behind a large oak tree.

"Where are you going to sleep?" Art helps me in and stands leaning over me.

"I don't know. A motel, I guess. There must be one in the next town."

His glowing egghead shakes back and forth. "Nope, nothing until Dodge City now. Move over. You're coming home with me."

I already know how this one is going to end, but I pretend that I have no idea at all. I move over and Art slides in.

We drive for several miles up a long dirt road to a large modern house set back on a hill. Three fierce-looking but very friendly German shepherds race to greet us. Art helps me out and leads me up the brick steps to the wood-and-glass front door. This is not what I had expected. I had expected a trailer with dirty sheets.

Inside, the house is filled with art. Art's art, Oriental rugs, a large stone fireplace, large modern leather couches, and handmade wood tables (also Art's work). So much for snap value judgments.

Art is watching me, grinning widely. He knows the whole thing. "I had a buddy in Nam. He died. He had an inheritance. He had written a will saying that if anything happened to him, he wanted me to have it. I got it. Not bad, huh? Not what you expected, either, I bet?"

I blush. I am ashamed of myself. "Not exactly."

We stand looking at one another. It is so obvious what is about to happen that we both laugh. Nothing like this has ever happened to me before. I have never been swept away by the moment. Even sex has always been thought out in a responsible manner. Birth control prepared. Perfume applied to all erogenous zones. Legs shaved. Teeth brushed. Makeup removed if possible to avoid extra time in the morning. *Oh boy.*

The house is lit only by the night light of moon and stars. Art takes my hand and leads me over to a great big brown leather couch. He pulls me down beside him and then he kisses me.

I have not been kissed by any man but Clifford in many, many years. I feel this strange man's mouth, his lips, his tongue. I start to pull back, running through my tape deck of fears: AIDS, herpes, chlamydia. I don't even know how you get chlamydia. I think of all my stern, motherly antiseptic conversations with Vivika. Then I feel his hands on me. So strong. So sweet. So free of any past, any hurt and responsibility, and I relax into this kiss of a lifetime. I feel as if I am raining from the inside out. As if some swollen cloud of moisture has burst inside me and is flooding my whole body.

He is leaking and I am raining, I think, and laugh into my kiss. Oh my, what a kiss. He undresses me with such forceful tenderness that I truly feel as if I have never been touched before. This is not a little boy making love, this is an *Air Ranger*. His body is foreign, its smell, its shape, like some exotic rare animal. I run my hands down his flesh-covered skull, down past the knotted wound on his spine, and hold his buttocks in my hands, pulling him to me as I come for the first time before he has even touched an erogenous zone; I am raining, rain falling in puddles and torrents over and over through the night. Forget Frank Sinatra and the plane ride, I think, before I fall into sleep with this strange bald man in my arms.

13

Never Say Good-bye

I stayed with Art for three days. I even went out with him one night as the Highway Helper's Helperette. The highlight of the evening was the delivery of a baby girl in the backseat of Art's jeep. I have never in my life felt so high. Or so useful. Fantasies of the two of us, as the Batman and Robin of the Plains states, flop in and out of my head. Mostly we just talked and fucked. Oh my, did we. If I had known about the true depth of the therapeutic value of a really great lover, I could have saved countless patients countless dollars. I was beginning to sound to myself like an eroticized Archie Bunker. *Forget that depres-*

sion shit, all you need, kiddo, is a really good screw! Well, maybe it was just a toy boat on the rapids, but it sure felt like healing. My face had a softness, a serenity that it never had before. Mother Teresa got it her way, I got it mine.

I also got to talk to Pop and the kids. The first time I called, Clive answered the phone.

"Clive, sweetheart, it's me! How are you? Oh God, I miss you all so much!"

Clive is quiet. I can hear him breathing into the receiver.

"Clive? Honey. It's me. Aro. Say something!"

"I need proof. This could be a trick to find out where we are."

The kid is clever. No doubt about it.

"Clive, honey, I called *you*. I must *know* where you are."

"Not necessarily. You could have found this number in my aunt's purse or she could have told you under torture or truth serum. I need proof."

"Okay. Okay. Good thinking, pal. Very smart. I'll describe the contents of your bedroom."

"No. You could have broken in and seen it. No chance."

"Okay. How about some secret thing just between us."

"Let's have it."

"Chicken à la Clive served by candlelight on silver plates."

"Auntie! Wow! It is you. I was good, wasn't I? I keep telling Vivika that the killer will try anything to find us! She's going to blow it if she doesn't listen to me. You better tell her! Where are you? No! Don't tell me! I don't want to know anything they could make me say under torture. Don't even give me a hint. Are you okay? We've been so worried. Poor Gramps has been too nervous to go swimming or anything. He just runs around Pepe's house fixing the plumbing and stuff. Have you been listening to the news? They thought they'd found a guy who was writing the lavender notes, but he was just one of those confession psychos. We're all sort of famous now. I get the news on Pepe's shortwave receiver. They described me as a 'brilliant young student at a prestigious Manhattan private school'! Vivika was really hot, because all they said about her was 'the sixteen-year-old stepdaughter of noted art historian Clifford Jergens'! She at least wanted a line like 'attractive stepdaughter.' Are you all right?"

"I'm just fine, sweetheart. I don't want any of you to worry about me. I'm in good shape and I'm safe and sound."

"Are you . . . alone?"

"Well, right now I'm with a . . . friend. People have been very kind to me."

"A male or female friend?"

"I thought we agreed, no questions. Honey, run and get Gramps and Vivika, I can't talk long, just in case. I miss you so, and I love you very much."

"Me, too, Aro. Please come get us soon! It's great here and all, but I want to go home with you."

"I know, pal. Soon, I hope. You just hang in there."

Pop and Vivika get on together. Pop gives me a rapid-fire report on every theory he, Pepe, the police, and the *Daily News* have on the killing, and Vivika just keeps repeating over and over, "Oh my God. I don't believe this is really happening! Oh my God!"

"I put you in the Lord's hands, Madonna mia. I been to mass more in the last month than in my entire life! Let your old man help! Tell me what to do! In the old country, I would be the outlaw. I would find the *fugitivo* who destroyed my family!"

"Mom, be careful. *Paleese!* You're such a baby. You

don't know *anything* about being on your own like that! There are so many gross-outs on the road. Remember when Kathi St. John ran away and she hitchhiked to her cousin's house in Florida? You would not *believe* the stories she told me! Maybe you should come here. No one's found us. It's great here. You should see my tan. Unbelievable. We miss you so much!"

"I know, baby. I wish I could be there. Just trust me a little bit longer. I need to do what I'm doing. I'll be fine."

"No hitchhikers, Mom. Swear to God, no hitchhikers!"

I glance up at Art, who is taking it all in and smiling at me. You couldn't really call Art a hitchhiker.

"No hitchhikers. I promise. Pop, if I need you, I'll call." I know he wants to help. "Hey, Pop, listen. I'm looking for a link, some clue. Maybe you could try to find some letters or stuff from Sarah Jane to Amora, or anything that rings a bell."

"I can do better than that. I brought all your old junk with me. Didn't want to leave it in case the reporters came snooping around. I got your scrapbooks, love letters, the works."

"That's fantastic! Start going through it and I'll try to call back tomorrow." "*Va bene,* Madonna. It's done."

"Oh, Pop. One thing. There are a bunch of letters from a boy named Lee Cohen. Don't read those, okay?"

"Can I read them, Mom?"

"*No!* I want blood oaths!"

"Okay. Okay!"

"I'll call again tomorrow. Love you all. 'Bye."

"Lee Cohen?" Art laughs and crosses to me, unbuckling his Army belt.

"Lee Cohen was the world's best kisser before you. Don't be saying things about old Lee."

Art comes around behind me and rubs my shoulders, letting his huge hands wander down toward my already responding breasts.

"He had freckles all over his face. Even on his eyelids."

"You know what we used to say in the Rangers about guys with freckles?"

"No? What?" I say, closing my eyes and leaning back into his lengthening penis.

"I'll tell you later."

And then there we were on the morning of my fourth day, Bottom the Weaver and the deluded Fairy Queen, trying to unravel from the power of an intimacy that may be possible only between two strangers who have not known one another long enough or risked enough for their defenses to cement. Art wanted to drive me on to Sante Fe. I wanted him to, too. But somehow, that newly functioning inner guide said no. So I said no.

"I'll call you when I get there," I said.

"No, you won't," he said. "The minute you get back into your own trip, you'll re-form what happened here. It's too far away from your world. You need your structure. You need a guy with a suit and a real job."

"No. Not anymore."

"More than ever, sweet lady. We had something really special. If this is all it's about, it's okay. If you ever come back, that'd be great. But you won't, and that's okay, too. Don't go off and do a whole heavy guilt trip about it. Let it be a rim shot. A real glowing memory."

"I don't know what to say. I always know what to say! I've never . . . this has been so wonderful. You are so wonderful. Maybe you're right about me. I'm certainly not in shape for life-changing decisions. But if you ever need anything, ever, I want you to know I'd be there for you."

"I know that. It's okay. The same here. You got enough money and stuff?" I nod, tears dropping all over my face.

"Listen. One idea. Just food for thought. Something doesn't hang together in this whole bazooka.

"In 'Nam I learned that whenever there's an act, there's a strategy, there's a goal. A game plan, so to speak. This was no impulsive violence. But there's no game plan. Find the game plan and you've got the killer. Even psychos, maybe especially psychos, have a game plan. This thing has all the balls in the air. Something's not karmic about it. Open your mind to the wildest possibility. I think you know who did this. I feel it in you, an answer trying to reach consciousness. Surrender to your unconscious. Don't try to be logical. Go *weird* with it."

"If I got much weirder, I'd go under with it."

"No way, Aroma. You are about as weird as an open window. Fear not."

I want so badly to give this man a gift. I get one thought. One weird thought. I take out a piece of paper and write Mona's phone number on it. "Art, I want you to call someone. My other friend from the road. Her name is Mona. I'm getting this strange wave of insight. If you're right about me, then you two may be made for one another. I couldn't think of two people I would more like to see happy. Promise me you'll do it?"

"You're a very wild woman, you know that?"

"That's a great compliment. I'll press that one in my scrapbook."

"I'll call her. You be careful."

"I'm always careful."

On this poignant exit line, I turn to walk valiantly down the steps to my car and trip, falling very carefully on my ass. I can only hope this is not an omen.

"Go weird with it," he had said. I'd try. Zooming along the highways, I was a different woman than I was a week ago, having crossed all kinds of dividing lines in my rigid pattern of rights and wrongs. An adulteress who dyes her hair. What next? All kinds of thoughts race across my opening mind.

Reuben Mars. Santa Fe.

I tried to go deeper into Santa Fe. Amora had lived there for about four years. As far as I knew, her second husband, John P. Harrington, Dr. Pompous Egomaniacal Tightass, still practiced there. Maybe the phone calls Amora made from Pop's house were to him? That one was easy enough. I'd check it out as soon as I got there. Maybe he was involved?

Anything else about Santa Fe? This was hard. Santa Fe happened during one of our down times. I never even went out for Amora's wedding. I didn't remember ever getting a letter from her. Then I thought of something. I pull the Toyota over to the side of the road and take the yearbook out of my overnight bag. I find the pictures of Sarah Jane. In the background of one, lying by a pool, is another woman. A slender brunette with long straight hair and angular, sort of Angelica Huston, features. She is smiling and holding a bottle of Lone Star beer in her hand. A southwestern beer. Something is familiar about her. I have seen her before. A name is making a violent attempt to form in my memory bank. Something with an L. Someone Amora knew in Santa Fe. The one or two times I talked to her during that time she had mentioned a friend, someone fancy—Amora was impressed. Someone who had introduced her to Dr. Hocus-Pocus. Could that be her? I leaf through the yearbook very carefully. Nothing. I pick up my overnight bag and turn it upside down. A small Polaroid falls out. It is a wedding picture of Amora, the good doctor, the dark-haired L-woman—and Sarah Jane Milano. So they were all in Santa Fe together. Another clue. Could a motive be far behind?

Yes.

I stopped for the night in Conlen, Texas. I lay on my motel bed, missing Art's shiny warmth, feeling sophisticated and mature and trying to remember anything from those lost years when my sister and I had split like a frazzled end, a cell dividing and stalking off, trying with all our might to pretend that we were singular. Images from the past floated across my buzzing brain.

I was up before dawn. I felt new energy. Compulsion. The old Santa Fe Trail was beckoning me onward. The road before me opened wide. I slid Willie into the slot and took off, trying to let my mind weird all the way out into the truth and into my future.

14

Georgia O'Keefe Wasn't Kidding

I hit Taos, New Mexico, on the heels of a true Indian summer thunderstorm. The air smells of wet mud and juniper, the thunder is bashing into the mountains and lighting the sky with colors from *National Geographic*, from old John Ford Westerns and cigar-store Indians. Names like siena, violet, amber, pop into my head from art class memories.

This is not New York City. This is someplace else.

I find the main plaza in Taos, which at a brisk pace a very old arthritic could circumnavigate in about ten minutes. It is so quiet that it is hard to accept that this is the fabled Taos. Retreat of Dennis Hopper and various famous and notorious dropouts of the seventies. Legendary home of Kit Carson.

I decided to spend the night, not only because I am completely exhausted, but because I am having an attack of fairly paralyzing anxiety about entering Santa Fe.

There is one hotel in town, a very pleasant sort of movie version of an hacienda, with a fireplace in every room and a heated pool.

I register as Marvella Baron, Newport, Rhode Island, and head for the pool. The rain has stopped but the air is heavy and damp. The water is warm and the color of lapis. Ponderosa pines surround me. I swim like a swan, a fish, a duck. Floating, gliding, building my courage for the task ahead.

It is dark when I return to my room. I take a long hot shower, a great deep breath, and pick up the phone.

A raw, husky voice answers. "Rancho Estrella."

"Hello. Is Mr. Stucci in?"

"Who is this calling?"

"This is a friend of Mona's, from Vegas. If you tell him that, I'm sure he'll want to speak with me."

I am not making the Voice happy. "Wait a minute."

My pulse is throbbing and I can hardly breathe. Somehow that little card had given me a sense of purpose; a destination, a form to my quest. I have not even considered what happens if he won't talk to me.

"Hello. This is Sarno Stucci."

"Oh. Hello. Thank you so much for speaking with me. I'm a very good friend of Mona's and I'm in Taos, and she said that I should call you; that you might be able to . . . that maybe I might be able to . . . that . . ."

"You a friend of Mona's, you do not need to explain.

You come to my home. You are my guest for as long as you like. Shall I send someone to get you?"

(*Never* underestimate the power of a cheekbone.) "Oh no. Thank you. That's very kind of you. I have a car and I could be there late tomorrow, if that's convenient?"

"As you wish. Just follow the main road to Santa Fe. On the road that leads to the Girard Museum take a left at the end and keep going. You'll see a sign."

"Oh, thank you so much. I should be there about five o'clock."

"Until then."

Sound of woman heaving sigh of relief. I get dressed and decide to take a stroll around the plaza before dinner. There is no one in sight, but the feeling that someone is following me is stronger than ever. Every few minutes a run-down pickup with an assortment of Indian children and elders with unsmiling faces zooms through. In every pickup there's also a skinny mean-looking dog. I feel a heaviness in my heart, like the heaviness in the air. Maybe it's the altitude. There is a sense of despair in this mountain paradise.

An Indian man dressed in hip huggers and a porkpie hat is putting away a large mat filled with turquoise jewelry and kachina dolls. I stop to look. Someone comes up behind me and taps my shoulder. I jump about ten feet.

"Hey, lady, come here." A young Indian boy takes my arm and pulls me away from the guy in the out-of-style jeans. "You wanna buy kachina, don't buy from that bandit. Buy from the crazy Arab down at the Shell Station. Don't trust those Zunis. They're all bad news. I'm Hopi, with a little Irish mixed in. You can trust a Hopi. Now, if you looking for something special, I got something you won't find on any reservation or in any of them fancy crafts places in Santa Fe or Albuquerque. Wanna see? Got it right here in my truck. It's Navajo. Made by a young artist. Illegal. Big trouble if he get caught doing this."

"Okay," says the new Aroma, road warrior and fearless adventurer.

The feisty brave practically leaps with glee into the back of his truck, which is empty except for the ubiquitous pup and a few small boxes. He pulls out a medium-sized crate and begins gently unloading a dazzling array of intricately fashioned and decorated figures. They are so simple and so beautiful, so filled with light and color that I am spellbound.

"They're beautiful."

"You better believe it. These are Yei Bei Chei Fox dancers. Navajo religous objects. Very sacred. See, the chief, he has the feathers in his band. Then comes the braves, the dancers. The clown, he's like the medicine man. He's got the purple shirt. He stands behind. Then the women. You know about the Fox dancers?"

"No. I'm from New York. I know about break dancers."

"What tribe?"

"Hundred-and-Forty-first Street."

"You're putting me on, right?"

"Right. Tell me about the Fox dancers."

"They dance in January. On the coldest night. In honor of the Coyote. See, the legend says that the Coyote stole fire from the Fire God to warm the people of the earth. He bewitched the Fire God and stole his fire. So the Navajos believe that if the Coyote could bewitch the Fire God, he could sure bewitch them. So they dance to honor him, to keep peace with him."

"Sounds practical. Does it work?"

"Hey, lady, it's a legend. I'm no expert. You wanna buy them?"

"How much are they?"

"Well, I'll tell you. I was taking them to this guy in Santa Fe. He has a fancy gallery. He's real hot for them. But if you want them, I don't have to drive all the way down there, so I'll do a deal. See, the artist is hard up right now. And these kind of things can't be sold legal; against the tribal laws, so I'll give them to you cheap. Two hundred dollars."

"A hundred twenty-five."

"Hundred seventy-five."

"Hundred fifty—final."

"Okay. Man, you got some Indian blood in you. Right, lady?"

"A little farther east."

I have never been happier with anything I ever bought in my entire life. I carry the box back to my room, place it carefully on my bed, and head for the restaurant, knowing that after dinner it will be waiting for me to open and extract my mystical playthings. I also like the concept. Hedging your bets, Navajo style.

The restaurant is quiet. A blonde hostess who, if she were not a mountain ski bunny would most likely be an ocean beach bunny, fixes me with a glazed, toothy smile and leads me to a table for two. When I tell her I will be dining alone, a slight loosening of the smile is noted. I have just changed category, gone from pampered matron to lonely weirdo in one single sentence.

This is my first decent meal since leaving Pop's. I decide to savor it. The waiter, a male version of the ski bunny, brings me a glass of white wine. I'm in no hurry. I relax and check out my fellow diners.

An old woman who appears to have no teeth is polishing off what seems to be a double martini. She is intently reading a book while she stuffs some kind of meat into her mouth. Is that what the bunny thinks my future will be? I shudder. The woman raises her hand and motions to her waitress, a sweet-looking dark-haired version of the hostess.

"Yes, ma'm, what can I bring you?"

The old woman sits up board-straight. "I don't want you to bring me anything. I simply want to explain something to you, not a criticism, but for your own edification and for the good of the restaurant."

The dark bunny's smile freezes into the beginning of a grimace.

"Do you see this lovely glass of water on my table?"

"Yes, ma'm."

"That is Taos mountain water. The finest public drinking water of any city in the country, with the possible exception of my home, Boston.

"I am not going to touch it! I did not request it. It is being wasted. In the middle of a drought, you have wasted a delicious life-saving glass of water. Do you see my point?"

"Yes, ma'm. Really sorry about that. Would you like me to take it away?"

"Yes. But for God's sake, promise that you will make good use of it. Water a precious plant with it. Or drink it yourself. I did not so much as touch the glass."

"Yes, ma'm. I'll drink it on my break."

The woman looks up and catches my eye. I do not want my eye caught. I do not want to engage in conversation with a drunken toothless water fetishist from New England. I look away. At the bar, I see another woman alone. This one is younger, an Afro-curly blonde and also very drunk. She is singing along with the tape deck and puffing smoke rings from a pink cigarette. She is drinking straight tequila with beer chasers. Tequila at seven thousand feet seems a bit risky. Three women alone in one dining room in a tiny mountain resort. Two drunk and one considering it. What can it mean?

I look at my menu. A group of oldsters in natty Eastern preppy attire enter and are seated by the ski bunny, who could be one of their grandchildren. They order Manhattans (which the bartender, it is soon reported, has never heard of). Lengthy descriptions are made. They are from Massachusetts (maybe the water lady from Boston will join them?). A table full of Norman Rockwell cutouts discoursing about Marblehead and sailboats, health problems and hearing-aid advances.

I feel sad. People like the Marbleheaders always make me feel sad. People with names like Bitsy, Buffie, Woozy, Pebble, Apple. People with inherited summer houses and "Episcopalian" written in the Religious Affiliation blanks. The Right People. People who have never knowingly spoken to a Jew or an Italian. People whose lives come with an unconditional guarantee that if you follow the path, you'll know what to do. Even though I know better. Even though I have treated many of their casualties. I still buy it for the first three minutes. They belong here. They actually look good in topsiders and Peter Pan collars. They give spine to the country. They vertebrate the Northeast. They create the Dun & Bradstreet of social paranoia and unknowingly wreck the lives of endless aspirers without ever noticing the guy standing behind the number 4 iron as they drop another perfect putt, lob a doozy over the clean white net. In their world, where William F. Buckley is a great guy and values seem made up by the L.L. Bean catalogue, people like me do not exist.

That makes me mad. That makes me feel guilty. I do not want to envy such people. I do not want to be mad at such people. I want to enjoy William F. Buckley. *Oh, that Buckley; he's at it again. Har-har.*

My bunno, bunnum (possibly Latin for male bunny) appears. "How is the trout?" I inquire.

"Real good. Real nouvelle cuisine," he says.

I order it, wishing there were someone there to appreciate that line. I think about ordering another glass of wine, but decide against it. I must set an example of proper conduct for women alone; one of the three of us should be able to walk out of the dining room in a dignified manner.

Two dress extras from one of Clint's old movies enter, playing the cool mountain cowboy parts to perfection. They take off their Stetsons, hang their sheepskin jackets on the coat rack, and slide onto the nearest barstools as if easing their hard tan bodies onto twin Appaloosas. They check out the swaying blonde. The swaying blonde checks them out. I fight the urge to remove her bodily from an evening for which one just knows she will be really sorry in the morning.

It takes them all about thirty-two seconds to hop along the beige leather Appaloosas to join forces. My trout comes, looking very nouvelle indeed. I decide to throw caution to the wind and order another glass of wine. I feel as if I've entered a combo *Separate Tables* and *Ship of Fools*.

I try to stop eavesdropping and think about what Art called the *game plan*. The missing motive. The *what if*.

The blonde and the Clintlets look over at me and then chuckle among themselves. That hurts my feelings.

The old water lady staggers out and a group of what Vivika would call "herbals" swaggers in. Two couples. All wearing the look of smug complacency often seen on the faces of big-city dropouts who have found *where it's really at*. People who have done the urban scene and split to become better persons in one of the paradise places. They have the look. New York Jewish girls dressed as Indian squaws. The husbands in the perfect faded jeans and denim jackets, but everything just a teensy bit too pressed. Lots of silver jewelry and ethnic woven *chazzerai,* as Aunt Minnie would say. They all look a little weeded out.

They make me depressed. I am certainly an emotional sitting duck this evening. Maybe it's the altitude. Everyone's getting to me. I always, however, feel this kind of downness in the paradise places, places that New Yorkers on bad days fantasize about dropping out to. La Jolla, Palm Beach, San Francisco, Malibu, Aspen. Places that exist without the energy of gritty reality, where the mailman will often mistake left for right and no one can give you directions farther than a two-block radius. Places where there is no reason for caring about stuff like that, where old reactionaries go to play golf under the shadow of Bing Crosby's ghost.

Taos is one of those. If heaven is like this, I may reconsider my options. I go brain-dead in paradise places, in towns like Carmel. The Carmeling of America. Too much cute. Too much white bread. Clogs the ducts. Clogs the colon. Brings me down.

The cowboys are looking over my way again. The blonde starts to lower herself from her stool and falls backward, her arms flailing wildly.

"Help her!" a shout somehow bursts forth from my trout-greased lips.

Cowpoke number two (an obvious shmuck of repute) slowly, and not very energetically, stops her fall with one overdeveloped arm.

I am now visible. I choose not to enter into any adventure for which I might hate myself in the morning. I pay the check and, with ramrod dignity, return to my room and my waiting treasure.

When I reach for the box on the bed, the gallery address where my young Indian *gonif* was heading with my Fox dancers gets me right in between my tired eyes. Reuben Mars Gallery. And some people scoff at the small-world theory. I lie on the bed and meditate for the first time in months. I feel as if I am being pulled down some cosmic dumbwaiter.

I take a long bath, shave my legs, pluck my newly shaped brows, polish my nails, and, loath though I am to admit it, partake of a lavender-scented douche preparation, giving my rusting IUD something to sing about. I take no conscious responsibility for these all-too-familiar rituals.

I get into my clean-sheeted wood-posted bed and for the first time in a week find the courage to tune in the eleven-o'clock news. All of it is bad, but I am not on it. A six-year-old girl on Long Island has hanged herself, becoming the youngest suicide on record (a claim just aching to be beaten); one or another Palestinian terrorist group has blown a hole in a wide-body airplane, sucking four people out into the wide blue. One minute you're sipping a Bloody Mary and scanning *People* magazine, and the next you're doing a half-gainer from fifteen thousand feet. Go know. The Russians have produced a documentary that follows a homeless man around Manhattan while he explains the way it is for the rich and the poor. New York comes off looking (to the feigned shock of the reporters and the city officials) like a glorified Gomorrah. New York *is* a glorified Gomorrah. If I were a Russian watching it, I would pay up my next twenty years' dues in the party and turn in my Hong Kong Jordaches for a loaf of day-old pumpernickel. In fact, I may do it anyway. Clive must be missing all of this, I think, drifting off into dreamland.

Dreamland. I am in a huge tepee with Art, Clifford, Reuben Mars, and Pop. I am naked except for a large red feather that barely covers my centerfold stuff. Art is gently caressing my face. Pop is in the corner cooking spaghetti, or maybe it's fettucine. Clifford is masturbating with one hand and holding a copy of *The Moon and Sixpence* in the other. Reuben is crawling up between my legs with a large jar of Vaseline. The tepee opens and the Clintlets storm in, with the blonde trotting behind. "Outta the way," they shout at poor Reuben, who crawls over to Pop, clutching his Vaseline to his chest. "I need olive oil, you putz!" Pop shouts, stirring madly. "Get that crap outta my kitchen!"

The blonde staggers forward, falling onto Clifford's erection. The Clintlets proceed to ravish me; one covering the mammary and mouth areas, the other concentrating on the birth canal. The blonde is making funny little whooping sounds. Clifford is now holding his book in two hands but is otherwise unreactive. I am crazed with lust and shame. "Art, save me." I moan (not really wanting him to—but trying to make a good impression in front of my father and Reuben). Art has disappeared. Suddenly the tepee opens again and Art reappears with a machine gun. He blasts away at the Clintlets, who roll off me and out of the dream. This would be fine, except that I haven't come yet. I lie quivering, waiting for Art to finish the dirty deed. "Gotta blowout at the reservation," he apologizes and runs off into the night. The blonde is still bouncing away on Clifford, so I can't ask him. I look around for Reuben. I am desperate with sexual frustration. I even consider asking Pop, but that would really screw up the pasta.

"Reuben, Reuben," I whisper, writhing in ecstasy. Reuben crawls back, still clutching the Vaseline. "Let's do it. I'm not afraid anymore. I'm not a virgin anymore," I pant.

"Then I don't want you," says the swine.

The tepee opens again. This time it's Lieutenant Mallony. "I knew you were here!" he says and whips out a pair of handcuffs.

"Please!" I gasp. "Before you take me in, please would you finish me off?"

"Glad to oblige," he grunts and unfurls the longest, reddest tongue I have ever seen.

"But there's no game plan," I sigh, swooning before the lucious licker.

"It's the wrong head," Mallony rasps and more than makes up for the inconvenience.

"Dinner's ready!" Pop shouts as I sink deeper and deeper.

When I wake up, I realize that it is possible to feel guilt and regret for what one did last night, even if one was home alone and fell asleep over the eleven-o'clock news. The poor blonde has nothing on me this morning, I think, as I load Mama-San and head west. I decide to take the direct way, through Chimayo, a dot on the map where there is a small church famed in native folklore for its magic mud, which, it is claimed, has curative powers over every affliction of man from paralysis to the heartbreak of psoriasis.

The scenery is magnificent. I can almost feel the pulse of hundreds of years of horses' hooves and wagon wheels crossing these plains and valleys, caught between cloud and rock, seeking water, a place to rest, a home in the middle of brutal sun and searing wind. Arid land, stone-hard like the faces of its people; Indian faces, etched in secrets lost to this land. Empty caverns still yearning for the sea that deserted it. Carved and pushed into alien places and abandoned.

Where campers pitch their Abercrombie and Fitch tents, prehistoric reptiles once swam. This land lies silent under the butts and beer cans crushed by affluent Adidas on the way back to their Winnebagos, doesn't take any shit. This is land that remembers. Land that will get even, have the last laugh, not like the dead, bitter acceptance on the Indian faces, bouncing up and down around the mountain curves, heading for Gallup to sell their wares.

The bellman warned me, "Don't take the road to Santa Fe on Friday or Saturday night. Every weekend, the Indians get tanked and take off down the mountain like crazy men. Every damn weekend, truckfuls of them get killed. They go flying right off the road. It's how they let their anger out, I guess."

Icarus in a hatchback, soaring into infinity, bone to bone in the land that was here first. Before Chase Manhattan, the Muppets, Chevron, and Rolaids. Before "Saturday Night Live" and Monday-night football, the Rosetta Stone, the pyramids, Hitler, and Mickey Mouse.

Before Christ, King Arthur, and Federico Fellini, sushi, Clairol, and rock 'n' roll. Before hydrocarbons, carcinogens, toxic waste, nuclear fisson, genocide, suicide, herbicides, and homicides. Before death, taxes, Adam and Eve. Before radio. This was right here, letting the work be done. Eons of sorrow and void, of moving earth and raging tide, of cold and whistling loneliness. Letting the land form. Making it more beautiful than any man-made thing. Not knowing it would become a Polaroid background, a depository for trash and camper piss, Army maneuvers and Indian despair.

I find the church at Chimayo and enter a dark mud-brick room, the walls covered with braces and crutches, blind men's canes, and yellowing photos of pilgrims cured. Signs warn against trying to take any of the miracle mud, which looks just like the ordinary kind. Outside, barefoot

Mexican children are selling cherries for a dollar a pound. Dusty dogs chase one another around the rickety frame houses. Eveything feels sucked dry. A kind of emotional dehydration. Every face looks menacing, as if they all knew the truth but me.

I stop for lunch at a landmark restaurant off the main road. I sit on a bougainvilla-covered patio, sipping ice tea and gobbling tortilla chips while I wait for homemade enchiladas soaked in *mole*. Tourists chat around me. Words reach my head. *Painted Desert, Petrified Forest, Continental Divide, Rio Grande.* Words from grammar-school geography books. Regional "in" spots that are the tourists' lifelines; the connective tissue of wayfarers everywhere. What do the mountains think of this all? What can they make of it? I am projecting now beyond other humans; I have become the voice of the Grand Canyon, the Colorado River, the land itself. Too much sun, maybe.

I finish off my enchiladas and my third ice tea. As I pay the check, the voice from my dream returns. "It's the wrong head," it says.

Down along the Rio Grande I go. It looked bigger in the movie. I am almost in Santa Fe. The end of the trail. The end of my trail as well.

What was that book by Willa Cather? *Death Comes for the Archbishop.* It's about the French bishop Jean Latour who traveled the trail turning Indian heathens into Christian heathens. The whole book comes back to me as I decelerate into Santa Fe. The missionary who lived high and fat on the Acoma Mesa, the village near the sky, where the Indians had climbed straight up the red rocks seeking a safe place, safe from Navajos and Lagunas, towering above their enemies; invaded only by the priests and missionaries, whom they obeyed and served gracefully. Then one fateful night the bishop, soggy from grape brandy, threw a pewter mug at his hapless servant for spilling gravy on a dinner guest. The poor boy fell dead. The cook saw from the doorway and told the tribe. After the guests departed, the friar was taken from his grand house and dropped like a stone from the mesa edge. The mountains don't take any shit.

And there was the tale of Doña Isabella, the vain and pretty wife of a Spanish landowner who could only protect her estate after his death by standing up in court and revealing her true age. She refused. She was thought to be at least ten years younger than she was. The priests prevailed and she finally relented and saved her fortune from her greedy relatives. Afterward she publicly admonished the priests for the *dreadful lie* they had made her tell.

Remembering this reminds me of Amora. That was an Amora kind of story. I shuddered. I have arrived. I still have a couple of hours to kill before my formal arrival. I decide to find the main plaza and take a look around, just in case I never get another chance.

I park the car near the main church, which is just as ugly as I had read it was, sort of Disneyland Gothic. I can feel my energy being sucked down already. So much for paradise.

I am getting bad vibes in Santa Fe Plaza. It is not what I had expected. A long line of Indians sit cross-legged under the wooden awning of an old government building, shaded from the sun, their jewelry and woven goods laid out before them. Directly across the plaza is a huge run-down Woolworth's. The park in the middle is filled with fizz-heads, a local variety of neo-seventies hippie types. At the far end, in front of the café boasting gyros and Indian bread, two tall, sunburned drunks are having a fight, kicking and punching one another. I bypass this scene and duck down a side street that is lined with expensive crafts galleries and jewelry stores. Ah. The *real* Santa Fe. And there before me, looming out of the candy-colored sky like a sea monster or an apparition, is the Reuben Mars Gallery. I am not ready for this. I slip into a health-food equivalent of a coffee shop and order chamomile ice tea.

Two women, attractive in a weathered, earthy kind of way, and very expensively clad in the latest Frye-booted, Ralph Lauren cowgirl elegance, stride in and sit at the table next to me. They are of the school that would tend to support Wanda Mackay's terrified rhetoric of the fate of discarded upper-scale women. From the way they touch one another's hands and smile knowingly, I assume they are lovers. That's what happens in places such as this, where most of the available men are gay, drug-addicted, married, or all of the above, and the nights are long.

"He's coming to take the kids for Christmas, and I'm nearly crazed about it."

"Is he bringing that bimbo from Club Med?"

"Bringing her? He's going to marry her!"

"You didn't tell me that!"

"I didn't know *that* until this morning."

"What a bastard."

"I'm scared. I don't know what I'm scared of, but I just feel panicky."

"Listen to this story. I was on my way to the Canyon de Chelle to take some pictures for my exhibit and I saw a sign for a cactus ranch, so I followed it; you know how I am about cactus. I went on and on for quite a while. And then, all of a sudden, just smack in the middle of the desert, was this cactus farm. I got out of the car and it was so quiet, so deserted, and filled with the most exquisite cactus I have ever seen. It's so bloody hot that you could bake corn on the road, and frightening; very barren, very primal. And then out of nowhere an old woman appeared, carrying a water can. She was quite fat and all covered up in long dark clothes, and as she got closer I could see that she was blind. Blind as sand. She greeted me and then just went about her work, caring for these incredibly vicious cactus. I was dumbstruck and I asked if I could photograph her and she agreed and I did. And then, when I couldn't stand it any longer, I said to her, 'Isn't it dangerous for you to work here, without sight? Don't you get pricked?' 'Oh yes, all the time,' she said. 'But shouldn't you be in a safer place?' I said. And this fat blind old woman smiled and looked right into me with her sightless eyes. 'And where would a safer place be, dear?'"

The other woman bursts into tears. I burst into tears. The woman who has told the story bursts into tears. The waitress who has overheard while she is bringing their food bursts into tears.

Then all of us feel a lot better. Women are great that way. We all share a story about ourselves and our ex-husbands. When I get up to go, the woman with the problem is smiling. Her fear is gone. Bring on the bimbos from Club Med. I now have the courage needed to enter the Reuben Mars Gallery. I know in the movies the fugitive dick would look up the suspect first. But in romance novels the idea of a possible *man* to help the heroine is the path of choice. I cop out. I open the door and the blast of conditioned air covers me. My heart is doing a conga drum solo. There is no one in view. I browse. The white adobe shelves are filled with vibrant primitive figures. Coiled wooden snakes, papier-mâché horses, brilliantly painted sculpted objects; objects that could have been done by fairy children. The pale wood floor is covered with hand-woven rugs. Indian baskets filled with Navajo pillows and fabrics line the walls. Cat Stevens is piped into the background. *If you wanna be high be high, if you wanna be low be low.*

"May I help you?" A soft voice behind me asks.

I turn. A beautiful young woman, darkly exotic and looking like an Inca princess, is smiling at me, her heavy long black hair pulled back in a ponytail, falling forward over one round shoulder. She is leaning on a pair of braces, her long black caftan covering her legs. There is a beautiful quiet about her. A palpable kindness. She makes me feel ashamed.

"You have beautiful things," I say, my heart moving into a cha-cha.

"Thank you very much. My husband is responsible for all of it. He chooses everything."

I can feel the bad news coming. I can feel a dream curling up and shriveling into burned rubbish behind my daydreaming eyes.

"Is Reuben Mars your husband?"

"Why, yes. Do you know him?"

If everything in life is timing, someone just stepped on my Swatch. "Oh, no. Well, that is, he taught at Berkeley many years ago. I had a class with him. He would never remember. I was just passing and I saw the name, so . . ."

"Of course he'd remember. He talks about those days often. He'll be back tonight; he went to Los Angeles on business. Please leave your name."

My name. I can't leave my name. I have done it again. Opened my mouth and let the babble out. What to do? I smile, instants away from bellowing anguish, smiling back into the shining open face of Mrs. Mars, a luminous planetary being, *a far better choice*, I hiss to myself in a quick searing blast of self-hate.

"Oh, no. I don't really think he would remember. Besides, I'm leaving now. I'll be staying with friends, so I won't be back here, so just tell him an old student—I mean, a former student—came by."

The Martian princess tips her head to the side and

watches me. There is no bitterness in her face and no fear; no rivalry or distrust. She is simply evaluating.

"Are you an artist?" She has chosen to respect my position. What class.

"Oh, no. Just a fan. My husband is an art critic and historian, so what I learned from Professor Mars has come in handy. Are you?"

"I'm a weaver. I don't know if that qualifies."

"I think so. Are some of your pieces here?"

"No. Not now. I'm preparing a show. But between helping here and the children, I may be preparing it for centuries."

"The children" is the last nail in the box. "Well, I've got to run. It was lovely to meet you."

"Yes. Please come back. I know Reuben will remember."

"I'll try."

I run down the street across the plaza, ignoring the leering halfhearted sexism of the fizz-heads, and lock myself in the safety of Mama-San. I am crying so hard I can't see. I am crying good-bye. No way to hedge my bet now. Consciously or otherwise. No more movie ending; the right man at last to rescue me from the mire. Somewhere hidden deep in my heart all of these years has been this secret yearning. The man who would have made it all right. The one I would have chosen if I had only known what I know now. The one who got away. I had headed toward him in blind panic. If Clifford was not going to do it for me, if I was going to have to go out there again by myself, now—I would risk it. Now I was scared enough to risk anything. I would not be alone dealing with the reality of middle age, empty nests, dead mothers, decapitated siblings, career letdowns, loneliness, and betrayal. I would be rescued in the last reel by the paunchy prince. I would not have to deal with all of this, all alone. I had followed a burned-out beacon. And now there was no place left to go but back to numero uno. Not going to make it easy for me, huh, big guy?

I cried. For the frightened old Aroma that Reuben had known. The one who was still becoming, still unpacking her teenage trunk and sorting through the crinolines and Capri pants. Time to say "so long" to all of those scrapbook dreams. I did my mourning in a green Toyota, so much a part of the present, it didn't even have a dent yet.

When it was all out, I drove to a gas station, washed my face in the "Out of Order" ladies' room, reconstructed it as well as I could, and headed for the next thing.

John P. Harrington was listed in the phone book, but it was not the same number. Still, he was my logical next choice. I pull Mama-San around the back of his building, an old adobe house turned into swank medical offices, and park out of sight and sun behind a huge cactus plant. I slip out of the passenger side and creep around to the back door. Takes a shrink to know a shrink. Nearly all of them have side doors so that weepy patients can make their exits unseen by the next victim.

The door is unlocked. My second ex-brother-in-law, whom I barely know, is in his office madly throwing important-looking documents into a cowhide or some-other-hide briefcase.

I sidle in, my shaking hand on Pop's gun, which I have moved to my jacket pocket. He looks up. He sees me. He has no idea who I am.

He looks more terrified than I think I look.
I say, "You have no idea who I am?"
"Yes."
"Yes—what, yes?"

"Yes. I have no idea who you am. You are. Who are you? What do you want?"

"I want to talk to you about my sister. Your former wife. Amora Sweet."

You know how in mystery stories they describe how "all the color drained from under Bart Sloane's Saint-Tropez tan." Well, that is no shit. All color drained from the doc's otherwise tawny and chiseled face.

"My God. It's never going to end, is it! You're too late. You tell them they'd have better luck draining a cactus!"

"Them?" I move ever so slightly forward.

The doctor is coming unwrapped. "Them. Them! The scum queens of Gomorrah! Don't play innocent with me! Sister, my ass. You're obviously one of Lella's flunkies."

The L-woman. *Lella.* That's the one.

Dr. John stops packing and slumps down in his chair, which seems to be constructed of different parts of various beasts of burden and dairy. Can't be good for his patients, I think, my mind frantic to keep him talking.

"Actually, I'm a friend, of, a, Sarah Jane's; she sent me over to—"

The doctor leaps up. "What do you think I am? Stupid? Sarah Jane's in New York! After what she's done, do you really think she'd send *you* to *me*?"

"Done?"

"She murdered your so-called sister—isn't that why you're here? If you are who you say you are."

Now I'm mad. "Now wait just a damn minute here. You mean Amora never told you that she had a twin sister?"

"Never."

"Why that, that! . . . okay . . . okay! Never mind

about that. I'm her goddamn twin sister. Don't you read the papers? So get that straight, Charlie! Right now I don't even care what my sister told you—but what do you mean, Sarah Jane murdered her? How do you know something like that? I've got the whole fucking NYPD and God only knows who else chasing me around, and you know something like that and you choose not to share it? What's going on here?"

The doctor calms down. The doctor gets it.

"You mean, you really don't know about the blackmail?"

"Blackmail? What blackmail?"

The doctor rises to his full lithe height and pulls a manila file out of his briefcase. It is filled with photos. The photos are of the doctor, the L-woman, Sarah Jane, and my renowned and respected sister engaged in a series of graphic orgiastic acts that would blow the tubes of "The Only Nude Talk Show." My mouth drops. My hand comes off the gun in my pocket and covers it.

"Oh my God."

The doctor, grateful that I am not about to add to his troubles, really opens up.

"It started so innocently." (I resist a sarcastic sneer.) "You see, I had a lover, Lella, and she brought your sister to a lecture I was giving. And we just clicked. Like a bolt of lightning. Lella was her friend. Lella is a very complex woman. Her family is powerful. Very powerful. And they control her totally. She saw me as her way out. So, it was a double betrayal. But she acted as if it was all just fine. Then an old school friend of Amora's came out. She'd been in Texas, gotten into some trouble, and she showed up here. She looked so much like Amora—it was very erotic. Like, well, like twins. That was in the seventies; everyone was doing a lot of drugs. The three of us got high one night and ended up in bed. It was wild. Then Amora invited Lella over, trying to make up with her. Lella and Sarah Jane really liked each other. It was a very Indian scene. I was like the master of this dark little menagerie. Three beautiful women and me. Then Clive went off to stay with his grandfather for the summer and we all got pretty crazy. But Amora, she couldn't really handle it. All the mescaline and the sharing me—not her nature—she was really not a seventies chick. She had a nervous breakdown. Just totally flipped. I put her in a private hospital here, kept it very quiet. Not a word got out to any of her colleagues. We even paid Sarah Jane so we could use her ID, and she left town right after. What we didn't know was that Lella had arranged for one of her family's thugs to photograph all of it. I didn't know that till six months ago.

"When Amora got out, it was no good between us. Too much damage had been done. We split up. I guess Lella thought that then we'd get back together, but I was tired of the whole scene. I went away for several years; wrote some books. When I came back, I didn't call Lella. Life went on until six months ago."

I am afraid even to swallow. He is confessing. I am the invisible priest. I don't want him to stop. Somewhere I think the motive may be hitching a ride into town.

"What happened then?" I slide ever so quietly into a fur-covered chair.

Dr. John picks up his dirty pictures and throws them into his briefcase. "I got a call from Lella. She'd been in Europe for several years. She said she was back in Santa Fe and wanted to see me for old times' sake. I agreed. She picked a restaurant out of town. When I arrived she was waiting with Sarah Jane. They let me have it. They had pictures, tapes. It was bad for me, but it was even worse for Amora. They had a deposition from Sarah Jane about Amora's forged medical records and somehow they had gotten her hospital file—the whole breakdown, everything. Amora was a superstar—it would ruin her. They wanted money. A lot of money. What Lella really wanted was revenge, but the money also would get her away from her brother and his mob. Sarah Jane was a junkie. She could hardly sit up. She was desperate."

"What happened then?"

"I called your sister to warn her. She did not take it well." (I could just imagine.) "She got pretty freaked; then defensive, then paranoid. She had a whole lot invested in not believing me. But then Sarah Jane showed up in New York, with another set of photos and documents, and Amora had to face it." Dr. John stands up and reaches for his coat.

"Please! There's so much more I need to know. The cops think I may have done it. This could clear me. You can't go now!"

"Listen, my dear sister, it is more than likely that I am the next candidate for Amora's gruesome fate, and I cannot even run to the police or the whole sordid mess will come out and ruin me, anyway. I'm getting out before the stakes go off the board. I had stripped my accounts and was all ready to pay when Amora was murdered. So now I am going to 'take the money and run,' as someone once said."

I leap up and try to stop him. "Please, just a couple more minutes! Something doesn't make sense! Why would Sarah Jane murder her? It wouldn't be in her best interests. And if she was that strung out, it seems unlikely that Amora, with all her weight training and stuff, couldn't have overpowered her. It all seems a little too together for a junkie. I've worked with lots of them. This is not how they operate."

Dr. John has turned off the lights and picked up his suitcase. I don't even have a kinky photo to convince Mallony I'm onto something.

"Frankly, I don't give a fried fart. All I know is that Amora called me a month or so ago; she was hysterical. She said Sarah Jane had been there and they were going to expose us if we didn't pay. She said they wanted a million bucks from her and she didn't have anywhere near that, but she had a powerful boyfriend and he was her only hope" (that explains her Jimmy Bob frenzy). "The hitch was that he was in the middle of a very messy divorce—the wife had a private dick trailing her and he might not be able to get his hands on that much cash. She was pretty desperate. She asked me to try to reason with Lella.

"I told her that was about as likely as offering a peace pipe to a Comanche war party. That was the last I heard."

He pushed past me and down the Southwest modern hallway toward the back door.

"Where are you going? How can I get in touch with you?"

He laughs. A snarly, snickery laugh. What a scary shrink he must be. "Off into the sunset, my dear. Forget it. I've got my own problems."

He was right. He did.

I scurried after him, stumbled on an Indian rug, and fell flat on my face. John, not slowed down by chivalrous instinct, kept going, right through the back door. *Pop. Pop.* Even though I had never heard a gun go off, except on TV, where they used special effects to make it all sound more dramatic, I had a very keen gut feeling that that was what it was. I stayed down, crawling, as fast as your average nine-month-old, to the window. I eased myself up, staying tight in the corner.

Oh my Lord. There was Dr. John, sprawled all over the adobe-brick driveway, and kneeling beside him, frantically gathering the money and papers in his briefcase, was the small man in the Calvin Klein trench coat who had been following Clive and me in New York! He jumped up, and as he stood, his hat got caught in the cactus in front of my car. The hat came off and a mane of long dark hair fell out. The small man with a big mustache was a tall woman with a big mustache. With or without—it was the L-woman. Lella. I froze, ducking back down to the floor.

When I peeked out again, she was gone. I decided to follow her lead. I raced to the Toyota and headed for Signor Stucci's ranch as fast as I could manage, considering that both my knees were knocking together and my entire body had gone into the human equivalent of gridlock.

15

Stucci's Honor

I'm late. The sun is falling like a burning skull behind the purple-gray horizon. I drive up a long wide street where elegant desert houses sit like sand sculptures; each unique, well spaced, but still somehow the same. Lots of room between. No one banging on the pipes in these parts.

It is hard to see in the twilight. There are no street lights or numbers. I drive up toward the mountains. Thunder rumbles above. A small sign, carved into a wooden post, appears at the top of the hill. Rancho Estrella. I follow the road for miles, down a dusty empty trail. Cold sweat crawls down my back and across my recently powdered brow. It is now really dark and the sky is strobed with lightning. I turn on my brights and slow down even more. The road forks and a small reflecting arrow points left. I am beginning to feel a tad Pavlovian about this.

One last turn and looming before me are two monolithic wooden gates. It is too dark to tell what kind of wall they are attached to, but they are serious. On either side of the gates are small houses inside of which are seated uniformed guards with extremely uncongenial expressions. Both of them approach. They each have double holsters and I know that somewhere there is an Uzzi, at least, aimed at my throat.

"Name," the one on the driver's side asks with all the warmth of a Buffalo winter.

I have no choice if I want to enter but to tell the truth. Still, I play for time. "Mona's friend. From Vegas."

Mr. Personality number one locks eyes with number two. Both check their clipboard. Both nod. I am squeaking by without my name or a lie.

"Get out of the car."

Only if you say please. I force my mouth shut and obey.

Out of the darkness two more happy-go-lucky types, each with a growling canine that makes Cujo look like My Dog Spot, approach my car and begin the kind of search heretofore reserved for known Libyan terrorists trying to get through Israeli customs.

My man, the one who talks, motions toward the guardhouse and a female version of himself marches out.

"Take her in."

The woman nods, looking like the "before" part of an Excedrin commercial, and leads me inside one of the *Star Wars*–inspired guardhouses.

"Your purse." Someone should teach these folks about sentence structure.

"My purse." Cold sweat is rolling like a glandular river over and around my entire body. *In my purse is Pop's gun.*

"I, uh, have a gun in my purse." (Heh, heh.) "I guess I should tell you that. It's my, uh, father's. He gave it to me for self-protection. I've been on the road for, uh, some time. By myself."

This does not seem to impress her. She rips open my purse, removes the gun, and examines every item from my Trident breath mints to one lonely Super Tampax lost for weeks at the bottom. She takes the gun.

"Undress."

Somehow I know that this is not the time for a self-righteous speech on human rights and invasion of privacy. This is not airport security, kiddo, this is most likely the mob. I undress. She examines me only a little less thoroughly than the dogs did the Toyota. What happened to the warm voice on the phone? The "any friend of Mona's" conversation?

I have gone too far for second thoughts, so I put my clothes back on as if this were a perfectly routine occurrence when dropping in on mutual friends.

"Wait here." You would think that someone who had moments before had her forefinger in your rectum would at least say "Nice to meet ya."

I can see, through the obviously bulletproof glass, my friend Irma talking to Laurel and Hardy. They all enter the guardhouse. I close my swollen eyes and try to calm down.

"Okay. Let's go."

I open my eyes. I am surrounded by the entire welcoming committee. They motion for me to follow them to a Chevrolet van parked off the side of the road.

"What about my car?" I manage to ask, visions of torture and imprisonment flashing before me.

"We'll wash it and gas it. It'll be here."
"Can't I just drive it in?"
I might as well have asked for a sperm sample.
"No one drives in. Rules."
I nod. I climb into the van. The gates open by remote control and we cross into the void.
"Put this on." I am handed a blindfold. I know it's nerves, but I have an overwhelming desire to burst into hysterical giggles and shout something like *You've got to be kidding!* I don't. I comply. Off we go. I am aware of the car turning many times, zooming uphill and then down. I am hungry. I am thirsty. I have to pee. My eyes are itching and I need a bath. I had somehow hoped for a more romantic arrival.

Finally we stop.
"You can take it off now."
I take it off. The door opens and the one who talks helps me out of the back. My makeup is smeared and I can smell the dried sweat on my back. If this guy is expecting Mona Part II, he is in for a major letdown.
"Thank you," I say.
A broad smile crosses the face. "My pleasure. Sorry for the rough stuff. Just doing our job."
"That's what Himmler said," I mumble.
"Say what?"
"Nothing. A little jest."
I look around. We are standing in the immense courtyard of a vast southwestern ranch house. In front of me, as far as I can see, is a mesa covered with pure white sand and cactus. It is so bizarrely beautiful that it seems unreal. The black sky above, the white moon-lit plain below, and this enormous pale-pink house stretching across the desert into nowhere. We walk up the sweeping brick driveway to the front of the hacienda. I can smell

wood fires. I hear music playing. My bodyguard strides to the wrought-iron bougainvillea-arbored entry and opens a panel on the wall. A mini computer and elaborate camera slide out and he goes to work, punching codes or whatever it takes to open the Herculean oak doors.

They part. The butler greets us. The hall behind him is lit with fields of white candles glowing from chandeliers and wall sconces, showering the space with mystical radiant light. "Over-forty light," Amora would call this. The butler beckons me forth. I feel like the guy in *Close Encounters* heading for the spaceship.

I follow him. Gunless. Carless. Scared shitless.

"I imagine you would like to freshen up before you meet Signor Stucci and his guests?" the butler says, endearing himself to me forever.

"Oh, yes. That would be wonderful, but they took my car and my suitcase was in it."

"That's already been seen to."

I should have known. It always is in the movies. I follow him down a long red tile hallway lined with Indian art and wall hangings. In the far distance, I hear laughter and music. I can smell garlic and onions. So this is how the Mona world works. We stop at a door with a shiny brass number 8 on top. The butler opens it and turns on the light. It's the kind of room James Bond uses for a nap while waiting for a deadly scorpion or Maud Adams to crawl by. Cool tile floors. Navajo rugs. A huge four-poster bed carved from tree trunks. Whitewashed walls filled with mirrors and western art. A mass of fresh flowers on the polished maple dresser. Motel 6 it is not.

"I think you'll find everything you need. There are some evening clothes in the closet, in case you don't have your own. Signor Stucci prefers formal dinner."

"Thank you very much." *What else? I never eat any other*

way. The thought of my usual dinner attire flashes through my mind and I fight back hysterics again.

"I will return to take you down for cocktails in an hour."

In an hour the new Aroma is ready. I have luxuriated in a sunken marble tub; washed my hair in a sky-lit shower; put to use every one of Mona's makeup tips, and then approached the closet. Inside is a selection of black, white, and red silk or satin dresses, each in both fabrics and in sizes 6 to 12. No anorexics or forgotten women dine in this joint. Below are matching pumps in sizes 6 through 8½. I ponder, Goldilocks before the porridge bowls, all thoughts of Dr. John's body, blackmail, murder, and my immediate future pushed aside by the power of a Cosmo girl fantasy.

I pick out a black satin size 10. It fits. I decide to press my luck and zip into a red silk size 8. It fits as long as I keep radar control on my stomach muscles and stay away from the second helpings. I decide to go for it with the size 8 red silk and matching size 7 pumps. There is even a drawer filled with very nice imitations (at least I *assume* they're imitations) of classic gold and pearl necklaces and earrings. I go for the works. When I have finished, I check myself out in the rosy glow from the candelabra and wall sconces.

This is not bad. I have never looked like this. I am astonished at what I see. I look glamorous. I have never looked glamorous before in my entire life. I stand there thinking about why that is. First, I'm too lazy. Second, it takes too much time and too much money—neither of which I have ever had in any measure. Third, Amora was glamorous. Ah. The lead weight shoots to the top of the pole and rings the bell. I always stayed clear of anything Amora did well. Better that than facing the fire of her ire.

I gave her glamour. Along with a few other things it might have been nice to try.

I think of every man who rejected me in my entire life. I think of Amos. I think of Clifford. I think of Reuben Mars. If they could see me now. The butler knocks discreetly, breaking into my ego exercise. I am so eager to try this new me out on a live audience that I even forget to be nervous.

"Madam looks very beautiful," the butler says as he leads me back down the hall and across the huge foyer and through another vast hall and around a massive inner courtyard filled with rare plants and rare caged birds and through another set of towering polished wood doors and into a magnificent living room all white like a desert snowstorm, lit by hundreds of white candles and an immense triangular white-tiled fireplace. Everyone is in pale colors, camouflaged by the whiteness and soft gleaming lights. I am like a comet, a fat drop of blood, a crimson slash. All eyes turn.

What's the Chinese curse? May you get what you want. I have always wanted to be the center of attention. Well, here I am, folks, and it is so unnerving that I would give almost anything to be a little white snowflake daintily and anonymously melting on the hearth.

All the men stand up.

A tiny, deeply tanned man with a pompadour of white wavy hair to match his white silk suit, his bright-blue eyes twinkling behind black horn-rimmed glasses, comes forward to greet me.

"Welcome, Mona's friend. You do my home honor. You are just as lovely as Mona said you were. I am Sarno Stucci. Allow me to present my guests."

I swallow hard. He has *talked* to Mona. This *is* the big time. He must know about me, because he doesn't ask my name. He comes up beside me and takes my arm, then very discreetly leans in and whispers into my pearl-covered ear, "Let us call you Maria Montez, shall we?"

I nod. Better than Carmen Miranda or Ima Sumac. Fine with me.

He leads me to the smiling figures, who almost swim before my eyes. There are three tall gentlemen all with the sharp-nosed, slender elegance of Roman aristocrats; a very old lady in a wheelchair, who looks exactly like Sarno Stucci in drag and must be his mother; two priests or monks, clad in flowing gray Friar Tuck ensembles; a wiry slick-haired younger man whose creamy linen suit is bulging at the seams over his musculature, a graduate of the "women are made for the kitchen and the bedroom" school. And wouldn't you just know, a tall brunette bearing an uncanny resemblance to the Stuccis and who could be a kid sister or daughter: Lella. When I recover I see a slightly overweight raccoonish-looking man who, after a moment's pause to reconfirm my suspicions, I realize is Reuben Mars. The Martian princess is nowhere in sight. Signor Stucci introduces his "friend from Las Vegas," Maria Montez, to everyone in the room. All we need is Hercule Poirot and Miss Marple and we could start filming.

I am so stunned by Reuben Mars and Lella that I don't hear any names at all. The woman in the chair *is* his mother. Reuben is introduced and doesn't even bat an eye. I don't know if this is a compliment or not.

"And last, my baby sister, Lella." We have just become the meaning of the term "eye contact."

Signor Stucci guides me to a seat between himself and his mother, a gesture for which I decide on the spot I adore him. The waiter appears for my drink request. "A Negroni," I whisper, causing approving smiles around the Italian section of the room. Signora Stucci does not speak

English. After a couple of sips of my Negroni, I relax enough to attempt my very rusty and purely colloquial Italian. More approving nods. All eyes remain on me and my strawberry dress. "My father is Italian," I say shyly.

"Ahhh. *Bravissimo*," chorus my guys.

Signor Stucci leans into my ear again as the butler announces that dinner is served. "We will talk later. Do not be afraid."

I am seated between a monk and the muscle man— not ideal for NYC small talk. Part of me is dying to confess my identity and let the chips fall where they may. Images start to appear from long-forgotten corners of my mind. Amora in Santa Fe. Now I remember. She did write me a letter about a Lella. She met her at a cooking class. Lella was a patient of Dr. Tightass, that's how Amora met him. Lella couldn't let her family know she was in therapy. They didn't approve. Amora covered for her. Wait a minute, Reuben must have been around then, too. Why didn't she ever mention Reuben? Why, indeed.

When dessert was served, I stole a momentary glance at Reuben Mars. He was deep in conversation with the priest on his left. I kept waiting for him to look my way; a slight smile, a quizzical Cary Grantish glance. *Pardon me ever so, but couldn't it be?* No such luck. All for the better, since I couldn't really tell him who I was now, anyway. Lella and I avoid all possibility of another eye attack.

Dinner, which was sumptuous, but not as good as Pop's, ended. We retire to the library, or at least the men do. Signora Stucci goes off to bed. Lella goes to help her. I am the odd donna out. I tactfully announce that I would love to get some air. I wander through the courtyard and down the center steps to an enormous cascading pink granite fountain. I sit there in the dark, breathing in the cactus blossom and rain-fresh air. I close my eyes. What was I into? Did Stucci know about Lella?

I hear footsteps on the stone. I open my eyes. Reuben Mars is standing beside me holding two brandy glasses in his hands.

"I thought you might be feeling left out, Ms. uh, Montez."

I avoid his eyes. This is not my plan. "Not really. It's nice to have a moment of quiet. I've gotten out of practice for dinner parties."

"If memory serves, you never were any bloody good at them. You always talked too much. At least that's changed."

He knew. He knows. He recognized me. How could he have recognized me? I don't look anything like that frumpy plumpy middle-class Eastern coed. Or do I? Glamour, my ass. Once a bagel, always a bagel—never going to be a baguette, cookie. Or did Stucci tell him?

"How did you know?"

"Well, the first clue was Spring describing this mysterious former student from Berkeley. There were not that many small pretty women in my class who would have remembered me or been so nervous about it. Then there was Stucci calling and inviting me to dinner, and then you. Looking very sangé, very chic, and slender and attractive, but still Aroma. What's wrong? You look like a little girl whose parents just admitted they knew it was her inside the Halloween costume."

"I feel that way. But I'm glad, too. It hurt that you looked right through me."

"So what's with the masquerade?"

"You don't know?"

"No. I don't know. Know what?"

"Oh, boy. I'm not ready for this. Do Stucci and his, his sister know who I am?"

"I don't know. But I bet Stucci has a plan for us all."

"Is he . . . is this?"

"Yes. But he's a brilliant collector and a wonderful friend. I stay out of his world and I like him. You can trust him."

"You wouldn't kid an old admirer, would you?"

"No. Want to tell a fellow old admirer what brings you here?"

I take a deep breath. "Some maniac cut my sister's head off and left it on my desk. The police think that I may have done it, because they can't find a motive or a body or anything. But they also think that if I didn't do it, then whoever did it may try to do it to me, too. I realized that the police couldn't protect me, so I took off, to try and figure it out for myself. I headed here: see, there were these notes with a Santa Fe postmark. And I thought that because she had lived here, there's a clue here. But also I came, I think, because I knew you were here and I've always thought about you, and my marriage is in real trouble—so I just came, but then I saw your wife, she's so lovely, by the way, and I realized that that was a real pipe dream; but my friend Mona said Signor Stucci could help me, so here I am and that's basically that—except for the blackmail and the shooting today—today, just before I came, I saw Amora's ex and Lella—she was there—she . . ."

He throws back his shaggy raccoon head and laughs out loud. "Now *that* is the Amora I knew and loved."

I can feel moonlight on my shoulders. "Loved?"

"Oh yes. You bloody marvelous broad. I was mad for you. You drove me quite insane with your chastity. Seems so ridiculous now, doesn't it? Time is the great comedian. Always has the last laugh."

"You said it. I feel really silly right now."

"Good. I like silliness in a woman. Makes me feel so macho. Sorry to interrupt; it's all a bit hard to absorb. Do go on."

I open my mouth to retort, but the butler appears and upstages me.

"Signor Stucci would like to see you, madam, and Mr. Mars in his study. Please follow me."

Reuben gives me a wink with one of his heavy-lidded dark-circled eyes. He has aged, I think, hoping he's not thinking the same thing about me. We trot along behind. Maybe the butler did it, I muse. Wouldn't that be a relief.

Sarno Stucci is sitting behind a massive marble slab transformed into a desk by four finely polished tree stumps. He is so tiny that he is semi-hidden by the table mass. The study is filled with books on Indian art and culture. There is the omnipresent walk-in fireplace and several oversize sand-colored chairs and couches, some facing the desk, others facing one another along both sides of the fire. It is clear that, mob or no mob, this guy is a black sheep. This is not your Ozone Park sensibility we're dealing with here.

The greaser with the muscles stands in the corner off to the side of Stucci. Lella is seated in a chair before the desk. Reuben and I are shown to two chairs beside her. We all sit there facing him like after-dinner guests in a Hollywood screening room, waiting for the show to begin.

It is obvious that he has a plan. I decide to continue in my new party mode and keep my mouth shut. Let him lead the way. Since this is not a guy whom people double-cross, I decide not to worry about my cover being blown. It is unlikely they would run to the cops. Pop would go wild, I think. Pop hates the Mafia. That reminds me to call Pop as soon as I can.

"Aroma, dear. May I call you that, now?" (He knows.) "Please don't be concerned about the others. I would not endanger you. Let me say to you that I owe your friend Mona a debt, and so I will begin to repay it by helping you if I can. She has told me your incredible story and I have taken the liberty of inviting some friends and family who knew your sister and may be of help."

I check the room. Reuben has a small ironic smile. Lella is grim-faced and silent, her hands tightly folded in her lap. I decide to keep my eye and my bet on Lella.

I nod. Garbo would be proud of me.

"Now, to begin. If you would be so kind as to tell us the entire story in your own words, leaving out nothing, not the slightest detail, within the limits of your ability to endure the painful memories. It is most important to know everything."

Sorry, Greta. This is the kind of thing I can get my teeth into. I begin at the Afro-Brazil class and spin a tale that would've kept Finch Hatten in Isak Dinesen's bed for weeks. I leave out all mention of Lella, Sarah Jane, and Dr. John. I do finish with an off-hand mention of blackmail. Lella flinches ever so slightly. It is clear her brother doesn't know—I have no desire to become the Greek messenger.

"*Molto interessante. Molto incredibile.* Now, if anyone has a memory of the poor woman that might be helpful, please speak now."

Reuben sits forward. "I'm afraid, Don Stucci, that I can't be of much use. When Amora came here, she was doing postgraduate work with one of the tribes, I believe. We met at a party, and we"—he casts a look in my direction—"were lovers for a brief time."

I'll kill her. What a bitch. She did it on purpose! It was all part of competing with me. Unbelievable!

"Anyway, then she met John Harrington; Lella introduced them, I believe, and that was that. She was never what you would call a southwestern type. She loathed it here. After she moved to San Francisco, I never heard from her again. In fact, I had given her a letter for Aroma, which was never answered, so I assumed the Sweet sisters had soured on me. Excuse the bad pun."

Letter? That witch! She never gave me a letter!

"Oh, one thing. Kind of funny, at that. When she first came here, she bought some land not far north of here, with a small ranch on it—thought it might be a good investment. She was too citified to live there, so she rented it to me. I stayed there for years. I wrote Amora when I left and told her that I would find a tenant who would live there and care for the place and the land in exchange for free rent. Spring's cousin moved in. But I never heard back from Amora. Just a perfunctory note from her lawyer. It was quite strange. Then out of the blue about three months ago, I received a notice of sale. The place had been sold and I was to vacate the premises—I must have still been on record as the tenant. I went out and helped Spring's cousin pack up. It was rather peculiar."

My mind was wandering. When I am extremely nervous, my mind wanders. *Spring Mars. What a wonderful name.* In the background I hear Signor Stucci asking Reuben a question.

"Reuben, by any chance do you know the name of the buyer? Was it in any of the documents?"

"Yes. Wait a minute. Let me get the dying brain cells stirred up a bit. It wasn't a person, it was a corporation; let me think. Something like Range Rider. No, Rough Rider. That's it. Rough Rider Enterprises."

My mind wanders back. "Oh my God! That's one of Jimmy Bob's companies!"

Signor Stucci leans forward. "What is this name?"

"Jimmy Bob—James Mackay. Amora's boyfriend. That's his company. I've seen it in annual reports that Amora had."

Stucci's lips had straightened into a thin white line. "I know this name. Paolo!"

The muscle in the corner almost jumps into action.

"Get Giuseppe on the phone. Try the Fish and Hunt first."

I whisper to Reuben. "What's Fish and Hunt?"

Reuben leans very close. "Mott St. Fish and Hunt Social Club. Heavy mob types. Very *privato*. They drink a little, play a little cards, and conduct international crime. You wouldn't like it."

Signor Stucci turns to his sister, who has not changed expression. "Lella, *cara*, you are so quiet. What do you think about all this?"

Lella folds her arms across her chest as if she were suddenly cold.

"I think," she whispers hoarsely but with chilling calm, "that you have the wrong head." And with that she stands and walks quickly out of the room.

All the men exchange puzzled looks.

I leap up and start after her.

Stucci raises a warning arm. "No, no, no. Let her go. I know my sister. When she is like that, it will do no good. When she is ready, she will explain."

Paolo returns and nods to Stucci.

"Please excuse me; I must take this call."

I turn to Reuben. "I never got the letter. I never even knew that she met you."

"I'm very sorry to hear that, but it does explain things."

"What things?"

"Why you never responded."

"What did it say?"

"More or less it said that I had never forgotten you and that if you felt the same, I proposed a rendezvous anywhere convenient so that, with the flush of youth gone, we might explore one another more honestly."

I will kill her. I'll kill her in perpetuity.

"She must have opened it."

"I resist believing that, but obviously you are right."

Tears rolled down my cheeks. "It's for the best. You found a lovely woman. It's right for you. Better than we would have been."

"Aroma. Things are not always what they seem. Spring was the daughter of a man in the Zuni pueblo—I bought craft pieces from him from time to time. He died quite suddenly and she was left alone. She was just a child, fifteen or so. Her father's stepbrother came to take over the shop and he raped her and beat her very badly. She ran away. She had nowhere to go. Somehow she found her way to me. I took her in and helped her get over it. She's crippled, you know—it was all too much. She didn't tell me she was pregnant until it was too late to do anything. I gave her my name to spare her the shame of having an illegitimate child. She had *twins*. We do not have a marriage. We do not live as man and wife. If anything, I am like a kindly uncle. I don't know what telling you this accomplishes, but somehow the fates have brought us together again. I want you to understand."

I understand. Oh boy, do I understand.

My heart is rolling over on itself. I reach for his hand. A paunchy prince he is for sure.

The door opens. Signor Stucci and Paolo are back.

"Please excuse me. I apologize for the interruption. But now it is very late. This has been most tiring for the signorina. Lella has gone to bed. Reuben, are you staying or driving home?"

Reuben discreetly retracts his hand. "Home. I promised Spring I'd drive carpool tomorrow."

"Giovanni will show you out. *Buona Notte, amico. Grazie mille* for your help. Signorina Aroma, please. I will see you to your room."

Signor Stucci takes my arm. His hand is small but surprisingly strong. Somehow I know that the night is far from over.

Signor Stucci guides me back through the mazelike hallways, but he doesn't stop at my bedroom door; he continues on to a small library, very different in feeling from the rest of the house. The walls and the furniture are covered in dark-green velvet. The tall bookcases are gleaming oak and the chairs and desk more Italian Renaissance than Santa Fe modern. He motions for me to sit and then seats himself across from me, his small white leather-shod feet barely reaching the floor. He seems tired.

"Aroma, my dear child, I have some news for you that is not good. It is very, shall we say, *complicato*. I have had a long conversation with my associates in New York. You must take my word that these men know everything about certain subjects. So what they tell me you must believe."

The cold sweat is working its way back over me. I swallow hard.

"There were things about your story that did not seem *simpatico* to me. Did not sound like a maniac. To be frank, the way your sister was killed, the body disappearing without a trace, everything so clean, so deliberate, that is the way professionals kill. That is what we call contract killing. This was confirmed to me by my friends back East. But it is even more complex."

I brace myself. I feel like I used to feel in geometry class when I would suddenly realize that my brain was about to close down. "More complex" might well be Geometry 2 all over again.

"A contract! We're talking about a wife and mother with a Ph.D. in psychology, not Al Capone. This is impossible!"

Signor Stucci raises one elegantly manicured hand to stop me. "Please. Try to put your middle-class reasoning aside and listen carefully.

"This man, Jimmy Bob Mackay. He is not what he seems. He has a nickname given to him by his employers. They call him Dragon Oil. He made a deal with some people many years ago. His organization is—how does the FBI say it?—a front for the family he drew blood with. But he got cocky. Forgot who he was pledged to. He started to operate without a consensus from his associates. He gambled, had big debts. And then he became involved with your sister and started letting the business slide, spent all of his time with the radio station, peanuts!

"This organization is not like my organization. They are Chinese. They are known as the Tong." (That would explain all the Orientals around Jimmy Bob.) "They are very devious. Very ancient in their code of ethics. Very brutal. They do not overlook such things. And they always have an inside man, watching. So they knew about you, about your sister and Mr. Mackay, about Paris. They found out that your sister and Mr. Mackay had made a side trip to Switzerland to deposit large sums of skim money, Tong money, and certain documents—fake passports, all the makings of new identities—in a Swiss bank. This did not please them."

"Well, then why wouldn't they just kill Jimmy Bob?"

"It is not so simple. He has become very public, very

powerful. They had an enormous investment in what he sheltered for them. They operate in a very deep, quiet way. Very little is known about how much they control; it is not like the Italians.

"And also his wife was squeezing hard. And she had much to squeeze. She didn't know anything certain, but she was suspicious and she was desperate enough to threaten him—to get him to stop with your sister or pay off big. He was greedy, and so was your sister. He knew your sister would be an expensive woman to keep. So they came up with a plan. They would hire you to throw his wife off and buy some time. The whole thing with you in disguise was planned so that anyone following would think you were your sister. They left for Paris.

"The Tong decided to teach Mr. Mackay a lesson. It would be no lesson to hurt his wife or even the child, because he disliked them both, but your sister was something else. It was decided to kidnap her and hold her until he was humbled enough to seek forgiveness. This was necessary because he was still extremely valuable to them. If he was killed, it would be a very difficult situation with the Securities and Exchange Commission, the FCC. They had made a big mistake, trusting an outsider with too much power. So their first choice was to bring him back into line. They were going to leave something—a finger, a toe, an ear—to let him know this was serious. But then she was murdered and this confused them. And also, they did not know that Mr. Mackay had at the same time taken a contract out on you."

"ME!" This is no longer geometry—we are talking advanced calculus.

"When you began at the station, did you not sign a number of documents, including a very large insurance policy?"

"I guess so. I wasn't exactly given a lot of time to study anything. I just signed."

"I'm glad you are a doctor and not a lawyer, *cara*. Well, it is standard except that they had increased the policy to more than three million dollars. The man was not *stupido*, he was trying to cover himself in case his wife or his employers tightened the screws."

"They? Are you saying my own sister was part of this?"

"That I do not know. It serves no purpose to torment yourself. But the plan was to make it look like a psychopath. Mr. Mackay's alibi was not strong. The police were pressuring him. So he took out a Tong contract on you to make it look like a psycho. It was to be a copy-cat killing. The Tong came to the hospital to kill you—but you had already left. I do not want to frighten you—but the Tong is still under contract. They are following you."

"Oh my God. Ever since I left, I've felt like someone was following me. I thought I was just being paranoid."

"No. But it is not like the Tong. They must be waiting for you to lead them to something else. Otherwise, you'd be dead by now."

I have stopped breathing.

"That lieutenant from New York—he's here, too."

From somewhere far off my voice appears. "But then, who killed my sister?"

"Well, *cara*. Either there was another contract, or . . ."

"Or it was the wrong head!"

"Exactly."

"Oh my God." I am starting to hyperventilate. I stand up, gasping for breath. Signor Stucci jumps up with the lightness of a springbok and leads me to the French doors, which he opens. I take several deep breaths. The cold sweat evaporates. I can feel the moisture being sucked back into my pores.

"But it looked just like her! Where would they find a head that looked just like her?" Silently, I answer my own question.

"Aroma *cara*. It was severed. A death mask. You looked at it for maybe five seconds before you fainted, and then again in the morgue. *Sì?*"

"*Sì.*" It all starts to fit. Sarah Jane. Dental records.

"You expected that it was her. Whoever left it there wanted everyone to think it was her. They found someone who looked enough like her to be believable. Things like that are done all the time."

"They are?"

"Ah. Yes. They are. So here we are. Mr. Mackay is missing. Your sister is either dead or missing. The contractor may still be stalking you, because only Mr. Mackay can cancel the contract, and he has not done so.

"Mr. Mackay went to see the Tong. He begged for forgiveness. He said that he would make amends. They told him to cooperate with the police and stay calm. He seemed to believe that the head was your sister's. He seemed terrified and contrite. He professed belief that the family had executed her as a warning. But we cannot be sure of anything. He was watched night and day, but two days ago he gave his shadows the slip and disappeared. So now you know all that I know. But you have my word, I will not stop until we know the truth. It is the honor of my comrades at stake. Their honor is my honor. And for Mona. I will find the truth for you."

"Thank you, signore. I am so grateful. For my father, too. If there is a chance that she is alive, that would be a miracle."

"Please, call me Sarno."

I have a moment's hesitation. Somehow calling him Sarno seems almost like a lead-in to carrying him off in my arms. "Sarno. I am very tired. I think I'd better try to sleep on this."

"But of course. I will take you."

When we get to number 8, another chill crawls up my stained silk back.

"Signore, Sarno. What you said, about the contract on me; could they find me here?"

"No one can harm you here! I have informed my people. They are doing what they can. But we need Mr. Mackay. Do not be afraid. We will find him."

I say good night. Will my virture be the price for protection? I wonder, remembering the lingering of my little host's hand in mine and the dreamy look in his crackling blues. That is the least of your problems, another voice points out to me. "Don't be afraid," he says. Me, who has read every trashy crime novel ever written. He might as well have told me not to swallow. In fact, that would be easier.

16

They Shoot Horses, Don't They?

So many things have happened to me in the last six hours that if I had paused for even a split second to think about it, I would probably have fallen onto my fancy borrowed bed and entered the land of disharmonic convergence. I didn't dare stop now. I turned off the lights and slipped out of my skintight—and now cold-sweat-drenched—evening wear and into a pair of jeans and a sweatshirt and sneakers. I put on my glasses, Pop's old Yankees cap, and, using one of the candles decorating my room, made my way down the now dark, silent halls in the direction I had seen Lella take her mother. I could have used Pop's gun, which had not wound up back in my belongings. I had no idea which room was hers. I tried each handle like Goldilocks; two were locked. The third was Mother Stucci, sleeping like a *bambina*; by the fourth, the candle was getting a little melty and so was I.

I put my ear to the door. I hear the sound of female sobbing. A sound with which I am familiar. Lella. I try the knob. Open.

Lella Stucci is curled up on an enormous thick white fur rug wearing a black silk pajama top. I tiptoe in, not wanting to frighten her, or myself, any more than is necessary.

She sits up and whirls around toward me, her strong, handsome face streaked with tears and black mascara. I jump back, dropping the candle, which luckily goes out and does not set the white fur and Lella on fire.

"Don't be afraid," Lella says in a hoarse whispery voice. This is obviously the advice of choice at Rancho Estrella.

"I've been expecting you."

Funny how different people are. When I am expecting someone, I never do it in a pajama top on the floor, sobbing my heart out.

I summon up all my adreneline. "I've got to talk to you about what you said tonight. About the 'wrong head.' I know all about the blackmail scheme! I know about you and Sarah Jane, and I saw you today; I saw you kill John Harrington. I didn't say a word about it to your brother. A little blackmail of my own, maybe. I want the truth! Where is Sarah Jane? What really happened to my sister?"

Lella stands up and walks, rather arrogantly, for my taste, over to her enormous white satin bed. She wipes her eyes on a monogrammed hankie and lights a cigarette, flinging the match into the fireplace, and begins pacing back and forth in the moon and firelight.

"I'll tell you what I know. It doesn't matter anymore. John is dead, and I'm trapped here forever. Nothing matters anymore except making sure that bitch gets what's coming to her!"

She can't mean Amora? What more could be coming to Amora? Even for Shirley MacLaine fans—Amora seems to have been paid back.

Lella shoots me one of those intense eye numbers. "'You didn't see what you thought you saw. I didn't kill John. I loved John. I wanted to hurt him, but I never wanted to kill him. I came to warn him. I was walking toward his office when he came out. I heard shots and ducked down. When I looked up, he was lying there. I ran to him, but it was too late. So I took the photos and the money and left. That's what you must have seen."

"Then who killed him?"

Lella snickers. "Who knows. Who cares? He's dead. But if I were you, I'd put my money on your chink-loving Cowboy Joe."

"Jimmy Bob?"

"Look, let's get this straight. I hated your sister. Your whore of a sister ruined my life. John was mine! I wasn't just his patient. I was his woman! I went to him secretly; I was in pain and I was desperate to get out of here. If my family had found out, they would have killed him and me. Psychotherapy is forbidden. Too many secrets could be told. We fell in love. Then I introduced him to my friend, Amora. It was just a game to her, to take him away from me; they broke my heart, but I never let on. When Sarah Jane came out, I used her as a way of staying close to them. It was evil. The sex, the drugs, the emotions. Evil. Satanic. John used all of us. One night I woke up in the middle of their bed. We were all entwined, like a spaghetti sandwich. I was really high on mescaline and I saw the whole situation so clearly. That's when I decided to have someone record it. It gave me a certain power over all of them. I hoped life would be kind and I'd never need to use it. But life wasn't kind; not to me, and not to poor Sarah Jane.

"When Sarah Jane came back, we had some long, long talks. She was almost nonfunctional. I nursed her and got her on her feet and then we set up the blackmail. Who would have known how famous Amora would become! It was perfect!"

I get up my confidence and slink (at least I am thinking *slink*) over and sit down on the bed and light a cigarette, totally forgetting that I don't smoke.

"What went wrong?"

Lella throws back her head and laughs. It is not a happy sound.

"Everything! We were in league with the devil. We were in over our heads. Sarah Jane went to New York to see Amora. I stayed here, sent the notes, and kept an eye on John. Then, Sarah Jane stopped calling. She didn't answer her phone. The hotel said she had not checked out, but that her bed hadn't been slept in for days. She just vanished. So I went to find out what was going on. I had my disguise. I watched Amora's apartment. Everything was strange. You came and went. I couldn't get close enough to know for sure if you were your sister or not. Then, at that volleyball game, you took off your disguise—I knew then something was very wrong and someone else was following you. I got scared and I came home. No response to my notes. No word from Sarah Jane—and then, the head."

I sit forward. "Yes! Do you think it's . . . it's . . ."

"I think it's Sarah Jane. And if it is—that means your sister hasn't paid for her crimes. But she will!"

Lella stalks across the room, her long tan bare legs

gleaming in the firelight, and reaches behind a kachina doll, pulling out a rolled-up piece of paper. I jump down from the bed and meet her halfway on the fur rug. We both drop to our knees and she unravels it. It's a hand-drawn map.

"This is a map of the road from here to your sister's ranch. I think the answer is there. I have two horses down in the back behind the stables all saddled and ready to go. All we have to do is stay on the road and head north—follow the North Star. You can see it very clearly in the desert. There's only one danger . . ."

Lella's long slender finger traces the side of the paper. "There's a huge canyon, a cliff that falls straight down several thousand feet. If we get separated, remember: it's to the left of the North Star; stay wide of it. The horses don't like it either; they'll keep clear unless something spooks them."

Lella jumps up and runs toward the window.

I stay on my knees in total shock. "The horses!"

"Of course, silly. We're going across the desert. The night is perfect. It's absolutely clear."

I have not been on the back of a horse since I was thrown by a Shetland pony at the Pennsylvania State Fair when I was six years old.

"I can't do that. I don't know how. I don't want to know how. I hate horseback riding!"

"I'll be right beside you."

That would have been more comforting if, only seconds after she had offered this wispy reassurance, an arrow had not come whizzing in through the window and slammed into poor Lella's silk-covered chest.

Like the Mad Hatter, I grabbed the map and, without missing a beat, I whizzed out of the room, down the hallway, out the back, across the property to the stables. The horses were waiting as advertised.

I attempt to get on. It is better that I'm alone. Watching me attempt to get on is not a much prettier sight than poor Lella and the arrow. Somehow, I get on.

Off I go into the wild black yonder. I say six Hail Marys, the Lord's Prayer, the Kol Nidre, and every mantra I have ever learned. I have to keep remembering to open my eyes. I gallop on. I am almost beyond nerves now. Sort of at the intersection of stark terror and oblivion.

I find the North Star, which I decide is the bright one, smaller than the moon. I hate myself all over again for dropping astronomy. I knew typing would come in handy, but stellar navigation had seemed rather remote at the time.

I wonder about the cliff. But the horse seems to be heading straight, or as they say, due north. I surrender to my fate. If the cliff it is, then so be it.

We charge up a hill and down below, in a desolate valley, not at all an Amora trip. I see a ranch, with a small light burning.

Somehow I am able to stop my steed. Now comes the hard part. The dismounting. I solve it by falling off. Nothing is broken. I brush myself off, and very carefully—not wanting the equine being to rear up or neigh or whatever other dangerous defensive actions horses take—I open the saddle bag and find a flashlight and a pair of binoculars. But no gun. No bow and arrow. Zip. I tie the beast to a cactus and crouch down, making my way slowly across the desert. At moments like this I sorely regret all of those missed aerobics classes. When I am about halfway, I use the binoculars. There is a very large, very unfriendly looking Chinese man sitting on the front porch, holding a rifle and wearing a sword. Around the side I see another one, who seems to be smoking a joint or Tai stick or something.

I am on automatic pilot now. I have gone too far to

stop. I am my only hope. I sneak around to the side of the barn, take off all of my clothes, more delighted than ever for my svelte new bod, pick up a good jagged rock small enough to conceal in my palm, and wiggle my way right up onto the porch, smiling at the Buddha boy like a high-rolling hooker at a dry-cleaning convention.

Either he is very horny, very stupid, or very stoned, but whatever the reason, he freezes, staring at me as if I had just dropped from a spaceship. I move right up against him, so close I can feel his sword against my ribs, and before he can say "Duck Sauce," I bop him with the rock as hard as I can. It seems to be hard enough, call it beginner's luck, because he slumps down against the porch rail and doesn't move. Now I have a gun. But since my approach has worked so well, and so quietly, I decide not to tamper with a good thing and wiggle right around to the back and repeat my performance on column 2. Same thing. Wiggle. Bop. Thump.

Now, I am Rambette. I carry my two rifles and sword holster back to the barn, put my clothes on, strap my sword on. I sling one gun over my shoulder (this is the part in the movies I can never understand. The hero always forgets to take the gun—too macho, I guess. Well, I do not intend to make the same mistake.) I creep around to the far side and climb up on the woodpile and peek in.

And lo and behold. On the bed, drinking her ubiquitous champagne and doing her nails, is my previously dead twin sister. I shiver, trying to get in touch with my feelings about her not really being dead. They are mixed.

There I am, crouching outside a ranch-house window in the middle of the night, in the middle of the desert, shaking with cold and fear; and there she is, drinking champagne and painting her nails. It was the nails that did it. Chanel Midnight Pink, no less. Bodies are all over the place, some headless, some bottomless. Clive and Pop are traumatized forever. I have a Chinese madman out to kill me, and *she is doing her goddamn nails!*

I bash in the window with my rifle butt and jump through. Oh, to have a video of that moment. The look on my twin sister's face as I dropped into her boudoir. I tear off my cap and glasses and start toward her. She leaps up and tries to run across the bed and into the bathroom. I head her off, pushing her back into the pillows.

"Don't hurt me! Please don't hurt me! I can explain everything!"

"Oh, great. Really glad to hear that! I was worried there for a second!"

I can tell she is trying to play for time. She sits up and smoothes her negligee. *If she blows on her nails, I'll blast her fucking brains out.*

She looks right into my eyes and then she gives me the old Amora, woman to woman, up and down. "You're so thin," she says.

"Talk!" I scream so loud my tongue hurts.

"Please! This is so hard! I never wanted any of this to happen. I never wanted you to be involved. I was desperate!"

"Listen you, you, floozy filth! Save it for the radio audience! I know all about the blackmail, and the whole sordid mess. I've even seen the pictures. Naughty, naughty, I must say. I was truly shocked. It was, in a funny way, kind of like doing it myself. So just cut all the shit! I know you and Jimmy Bob murdered Sarah Jane and Dr. John and Lella Stucci, and, at any moment, probably me! I even know about Reuben! Reuben! You knew how much he meant to me! I never would have married Clifford; my whole life would have been different, how could you have hated me that much? You wanted me dead, for real! But not just dead, even; dead, fantasy dead, I could understand. I wanted you dead plenty of times, too. This was worse! You wanted to ruin my life! I . . . I"

The pain finally catches up with the anger. I am sobbing so hard I can't see. Amora, never one to pass up a photo or any other opportunity, rolls off the bed and grabs a gun from under the mattress.

She jumps up and we stand facing one another. The cowboy and the lady.

"Yes. I did want to ruin your life! I hated you! God, how I hated you! You were always there as a reminder of who I really was, who I might slip back into being! How ironic, to be saddled with a distorted mirror image. Someone as unique as I was! And you, not even trying to change! And you're the one they loved. Pop loathed me! You got it all! No matter how hard I worked, how hard I tried! You got the love. Nothing I did pleased them! You! With your envy and your dumpy mediocrity! I did everything I could to leave you behind! But you wouldn't go away. You were always with me in my head! Everyone liked you better. Even my own child! How do you think that felt? And then, finally, when I thought I had it all, had so much that no matter what contempt you and Pop had for me, nothing could touch me, Sarah Jane showed up. Sarah Jane! My one friend. My idol. And there I was again, fighting my way out of the past. And the worst part, the very worst part, was having to turn to you, to share with you! Watching you move into *my* world. A world I earned! Not you! Me! I was losing everything! If I lost Jimmy Bob then, I'd have nothing left. So what do you think I'd do! When Sarah Jane came to pick up the money, we injected her with tranquilizers. I cut her hair like mine, put my blue contacts on her eyes. I'd already switched the dental records. She looked more like me than you ever did. It was perfect! I left her with Jimmy Bob and came out here. He was going to take care of everything and meet me. We had a doctor from Brazil waiting in Mexico to change our faces and we'd pick up the money and be gone forever. Jimmy Bob just had to wait long enough to collect all the insurance. But then, you—you got away! And everything fell apart! You ruined everything! You've always ruined everything!"

I am, despite my state of mind, trying to be fair. I am trying to hear her side. All those years of training—*there are always two sides*—I am trying. But this part, this "You ruined everything" part was too much.

"Me! Me! All of my life, I stood in your shadow! You ridiculed me. You pushed me away. I could never compete with you, so I just gave up. I was so afraid that if I tried, if I threatened you at all, I'd lose you and the whole complex contest. I just withdrew. I never gave myself a chance, and rather than that making you love me, it just made your more patronizing. I envied everything about you, and I felt so guilty. We were almost the same person—I mean, we started out like that—and you had taken that person and made something magical from her, and I had let her down. I was a coward. I was a failure to myself. You did have everything but love. That was your choice! You pushed us out. We reminded you of something you wanted to forget. Of course Pop chose me, I needed him. I cared! Whom would you choose? You never let us love you.

"And Clive! Clive! That child needed you so much, loved you so much! You treated him like an annoying pet! *You* ruined yourself! Don't you dare try to blame any of this on me! Don't you dare!"

I throw my gun down and grab her arm. We fight for

the gun, which goes off. Amora drops it and we roll around on the rug, forty years of rage and pain finally making its way to the surface; we roll, pounding on one another. It truly feels like self-inflicted wounds.

Footsteps. Very loud boot steps. We roll off one another, panting. I slide back toward my gun, but I'm too late. Jimmy Bob Mackay is standing in the doorway with a machine gun in his arms.

"Well, well, well. What have we here? It's the Doublemint twins, having a little squabble. I would have thought you'd have learned your lesson by now, Aroma. But I guess a mere arrow through the chest isn't enough to stop someone as foolhardy as you, now is it?"

I imagine what he means is that a machine gun is. If so, he's absolutely right.

"You know, you've caused us a mite of trouble, little lady. Not to mention several million dollars in insurance money. You've gotten to be more trouble than a pig in shit."

I start to retort, but my inner guide stops me. Somehow, being expendable makes folks open to you.

"Now, you are the only thing standing between your sis and me and our escape across the Rio Grande. Not the way we had it planned, but I reckon we can scrape by on twenty million pesos for a few years, anyway. Don't want to get too greedy."

If every dying man has a last request, I have a last question. "One thing that I can't figure. How did you get her head in there without anyone seeing you?"

"That was the easy part! I plopped it into my Le Sport exercise bag and dumped the body in the incinerator in the basement. Then I just strolled on over to WNRD. Don't forget, it's my building. I know every nook and cranny. I came right along through the basement and up the emergency stairs, they're right beside the office. I was in and out in no time at all.

"With you, it would have been easier; Chen wouldn't have had to dispose of the body. We wanted them to have every square inch of you—the note was for the cops. That was my one mistake. I never figured you'd leave like that."

I am stunned. "Chen? Chen!"

"Sure 'nuf. Chen is my main man. The Tong sent him to me years and years ago. He's my blood brother."

Before I can absorb this new information, a tall figure dressed all in black leaps in my broken window and points an Uzzi at Jimmy Bob. Amora, who has been hovering behind J.B., races forward. "Darling!" she gasps. "Thank God! I thought you'd never get here! I couldn't have taken another minute with him. Kill him quickly and let's go. Everything's arranged. I have the keys to the accounts, passports, everything."

The figure takes off his hat and glasses. It's O'Ralph.

Jimmy Bob and I in harmony: "O'Ralph!"

As Amora rushes to O'Ralph, her chiffon job gets in the way of his target range, and in that split second, Jimmy Bob, in a frothing jealous frenzy (after all, like him or not, the guy has killed three people and taken on the Chinese Mafia for the ungrateful bitch) blasts O'Ralph, who falls dead without having said one single word.

Amora, who has just watched her ace fall out of the deck, whirls on her cuckolded lover. "I didn't mean it! J.B., I was just trying to distract him, darling!"

This is the meaning of "too little, too late." Jimmy Bob takes aim and fires; right between her fake blue eyes.

Primal instinct rises. I dive down and retrieve my gun.

"You killed my sister, you rotten son of a bitch!"

Jimmy Bob is frozen in true Othellian despair. The reality of what he has just done overcomes him.

Before either of us can make our next move, Chen leaps into the room, dressed like an extra in an old Bruce Lee movie.

This brings Jimmy Bob back to life. "Kill her!" he demands, pointing at me.

Chen, my former trusted ally, turns his previously adorable but now menacing grin on his boss and says, in perfect English, "So very sorry, James; I have been offered a far better deal." And with that he whips out some sort of very serious-looking strangulation device and simultaneously, with one swift barefooted kick, knocks both of our guns out of our rigid white-knuckled hands.

Jimmy Bob, hero of the West, pushes me aside and hurls his enormous frame out of the window. I follow him, landing on top of him on the ground. "You rotten no-good, cow fucker!" I rant, holding onto his neck for dear life. Jimmy Bob is staggering, trying to get to his car with me attached. "You animal! You slimy creep!"

I slide down and race for the car door. Jimmy Bob races for the car door. I manage to fling it open just as Chen and the two horny Chinese thugs surround us.

"Hands up!" they demand.

I've already done the no-clothes number. I am completely out of tricks.

J.B. and I oblige.

"Move away from the car." Chen is not amused.

Jimmy Bob is whimpering and making an assortment of thoroughly unmanly sounds. "Chen! You were like a brother! Whatever the Tong offered you, I'll give you double. Come to Mexico with me. Let's leave all of this behind us. We're blood brothers; we've got a history together."

Chen does find this amusing. "Blood brother, my yellow ass. Only your blind occidental arrogance could have made you think that. You treated me like a coolie. The Tong is my brother. I have always belonged to them. You deserve to die for your betrayal."

Jimmy Bob, in another chivalrous gesture, pushes me into Chen and the boys and dives into the car. Instinctively they go for him, and I, knowing this is my last chance, crouch down and run like hell, like the wind, like an African track star. I run for my messed-up middle-aged out-of-condition little life. I hear shots and then a car motor just as I reach the crest of the hill, where my friend Flicka is waiting patiently. Now all I have to do is get on and off I go. Well, I get on, all right. Fear is great for grace. I hurl myself across and take off like a meteor, heading straight on into the night.

The car sound is getting closer. I realize that I am all turned around and I have totally lost the North Star. I am going very fast; I search the sky with my glassless, nearsighted eyes. I can't even seem to find the fucking moon. *Panic. I must not panic.* I look up again. No moon. But we seem to be heading back the way we came; moving slightly uphill, rather than the long downhill gallop we took when I started out. If that's true, then the cliff would be on my right. The jeep is louder. It is very close now. I can hear Chen yelling instructions at the others in Chinese. *Panic. Must not panic.* Take a deep breath, little lady. Think. An idea. One involving a high degree of risk. (So what else is new?) I think of the story the divorced lady told this afternoon; was it possible that I was still working on one day? The story about the blind lady in the cactus patch. "And where would a safe place be, dear?" That decides me. I pull back on the reins and say "Whoa!" just like Annie Oakley herself. I stop my nameless nag and point him or her directly at what I am praying is the path to the cliff. I stay there until the jeep is so close that I can feel the dust from the tires—the Santa Fe equivalent of the whites of their eyes. And then I start forward again, very fast. I have no idea how far away the edge is, but it's too late to reconsider. They are close enough to shoot me, but thanks to my lack of horsemanship, I am bobbing and swaying enough to make this rather difficult. I know that any minute they will overtake me. Suddenly, as if the God Equus were watching over us, my horse, sensing such things as cliff edges, rears up and bucks backward, throwing me off sideways. Off he goes, as fast as he can in the opposite direction. The jeep, not understanding the meaning of this act, keeps accelerating. In fact, even as I pick myself up and run frantically for some sort of cover, I do not hear the brakes. I turn around to see the jeep, Chen, and the Wontons soar off the side and drop out of sight. Some time later, I hear a splat, followed by an explosion.

I am all alone in the black starry night. And I am still alive.

Far off I hear engines. They grow louder and louder. I wait for them. I feel totally calm. A fleet of dune buggies carrying Signor Stucci and his boys, Reuben Mars, and Pincus Mallony appear like mammoth night creatures. I am really glad they are here. But I am even more glad that I took care of it all by myself.

Epilogue
or
Ending With a Less Grisly Beginning

The whole aftermath is still kind of a blur. Police in and out. Reporters everywhere. We were back in the headlines again.

I stayed on at Rancho Estrella for another week. I saw a lot of Reuben. I know this may sound ridiculous, but I truly believe it is my first real romance. We still haven't made love. Somehow it didn't seem right. We both have a lot of sorting to do before we can really know what we're in for. But it was the most magical week of my life.

The drive back in the green Toyota was a very different trip. First, there was more truth to tell myself. I realized somewhere along the way that the crisis, the gigantic disruption of my daily routine, however terrifying and bizarre, had been in some ways easier than maintaining an ongoing relationship with the joy of living each moment fully. I had been thrust into a total surrender to the present tense in a way that I had never quite been able to do before. I had risked. Not just playing it safe and watching the real action from the sidelines, living a half-life like a matron at the matinee.

I wanted to be able to go home to dirty dishes and trips to the shoe repair and find a way to make my daily life as alive as my outlaw life. Pop did it. Maybe now that I had proved whatever it was I had needed to prove, I could be humble enough to ask for guidance. That I could still learn was what I had learned.

I was a forty-year-old woman who, just as she was settling down for the long winter's nap, had been picked up by the loosening folds of her tense little neck and thrown off a cliff into the vortex.

And I had made it back to the road. I was alive. I was damn lucky, too. I had let myself off the big hook. I was absolved. I was sorry about Amora. Dearly sorry. But it wasn't my fault.

For now, God had chosen. And I was whizzing down the highways, going home to rebuild my life. Hopefully to do a little better than before.

If I could put all of this stuff to good use, then maybe Amora's tragedy would not be such a waste.

I hit the New York state line and went directly to Pop's, where he and the kids were waiting with wide eyes and open hearts. I needed to ease myself back into reality the same way the returning vets did, I guess. Everything seemed sort of blurry, as if I were watching from under water.

Clifford came. I must give him his due. He was really very upset and very sweet. It felt so strange. I had played house with this man for five years. I had been totally faithful and involved in the marriage. I had had credit cards, magazine subscriptions, and tax returns with this man. It all seemed like a mirage. The closer he got, the fainter he got. I realized that we had never really committed ourselves. Neither of us ever trusted enough to be truly vulnerable to one another. We painted ourselves so far into our Impressionistic little corners that there was no way to find our way back. So much for "this time I've got it right."

When we faded out of the newspapers, I went back to the Village. Clifford helped us pack; we didn't really have very much. As a Nordic attempt at humor, he even offered me his grandmother's footstool.

Ironically enough, Amora had named me as the beneficiary of her old life-insurance policy and requested that I be given custody of Clive. The policy was one million smackaroos, with a double-indemnity clause, so I have now joined the satin-sheet crowd myself. Poor Amora; I guess she'd really hate it, wherever she is. Maybe not. I hope not. I think about that last night often, and my one real regret is that we didn't have time to get beyond the hurt and anger. If the night hadn't turned into *Hellzapoppin*, I think we could have ended up friends.

Well, I'll never know. Clive did go home to see his real father; I guess Amora left me the money because Clive has a rather fat trust fund from his father's parents, at least that's what I've told him. It'll all go to him someday, anyway.

Now that I've had a great big lick of the outlaw life, I admit I've had some thoughts of the Swiss bank account with the twenty million pesos. I wonder if the Tong knows where it is? I wonder if I could find the keys? Just night thoughts, mind you. Just night thoughts.

Vivika, Clive, and I moved back uptown, but it was too much Amora to be healthy for any of us. We sublet it and moved to a very pleasant loft in Tribeca filled with light and air.

Radio job offers have been pouring in. I'm almost as big a name as Amora had been. Maybe even bigger. Notoriety equals celebrity in our *People* magazine world.

I am back at my old job for now, until I can sort things out. I don't want to become one of those dehydrated instant celebrities, just add headlines and stir. But I do love the radio. One offer, in Boston, sounds kind of nice.

The kids really like my new look and I've kept it. I've even managed to keep my new weight, and with a little more time and money, my wardrobe has classed up its act. How nice to discover the wonders of eyeliner and lip gloss at just the moment the calendar and the bathroom mirror have let it be known that the days of the Natural Look have just turned into the "before" page of the *Ladies' Home Journal* makeover.

I was right about Art and Mona. They are living together.

And that is about that, tabloid fans.

My first real day back in the city I took the subway uptown. A street crazy with a battered old saxophone got on wearing a purple beanie with colored balls bobbing on wires and red bunny ears. He shouted at us, "I am an extraterrestrial from the planet Artemetrius. Here is the music of my world!" He blew on the saxophone very loudly and very badly from Bleecker Street to Fourteenth. A Korean woman across from me never even looked up from her *Daily News*. "If you want me to stop, please make a donation. Help me get back to my planet. I have been away too long."

I gave him five bucks.

I understood that guy. I'm finding my way back, too. But I knew right then that I was home.